PRAISE FOR *THE*

"Fleet and fun, *The Fireballer* will appeal to fans of *The Natural* and Robert Coover's *The Universal Baseball Association*. Frank Ryder is a classic American hero—the phenom who has to overcome his own terrible past. Mark Stevens has done the impossible: He actually had me rooting for the Orioles."

—Stewart O'Nan, coauthor of *Faithful* and author of *Ocean State*

"Seldom do I read a book that knocks my socks off the way *The Fireballer* did. This is a feel-good baseball story with a hold on the vernacular, the heart, the soul, the big picture, and the subtleties of America's favorite summer pastime. The characters are beautifully etched, and pitcher Frank Ryder may be the most likeable hero since Gary Cooper gave life to Lou Gehrig on the big screen. I guarantee that you don't have to be a baseball fan to be swept up by this moving tale. With a full heart, I recommend—no, insist—that you read *The Fireballer*."

—William Kent Krueger, author of *Fox Creek* and *This Tender Land*

"Mark Stevens's *The Fireballer* is a timeless baseball story told with a love of the game and fast-moving prose that will leave you cheering and crying at the same time. Frank Ryder is the most appealing of heroes, taciturn and loyal, talented and haunted—truly haunted—and with a fastball that will change the game. With its authentic baseball scenes and its rich heart, *The Fireballer* is a novel that rests comfortably with other classics of the game."

—William Lashner, author of *The Barkeep*

" *The Fireballer* is not just a great baseball yarn that any fan of the game will enjoy—it is also a richly layered exploration of character, regret, and redemption."

—Lou Berney, author of *November Road* and
The Long and Faraway Gone

"The old game of baseball keeps coming up with new stories about the next twist or turn in the sport. In *The Fireballer*, Mark Stevens has invented a startling 'What if?' that stretches the limits of the game. More than a baseball book, the novel is a journey through the mind and heart of a gifted, but tragic, athlete who finds a road to redemption."

—Stephen Singular, *New York Times* bestselling author

"*The Fireballer* is a compelling story that I found hard to put down, rich with authentic baseball details and full of heart. Mark Stevens hits it out of the park with this intricate and moving tale of redemption."

—Robert Bailey, *Wall Street Journal* bestselling author of *The Golfer's Carol*

"Mark Stevens has crafted a powerful, heartfelt story—with a memorable baseball backdrop—that carves out a place alongside classics like *The Art of Fielding* and *The Natural*. Stevens knows the game—but it's his deft narrative and characters that help this book truly sing. I couldn't put it down."

—Alex Segura, bestselling author of *Secret Identity*

"You don't have to know baseball to love *The Fireballer*. At the center of this big-hearted book is Frank Ryder, a star pitcher tormented by a mistake in his past. Readers root for Frank not for his fastball, but because his redemption delivers us all."

—Stephanie Kane, award-winning mystery writer and author of *True Crime Redux*

PRAISE FOR MARK STEVENS

"Mark Stevens writes like wildfire."
—Craig Johnson, author of the Walt Longmire novels, on *Lake of Fire*

The Fireballer

a novel

MARK STEVENS

LAKE UNION
PUBLISHING

Text copyright © 2023 by Mark Stevens
All rights reserved.

Published by Lake Union Publishing, Seattle

www.apub.com

Amazon, the Amazon logo, and Lake Union Publishing are trademarks of Amazon.com, Inc., or its affiliates.

ISBN-13: 9781662512520 (hardcover)
ISBN-13: 9781662505638 (paperback)
ISBN-13: 9781662505621 (digital)

Cover design by Shasti O'Leary Soudant
Cover image: © Bokeh Blur Background / Shutterstock; © Triff / Shutterstock; © KK.KICKIN / Shutterstock; © Taurus106 / Shutterstock

Printed in the United States of America
First edition

This one's for Irv.

PROLOGUE

Frank Ryder stands flush against the chain-link fence. He rarely puts himself in this situation, temptation so close.

In the distance, Frank's classmate Chris Ellroy strolls from the on-deck circle to the plate. Ellroy's size and shape are unmistakable. He is a bear.

A heavy quiet has settled over the game. There are enough moms and teachers and students to justify the bleachers, but barely.

Frank has had one thousand daydreams about joining the varsity squad at Thomas Jefferson High School. About helping the team turn things around. But Frank knows why it can't happen.

Ellroy, a lefty, takes practice swings with fury. The May afternoon in Denver is hot and still. A bank of dark clouds gathers in the foothills, but they won't cause trouble for at least an hour. One thing Frank likes about living in Colorado is that you can see the weather coming. That wasn't the case in Georgia.

South High School's center fielder, recognizing Ellroy's size and those impressive practice cuts, puts his back to the plate and finds a spot he likes better, closer to the fence in center field.

"Sup?" says the kid from South. Long brown hair bounces off his shoulders. He is skinny, lacks meat.

"You guys taking it to us," says Frank.

The Thomas Jefferson High School Spartans are down 12–2.

"Lucky," says the kid. He's still deciding how far back to play. "It ain't over."

"Until it is," says Frank.

Frank is six one. He's got longish hair underneath a Colorado Rockies cap, worn as a signal that he's trying to fit in. He's fresh from a long workout. Sweat makes his Bob Marley T-shirt sticky.

The South High pitcher uses a full overhead windup. He looks poised. Frank, as always, imagines himself on the mound.

Frank's classmates have no clue. His twin brother, Josh, is the only other student in school who knows what Frank wants. The ache Frank feels is painful. It's as if a doctor went in and exchanged his heart with one a few sizes too big, and now it's fighting to beat its way out of his chest. All Frank has ever wanted to do is play baseball. He dreams it, studies it.

But doesn't play it.

Ellroy takes the first pitch like a statue. It's a strike.

On the second pitch, Ellroy lifts his right leg. He drops his head. His bat cranks. There's a sweet sharp ping of ball on aluminum.

The long-haired South High School center fielder scampers at an angle, his glove up to shield the sun and track the little white missile.

Frank moves too. He shrugs his backpack from his shoulder, turns to run.

Frank finds the spot he wants, waits a moment, adjusts one stride to his left, and catches the ball with two bare hands.

Whooping and hollering reach Frank as he looks up.

The TJ dugout goes bananas. Even if the score is now 12–3, it's something. Ellroy stomps on second base, keeps running.

"Here."

The South High kid pops his glove in the air for an easy target.

Ellroy rounds third. Matching mini clouds of brown dust puff up from the sandy infield as he jogs home.

The kid's glove flaps again three times, *whap whap whap* like a hungry bird begging to be fed. "Hey," says the kid.

Fifteen feet behind the fence, Frank takes three quick steps. He fires.

The kid shouts, "Hey!" again. This time, angry.

The ball climbs to ten feet off the ground and keeps sailing. The shortstop stands ready to catch it, then realizes at the last second he will need to get up a few inches, so he hops but not high enough, and a moment later the ball lands with a smack in the glove of the catcher, who is standing on home plate. The catcher opens his glove to study the ball as if he's found a strange egg.

The outfield kid stares at Frank like he's a zombie. "What the actual fuck?" he says.

Frank shrugs.

In the distance, Chris Ellroy stands by the dugout. Ellroy's arms are extended wide and up in the air in a giant *V*.

Ellroy isn't alone. All of Ellroy's teammates stand outside the dugout. They are all looking out at Frank. Shouting. Whooping. Pointing.

Frank catches the overall tone. The gist. Whatever the precise words, he's not sure. It's a combination of amazed and pissed off.

Frank picks up his backpack and starts to run back up the hill to the school, as sure as anything he has just made a huge mistake.

It's one that might ruin his life.

MAY

The difference between the impossible and the possible lies in a man's determination.

—*Former pitcher, Los Angeles Dodgers manager, and Hall of Fame member Tommy Lasorda*

Chapter 1

Frank Ryder claws the dirt with his cleats and stares out at the man on the mound.

He takes a breath, swings his medium-barreled maple bat three times through the zone.

Ryder waits. His heart thumps. If the fans went still for a moment, they might be able to hear it clear out above the ivy draping the outfield walls.

This is Ryder's first official trip to the plate as a batter in the major leagues.

And he knows what's coming.

He is the target.

The focus.

The one.

—⚓—

Outside Wrigley Field, though the game is well underway, ticketless fans scurry about. They're fueled by a deep fear of missing out. Regular folks from Portage Park, West Loop millennials, swank Streeterville C-level types, hipsters from Bucktown. Out-of-luck regulars from Wrigleyville too. Even fans from southside White Sox country—some Hyde Park academics, retirees up from quiet old Beverly, the profoundly curious from Mayor Daley's old Irish neighborhood, shot-and-a-beer Bridgeport.

Suburbanites have battled expressway traffic all the way into the city from Naperville and Barrington, from Oak Lawn, and from downstate too. People from places like Normal, a father and son from Grand Detour, a farm family from tiny Lost Nation. Cardinal fans, too, have made their way from downstate. The truth is, any baseball fan with means has made their way to Chicago to call in favors.

The hopeful approach late arrivals who might be willing to part with their tickets. Perhaps there's a clueless couple who chose a random game for a casual baseball date, and perhaps they need some easy cash—$800 per seat. Or perhaps they aren't true baseball fans. They don't get it—the game of baseball is now teetering in the balance for one simple reason. Because Frank Ryder is a certified freak. Perhaps they don't understand the game. They don't *get* baseball. They never will. The key is to spot these individuals first and extract the tickets from their hands before a bidding war begins with a panicky competitor.

But this scenario isn't likely. The eager ones who believe they are missing out on history have been checking their phones for the score. The game is ticking along. The game is going, in fact, much too fast. It is now the fourth inning. Hope for finding a way inside grows faint, prepares to vanish.

The Friendly Confines buzzes. All the other stops where Frank Ryder has pitched have been the same—packed stadiums, media frenzies, spectacles to the core. The nearby watering holes are mobbed. The Cubby Bear is jammed. So are Murphy's Bleachers, Sluggers World, and Bernie's Tap & Grill. Unlucky cops watch the streets. More fortunate uniforms work inside, where at least they can claim they saw Frank Ryder. The giddy atmosphere is tailor made for pickpockets, drunks, and dealers.

In the crammed press box, a veteran baseball reporter from the *New York Times* flew to Chicago to cover the game, but he's keen to find someone who can spill the beans on the phenom's dark side. Was there some crazy experimental surgery? Twitter has tried to get the rumor rolling about the kid spending a few months in Mexico and how the time can't be explained. Is the kid on drugs? Who are his enemies? Friends? Girlfriends? Reporters have been to the suburbs of Atlanta and the city of Denver too. They have tipped over all the obvious rocks and poked around underneath. They have skimmed the surface of the kid's upbringing and his middle-class youth. Everybody knows about the one tragic, fluky incident way back when. There must be more. There is *always* more. Watching the kid stand in the batter's box, however, the reporter gives him credit. He looks confident.

And that ain't right.

Up in the luxury boxes, the retractable glass windows are open wide. Corporate schmoozers stand and watch, sipping beers and booze from plastic cups. One investment banker has bet an ambulance-chasing attorney a hundred bucks Frank Ryder strikes out in three pitches *and* never gets the bat off his shoulder.

Out in dead center field, in the next-to-last row of bleachers, a plumber from Fuller Park sits with his thirteen-year-old son, who has the old man's kinky red hair and a face as round and open as a dinner plate. The father works on a Vienna Beef with mustard and onions. The kid grips a fat messy Chick-Ago Sandwich with two hands. Dad and the stranger next to him agree on one thing: the kid's arm is due to shatter any day. And they agree on another thing too. That they never thought the pitch-speed record of 106 miles per hour, if you really believe Aroldis Chapman once threw a pitch that fast when he was with Cincinnati, would ever be broken. "No way the kid can last," says the stranger. "It isn't possible." Dad thinks that would be something, to watch the kid get carted off the field tonight, a quirky bit of crazy baseball history over and done with in a flash.

"Now it's the kid's turn to face the music." Dad's tone to his son is equal parts instructive and feisty. Dad figures this is a teachable moment about baseball and its ways. "You know that kid is shakin' in his boots. The sport of baseball itself will have a thing or two to say, and it's going to say it right now. And if that kid ain't scared, then we know for sure. He's a one hundred percent bona fide fuckin' mutant."

—⁂—

Frank Ryder will not give in. Once the message is delivered with the first pitch, there will be pitches he can hit. Ryder plans to smack a line drive back up the middle, maybe whistle one past Simons' ear.

Give *him* pause.

The *him* is Tim Simons. For years, Simons was an Atlanta Brave. In Frank's bedroom in Alpharetta, before all of what happened and before his family moved from Georgia to Colorado, Frank would practice pitching late at night. With a ball in his hand, Frank would study YouTube clips of the best pitchers. He would mimic their windup and delivery, racking up the imaginary strikeouts in his head.

His favorite? The one he studied the most? The ultrasmooth motion of Tim Simons.

Part of it was Simons' high leg kick. Part of it was the inscrutable face and the Popeye mandible of the man who threw tracer fire. For four sparkling years, the lanky hurler with the flowing hair and scruffy beard was a tough pitcher with filthy stuff. For four years, he was one of the best pitchers in both leagues. The following year, he hit the wall in July. He went on the injured list for six weeks. His season collapsed. Two years ago, the Cubs took a chance via trade. Maybe it was the change of scenery. Something revived him. He returned to dominant form.

Ryder remembers shouting at home with the crowd at the park. "Simon says!" they yelled every time another unlucky batter stared at a called third strike or flailed with his bat at the breeze. Most of the time, Simon says, "Sit down, take a seat back on the bench with your lame-ass teammates."

And *there* he is.

Ryder stands erect, bat relaxed on his shoulder. The commotion Frank Ryder has caused as a pitcher—*that* was something he could anticipate. Coaches warned him, but down deep Ryder knew: this would be baseball's chance to smack back.

The crowd understands. Their roar is full throttle. An extra layer of dampness oozes onto Ryder's hands. An unfamiliar thudding clatters his ribs. His knees aren't rock solid, but at least they don't shake.

He hopes.

Through the course of the first six weeks of Ryder's first full season in the big leagues, after he was brought up to join the expanded roster the previous September, the schedule and a crafty manager have kept him from stepping into the batter's box. All the commotion Ryder has caused has been from the mound.

As an American League pitcher, he is never required to swing a bat unless his Baltimore Orioles are playing in a National League park, such as Wrigley Field. In the National League, there are no designated hitters. All pitchers hit. Ryder dislikes the whole DH concept. He would prefer to have been drafted by a National League team so he'd have regular chances to prove his athleticism at the plate as well.

But here he is.

Ryder's teammates have fashioned one run—a bunt single, a stolen base, and a well-stroked double to right-center. So the game is already over except for the final tally. It's the fourth inning, but the Cubs won't score. They might not get a man to first base.

"Nice day." They are only standing a few feet apart, but catcher Tim Barrett shouts the two words. The roar from the crowd could cut steel.

"Hear anything?" says Ryder.

"Nah." The Simons-Barrett combo is the Tim Towers. Barrett is six two. Simons is six four. "You?" Barrett squats, flaps his fat glove.

"Something, yeah. But it's hard to pick up."

"Welcome to the way the game is supposed to be played."

"Thanks," says Ryder. "I mean, thanks, I think."

Ryder waves his bat through the zone one more time.

He waits.

Simons milks the moment, lets the pressure mount.

The crowd's clamor subsides. Perhaps they all have a twisted need to hear the brittle crack when a Simons fastball finds Ryder's ribs.

Simons stares in for the sign.

Ryder crouches. Cocks his bat. Waggles it.

The left leg lift and kick is the leg kick, *that* leg kick—the one he studied for years. Where in the hell is the ball in the whirling mass of humanity?

The left leg lands.

Simons is focused on Ryder's head.

The ball is halfway to its target when Ryder reels backward, lets the bat go flying, smacks the dirt hard with his chest, like an ugly belly flop in an empty pool, and waits for the crowd to erupt.

Chapter 2

Bottom of the fifth.

Torres, the Cubs' longtime shortstop, stands in the box.

Luke Wyatt flashes the signal.

The 1.

Fastball.

Ryder starts his motion. It's automatic. Every muscle knows its role.

First pitch, 106 at the knees with a twisty tail.

Strike one. Ryder glances up at the scoreboard, where the speed is posted from the radar gun. He can feel the speed in his bones, but he likes to check.

Second pitch, 108 in the dead middle of the plate.

Torres pretends to see it, swats the air.

Strike two.

Third pitch, a cutter at 105. Torres swings with no real plan in mind. The ball rests unharmed in Wyatt's glove long before Torres' bat comes through the zone.

You're out.

Wyatt fires the ball to Bayless at third for the toss around the horn, to Ortega and Cruz and back to Bayless in a happy rhythm.

Walking behind the mound, Ryder mops sweat from his brow with the sleeve of his shirt. Shakes his blond, floppy, shoulder-length hair.

Plucks at his jersey where it's soaked in sweat. The Chicago night is as muggy as a swamp.

Next up, Barrett.

First, 110 for the joy of it. Toes to fingertips, thighs to wrist, leg kick to release, Ryder's body knows the effort required for top speed. The timing. The torque. The reach. It's music.

There's a beat to it, deep in his soul.

Ryder tosses six or seven of these utterly unhittable beauties at top speed each game. His record is eight.

To connect with a pitch moving 110 miles per hour, time is reversed. At 110, in a game that disdains hours and minutes, time evaporates. The ball will smack leather as fast as a batter can swing. It's arithmetic. And physics.

Barrett, like so many before him, goes jelly at the knees. Jelly ligaments. Jelly patella. Jelly joints. There's uncertainty in his stance. The bat doesn't flinch. The crowd gasps. Guffaws roll out from Ryder's bench. His teammates dig the spectacle. They are lined up on the edge of the dugout like joyous kids.

Inside, Ryder smiles.

Outside, at every moment on the mound, he is the bearer of bad news. He maintains a grim visage. In fact, he learned that inscrutable, vacant expression from Tim Simons. On the mound, Ryder's facial expression never changes. One strike builds confidence for the next. Effort evaporates. Rock and throw. It's synchronicity.

When he's out of the mound, the only thing he guards against is thinking about a kid in a grave in Atlanta.

Ryder is better at pitching than he is at forgetting. He's not sure he wants to forget.

For the second pitch, Wyatt calls for a curveball, flicking two fingers in a flash. The pitch floats for a moment like a white pizza pie. Ninety-nine miles per hour. Barrett bites. His timing is decent, but the ball drops like there's a fluke in the gravitational force. Barrett's swat gets nothing but air. Barrett steps away from the box, retightens his batting glove to make it look like he's got a plan.

Third, a cutter at 102. Barrett's hacking, random swing clips the ball as it comes to the plate, and the ball dribbles out in front of the mound. Wyatt pounces on it like a starving cat and fires to first for the easy out.

Again, the ball goes around the horn, and Ryder steps off the mound.

Mop. Readjust. Shake. Pluck.

A jumble of thoughts knocks on the door of his mind. Maggie, who is likely watching. At least, she's half watching in her own support-ive-girlfriend way. She's certainly doing one or two other things at the same time—reading or studying. His brother will be watching.

Ryder glances up at the Chicago night.

Focus on the game.

Next up, Simons.

It is Ryder's chance to respond.

Frank Ryder and the surging Baltimore Orioles, who produced a pitiful 49 wins out of the 162 they played last season, are up 5–1. An Orioles win tonight would give them 23 wins for the season, and there are 19 weeks of baseball left to play. The team is on track for 95 to 100 wins, which should put them in the playoffs. The sole flaw in Ryder's line so far tonight is the lone run, the first he has given up in his first ten starts. It was the result of unadulterated luck, even if the hitter who happened to connect will claim he knew what he was doing.

The only other blemish is the dusty patch on the front of Ryder's gray road jersey, from hitting the dirt to stay clear of Tim Simons' ultraclear message.

We don't take to flashy upstarts.

Or the message could also be, *You ain't nobody until you have a couple hundred wins under your belt.*

Or a combination of both.

That bit of chin music prompted a hellacious rant by Ryder's manager, Art Stone. The benches were ready to clear. Simons was warned, but Stone wanted an ejection. The pitch was *so obvious.* Stone, a paunchy old-timer, stood toe to toe with the ump and unloaded but, somehow, avoided the heave-ho.

Now, it is Simons' turn in the box.

And Ryder's turn to say *hello.*

Wyatt wants the 1.

Tim Simons is one of the better-hitting pitchers in the league. He owns a lifetime .180 average and six home runs. He carries himself well at the plate, with a touch of swagger.

With the first pitch, however, Ryder shows him 109. Pure gold. Center cut.

Simons does his impression of an old statue.

Why hurt him? Why watch the benches clear? Where does tit for tat lead? Where will it end?

Second pitch. Why not flash the goods again, let Simons feel what it's like to stand next to a bullet train?

This time, a mere 105. This time Ryder dots the corner high and tight.

Strike two.

Wyatt shows fist.

Beanball.

Wyatt wants Ryder to defend himself.

Ryder shakes it off. He stares in.

Wyatt makes him wait. The pause is Wyatt saying, *Fuck you, give me what I want.* It lasts two seconds, but it's there. Wyatt is speaking for the whole team. Maybe he's channeling all the fans back in Baltimore. Everyone wants payback for Ryder kissing the dirt.

Ryder wants another sign.

These longer pauses are sometimes trouble. Ryder likes to stay in a rhythm. There is a cadence to his work. He never likes to leave too much time for the ghost to appear. The ghost has a mean sense of timing. Ryder likes to keep moving, like there is some special law of physics governing the space between human beings and the supernatural.

At long last, Wyatt puts down the 1.

Ryder's next pitch wouldn't impress a scout watching a high school game.

Simons thinks he's got a clue. He pulls the trigger, but so early that Simons' bat is clear through the zone before the fat marshmallow pitch floats across the plate, waist high and dead center over the plate, and lands in Wyatt's mitt.

The guys in the Oriole dugout cut up and smack the rail with a howl or three. Ryder buries his smile, pulling his jersey up over his face to wipe off the sweat so nobody can see.

Ninety.

His teammates are still cracking up when Ryder reaches the dugout, and he tries like hell to avoid joining the laughter.

— ᚙ —

Umpire, catcher, batter, plate—and the sixty feet, six inches separating him from them.

The fundamentals don't change from mound to mound to mound.

The backdrop, the breeze, and the mood change from park to park. So does the weight of the air. The intensity of the crowd.

The peripherals don't alter the essential equation of baseball. Sixty feet, six inches. Batter stands there. Pitcher throws from here. Three strikes, you're out.

Occasionally, in his brief time in the major leagues, Frank Ryder pauses for a moment to rub down the seams on a fresh ball. He thinks of how he got here. He thinks of how he almost *didn't* get here. But at the red-hot core of the game is a simple question: "Can you hit my stuff?"

Chapter 3

Ray Gallo pops a handful of cashews, chews the buttery bits, and washes them down with a sip of bourbon.

On ESPN, Matt Vasgersian is running through an analysis of Frank Ryder's last pitch to Tim Simons. The video is frozen on perhaps the funniest frame Ray Gallo has ever seen—Simons' bat in full extension as if he has finished a home run swing, and yet there is the ball hovering like a full moon over home plate. Parked. Simons' head is down. He is staring right at the ball. It's the moment when Simons realizes he's been played.

Vasgersian is chuckling. "At ninety miles an hour, it probably looked like a pitch thrown by a fifth grader in a game of underhand softball." Vasgersian is a likable, hardworking reporter. "At ninety miles an hour, Simons had a full point-four seconds to decide whether to swing, where to swing, and even how to swing. For a hitter, it's the equivalent of a long walk on the beach, those point-four seconds. But when Ryder takes time off the table, every scrap of it, he can toy with even the best hitters like they're puppets on his string. That's the genius of Frank Ryder."

The replay of the fat baseball sitting over the plate, almost like it was parked on an invisible tee, is followed by the slo-mo replay of Tim Simons thrashing his bat into an innocent bag of sunflower seeds in the dugout. Simons finishes his tantrum holding twelve inches of his Louisville Slugger and its sharp, jagged end as his teammates run for cover.

"Serious humiliation right there," says A-Rod. ESPN has cut back to the booth, where the former Yankee star is huddled with Vasgersian and Jessica Mendoza. "Pupil schools teacher. We all know how much Ryder idolized Tim Simons back in Atlanta, and I'm sure it's one of those moments that will be remembered here in Chicago for a long time to come."

—m—

Chicago. It's either too hot or way too cold. Either way, inhospitable. Where are the trees? The flowers? The greenery? One big lake doesn't cut it, but what's happening with Ray Gallo's team is better than any view.

With each Ryder pitch there is almost a need to laugh, partly at the spectacle of it all and partly at his own weird luck. On TV, it's like you're watching a joke. It's like every pitch is a coked-up hologram video, the ball a subatomic particle, an unhittable blink of white nothing, and really at the speed it goes you're not even sure you can pick up the color. It is as if Frank Ryder's pitching motion is double speed, the ball is triple speed, and everything else moves to the beat of a regular world.

In fact, in the bottom of the seventh, the first two batters tap identical *excuse-me* dribblers back to Ryder. The third batter fans in four pitches. Seven pitches, three outs.

In the top of the eighth, Simons looks weary.

"You can see him struggling to find his release point," says Mendoza. "His velocity is down. It's like he was trying to keep up with Ryder and now he's gassed, but it's been about eighteen starts since Simons made it through the eighth inning, and you have to go all the way back to 2018 for his last complete game."

Simons quickly walks two batters and gets yanked for a rookie out of the bullpen. The new pitcher gives up a bases-clearing triple on the first pitch. Orioles 8, Cubs 1.

Gallo's phone chimes, spitting up a number and a name. The ring brings Gallo back to the moment.

At seventy-one years of age, Gallo occasionally forgets where he is and who is around. It's as if he has slipped into a trance—and he doesn't really mind it, as long as it's not the beginning of dementia or some related bullshit. He blames this one on the kid, Ryder, and the mesmerizing spectacle of watching him pitch.

The phone chimes again. Tommy Rafferty.

Gallo's assistant, Aiko Tanaka, relaxes on the nearby couch. She is the one who programmed his phone so each ring brings up the caller's identity. Aiko is working on a plate of room service salad—kale or arugula, something undernourishing and carb-free. She is ever perky and always polished. Gallo finds her insights interesting. And it's hard to imagine someone who loves the game more.

"Tommy Boy," says Gallo. "Strange that you should call."

A laugh. A polite one. "Welcome to Chicago."

As with most calls, Gallo punches the speaker icon so Aiko can hear. He hates holding these devices to his ear.

"You think I'm in Chicago? Spending money in *your* town?"

"I have friends at Midway."

"Maybe I sent my Gulfstream to pick up a pizza."

"Friends at the Langham too."

"Is the Cubs a baseball team or a goddamn spy organization?"

"These days you gotta be both."

"Here on business," says Gallo. "It's purely coincidental."

"Is that right?"

"What's it to you?"

"I thought you were stepping away from the day-to-day stuff."

"Sometimes it helps to bring in the heavy hitters."

True. Gallo made his fortune dreaming up and manufacturing the active ingredients for cosmetic companies—proteins, liposomes, bioactives. His company is behind the scenes, but his work shows up in big-brand makeup and shampoo and lotions.

Gallo wants a change of topic.

"Your boy Simons was trying to put Ryder in the hospital. You calling to apologize?"

Tommy Rafferty is the chairman of a conglomerate with an ownership team, and Gallo can't imagine the complications. Rafferty's siblings are on it, too, but Gallo is most familiar with Tommy, who is twenty years his junior and made boatloads in investment banking.

"I'm sure it was a mistake," says Rafferty.

"Yeah, Tim Simons. Did he have three wild pitches all of last year? Four?"

"Not every pitch goes where you want," says Rafferty.

Unless, thinks Gallo. Unless you're Frank Ryder.

"I'm calling with a welcome greeting and to say congratulations on Frank Ryder."

"I didn't train him."

"You found him."

"*Drafted* him. And all of Oriole Nation would have squawked if we had picked anyone else."

Ryder had been a high-risk prospect when he graduated from Thomas Jefferson High School in Denver, due to the speed of his pitches. He walked too many. Scouts kept tabs on him at Metro State. The Roadrunners rarely produced major-league talent, but Ryder's fastball generated buzzworthy chatter. Frank Ryder was drafted after his junior year, but he opted to finish college rather than take a lowball offer from the Phillies.

During his senior year, something clicked. He didn't lose a game. His fastball hit 104. Attendance at Roadrunner games went crazy. Frank

Ryder's name sat on top of every list of pitching prospects. On top, in fact, of all potential draftees.

"Hell of a start to the season," says Rafferty.

"The key word is *start*," says Gallo.

"Seriously, are you worried?"

Gallo is always afraid. It's in his nature.

"The healthy variety. Keeps me sane."

"Your boy is on track to smash the single-season strikeout record by early August."

"Worry based on facts," says Gallo. "Facts about pitchers and injuries."

On television, the Cubs' Kurt Costa stares at the first pitch, if it's possible to stare at something you can't see. The pitch is proof of Ryder's new clubhouse nickname, CSI. *Can't see it.*

The superimposed screen graphic shows the pitch arrived at 107 in the corner of the strike zone next to Costa's knees.

"Yikes," says Rafferty. "Guess your boy wasn't too happy with Costa's first AB."

"How come you're not at the game?"

"I don't see the point," says Rafferty.

"There's a point to baseball? Tell me."

Other than making money, of course.

"The point is entertainment," says Rafferty. "And in our case, entertainment involves creating tension. On any given night, et cetera."

"So you're calling me to welcome me to Chicago and, what, warn me too?"

"There's the Gallo paranoia we all love and admire," says Rafferty.

"Did I misinterpret your message?"

"You must know something is coming," says Rafferty. "You hear the talk."

"Talk about what?"

"About what to do."

"There is nothing to do but sit back, blow the suds off the top of another cold one, put some popcorn in the microwave, and marvel at an athletic specimen."

The camera is zoomed in on Costa's face. He is hyperalert. He swings at the next pitch long before it arrives. It's an ultrarare changeup. Ninety-four.

"Maybe," says Rafferty. "Until attendance crashes. And what if there are dozens of Frank Ryders running around, and suddenly every game is a done deal before it even starts? Maybe we should set an upper limit on how fast a pitcher can throw."

"Is there an empty seat at Wrigley? Even the rooftops, for crying out loud."

"It's the first time around," says Rafferty. "Curiosity factor for now. We've talked to our fans."

"Focus groups? Impressive."

"The bottom line is eyeballs on televisions and fans in the stands," says Rafferty. "Watching Frank Ryder pitch is going to draw some interest at first, but then why watch the game? I'm not talking about the baseball purists; I'm talking about getting the average guy out to the ballpark with his wife and kids or his buddies for beers and hot dogs. They want to see their team smack the ball around, score some runs."

Costa doesn't get his bat off his shoulder for strike three, a snaky cutter at 103 that nips the outside corner of the plate.

"He's one pitcher," says Gallo.

"I'm sure you think nothing needs to be done."

"So you are calling with a warning."

"It's not a warning. It's a discussion."

"It's not hard to read between the lines. Or, in this case, hear between the lines."

"Think about it," says Rafferty.

"I've thought plenty. He's one pitcher. Cy Young was one pitcher. Nolan Ryan was one pitcher. Bob Gibson was one pitcher who had thirteen shutouts in 1968. Thirteen! There was no talk of *something needs to be done*."

"Frank Ryder has changed the game," says Rafferty. "It's not the wins and strikeouts and the lack of hits."

"He gave up a home run tonight."

"The definition of fluke."

"So your pitcher shuts us out, you win. Ryder loses."

"It's the balance between hitter and pitcher. At Ryder's speed, there is no game."

"Batters are always on the losing end. They live with failure."

"But at Ryder's velocity, the game evaporates. It's like having a soccer game and telling one team there is no goal for them to kick the ball into. It's like putting the basketball rim at ten feet for one team and fifty for the other. It's like a football game with eleven guys on one side trying to move the ball against thirty-three."

"They didn't tell Rickey Henderson to stop stealing bases."

"It's a different wrinkle."

"Or Barry Bonds to stop hitting home runs."

"In a way, yeah, they did."

Gallo's Orioles are back at bat. They are spunky tonight. A team-wide confidence has oozed its way into the dugout. He can see it in the little moments after the players come off the field and the way they watch and hang out on the lip of the dugout when it's their turn to bat. There is hope in their eyes and maybe a spark of determination Gallo hasn't seen in years.

Gallo stands. He is a large man. Old bones complain. He will never move through life as unburdened as his wife, Lisa, who tonight is getting in a few miles on the elliptical in the exercise room and taking a swim in the hotel pool, all while listening to audiobooks on her waterproof earbuds.

Gallo's nose is knobby, his eyes droop, his jowls balloon. He moves close to the floor-to-ceiling window, feels a cool flow from the air-conditioning vent. He stares down at the Chicago River, the bridges going across. He knows how all the other twenty-nine owners would react if they had Frank Ryder on their team. He knows how he's *supposed* to react. He has seen the feminine but focused sparkle in the eyes of his GM. *Hope. Momentum.* Now there is reason to put together a plan to build around Ryder. The kid has nine wins in late May, and if he can lift the Orioles up by a total of thirty or thirty-five more wins over the previous year's team, when the Orioles started showing signs of life, they will be smack in the middle of the pennant race in September. One sore elbow? One off-field accident? One strange line drive back up the mound that catches Ryder's ankle or a rib?

Or face?

Baseball can't guard against any of those wrinkles or the delicate psychology of these precious athletic minds. Baseball is a humbling game, they say. Why not be an average team? Entertain, sure. Give fans hope, sure. But really *going for it* means pressure and driving yourself crazy. Much like his business, Gallo only knows to hire good people and support them. Does he believe that shelling out megasalaries for top talent would guarantee a better record? No.

"So if you think it's a problem, how you going to fix it?" says Gallo. "Yank him if he tops one oh five? Suspend him for the season if he tops one oh six? How do you tell a professional athlete he can't do what he's good at? Can't give it his best?"

"What I'm saying is the commissioner is poking around."

"Poking around *what*, for Chrissake?"

"He knows you have to nip this in the bud, and maybe the Rules Committee needs to take a look."

"Well, nip *this* in the bud, if that's all you got."

That draws a chuckle from Rafferty. "I'm just saying there might be a topic on the agenda at next month's meeting."

"Give me a break."

"You had to see this coming."

25

"I did? Next you're gonna say pitchers can't exceed ten strikeouts a game, or maybe they have to pitch underhand like a goddamn softball game?"

Gallo comes back to the TV, remains standing. Aiko replenishes his drink. He rolls his eyes.

Aiko shakes her head. Shrugs. Smiles. She is cute, trim, and always well put together. To Gallo, she is youth and springtime and optimism.

The Orioles have the bases loaded, nobody out. This kind of delicious anticipation used to happen once a season; now it seems to happen with regularity.

"Commissioner put you up to this call? You're willing to be his emissary?"

"See you in New York. Bring all your best arguments."

Aiko rolls her eyes like a teenager told to clean her room. The look is precisely what Gallo is feeling.

"The commissioner is going to stir all this up midseason? What a pathetic lunkhead."

"I'll be sure to relay your kindness," says Rafferty. "You know we can't let it linger."

On TV, Orioles center fielder Diaz slashes a line drive in the gap in right field, clearing the bases with a triple. The camera finds Frank Ryder in the crowd of ballplayers greeting teammates who have scored with high fives and hugs. Ryder looks as happy as a person can get. Another camera finds a group of four men in the stands. They are all wearing Cubs pinstripes T-shirts with a giant blue circle, the red capital *C*, and red *ubs* letters inside it. There's not a smile among them.

Chapter 4

At certain times, and he is never sure what factors help him keep his composure, Ryder can let his mind settle on what happened without going all the way down to the darkest end of his own tunnel of sadness.

He has googled himself—Frank Ryder Webb Bridge Park.

It's there on the internet for anyone to ponder. One minute, innocent Frank Ryder pitching in Alpharetta, Georgia. One minute, ordinary Little League kid. One minute, as far as he remembers, happy kid, normal kid dreaming of baseball and all his favorite players on the Atlanta Braves and doing whatever it took to stay on his parents' good side with grades and chores so they would keep driving him to games and practices. Anyone looking at the video wouldn't guess that anything unusual is about to happen. The only video of what happened was shot on an iPhone, and the quality is good—a bit too good, as far as Ryder is concerned.

The baseball field in question could be any diamond in the country, a bunch of twelve-year-olds doing their best imitation of big-league baseball players.

One minute, it's so routine.

And then comes the worst thing.

The worst day.

The worst everything.

The worst moment.

Once it's happened, of course, there is lots of video and lots of photographs and television news cameras too. All those videos and news reports come later. One video spawns thousands of other versions of the story. It is "Video Zero," the first infection of the brief epidemic of coverage.

The news clips are all online too—sad-faced reporters next to the field where Frank Ryder used to play.

—⁓—

Today, the reporters aren't sad. They are hungry.

"That first pitch from Simons?" The reporter is a pen-and-notebook guy. "Did you know it was coming?"

"No," says Ryder.

Of course he knew it was coming. But admitting it would acknowledge the unwritten rules, which ballplayers don't discuss.

"Bother you?"

Never show weakness.

But Maggie has urged him to lighten up in these moments. *When the game's over,* she says, *you can relax. Let them see another side.*

Ryder thinks he's trying to heed Maggie's advice.

"No," says Ryder.

"Did you think the ump's warning was fair? Right?"

TV reporter, much slicker. Tie, but no coat. The visitors' clubhouse at Wrigley is cramped and close. Ryder is sweating from every pore.

"Not my call," says Ryder.

"But you didn't retaliate."

"Pitch might have been a mistake." *It wasn't.* "What's to retaliate? I was okay."

Ryder is in his street clothes now, a shiny blue suit. Italian cotton. White shirt. His tie, burnt orange, hangs loose. The clothes and the expensive tailor were not his idea, and he realizes now, at this inopportune moment, that they aren't him. They are pretentious. He is not Justin Verlander. He is not *GQ*. His agent brought him an offer to endorse cologne; he wants peanut butter. Or tools. Something real or useful.

"Stone nearly got ejected arguing on your behalf."

"Yes," says Ryder.

"So he thought Simons was throwing at you on purpose."

Ryder shrugs.

"You didn't want to retaliate?"

Ryder stands by his locker. There were so many reporters around him he isn't sure who asked that question. "I'm out there to pitch," he says.

Maggie will scold him later, no doubt.

Plus, he will never mess around near a batter's head again.

"The home run?" A female reporter. She is from TV, given the hair and makeup. Also given the microphone and cameraman behind her. Red hair, warm ivory skin, light freckles, tall.

"Yes?" says Ryder.

"First hit you've given up in your last three starts."

"There are going to be hits." He smiles. "Apparently."

The reporters laugh, and that makes Ryder hold the smile, look up and around. "I am not a machine," he adds.

"This one landed on Kenmore. It's up there with Dave Kingman in the record books."

"Costa is a good hitter." In fact, Costa is one of the best. He's a crafty hitter, not a slugger. He plays every pitch like he's there to win.

"Do you think he was guessing?"

Guessing is the only way. Timing, location—everything.

"I'm afraid you would have to ask him," says Ryder. He is polite. Earnest. Soft spoken. "I have no idea."

"Was the location where you wanted it?"

"Yes," says Ryder.

They all are.

Well, most.

"Costa says you can be beaten. He says it's a matter of batters answering the call. Upping their game."

"Fine with me," says Ryder.

Except how, exactly?

At 110—and Ryder hit 110 on the gun three times against the Cubs tonight—there is only hope.

And luck.

"Did you think Costa was boasting when he rounded the bases? Pounding his chest when he came to home plate?"

"I was getting ready for the next batter," says Ryder.

But he saw the whole thing. And there was mumbling in the dugout in the top of the following inning, that Costa needed to get drilled.

"Is there a secret to beating you?" All the way back to the pen-and-notebook guy.

"What do you mean?"

"What would you do if you were a hitter?"

"Sorry to say, but that's not my job. And if I knew, why would I help my enemy?"

Ryder smiles. The reporters laugh. Maggie would approve. Ryder likes the feeling, too, but it only lasts for a flash.

"Do you think what happened to you in Alpharetta—" This is a new voice. He is older. Suspenders over a white shirt. Heavy stubble, no doubt part of his look, on olive skin. Microphone.

Ryder holds up a hand. "I don't go there."

"It's not about *what* happened; it's whether you'd be here today if that *hadn't* happened. What do you think?"

"I don't discuss it."

The reporter's microphone comes closer like a cattle prod. "But it's not about the incident itself. It's how the incident impacted your life."

Incident? Sounds so minor. Do *incidents* generate ghosts?

"No," says Ryder.

"No, what?" says the reporter.

"No, I don't discuss it."

"Do you think what you have become, a pitcher who has made normal baseball offense impotent—do you think any of this would have happened if not for—"

The whole room can fill in the blank. So can everyone watching on *Baseball Tonight* or streaming it online. His parents? They didn't start out as sports people, but they watch when he pitches. His brother too. And Maggie, back home in Denver in her apartment. She tracks his coverage, subscribes to MLB so she doesn't miss a game. They are always pointing the camera at him, even between games when he's sitting in the dugout, yukking it up. Ryder swims in a fishbowl. At MSU, as his rankings climbed among draft prospects, it wasn't hard for reporters to track his story back to Alpharetta and find out about the move to Colorado.

"I'd be glad to answer any other questions," says Ryder. "About tonight's game."

At some point, the questions stop. Each city has been a bit different, the level of aggressiveness from the media. They all want a piece of him. From a physical perspective, this part of the whole job is easy but tiring. He gets weary of hearing his own voice. It's a struggle to respect each question as if he hasn't heard it before.

Tonight, the locker room is hot and close. Even though he has showered, Ryder is sticky and overheated. Fleeting panic arrives with a flash of claustrophobia. Once, the ghost appeared amid the cluster of reporters. In Arlington, Texas. There is almost no *there* in Arlington except more used car lots in a row than Ryder had ever seen, but that's where the ghost showed up, in the visitors' locker room holding a microphone and listening to every one of Ryder's answers. The ghost wore sharp school clothes and a black backpack. The backpack looked heavy, the way the straps pinched down on the fabric of his white shirt. The ghost's black skin was perfect, his forehead smooth and shiny. The ghost did not move. He didn't say a word, asked no questions. He held the microphone and stared.

Ryder had a hard time holding back the tears. His voice was thinner than usual.

Ryder's trick now is to wait for a pause long enough to say, "Thanks, everyone," then turn to his locker to grab his bag and phone. "Thanks, everyone" is becoming a signature. A smile helps. He has fed them enough. They don't complain.

The one guy with the cattle prod microphone, however, isn't getting the message.

"Seriously, it's a cause-and-effect question," he says. "Do you think you'd be here today without the other? Did the Alpharetta thing give you more, I don't know, *determination?*"

"I don't talk about that," says Ryder. The smile is gone. "In any way, shape, or form."

—⁂—

Tonight, Ryder is in time for the team bus. He prefers the bus over a cab. Likes being with his teammates, about the only ones who don't make him feel like he belongs in Ripley's Believe It or Not! Odditorium—an Arlington attraction he spotted in a hotel brochure.

There are fans with Sharpies uncapped and ticket stubs to sign. Baseball caps and baseballs too. He signs a few, makes it clear he is in a hurry, and there's Jessica Mendoza by the Billy Williams statue, and she walks with him to the waiting bus. The bus idles with a metallic purr.

Ryder is a big fan of Jessica Mendoza's work and style, her enthusiasm for the tiny elements of the game. Ryder is so close to the safety and sanctity of the bus and the air-conditioning, and yet it's Jessica Mendoza, a former softball outfielder, a damn good one. She played for Stanford—a good pitching school Ryder dreamed of attending.

"Can I give you a call in the morning?" she says. "Buster wants you back on the podcast if you're up for it."

"Buster" Olney. *Baseball Tonight.*

"Sure," says Ryder. "Though there's not much new to say. I mean, since last time." Or the time before.

Mendoza smiles. She is wearing a simple white shirt. "Good game tonight."

"Thanks."

"You're good with the press too."

Maggie might disagree.

"I try."

"You look like you saw this coming."

"I like to plan," says Ryder.

"That's a lot of pressure."

"Part of the job," says Ryder. "Call me any time in the morning after eight. Buster has my number."

"You realize they're coming for you?"

Ryder stops. "Reporters?"

"The owners."

Ryder glances up. In the window of the bus behind Mendoza and above her are Tackett, a utility infielder, and Diaz, their center fielder. Tackett taps the top of his bare wrist. Diaz slices his throat with a finger and laughs, big shiny teeth flashing.

"We have sources saying they will make a move," says Mendoza.

"And do what?"

She shrugs, like, *Who knows?* "You must have anticipated a pushback."

"Sure," says Ryder. "I mean, I read some of the stuff out there, but what do you think the owners want?"

"There are theories all over the place. They run the gamut."

"Theories?"

"Set a top-end limit. Say, one oh eight," says Mendoza. "Or one oh five. Or move the mound back. They're worried about the long term. Attendance. TV ratings. There are rumblings. They are going to try something. Reassure everyone they will keep the game intact."

—ɷ—

It's four miles to their hotel in the Loop, but with Chicago traffic on a Friday night, there is ample time for stories on the bus and some whooping and high fives. It's fun to play a good team and kick their ass. Pumping each other up is their reward. So is running down the Cubs and Kurt Costa, though Ryder has long admired Costa's on-field tenacity.

Ryder sits alone, his face against the cool window of the bus. He is tired to the marrow. He could fall asleep in two minutes if he closed his eyes, but instead he lets the city drift past, a slow-moving blur of light. Muffled horn honks and the occasional shout from the sidewalk penetrate the sealed bunker of the team bus, the grind of the idling motor a kind of gentle white noise all its own. Ryder hopes not to spot the ghost dodging traffic on Lake Shore Drive, jogging alongside the bus or waving at Ryder with a big smile. One thing about Ryder's ghost—he looks so damn ordinary. He wears school clothes. His backpack looks heavy enough for college, let alone eighth grade.

Ryder plucks his tattered copy of *Dune* from his bag, punches on the overhead light. He loves how quickly he can be back on the inhospitable planet Arrakis, but at the pace he's reading, the thick novel won't be done until the season is over. He loves what the book has to say about managing fear, and Ryder feels empathy with the main character, Paul, who is adapting to a whole new alien culture. Ryder dabbles at video games. *Fortnite. Minecraft.* His heart's not in it, unlike many of the others. He likes the simplicity of a book, how the images are all in his head and not forced down his throat. The book is a suggestion from Maggie, who has a whole shelf devoted to *Dune.*

"Ryder."

Stone sits down in the empty seat next to him. Ryder nods, holds up his bottle of water in a toast. Later, in his room, he'll have one cold IPA and watch the video. Ninety-two pitches. The physical fatigue will ease and his brain will take over, wanting to think through everything from the game.

"Skip," says Ryder.

"Lots of zen in *Dune,*" says Stone.

"My girlfriend told me the same thing," he says. "To watch for the zen stuff and something about time. I'm digging the sandworms and trying to imagine how bleak it is up there."

As if it's a real planet.

"Great game."

Ryder says nothing.

"Your wipe-out pitch was the cutter tonight," says Stone. "Twenty K's, and sixty percent of those you closed with the cutter."

"It had good bite tonight," says Ryder. "The heavy air."

"Your spin rate, zone velocity, stride length. All good."

The Orioles support a data team, but it's one-third the size of the fleet of analysts the Yankees and Astros are said to deploy. There are rumors those teams have up to twenty geeks running around crunching numbers and developing spreadsheets, warning of injuries, proposing trade ideas, on and on. Ryder is okay with data. But if he concentrates on all the numbers, he will lose the flow and freedom of pitching.

"Felt good," says Ryder.

"You afraid to throw at Simons?"

"Not afraid."

"Afraid of hurting him?"

Ryder shakes his head. *Of course* he's afraid of hurting Simons. "Not really."

"It doesn't have to be one of your bullets."

Art Stone was a big-league catcher, most of his career with the Washington Nationals, before working his way up the coaching and managing ranks. He played hard, played scrappy, played hurt, played like every game was life and death.

"Of course."

"Then you have to respond. He expects it."

"Probably."

"And right now he sees you as weak. He's shaking his head somewhere. And he's thinking you aren't tough enough for this game."

Stone is old school and top down. Players as chess pieces. Before getting drafted by the Orioles, Ryder would have said it wasn't clear the Orioles had a burning desire to win. Two decades of mediocrity, except for one brief appearance in the playoffs when they didn't win one game, suggest that Ray Gallo, the owner, is happy with average.

"We kicked their ass."

"Even the fans expect you to return the favor."

There is beer on Stone's breath. In the seat across the aisle, Diaz is reading a magazine. His pinpoint overhead light puts Stone in silhouette.

"Wyatt said he asked you for it."

"He did."

"You have to plunk him, Frank. It's a fact of life. A fact of baseball. Your team had a chip on its shoulder. You understand, right?"

Ryder bristles at the lecture—but bristles more at himself, for not being prepared. He should have seen Stone's admonishment coming.

"Because Simons came after me."

"And because they want to *protect* you." In the darkness of the team bus, seats so high each row is its own cocoon, Stone's voice is firm. "Every single one of your teammates was ready to come out on the field and back you up if Simons or anyone took offense at you replying with your own goddamn beanball. Your own goddamn message. They were hoping for it. That's when the team comes together. When we got each other's goddamn backs. It would have been good for the team."

"Even if I'm fined. Suspended."

"Think long term. So you miss one start. You're telling your teammates who you are; you're telling the fans who you are. What you're made of."

Ryder swallows hard. What he wants to say is, *I'm made of outs. I bring you outs. I bring you wins. Eye for an eye leaves everyone blind.* "Okay," he says.

"He tried to bean you at ninety-eight."

"Thanks for noticing."

"So you come in at one oh two. Midthigh. Fat bruise. All even fucking steven."

Ryder won't let himself get trapped like this again.

"It's for the team," says Stone.

"Yep," says Ryder.

"It's not the Georgia stuff, is it?" says Stone. "I mean—"

Stone doesn't know what to say. Most people don't.

"Nah," says Ryder, taking Stone off the hook.

"Afraid that'll happen again?"

All the time.

"Nope," says Ryder.

"And it's not, like, an ethical thing with you?"

"I get your drift," says Ryder. "I got it now."

Stone rises to head back up. He likes to sit in the front seat with an open view of the road. "Okay," he says.

—⚓—

With the win, the Orioles move ahead of Tampa Bay in the AL East. Only Boston and New York now own better records than Baltimore. There is an upward trajectory now. And this climb is happening at a time of the year, in late May, when Baltimore Oriole faithful expect to see the team sag and fade, make a firm commitment to playing mediocre baseball for the remainder of the season, only occasionally winning a series and never against the teams above them in the division. In fact, they are typically chewed up and spit out by the likes of the Red Sox, the Yankees, and the Rays. Only Toronto started the year with a horrible April and immediately packed up all belongings and pride and moved to the basement of the division.

The pressure is on Ray Gallo to support the momentum, to catch Boston and New York and their home run–clobbering lineups.

The pressure is also on their numbers-crunching general manager to find another starting pitcher and maybe a reliever too. There is one prospect in the minors, a third baseman, who is launching homers on a regular basis. And Stone is pushing hard for the GM to go out and snag an overlooked outfielder from the Mariners, a guy Stone believes is underused, has plenty of pop, and might be available for cash considerations.

All the reporters and columnists and commentators credit Ryder. He is the lone significant new arrival. He's one guy, and he pitches every fourth game, but his presence is rubbing off. His teammates are sharper, more focused. Hope is high-octane fuel.

Wrote one reporter for the *Baltimore Sun*:

> Frank Ryder's pitches aren't just game-changing. They are game-ruining. They are the blink within the blink.
>
> They are mini meteors of mind-blowing mayhem. They turn hitters into mere props, useless afterthoughts. While other pitchers ply their trade with ordinary All-American Remingtons, Ryder went out and brought back a smoothbore antitank assault rifle.

The bullets coming off his long fingers are fired at four times the speed of sound.

Ryder's pitches are something you have to see to believe, but the problem is, well, seeing them. The problem for hitters? The problem for hitters is there is no problem. There is nothing left to figure out. All the analytics in the world won't help. The problem is there is no time. Frank Ryder has eliminated time. He has taken what precious scant few microseconds a batter is given to work with and he puts that time in the garbage disposal with the batter's ego and pride and he hits the switch, turns it all into chunky bits, and washes it down the drain. Until Frank Ryder, batters luxuriated in .3 to .4 seconds of time to do their thing. Frank Ryder takes time off the table.

Frank Ryder is giving long-suffering Oriole fans a couple of things they have lacked for approximately two decades. A steel backbone. And a reason to believe.

Right now, for Baltimore, he's the only man that matters.

Chapter 5

In his hotel room high above the Loop, Ryder stretches. He is tired but recognizes his mind is still whirring—the reporters, Mendoza, Stone. The reporters, *the ghost*, Mendoza, Stone. Simons, the reporters, the ghost, Mendoza, Stone.

One thing about the ghost: he prefers public spaces. So far, he hasn't slipped into one of Ryder's hotel rooms or caught him off guard in his condo in Baltimore. If only Ryder never had to venture out. Maybe the key to no ghosts is self-confinement.

Ryder is barefoot in black shorts and a black MSU DENVER T-shirt with block letters. The Orioles' video department has loaded every one of Ryder's pitches into one loop and loaded the video on a flash drive. Ryder slides the stick into his laptop on the edge of the bed, but before he gets into watching the video, he limbers up on the floor. He travels with a yoga mat for this reason.

Planks. Lunges. Dead bugs. Ryder stands for scapular wall slides, and, back on the floor, grabs his foam roller for the quadruped reach throughs. Every motion is gentle, careful, respectful of his body. Ryder's body has poured itself out, and Ryder likes to say *thank you* back.

Propped up on his bed with a beer, the solid tug of fatigue a steady presence, he studies his work. Each of his ninety-six pitches runs first in regular speed and again in slow motion. Strung together like this, the regular-speed series runs about five minutes long. The slo-mo is twenty.

The regular-speed version is from the batter's point of view, the slo-mo version from the third base side. Ryder studies each pitch. Arm slot, release point, rhythm. He looks for irregularities. Each pitch includes an embedded graphic showing release velocity and plate velocity. There is a Baltimore Orioles internal website he could log in to if he wanted to study data like a college professor making a bid for the Nobel Prize. *No thanks.*

There is no sound. Ryder can add his own soundtrack, the roar at Costa's home run and the ho-hum quiet when he was dispatching Cubs back to the bench in batches of three. There isn't a muscle or ligament not engaged in pitching a baseball. Fibers fire together in a symphony of motion, as if it is one thing and not a bunch of parts. And they need to do it the same from first pitch to last. His mind needs to grasp the pieces of action, but so does his body. When it's working, pitching is as automatic as walking or climbing a set of stairs. When it's flowing, the unconscious self takes over.

Tonight, at Wrigley, it was all rhythm. There was one fat fluke when Costa swung with authority. But on the replay the bat starts to move when Ryder's arm is at high noon, straight up. Costa didn't track it out of Ryder's hand, adjust, clobber it. No. Making contact was naked luck.

Ryder's phone chimes. He glances at the ID and scolds himself. Checks the bedside clock. It's 12:02 in Chicago, 11:02 in Denver.

"My bad," he says by way of answering.

"As always." There is a protracted sigh. And a laugh. "Just out here waiting and waiting."

"Would you believe me if I said I was about to pick up the phone?"

"Probably not."

"You're a smart one."

"It ain't brains. It's intuition. Part of the *whole package.* Boys are kept in the dark, but there is a special class for all little first-grade girls. You guys are too busy picking your noses and groping around in your own pants to notice, but all the women who teach elementary school pull all of us first-grade girls aside and make sure we are in tune with our intuition, and aware it's something we got that boys don't have and will never get. Our only true superpower."

"Who knew? Reason to be careful."

Ryder closes his eyes. He'll never tire of her husky, too-cool voice. Ever since he was a junior at Thomas Jefferson High School, Maggie Moore has been on his mind every single day.

"And I just told you something you now need to forget you ever heard," she says.

"I brought along my neuralyzer," says Ryder. "I'll spray myself later. Wouldn't want to violate any trust."

Men in Black is one of her favorite movies too. She goes into the Rip Torn bit: "You're a rumor, recognizable only as déjà vu and dismissed just as quickly. You don't exist—you were never even born."

"Then how did I get to Chicago?" says Ryder.

Maggie ignores him. "We at the FBI do not have a sense of humor we are aware of," she says.

Ryder imagines Maggie lolling on her bed. She likes to stretch flat on her stomach and hang her upper torso over the side, talk with her head dangling.

"Cool, whatever you say, Slick," says Ryder, giving his best deadpan Tommy Lee Jones. "But I need to tell you something about all your skills. As of right now, they mean precisely . . . dick."

"And that's something nobody is ever going to say to you," says Maggie.

"Please."

"We all watched out here tonight. Weren't you pissed off when Simons knocked you down? I mean, *what the hell?*"

"They want you to know your place."

"They? I thought it was one guy—that Tim 'Simon Says' dude you used to worship."

"He was sending a message from all of baseball. And all the baseball gods."

"What message?"

"Upstarts need to know their place."

Ryder wishes she would FaceTime or Skype so he could see her, but Maggie prefers voice only. She won't send him pictures of herself, and prefers email to text too.

"When the announcers were wrapping up, Jessica Mendoza said the game is going to respond, maybe change the rules. Can they do that? Change the rules because of you?"

Maggie is a runner. She played lacrosse for a year in high school before switching to cross-country. She wasn't a baseball fan or team sports fan when they met. That's changed.

"They can try," says Ryder. "Any rule change has to go through a whole process—owners and players. Committees and stuff. Seems ridiculous, but yeah, they change the rules all the time. Like that whole DH business in the American League."

"Don't you like to hit?"

"Of course," says Ryder. "Cubs, Rockies, Braves. Any of them. Saint Louis, one classy organization. Sure—would love to have pitched for a National League team."

Maggie Moore knows everything. Except the ghost.

"Get yourself traded."

"It's called a contract," says Ryder. "A deal. What else did Mendoza say?"

"There are two other announcers. It's not the Jessica Mendoza show up there. And she's married, Frankie Boy. *Married.*"

Maggie is teasing him. But Maggie is the one who declined his offer to come live with him in Baltimore. His condo there is big enough for a large family, but she wanted to stay close to her mother. Between six weeks of spring training and the Orioles' travel schedule, Maggie figured it didn't make that much difference where she lived. And, despite the familiar banter, there are unspoken spaces between them.

"Mendoza is married, huh?" he says. "You really pay attention."

"They showed pictures of her with her *kids*." Maggie draws the word out. "And her very *adorbs* husband."

"So?"

"So, I can read you like a book over the phone from a thousand miles away."

"And what about you?"

"What about me *what*?"

"The guys you're fighting off."

"Two dates every night; on the weekend it's three," says Maggie. "It's tiring. Being a gangly, slightly awkward girl with no boobs to speak of and a schedule like mine? I am thinking of passing out numbers, like at the DMV. Neighbors complaining about the long lines."

"I knew it."

"Oh, and another thing," says Maggie.

"Go ahead."

"Am I keeping you up?"

"Not a bit." After a game, his body is tired, but it takes hours to unwind. The middle two nights between starts, he'll sleep like all the logs in all the forests. The night before his next start, he's lucky to get a few hours. "What is it?"

"Don't take this the wrong way."

"Here comes the critique of my media skills," says Ryder.

"Have I mentioned this before?"

"Once or a thousand times—I'm not sure."

"You got a few laughs tonight. Good."

"Thanks."

"But generally you look so serious."

"Serious?"

"You're all tense. I want to zip out there and give you a massage. Twitter is on your case. They want flash to go with the arm. They want to see you sparkle. Shine. Own it."

"Just who is Twitter?" *A teeming cesspool.* "Can we get back to the part where you're going to meet me somewhere and give me a massage?"

"Sure."

"For the record, I ain't stopping you."

There have been two trips for Maggie so far—one on the road to meet up with him in Boston and one to Baltimore. Neither went as well as he'd hoped. She was uncomfortable in his fancy condo. Her sights are set, with a hard-nosed zeal, on working in health care at some level, perhaps physical therapy.

"You don't have to be so serious, though, do you?"

"I guess not." Ryder hasn't given it much thought. "I mean, I don't want to come across as cocky."

"Your answers are so short."

"There's not much to say."

"You look like a witness in a murder investigation, not someone who is putting baseball records under his name every time he goes out there."

"I'm being me."

"You're great. You're real," says Maggie. "But you'll get more people on your side if you show them your heart."

"Why don't you come out here, and we can rehearse?"

Maggie laughs. "I know what kind of practice you're talking about. And you don't need any practice."

"Everyone can always get better at everything."

"Maybe."

"And speak up a bit," says Maggie. "Out there on the mound you're, like, in charge of everything, and then when we hear you talk, you look like you're so uncertain. It's okay to flash that smile every now and then. Tonight, when I was watching, I swear I thought you had seen a ghost."

Chapter 6

At age twelve, he was Frankie or Frankie Boy. Some of his teammates called him Flame, a nickname he cherished.

When Frank Ryder of the Baltimore Orioles lets his mind drift to that day, a drift he avoids as much as possible, all he sees is Deon Johnson's vacant stare. As far as the internet goes and as far as the media is concerned, too, Deon will forever be known by his yearbook shot.

It's not a good image. Deon is gazing above the camera and off to the side. His smile is forced. His eyes are half-closed. The photo is like a last cruel trick from life. It's his internet tombstone.

Ryder has played the movie clip in his head 1.3 billion times.

The clip starts with Deon coming out to play first base in the bottom of the sixth inning. It's a hot summer day. Ryder is pitching for the Alpharetta All-Stars traveling squad, and the team is playing the Buckhead Braves. Buckhead is Atlanta's own little Beverly Hills. The All-Stars show no mercy. The Buckhead bunch looks bigger, looks tougher, and wears matchy-matchy uniforms right down to the baseball pants. They all drove up in shiny black vans and strutted onto the field like they owned the place, but the All-Stars, in fact, are up 12–1 when Deon comes out to play defense in the bottom of the sixth inning.

The first out is a foul pop-out to the third baseman. On the All-Stars, at least, nobody cares. The game is in the bag. *Let's wrap it up and get out of here.* The second out is a fly ball to center field.

Ho-hum.

Frank Ryder is the third batter of the inning. On the first pitch he sends a ball to the gap in right field. Frank scrambles his way around the bases for a stand-up triple. The batter after Frank is Frank's twin brother, Josh. Josh, who is also the All-Stars' catcher, hits a grounder to short. The shortstop scoops the ball up on a room service hop and fires over an easy throw to first. Josh's frame is bigger than Frank's. He's a big boy and doesn't run fast, but faster than you might guess by looking at him. Nevertheless, the shortstop is in no rush with the throw, and it's right on target.

But Deon Johnson melts down. He tries to put a foot back and find the bag, but he's out of position and too far in front of the base. Panicking, he tries a quick peek around for the base, but by now the ball is almost to him, and when he looks back it's too late, and the ball wings off his shoulder.

Josh takes the extra bag to second, and Frank jogs home with run number thirteen, a rub-it-in run they don't need.

As Frank crosses the plate, Deon's dad bellows across the field, "Chin up, son! Keep your head in the game!" It's such a loud shout that Frank looks around. The dad's words are innocuous. They are the kind of thing you hear all the time, but they don't go with the next image of Deon's dad slamming his clipboard down on top of the waist-high chain-link barrier guarding the Braves' dugout.

Deon's dad is the Buckhead coach. He is the type of coach who comments on every umpire call. Who huddles up his players every inning for a pep talk. Who is so intense and belligerent he probably thinks indignation alone develops talent.

Deon is struggling. He's been in the game for a few minutes, and he's already let his team down. Everyone in the stands, a few dozen parents, knows Deon Johnson is not comfortable out there on the field. After muffing the throw, he doesn't know where to stand at first base.

It's like he's never been coached a day in his life, but how can that be? He's wearing one of those uniforms. He looks like he fits in. What gives? In the top of the seventh, the All-Stars need three more outs to post a W. In baseball, of course, anything can happen. Especially in Little League. There is always hope, right? To be official, the visiting team still needs to have their chance. There is always a chance. Bunches of runs are possible. But they will have to score thirteen runs against a guy who throws like he plays for a good high school team.

First up in the battle for thirteen runs is Deon. He wears a powder-blue helmet that looks like it's a size too small. The boy is built more for football than baseball, with an expansive chest and big, rounded shoulders. The whole package is unsteady and fearful. He stands in the batter's box from the left side with his bat on his shoulder and his big eyes staring out.

Ryder didn't pay attention to those kinds of details at the time, but all this was captured later, when the video was played on the news channels and ad nauseum online.

Why would anyone be taking video? Why would anyone think it was necessary to capture these moments? Deon's mom was at home, Ryder would find out later, and the video was shot from the aluminum bleachers along first base. It's not even a Buckhead mom or a Buckhead dad who records the moment.

It is random video from the dashboard cam of life.

Frank Ryder saw no need for mercy. How could he? Why would he? Twelve strikeouts in the books; why not go for more? He was playing a sport he dreamed about twenty-four hours a day.

There was, at the time, already a minor buzz about Ryder's arm. Thus, *Flame*. His coach never said much other than, "Keep it simple." The other kids worked on their form or their release point. Frank Ryder's velocity was fine.

Deon steps in.

Ryder peers in.

His brother shows him the glove and scoots over two inches, still in his crouch, wanting the pitch on the inside. He gives the signal, the same as all the signals. The 1. Ninety percent of the time, it is the 1. Josh gives a quick jerk of the thumb to show where he wants the pitch—high and tight.

Ryder's one weakness is walks. He can be erratic for a batter or two, no question, when he doesn't focus.

Ryder's first pitch to Deon Johnson gets loose.

It comes off his hand weird.

If Ryder concentrates—and it doesn't take much—he can conjure the feeling in his hand as it sent a signal back to his brain. The signal said, *Uh-oh*. Or, *What the hell was that?*

The feeling in his hand comes with the odd and unnatural smell of sweat mixed with the polyester uniform and the sensation of standing under a beating midday sun with the bill of your cap as your only protection. The feeling in his hand triggers it all.

The silence too.

Deon freezes.

His face is turned square to the pitch. Ear flaps and all, the helmet may as well be sitting on the bench in the dugout.

The ball smacks Deon square between the eyebrows.

Whenever Ryder replays the moment—not the video—it's accompanied by the wicked, wicked sound of ball on skull.

Deon drops to the ground as if his bones are vapor. It is a straight-down crumple of the human form. Deon's body loses all ability, instantly, to lord itself over gravity.

A long, long quiet.

The longest, worst quiet.

The next movement in the video is Josh and the umpire moving as one, as though choreographed, toward Deon. At the last second, the umpire grabs Josh from behind to prevent him from trying to roll Deon over—amateur hands might make things worse. Deon's father sprints from the dugout like any father would. Frank is on the mound, and by the time Deon's father reaches his son, Frank is sitting on the dirt with his knees up to his chest in a tight ball.

The news stations run the video, everything up to *the moment*. The video freezes with the ball between Frank Ryder's hand and Deon's head, a white sphere suspended halfway between mound and batter's box, a bullet of doom.

The police show up alongside the ambulance, which is nothing more than a fancy coroner's wagon or a hearse with flashing red lights.

Frank's name is mentioned, and the whispers and recriminations begin, fueled by those who said they had known all along. Frank Ryder should never have been pitching Little League.

Not with that arm.

JUNE

Pitching is the art of instilling fear.

—*Los Angeles Dodger and Hall of Fame pitcher*
Sandy Koufax

Chapter 7

The Gulfstream banks around to the west, lines up heading due south. Ray Gallo catches a glimpse of the Manhattan skyline, looking hot and still, before the jet comes in over the tops of the apartment buildings in Hackensack and lands on Runway 19 at Teterboro Airport.

A limo takes Gallo and Aiko across the George Washington Bridge toward Manhattan, but the traffic is so thick it's an arduous slog. They could take the Lincoln Tunnel, but being underwater gives Gallo the willies. Aiko scrolls through Gallo's emails, typing Gallo's dictated replies with her whirring thumbs.

"Commissioner's office sent a text to remind everyone that there will be a news conference after the meeting," says Aiko. She wears gray pinstripe slacks and a short-sleeve lilac pullover with a V-neck. A portrait of focus.

"Good," says Gallo. "I hope it's to explain that nothing was done. And nothing will ever be done."

"We can hope."

"They're foolish to call the meeting, let alone give it serious discussion."

Gallo feels restless, antsy. This season, he's in the news more than he prefers. Baseball Nation had once seemed to forget about the Baltimore Orioles. No longer. The bloggers and reporters have been relentless. Crazy ideas are being floated, how to take advantage of their prize. Everyone's got a theory. His GM is allegedly cooking up a scheme.

Wasn't being the first female GM enough? She manages armies of data analysts, as if the soul of baseball can be found on a spreadsheet. Numbers are Alicia Ford's whole deal.

"They are playing 'What if,' that's all," says Aiko.

"What if they keep their mitts off the game?"

"It's not the same as controlling the number of mound visits." Aiko is always blunt. She thinks and works in a zone where she is never afraid to speak her mind. "This is existential now."

The back of the limo smells like sweet lilies. Aiko is so tiny in her seat it feels like there's an acre of bench between them.

"What if they just leave everything alone?" says Gallo.

"Major League Baseball? Why else do we have a Rules Committee? They could set a maximum speed for pitches and give the batter a ball if a pitch comes in *too* hot. They could lower the mound again or move it back." Aiko always talks a hair too loud. He likes her assertiveness. "In Japan, though, I have to say I think fans would pack every game to watch, even if they know their team will lose, when Frank Ryder comes to town."

"For real?"

From the bridge, the Manhattan skyline looks overbuilt. He's about to be trapped in a kiln.

"They are more respectful of individual accomplishments and pure feats of athletic prowess." Aiko's English is all-American. She's a Southern Californian from La Cañada. Her father is from old money. He is a hotshot at the Jet Propulsion Lab. He doesn't have to work. Neither does she.

"So the owners wouldn't have to worry?"

"I can't say for sure."

"You studied this on your trip?"

Aiko traveled with her parents to see the country for the first time earlier in the year.

"Baseball teams are much tighter in Japan, almost like a family," says Aiko. "It's the group mentality, samurai warriors all fighting for the cause. When you're on the team, it's a long-term thing. There isn't this trading and bouncing around between teams. So I feel Ryder's talents would be appreciated like a rare gem. He would inspire awe and wonder. A puzzle to be solved and respected."

"And the salaries?"

"Are not the focus," says Aiko. "You play for a team, you are set for life. You have one of the best jobs in the country. You train hard, work hard all year long with a very short break. Much more togetherness and training in the off-season too."

If the Orioles had won a few more games last year, thus not owning the number one draft pick, they could have avoided Ryder altogether. Three more wins the year before Frank Ryder emerged as the slam-dunk consensus pick would've made Frank Ryder some other owner's fun-not-so-fun conundrum. If another team was managing the Ryder business, would Ray Gallo be among those trying to rein in Ryder now, trying to use a rule change to counter a freak of nature?

It's hard to imagine one pitcher will damage an entire sport, but there's the whole precedent issue—an urge to lay down the law before bullet pitches become the norm. Once or twice a month, Gallo gets an email or text with a link to a story about some high school or college phenom who is the second coming of Nolan Ryan. They are out there.

The season wins record for a pitcher sits at thirty-one, unless you go back to the nineteenth century, when the pitching paradigm was a different beast. Could Ryder get to thirty-seven or thirty-eight wins? About half at home and half on the road, say. So he might "ruin" twenty games a year on the road at the very most?

Or is it the fact that the Orioles are clawing their way up the American League East and are about to crash a battering ram into the top of the standings? That the two spots ahead of the Orioles are held by the Red Sox and Yankees, who fight for supremacy each year like two angry weasels in a shoebox? That those two teams write massive checks and make obscenely outsize obligations to the best players money can buy? Those two teams would not appreciate being taken down a notch by raw talent.

—∞—

The offices of Major League Baseball are near the top of a skyscraper in Rockefeller Center. Making the move from Park Avenue, MLB somehow found a way to more than triple the office space it needed. Same number of teams. *What gives?* The "old" offices lasted less than twenty years. Gallo remembers the renovation price tag for the Park Avenue HQ with the mini baseball museum and all the displays, as if it's open to fans like some sort of Cooperstown East. It's not.

Every time Gallo comes for a meeting, he thinks of the waste and silliness of the corporate overlords chewing up so much revenue every month, even the additional cost of paying New York City salaries. Is there any reason MLB couldn't make its home in a quiet Iowa farm town, perhaps rehab an old warehouse and call it good? It's not like the entire MLB staff marches out to see the Yankees or the Mets every night, and it's not like the press wouldn't follow them to Nowhere, Iowa, to decide whether the phenom of the century is still going to be allowed to keep throwing a baseball the way he wants and the way he was raised and trained to do.

—∞—

The new offices replicate the old. The World Series trophy sits behind a locked glass case. The names of every World Series winner and the year they won are engraved on a wood panel in the entry hall next to a list of every Hall of Fame inductee. A sitting area off the main hall comes draped with oversize photos of the old Negro Leagues—an apology exhibit if Gallo has ever seen one. Down the hall toward the meeting rooms, a series of headless mannequins displays uniforms for every team. Some of the mannequins have their caps over their hearts as if their headless bodies are singing along to the national anthem.

Singing with precisely *what* anatomical function?

—⁂—

The table is oval and shiny like an acre of fresh caramel. The walls are the same gooey brown. The room is cool and the lighting is subdued. It's a windowless, climate-controlled star chamber. The more the meeting goes on, the more absurd things become. They would be better off sitting together on his expansive back deck in Tuscany-Canterbury with a few buckets of blue crabs and a keg of Natty Boh. It's a fantasy. The disdain in the room for the city of Baltimore is palpable. Nobody would ever agree to meet there. It's always New York.

"It's not even a question." This is Jimmy Wharton, Texas Rangers. Cowboy schtick, right down to the oversize belt buckle. "He's a generational kind of player, but you can't call it sport. Not if the offense has no chance."

They have all been asked to go around one at a time, provide their views on the subject. *General impressions*, per the commissioner's orders. Any meaty discussion, of course, would be grist for the Rules Committee, not the owners. But the owners could throw a sizable stink—and plenty of hitters, who don't need their batting averages to dip, are no doubt mobilizing within the union to stop Frank Ryder.

After each comment, eyeballs circle to Gallo's spot. Gallo is the ugly murderer sporting a face tattoo like a nihilist skinhead, and everyone on the jury wants to know how he's reacting to the latest testimony against him by evaluating every scowl, wince, and flinch. Gallo gives them shivering shit balls in return. What did they call it in Yiddish? *Bupkes.*

"I can see the danger, but it's one pitcher." Peter Brawley is twenty years below the average age in the room. Cleveland Indians. "Leave him alone. And the chances of Ryder going injury-free are precisely zero."

"I wonder if we don't want to consider the message we're sending." Jerry Hyde. Seattle Mariners. Made his fortune building tax shelters for the ultrarich. More recently, accused by the players union for colluding with other owners to keep salaries down. He is a small man with rabbit teeth. "Tommy John surgeries are performed on teenagers more than on any other age group. If we say one ten is fine, we share some responsibility. Picture some reporter down the road writing about a high school kid who had his elbow reconstructed, and he's dealing with rehab and won't pitch again for eighteen months, and the kid says, 'I was trying to throw like Frank Ryder.' We would share some blame."

Next up is a Ziegler.

"Here we go."

Gallo is surprised to hear his own voice.

"What?" says Ziegler.

"We can skip over you and save ourselves five minutes because your comments are predictable. Red Sox?" Gallo looks straight over at Fergus Rowley, white shirt and round glasses with blue frames. "You too."

"We aren't talking about a midseason change." It's Commissioner Bobby Morris with the even tone. Pretty boy. He reminds Gallo of the host on *Wheel of Fortune*. "We are looking down the road."

"And word gets out the owners favor shutting down Ryder or cutting him off, you don't think that'll get inside the kid's head?"

"Word isn't getting out," says Morris.

"Of course it's getting out," says Gallo. "Nothing to stop anyone from expressing an opinion anyway. And we all know the Yankees would offer Ryder forty mil a year for five years and fight us all to leave the kid alone."

"We will see what he can bring when he's no longer under your control," says Ziegler. "And we'll see whether you have the intestinal fortitude to offer him the kind of contract he might deserve when he's eligible. Are you willing to invest in your future? In Baltimore's? No doubt Staller will have more than a few things to say about that."

Mickey Staller, Ryder's agent. There is buzz Ryder might be the first pitcher to crack the $50 million mark.

"Then why don't you entertain us all with your magnanimity?"

"On the side of the fans," says Ziegler.

"Told you," says Gallo.

"Even one oh five or one oh six, it's a nightmare for batters."

"Costa went yard on Frank the other day."

"Watch the replay," says Ziegler. "Costa was as shocked as the rest of us, gave that little shrug rounding first base."

Cal Ziegler believes small-market teams mooch off the big boys. He wants to push for a different formula for how much of the collective pie each team gets to eat.

"Then make it five strikes instead of three," says Gallo. "Or go back to the 1880s, when the pitcher tossed underhand and the batter could request a pitch in a certain spot."

"You watch," says Ziegler. "The TV revenue is going to drop when Ryder pitches. And overall attendance was down last year anyway—another six percent? How many hot dogs is that? How many beers at ten bucks a pop?"

"Ryder's games are packed. Home and on the road," says Gallo. "Quite the contrary."

"Imagine Mom and Dad going to a baseball game and they got two kids, both baseball-loving boys," says Ziegler. "The Orioles are coming to Anaheim for the weekend, and they all want to go see Mike Trout play."

"Our beers are six bucks." This is the Angels. Sam Greene. "We sell more beer than all of you."

"Dad is an Angel fan. They see Ryder is pitching on Saturday night. You think they're going to get tickets for the Ryder game—or maybe take their boys out for one of the games when Trout has a chance of getting wood on the ball?"

Ziegler's condescending tone prods Gallo to flash on his GM's request—permission to go after two key players she thinks can help them chase down the Yankees and Red Sox.

Leaning back from the table, ignoring the rising chorus of conversation around him, Gallo texts Aiko:

Tell Alicia I'm ready to meet.

Chapter 8

"How's the arm, Mr. CSI?"

Doug Pagnozzi, a jaded veteran with thirteen big-league seasons under his belt, is working on a bag of sunflower seeds.

"Normal day-after stuff," says Ryder.

"Feels the same?"

The Orioles are Pagnozzi's sixth pro team.

"The same as what?"

"Normal."

"It feels good," says Ryder.

"No soreness?"

"Nothing more than what I expect."

From his spot in the bullpen, where he likes to sit the day after a start, Frank Ryder takes in Camden Yards like he's another fan sitting out in the bleachers. It's Sunday. This could be church. The crowd is humming the standard lyric-free hymn, the exuberant buzz of thirty-five thousand baseball fans stirring, waiting, and chatting. Incense is whiffs of mustard and beer, Boog's BBQ, and french fries.

Joe Rhineland is on the mound. He has tossed a smooth three-hitter through six. Rhineland pitches the next day after all of Ryder's starts. He's got a curveball as nasty as what Félix Hernández once threw and an unhittable fading changeup he learned from Zack Greinke, when the two played for a season together in Arizona. The day after Ryder's screaming fastballs, Rhineland's pitches dangle like a squiggling worm on a fishing hook. Seductive. The batters believe in their bones they will exact revenge for what Ryder did to them the day before. They believe they must restore their dignity by taking their hacks, but no. All the hitting coaches warn their batters to lay off and be patient at the plate, but seeing a seminormal pitch is pure temptation after a day of Frank Ryder. Rhineland induces his outs with little dribblers to the infield, mixed with six or seven strikeouts. He never lets batters get comfortable at the plate.

Tomorrow's starter is Kevin Wright. The Ryder-Rhineland-Wright trio has been dubbed the *Three R's* by sportswriters, who must love snickering every day at their own joke. The saying "Three R's and pray for a W" is a thing, even if it doesn't quite have the ring of "Spahn and Sain and pray for rain."

"When did you first reach one hundred?"

Pagnozzi is big and lumbering, with deep-set eyes and a wide face. He is an artist on the mound, mixing speeds but never topping ninety-two or ninety-three.

"I reached a hundred a few times in high school," says Ryder.

"Training how?"

"Long toss—lots of long toss. Pull-downs. Weighted balls. I had a coach who threw javelin—made the national team. He was all about quiet intensity and the purpose of what you're doing."

"You had scouts come around in high school?"

"In college. In high school, I was decent." Ryder prefers underplaying it. "My walk rate was iffy."

"But you had other choices than Metro?"

"Academically," says Ryder. "Baseball wasn't going to pay for college."

"That's when you found the real velocity."

"It kind of all came together."

"I never heard of Metro State."

"Rocky Mountain Athletic Conference," says Ryder. "One of the oldest in the country."

"Was it your coaches? They wanted you to keep pushing the speed?"

"Not in so many words."

"But they kept finding ways to pick it up?"

"Little things, yeah," says Ryder.

"Strength and technique?"

"One coach for each."

"They worked together?"

"Like bread and butter."

Most baseball players don't read. They don't pay attention to other players all that much, unless they are close buddies. There are cliques. Video games are the big distraction. So is beer. And movies. And spotting beautiful women in the stands and figuring out how to get a message to them. The stories about his Metro State coaches, however, have been splashed all over the news. Ryder is happy for the conversation. Rookies know their place. Being agreeable is one of those places.

"What's that feel like?"

"What do you mean?"

"To throw that fast?"

"It's no different," says Ryder.

"That doesn't seem possible."

"I mean, it doesn't feel any different in my arm or anything."

"The same as if you were pitching in high school?"

Seeds sputter. The PA announcer introduces the next batter with a ho-hum monotone bestowed on all visiting batters. June sun says, *You ain't seen nothing yet.*

"Yeah," says Ryder.

"How fast back then?"

"Ninety—ninety-one."

"And your control steadied out when?"

"At Metro. Got better as a junior. Much better as a senior." Ryder waits, unsure where this is going. He also doesn't want to come across as cocky. But Maggie said to *own it*. "Might lose it any day."

"I have friends who knew Ankiel," says Pagnozzi.

Rick Ankiel went from top-flight, bad-ass hurler to confused head case, a guy who woke up one day and couldn't get his arm to do what his brain wanted it to do. It was as if his muscles had forgotten all their timing and coordination. The breakdown happened on national television in living color. During a playoff game.

"Dude fought the monster—fought it hard," says Pagnozzi.

"Came back too. All the way."

"But never shook the monster," says Pagnozzi. "Just controlled it."

Ryder is all too familiar. He read Ankiel's book. Ankiel stared down the boogeyman. Psychologists tried to put him back together. Ankiel came back as a pitcher and later switched to the outfield, picking off runners with laser beam throws from deep in center field.

A crack of the bat sends a ball high and deep straight toward them in the Oriole bullpen.

"Of course it's Bogworth," says Pagnozzi.

Brandon Bogworth is the Detroit Tigers' first baseman, a power hitter. His hit appears bullpen bound. None of the pitchers in the Orioles' pen moves a lick. They are a portrait of disinterest. Ryder peeks at Rhineland, who is on the mound with his hands on his knees facing the outfield, looking dejected.

Orioles left fielder Lanny Wilson is in full sprint mode, heading straight to the bullpen wall. From Ryder's perspective, Wilson disappears for a second before the wall rattles with a bone-cracking thud, and Wilson's wide-open glove stabs the air—the glove is all they can make out of Wilson, given the wall—and snatches the ball from its flight.

"Jesus," says Pagnozzi.

The crowd erupts. Ryder imagines the cart racing on the field and the grim medical report in Lanny Wilson's future when the little left fielder comes scampering into view, heading back to the dugout with the third out in his grasp and his body, at least today, no worse for the pummeling. Rhineland pumps his fist in the air, and the whole team jogs off the field, the crowd going nuts at Wilson's effort to protect the 1–0 lead. They cheer again as the giant scoreboard replays the catch, giving Ryder a chance to see, in slo-mo, Lanny Wilson's imitation of a crash test dummy.

Pagnozzi grins like a rookie and not a journeyman pitcher in June. "Jesus," he says again. "This team. Something special this time. And of course he's leading off the bottom of the frame."

It's an old baseball fact—you make a dazzling play in the field, you're first up in your half of the inning. Fate. The baseball gods. "They will be playing that clip for years to come."

The bullpen phone rings. The bullpen coach points at Pagnozzi, twirls his index finger in a circle. Pagnozzi will pitch the eighth.

"Joe is cruising." Pagnozzi stands, starts windmilling his arm. "Why give him the hook? Eighty-one pitches when he could do a hundred or more."

Nobody listens.

Ryder shrugs. Maybe the data nerds prefer certain matchups they want to exploit with Pagnozzi's left arm. Or maybe Stone has a feeling.

Pagnozzi's empty seat is filled.

Deon.

Deon's backpack is on his lap. He's clutching it tight to his chest. Deon is wearing his blue batting helmet.

Ryder's heart climbs up the back of his throat. He can't move. Ryder listens to Pagnozzi's cleats scrape the dirt of the bullpen mound as he throws.

Ryder waits.

Deon turns to stare at him. He thrums his fingers on the top of his black backpack.

"Must be nice," says Deon.

Deon's stare locks on Ryder like he's the best interrogator who has ever lived.

What's nice?

Ryder thinks it.

Deon hears him.

"Relaxing." Deon stretches the word out so far it could be its own sentence. *Reeee-laaaax-innnnnnnnnng-guh.*

Relaxing?

"You're cashing checks for sitting around," says Deon. "You're doing nothing today except watch, and yet you're getting paid."

In fact, Ryder works hard not to think about the money side of things. He gets the base rookie salary, of course, but the signing bonus was ridiculous. It was Monopoly money. Ryder has eyed some of the futuristic, beyond-snazzy cars his teammates drive and realizes he could pay cash for his own fancy wheels, but he doesn't have the nerve to spend that much all at once.

"You can't *not* think of it," says Deon. The stare is intact. "It's gotta be stressing you out. I mean, if you keep pitching like you have been, no doubt you can parlay all these ridiculous numbers and wins and strikeouts into a big, juicy contract."

Ryder wants to look around. The kid said *parlay*. What kid uses the word *parlay*? Ryder wants to see if anyone else is watching him watch the ghost.

Deon's stare is testing him.

"Of course I'm real," says Deon. "Don't give me any of them hang-dog eyes. What have you got to be sad about? I'm as real as one of your motherfucking heaters."

Parlay. Motherfucking.

Deon's expression is blank and icy. Gangster. His forehead is smooth.

"And you don't think you'd be here if it wasn't for me?"

What?

"You brushing me off? Pushing me to the back? Trying to forget? Now that you're big time and all the reporters want a piece of you and every time you pitch it's like more coverage than game seven of the World Series, now you're going to deny, deny, deny? Sure *looks* like I might have had something to do with all of this, because *here I am*."

Ryder stands. He needs to move away from the spot. If it was cool to do so, he'd open the bullpen gate midinning and sprint to the dugout or the clubhouse or out of the stadium and down some backstreet alley where he can't be found.

Ryder risks a look around. Deon's spot is empty. A shudder hits Ryder's chest like he's attached to a vibrating strap, but there's no switch to turn it off.

Chapter 9

Pagnozzi loads the bases with a walk and two cheap infield hits in the top of the eighth. The crowd has grown edgy. Baltimore fans are familiar with failure. It's a weird sensation, accepting defeat before it arrives. Ryder knows it. Every ballplayer knows it. Failure is woven into the fabric of the game.

No doubt the crowd wants a hook. Pagnozzi is a journeyman, they are thinking. Is he invested in cleaning up the mess he's made? The crowd wants someone to come in and slam the door.

Pagnozzi escapes with an infield pop-out and a double play. The team heads off the field with the crowd roaring. Kyle Sundeen, their closer, zips through an easy top of the ninth to secure the 1–0 win.

—m—

Ryder slips into the weight room to wait for the reporters to clear the locker room. It's not his first trip here. No sign says MEDIA KEEP OUT, but it's an unwritten rule. Same with the trainers' room. Pagnozzi might still be grumpy about almost blowing the game, but the victory is jazzing the clubhouse. The music is up a notch, the chatter is good.

The lone teammate doing postgame work is Julio Diaz, the team's most disciplined athlete. Diaz has an uncanny knack for trajectory as balls come off the bat. His ultimate zone rating is gold. He's the team's leading hitter. He swats balls with game power. He's not a batting-prac-tice spectacle who fizzles when it counts. His big free agent contract was north of $150 million. He's the team's fashion plate and also the most likely to be seen with Hollywood celebs.

"I thought Wilson was a goner," says Diaz, unplugging a pair of old-school buds from his ears. Ryder can hear the tinny thump of a beat, a flare of horns.

Ryder shakes his head. "Check the fence for bruises."

Diaz is running through simple stretches—groin, glutes, and lower back. Most players blow off this step, as if they are immune to injury.

"You hidin' in here?"

Ryder looks around. "Is it that obvious?"

"I know I would. If I was you."

"Even on days when I'm not pitching, seems like they all think they have a question nobody else has ever thought up."

"Ninety-nine versions of the same three questions," says Diaz.

Diaz is from Santo Domingo. His English is accented but it's smooth. Diaz studies everything. Nutrition, stretching, videos of oppos-ing pitchers, and the game's essential strategies. If there is a dark side to Diaz, Ryder hasn't seen it. Diaz makes it all look easy, including the interviews.

"Seems like you don't mind the attention."

Diaz shrugs. He has quick-changed into black shorts and a plain blue T-shirt. Ryder feels oddly overdressed, out of sorts, in his uniform. "They love failure. They live for failure. You okay dealing with them?"

"Some days it feels like they want to shove a hot knife between your ribs."

"They come on like friends," says Diaz. "Like they have a *right* to be friends. Like they control your story. I give them the Julio Diaz they like, but they don't know me as a person—not a *real* person. So I cooperate. It's a game. They need us, we need them. We are meat and they feed on us. And where would we be without their help projecting our image? That's what it is. An *image*."

"It's strange." Ryder remembers his mother telling him he was mentioned on the cover of *People* magazine, but Ryder never remembered talking to anyone from *People*. "A strange feeling at least, how they come on."

"Plane lands on time, it ain't news. They want disaster. Errors. Disputes. They wanna see bodies in the wreckage. A few survivors makes it better."

"So you're saying I should keep my head down."

"Yeah," says Diaz. "Keep your head down and your chin up. It's a contortion. And keep smiling."

Ryder sighs. All the advice. Would Maggie agree with Diaz? Ryder isn't sure.

"Don't give them material," says Diaz. "Talk about what happens between the foul lines, you'll be fine. Don't drink and drive. Be kind to your girlfriends, treat your family well. If it starts getting into any off-field crap, it gets ugly. Every time."

—⁊⁊⁊—

Ryder showers and dresses. One thing about playing at Camden Yards, with nobody to go home to, Ryder can take his time.

It's a short cab ride to his condo, but team image comes first. No jeans and T-shirts, even for home games. He slips into tan slacks and a burnt-orange pullover. The clubhouse is serene, civilized. The media have scurried off.

He's due to meet up with Wilson, Rhineland, and Pagnozzi for beers and dinner. There is talk of hitting a club after the meal. It's still two days until Ryder pitches again, so tonight is a good night to unfasten the ankle weights. He needs to lighten up, per Maggie's prescription.

But he can't shake the ghost. He revisits every question and every exchange with Deon.

Parlay. What the hell?

—m—

After a day game, the guys with families all head home. It's hard to get family time during the season. For players who aren't married, they may as well be on the road, except you get to go home to your own bed and not another hotel room. Tonight, Ryder is going to put himself out there, see what happens, and maybe drown the ghost in a couple of drinks.

"Hey, Frank."

Stone waves Ryder back to his office, around a corner and down a hallway. It's a cozy office with one desk, two big leather chairs in front of it, and a couch off to the side. Framed photographs clog a wall—Brooks Robinson, Cal Ripken, Mike Mussina, Jim Palmer, Eddie Murray. On and on.

Ryder wonders if Stone wants to ask him about how a young boy got into the bullpen. Ryder gets an idea—to watch the game tape later and see if the boy shows up, or at least see how silly Ryder must have looked while Pagnozzi was warming up.

Sitting in one of the chairs is Alicia Ford. She is tall with short dark hair and a clean, sleek look. She stands and shakes Ryder's hand with a firm grip. A short-sleeve pullover shirt hugs her body. It's white with bold black vertical stripes like a football referee's. She is wearing a pair of tight-fitting black slacks, too, and an Oriole baseball cap.

She's easy on the eyes with a generous smile. Starting with spring training in mid-February, it's been four months of guys and guy time and sweat and grind. He's met with Ford many times and finds each encounter a bit of a boost. What better combination than a beautiful woman and someone who thinks about baseball as much as he does? Ryder reminds himself she is double his age. And married. Ryder misses Maggie.

Next to Ford in the second leather chair is Jimmy Lackland, the pitching coach. He looks dejected. He is a big man with broad shoulders. The beer can in his hand is a receptacle for tobacco spit. There is the ever-present wad in his cheek. His cap is pushed back, and what little hair he's got is matted down and sweaty, but Ryder has never seen Lackland exert himself. Not once.

Like Lackland, Stone is still in his uniform. A can of Miller Lite sits in front of him. The room is devoid of fresh oxygen, but Ryder gets a whiff of Ford's woodsy scent like a pine forest.

The Ford-Stone-Lackland trio is odd. Ryder tries to imagine whether Stone is okay with putting his trust in a woman to assemble his team and help call the shots. Stone started coaching in the big leagues one year before Ford was born.

Ford leans back in her chair, folds her arms across her chest, and studies Ryder. "Are you paying attention to all the noise out there?" She has a husky voice. Her face is wide and open like Jessica Biel's. There's an eagerness to every expression.

"Noise?"

Ryder isn't sure if he's supposed to grab a seat on the couch. If that's an option. He remains standing.

"Controversy," says Stone. "Opinions."

"Sure," says Ryder.

He glances now and then at the vitriol on Twitter, links to crap from writers around the country saying baseball has to figure out "the Frank Ryder Problem."

"It doesn't bother you?" says Ford.

"It's ridiculous," says Ryder. "Some of those fans get so angry. I mean, are they supposed to be guaranteed seeing a home run by their big bats every time they buy a ticket?"

"It's the twenty-third of June," says Ford. "Sixteen wins. A good season for most. You think you'll have no problem at this pace?"

"Coach has me on a good routine between starts."

Workout on the first day off. Throw thirty pitches or so on the second day off. Sprints and light workout on the third day off. Watch videos of the batters from the next opponent and major rest on the fourth day off. And every day and every waking minute, be on guard for a little stone-faced Black kid with a chip on his shoulder who nobody else can see.

"We've been looking at some ways to think about this differently," says Ford.

Ryder doesn't want anything different. He doesn't want anybody thinking. "What do you mean by *this*?"

"Your presence," says Ford.

"Your talents," says Lackland. "And for the record, this ain't my idea."

"Got it, Jimmy," says Stone. "Jesus."

"I want the kid to know where I stand," says Lackland. "It's a pitcher thing. Pitcher to pitcher."

Lackland, with nine years in the big leagues as a starter for the White Sox and the Angels, hasn't been able to show Ryder one thing about how to improve. But Ryder always listens. It's what you do.

"Your power suggests that maybe we deploy you in a different way," says Ford.

Ryder hates these manipulators with a passion. They are overthinking everything. Some teams deploy a pitcher who only throws the first inning or two and isn't expected to go deep into a game.

Ryder shrugs. "Some teams seem to like it."

"And you?" says Ford.

"Jury is out," says Ryder.

"And won't come back until one century after my unborn grandson is in college." Lackland punctuates his point by spitting into his can.

Ryder doesn't want to go down this road. One of the reasons he liked being chosen by Baltimore, if it had to be any American League team, was their conventional mindset. "Mixed results, right?"

Stone lets out a sigh like he's been holding his breath. "Not exactly," he says.

"So we've crunched some numbers," says Ford.

"Please," says Ryder. A bubble of panic rises in his chest. Does he have a right to say what he thinks? He'd rather head back to the bullpen to see if he can find Deon than listen to this crap. "No."

"It's an idea," says Ford. "We are proposing to start you every other day, but just for the first forty or forty-five pitches—three or four innings max."

"Given the shutout innings you'll throw, it will give us nine innings of offense to five or six innings of offense for them." Stone straddles two worlds. He came up old school, needs to save his job by not dismissing the new school. "And about five more W's by the end of the season. I mean, we know it's not going to work every single time, but it should work eight times out of ten. And we'll need those extra W's in September."

"Based on our calculations," says Ford.

"Based on *their* calculations," says Lackland.

Ryder feels numb. Whatever sourness was brewing in his stomach from the ghost reactivates now like he swallowed a box of baking soda and he's been waterboarded with vinegar.

"No," says Ryder. The whole idea of walking away after a few innings? Lame. "Seriously."

"Told ya," says Lackland. "It's a pitcher thing."

"More games," says Stone. "Shorter appearances."

Complete games are the goal—nine innings of dominance. It's a rarity these days, but it has always been the way Ryder thinks.

"Three innings?" says Ryder.

"Maybe four," says Ford. She taps a pen on a notebook on the table. "More on pitch count than total outs."

"What about—?"

"W's," says Lackland. "Your record."

"Yeah," says Ryder. "Exactly."

"The win-loss record is antiquated," says Ford. "It's a tired way of thinking about the point of the game."

"You have a dynamite ERA and off-the-chart WAR, and your win record is of course ridiculous," says Stone. "It's all that matters—to you, your agent. All the Orioles organization wants is to keep winning games and end up on top of the division. Wins. *Team* wins."

Ryder can't picture it. He can't imagine coming out of the game when the job isn't done. He lives for exhaustion. Nine innings is for men.

"Who starts the days I don't?" he asks.

It's a make-conversation question. Ryder is buying time.

"The other starters," says Ford. "The idea is to use more pitchers every game, keep everyone sharp."

"It's kind of like I'd be a middle reliever in the beginning of the game," says Ryder. It sounds so half-baked.

"Think your arm would be okay?" says Ford. "You'd be lights-out, of course, at the beginning of the game."

Lackland shakes his head, tips his chair back so he's leaning against the wall. His sixty-year-old legs dangle like a schoolkid's. "It's not the way pitchers think. And, Frank—you don't have to agree."

"Forty pitches every other day?" says Ryder.

"Something like that," says Ford.

"It's all theory," says Lackland. "Way too much data analysis, if you ask me. Nerdy shit. You got a goose that lays nine golden eggs every time he takes the mound, and now you're asking him to get into a whole new rhythm."

Ryder has always wanted the legacy of a long career and hundreds of complete games—Bob Gibson, Steve Carlton, Tom Seaver.

"You'd want the whole team to buy in," says Ryder.

Stone and Ford exchange a long look. Stone says, "You tell him."

"There are some plans in the works," says Ford.

"Trades?"

"Upgrades," says Ford.

Ryder mulls it over. All he's ever wanted to do is win games— and be the complete-game pitcher every chance he gets. "The owner is behind this?" He's not sure he's allowed to probe around in ownership thinking, but what the heck. "Gallo?"

"This season is our chance," says Ford. "This one and maybe next. This is all in confidence. We want no rumors, no chatter."

Ryder nods. "Glad to hear about the upgrades, if that's what you're calling it. But I don't like the three-inning deal. It ain't for me."

Lackland gives a little fist pump at his chest, winks at Ryder. "The data geeks spend too much time looking at numbers and not enough time watching the actual game," he says.

Ford shrugs. "Keep all this here," she says.

Ryder nods.

"And speaking of quiet," says Ford, "you notice the new theme song last night before your start?"

"Not really," says Ryder.

"Deep Purple," says Ford. "An oldie called 'Hush.' It'll be your own 'Enter Sandman,' like Rivera used," says Ford.

Ryder always wondered what it was like for a kid from a Panamanian fishing village whose trademark entrance fanfare, to what became a Hall of Fame career, was by a heavy metal band from the United States. Mariano Rivera began his career as a starter.

"'Hush'?" says Ryder.

"About how you quiet all the batters," says Ford. "The production crew cued that up during your warm-up tosses last night and Twitter lit up, fans saying it's got to be your thing. Made the local news last night too. And ESPN. And the morning paper."

"Loved that song back in high school," says Stone. "Trippy."

"The tune has to be something you can get behind," says Ford.

"I'd hate to disappoint Twitter," says Ryder.

Ryder wants the meeting over. In fact, he never wants to be invited back here again.

"Okay," says Ford. "I think we're done here."

—⚬—

Ryder collects his backpack, finds a cab, and is pleased when the driver makes zero attempt at small talk. He is lost in the conversation in his head. Should he be a better team player? Is this what baseball is coming to, all the weird theories? Messing with the game?

If the Orioles want to fight it out with the big boys, the Red Sox and the Yankees, how can he be the one to block the plan?

Pitching is *complete games*. Ryder pictures himself walking off the mound after three innings—getting replaced so early.

It would equal failure when it's not. It would be all foreplay, no finish.

—⚬—

The taxi pulls to a stop at Harbor East before Ryder notices they've arrived, like a magical transport beam. In fact, he's not sure how long they've been stopped. He comes around to the moment, realizes the driver is climbing out of her seat behind the wheel and she's making the trek around the car to open his door like maybe he's a prima donna.

She opens his door. "Twelve dollars today," she says.

Ryder digs for a twenty. "Sorry," he says. He's unfolding himself from the cramped back seat. "Got lost in my thoughts there. Keep it."

She eyes the twenty. She is his mother's age or older. She comes up to Ryder's chest. She is wearing worn blue jeans and a T-shirt with a faded, outsize photo of Frederick Douglass. Never Say Die.

There is a pause. Ryder recognizes this hesitation, starts to dig around to see if he's got a Sharpie. Where is she going to want it?

"I want to ask you something." She looks down, nervous.

"Sure," he says.

"The taxi is my second job," she says. "I work days in school. Teacher's aide. My husband is in public works. Road crew. He's a supervisor, but still. You get the picture?"

"Got it," says Ryder.

"Two kids," she says. "Middle school now."

"Got it."

"We all love baseball. My husband Ron more than anyone. Diehard Orioles. Bleeds orange."

This could go one of two ways.

"You make us realize anything is possible," she says. "We don't get to many games, of course. It ain't cheap. But we are saving up to make plans to come see you pitch, sit out in the cheap seats—we don't care. Watching *you* sends a message. To our kids too. We love what you say after the games. My husband tells our kids you are a role model for them. He tells them the secret to everything is focus and apply themselves. That they can do anything."

"Ma'am, that is very kind. Some don't quite see it that way."

"So I was thinking, the last few minutes here in the car."

"I'm so sorry I was zoned out—"

"No," she says. "I'm wondering if you would come to our school? Talk to the kids? They love you. I'd have to check with my principal— maybe when school opens back up in September."

"Sure," says Ryder. He's done two school visits and one to the children's wing of a hospital, a tour that required Ryder to check all his emotions at the door.

"You would?"

Ryder gets her name. Martha Greer. Shakes her hand. He asks for a card. Diamond Cab. "Most of the kids don't read. Don't want to."

"I'll be in touch. Or the team will. September."

"I see the kids out on the playground pretending to be you. Little Frank Ryders. Like some sort of superheroes. Some of them get a running start to pitch, like they don't have to have one foot on the rubber." She smiles now, relaxed. "They want to get extra speed on the pitch, but of course it's third grade, but still. So damn cute. You'll see."

Chapter 10

Ryder changes out of his street clothes to gray workout shorts, a plain white T-shirt, and sandals. His gleaming condo on the twenty-second floor offers a stunning view of the Inner Harbor, but none of the windows open, so the inside is sterile and sealed off, even with floor-to-ceiling glass. Other than his clothes and a few books, the unit is devoid of personal stuff. It's no wonder Maggie hated it. It's the opposite of cozy. No matter the temperature of the city, it's chilly inside.

Ryder goes out his condo entrance down the hall to stairs by the elevator. He's got his phone and a can of good beer. He follows the stairs to the roof. Two women are sitting on the edge of the hot tub, legs dangling in the steaming bubbles. The tub jets grind. The women hold matching pink plastic tumblers. Ryder spots a bottle of wine jutting from the top of a cooler. It could be champagne. They acknowledge Ryder with smiles, ask if he would like to join them. He would very much like to join them. He would like to pretend he was that carefree, that flexible. They are both wearing tiny bikini tops. They are both trim and fetching. He could entertain himself and forget about the new pitching idea coughed up by the data geeks. Ryder smiles back, slides by. "Aw, come on," says one. "And you look mighty, mighty familiar, by the way."

"You don't live here?" he says, looking back.

"Visiting our mom," says one. They are *sisters*.

Ryder hoists his unopened beer. "Enjoy the night," he says.

—∿—

The building is full of people who leave each other alone. Ryder has signed a few autographs in the lobby and in the elevator too. He's had a few conversations in the hot tub. The women who live here tend to be older. Thirties. Forties. Singles. They tend to be women who seem to be looking for something. For *next*.

All five Adirondack chairs are open. He takes the one closest to the corner, where he can put his feet up on the railing. He cracks his beer and listens to the real-life squeals and sirens of the city streets, the gentle clattering crackle of places to go and things to do. He watches motorboats putter back from pleasure cruises out on the wide-open water. The occasional yacht.

The air is odorless except for a tang of salt. A gentle breeze kisses his face. He sips his beer, wishes he had brought along nuts or a wedge of cheese.

Ryder wonders what he would even say to kids at a school. Is he supposed to have a pocketful of platitudes to keep them out of trouble? To put them on a path so they can buy a yacht? What might they want to hear? Maggie might know. Or his mom. Maybe the Orioles have a script for these kinds of things. The thought of a school visit makes him squirmy. What's worse is the stupid idea of pitching only a few innings on the day of his "starts." Ryder has half a notion to climb in the hot tub with the sisters. Distract himself.

Ryder's phone chirps with a text.

CALL?

It's his brother.

Ryder sends back a thumbs-up. His phone buzzes.

"Calling to brag about going four for four or some shit like that?" says Ryder.

"How about one for five?" Josh is the starting catcher with the Birmingham Barons, the Double-A team in the Chicago White Sox system. "And I had a passed ball."

"That's a pretty sucky stat line if it's true."

"At least we won." The White Sox drafted Josh after a year at Arizona, where he'd been a damn good hitter and decent catcher. "And that passed ball was BS."

"Whatever you say," says Ryder. "Who did you beat?"

"Chattanooga. The Lookouts." Josh says *Lookouts* to make it sound scary and intimidating, which it never will be. "Four to one. Three of those runs are RBIs in *my* book, thanks to a no-doubter over everything in dead center field."

"Way to go. Charlotte next," says Ryder. "Then the big time, and I'll look forward to striking you out."

Josh ignores the bait. "They got a guy with Chattanooga throws one oh two like a walk in the park."

"And now is the part where you tell me the speed of the pitch you hit."

"One oh one. You should have seen the thing come off the bat."

"Long as you didn't dance around the bases," says Ryder.

"Most respectful-looking home run trot you've ever seen. Ho-Hum City."

"Good thinking," says Ryder.

"Though there was a bit of carrying on in the dugout."

"That's understandable. And to be forgiven. But that's not why you're calling."

Josh never calls to boast. "Not really."

While he's waiting, Ryder wonders if Josh ever sees the ghost—the same one, of course. It would be plain weird if Josh saw a ghost and if the ghost was taller or older or wore different clothes. But how the hell would Ryder bring up such a nutty topic? Is the boy who hurled the fatal pitch the only one to be haunted?

Josh launches into a story. A reporter from the *New York Times* came to do a profile of "CSI's twin brother" and that brother's efforts to get to the major leagues, to live in the shadow of a phenom.

"It's not like we get a lot of media down here," says Josh. "I knew he was a new face. Older guy. Polite. Came across like a thinker. All that. Introduced himself and told me what he was doing and seemed so low key. He came to two home games, followed us to Biloxi for a third, and then I saw him a week later. He asked to meet for coffee on an off day."

Ryder understands where this is going. "You thought he was a friend." Ryder says this as a statement, not an accusation.

"I mean, he heard me say over and over again that I was living my life and you were living yours, that I didn't expect to get any kind of special pass to the big leagues because I got *you* for a brother."

Ryder pictures Josh—an inch shorter, clean cut, burlier than Ryder, and rarely relaxed. They are definitely not identical twins. Josh struggled in school before Deon Johnson. He struggled more after. He gets trapped by a wicked combination of self-doubt and indecision.

"And?" says Ryder.

"He got me going."

Ryder imagines the fake sincerity on the reporter's face. "In detail?"

"I didn't think I'd been talking all that long," says Josh. "It sort of all came out."

Reporters have never had much to chew on. Their parents offered a moving statement at the time, the day after it happened. Their parents spoke for the family. There wasn't much a twelve-year-old could or would say, anyway. Most of the attention was focused on the kid who threw the ball. Later, Josh was one of those details that made the rounds as the story was embellished: *The poor kid's twin brother was the catcher. He was right there.* Their parents protected their sons and protected themselves too. They homeschooled their sons for a year—eighth grade—and moved to Denver during the summer before their freshman year for a clean start.

Ever since, Ryder has avoided all media attempts to drag him through the memory muck.

"He asked about me?" says Ryder.

"He asked about everything," says Josh. "He was smooth."

There is no dark secret that's being protected. But having it spilled all over the page will make it seem like it happened yesterday. Again.

"I'm sorry," says Josh. "He started out focused on my career. I mean, of course I knew it was about you. He wouldn't be writing about a minor-league catcher if that catcher didn't have a famous brother. He sucked me in."

"Jerk," says Ryder. "Call him back, tell him you went too far?"

Josh considers it. "How would I do that?"

"Tell him you got carried away. Tell him *something*."

Josh hesitates. Ryder can hear the uncertainty. "I don't know," he says at last.

"What did he ask the most about?"

"How we dealt with it," says Josh. "How we coped."

"Did we?" says Ryder. "Did we cope?"

Chapter 11

Ryder is right *there*. He is at that point of no return. The sign in the road points two ways—drunks to the left, no hangovers to the right. It's written in all caps. He ponders it. He's not pitching until Tuesday. He pours another glass of wine. There is that delicious moment where his woes float away of their own accord. He needs that. He wants to stop thinking about what his brother might have told the *New York Times*. The writer will undoubtedly recap the entire awful story again, trying to understand something that can't be understood.

Pagnozzi is going through the tenth reenactment of Wilson's catch, the carefree abandon of Wilson's locked-in zeal. Wilson and Rhineland are rolling, in tears, as Pagnozzi stabs his hand in the air to mimic Wilson's flying glove yet again and how his body slammed back to earth like a sky jumper who forgot to pull the cord.

"Got me the W," says Rhineland.

"Feel free to buy the next round—or dinner is fine too," says Wilson. He is still laughing. "As a way of saying thank you."

"You want a tip?" Rhineland's short hair is spiky and well gelled. He's got a thin, long face with jutting cheekbones that look prominent enough to grab. "I gotta tip now for your effort? Like it's a goddamn Starbucks or a shoeshine stand?"

"Something like that." Wilson has chiseled good looks and an easy, warm smile. Tonight he's wearing a bright-pink business shirt with a green paisley tie, which look even brighter against his smooth ebony skin. "Pitchers making that serious dough? I think it's a good idea. You should keep a wad of cash with you on the mound, wave some Benjamins in the air as extra incentive."

"Shit," says Rhineland. "You're the one on the highlight reel. Best play of the day, week, all of that. You're playing like it's a contract year, not the first of a five-year deal."

Wilson drops his jaw in a moment of pretend shock, but he knows it's true.

They are crammed in a booth at an Italian strip mall restaurant called Caruso's. The location and plain surroundings belie the forty-dollar entrées. Wine list like a telephone book. The space is much bigger than the exterior might let on, with a big, wide bar that is hopping. It's a scene. Little black dresses. Legs, shoulders, hair. Caruso's *carousers*. They are all on the prowl. Laughter ebbs and flows.

The buzz helps. The restaurant treats the foursome like family because Rhineland is a regular. They are tucked away in a booth in the back. They started with complimentary martinis. They were little ones, but straight rocket fuel. The eighty-five-dollar bottles of barbera followed.

Are they working on their third bottle, or fourth? Ryder gets that floating sensation, tells himself to slow down.

"Five years?" says Wilson. "I signed for five *years*?"

"Good money too," says Pagnozzi. "Especially if they signed you for your bat but you're going to add an elite glove to the package."

"I saw on Twitter that your wall-bashing grab had a catch probability of seven percent," says Rhineland. "You keep that up, you're going to be the biggest bargain in the majors."

"I signed for five years." Wilson shakes his head. "I want to make the playoffs at some point before I die."

"Seen our second-half schedule?" Pagnozzi is the journeyman in the bunch. He was a middle reliever for the Dodgers the year they collapsed against the Astros in the World Series. "Two road trips from hell. May as well get Magellan to manage."

"You checked the Orioles' storied history for finishing strong?" says Rhineland.

"Of course," says Ryder. The months leading up to being drafted, Ryder read everything he could get his hands on about the Orioles—both history and recent woes. "Not a great twenty-first century—so far."

"You think?" says Wilson. And laughs. "Mediocrity 101. Did I really sign up for five years of this? I'm gonna go out like Willie McCovey or Rod Carew."

"I wouldn't worry about that," says Pagnozzi.

"And *you're* gonna go out like Juan Marichal," says Wilson to Ryder. "Years and years and no ring, maybe a few minutes in the playoffs, and *poof*, you're gone."

"Or in the Hall of Fame," says Pagnozzi.

"Give me two World Series rings instead of going into the hall," says Wilson. He means it. "Even one. I don't want to play a hundred sixty-two games every year, humping from city to city and hotel after hotel, knowing we're going to let other teams run us out of the room come August and September."

"What choice you got?" says Rhineland. "Maybe we put on a run—maybe it all comes together, now that we got the savior here."

"Hey," says Ryder. "None of that. Just another goddamn pitcher."

"And LeBron is just another basketball player," says Wilson. "Too bad the clampdown is coming."

"By that you mean?" says Ryder.

"They can't let you keep doing what you do," says Wilson. "And you pitchers are outnumbered. The union is hitters. And hitters don't want their averages to crash, even if there are a bunch of Frank Ryder clones out there working their way up to the show. Much as I love playing behind you, Frank, enjoy it while it lasts. They'll punish pitchers for throwing faster than one oh five or move the mound back behind second base. The union is on fire. If I was Stone or Gallo, I'd be finding a way to dump all my chips on the table this year. Know what I'm saying?"

"They're making moves now."

Ryder blurts it out.

"Bullshit," says Wilson.

"It's not." Ryder wants their confidence. Teammates first. The wine is talking. He doesn't want to think about the union or the politics of the game. "I got pulled in."

"Moves?" says Pagnozzi. "That means they're shipping my ass out of here."

"Or mine," says Rhineland.

"They aren't breaking up the Three R's." Ryder isn't sure of that statement, but he tries to sell it with a firm look. "I was told to keep this to myself."

"Of course you were," says Pagnozzi.

"What's that mean?" says Ryder.

"It means you're in the loop because the entire team's strategy is built around you. The fact that you exist. You and your freakishness."

"Freak?" Ryder is offended. He didn't train to become a *freak*. He trained to get better. "Why, thank you very much."

"Don't try to deny it," says Pagnozzi. "Own it like Muhammad Ali. Say it to yourself: 'I am the greatest.'"

"I've been here for a minute." Ryder massages his right hand with his left under the table. "And it's not my style."

"What else did they tell you?" Wilson is as eager for information as he was for the ball when he crashed into the wall. "They didn't call you in to tell you about the possibility of some trades. In June? I don't think so."

Ryder lays it out for them—Ford's plan to use Ryder for a few innings every other day. By the time he's done, Pagnozzi is slumped and staring at the ceiling. Rhineland covers his face with both hands.

"When was the last time you pitched every other day?" says Pagnozzi.

"High school," says Ryder. "Only in the playoffs."

"And how hard were you throwing?"

"Fast enough. I told her I wasn't into it."

"You told Alicia Ford to shove it?" Pagnozzi is dubious.

"In so many words."

"It would be a stupid waste of *you*," says Pagnozzi. "The offense has to deliver, and every other day the entire bullpen needs to cover six innings? Fuckin' risky."

"And we'll probably cough up a couple of our prospects," says Rhineland.

Rhineland, who listens to the Buster Olney podcast on a regular basis and has made no secret about his interest in becoming a broad-caster when his arm drops off, mentions the names of a few pitchers they might have in mind.

Ryder stands up, points to the restroom, taps his chest with his fist. Smiles.

And gets tapped on the shoulder.

It's a man with his son. The kid is holding a copy of *Sports Illustrated*, the new edition with the cover photo of him staring in for the sign. The cover headline: IS FRANK RYDER'S ARM A SIGN OF BASEBALL'S END-TIMES? And, in smaller type: How High Can the Orioles Fly?

Ryder signs it with the Sharpie from his pocket. The signature is a weird one, given the drinks.

"I'm sure the *SI* cover jinx has no power of you," says Dad. "Not with your firepower."

—⚏—

Ryder hits the restroom, all heavy gleaming tile with a row of eight individual sinks. Tinny Frank Sinatra croons "Fly Me to the Moon." Maybe Frank is singing out there in the dining area, too, but the clatter of the bar and the general hubbub make it impossible to hear him. Ryder has memories of when he would stay at his grandparents' house in Alpharetta, and Grandpa Joe would play Frank Sinatra on vinyl and Ryder would watch the records go around.

Luck be a lady
. . . tonight.

The long evening and all the wine make him tired. He worries about having shattered the confidence he'd been granted by Ford, Stone, and Lackland. He wonders if he can Uber off by himself before the evening enters its next boozy phase. How would it look to peel off now?

An old man is sitting on a stool near the door inside the restroom. He is Black and frail and could be asleep. He is sitting so still at first Ryder catches himself, to make sure it's not another ghost, maybe Deon Johnson's grandpa. A wicker tray for tips sits on top of another stool.

The man grabs four paper towels from a shiny dispenser and hands them to Ryder when he's done washing. Gold, round, wire-rim glasses hug his face. He's bald. He is wearing a white shirt, black slacks. He smiles, his eyes as bright and clear as a baby's.

"Ha!" he says, coming alive like someone turned a key on his back. "Smoke! It's you. Smoke."

"Smoke?" Ryder says it like a reflex, to see how it sounds. "Smoke" Ryder. *No thanks.*

"Where in tarnation did you come from?"

"Tarnation?" Ryder drops a ten in the basket.

"Yeah," says the man. "Tarnation. Damnation. *Eternal* damnation, is more like it. Where in *tarnation* did you come from?"

"Georgia." Maggie would not be proud of him—getting plastered. Ryder is not sure this conversation is happening. "Georgia, and then Colorado."

"They got coaches know their *bidness*." The man holds up a crooked index finger. He points it at Ryder's face. The digit is a skinny eyeless snake. "You the smoke and fire all at once. You the brimstone itself! You bring the wrath of God with every goddamn pitch. You know that, don't you?"

Chapter 12

He's got the wrong table. No, his spot is taken, and so is the spot on the opposite side of the booth, where Rhineland and Wilson have squeezed in to make room.

The young woman in Ryder's spot scooches over to make room, and he recalls one night in Toronto when the party started early and ended late. That night, his inner judge closed the shades in his bright courtroom, popped a handful of melatonin, and lay down for a long nap. It was a night he can't understand or explain to himself, much as he has tried. It was a night that made him stop and wonder how he'd put himself in such a situation, no matter how much he'd enjoyed it in the moment.

Rhineland introduces Gretchen, sitting next to him. She's a stunning woman with long straight red hair. The hair comes so far around to the front of her head, and falls so effortlessly, that she looks like she's peeking out through a colorful waterfall. She offers him a big smile, sips from a martini glass where the silvery liquid soaks three plump olives. She hiccups, laughs, straightens her back, puts a fist to the center of her well-freckled chest three times fast, and laughs again. "I'm fine," she says. "Pleased to meet you. Maybe a little too pleased."

On Ryder's side of the booth is Olivia. "Don't mind my friend Gretchen," she says. A light hand taps Ryder's biceps. "She'll be fine."

Olivia sips from a tumbler. A lime wedge is perched on the edge of the glass like a parrot's beak. Rum and Coke?

Pagnozzi offers his wineglass in a toast "to friends." Pagnozzi winks. Wilson looks at Ryder and rolls his eyes. The table smells like lavender and something orange or citrusy, a welcome infusion. If Ryder has one more sip of anything alcoholic, he might need to bolt back to Mr. Tarnation's bathroom.

"Good friends?" says Ryder. "How so?"

"Ah," says Rhineland. "Old family connections. Gretchen is the sister of my best friend where I grew up in California—an avocado ranch in Goleta. Olivia is one of her pals from UMBC."

"Go Retrievers," says Gretchen, and hiccups again.

"UMBC? University of Maryland"—Ryder hesitates—"Baltimore something or other?"

"County," says Olivia. "Nobody gets the County part. UMBC."

"You knew each other in California?" he asks Rhineland.

"She was five years younger than me. I mostly knew her brother," he says.

"Bratty and clueless," says Gretchen.

Gretchen and Olivia must be twenty-one years old and a minute. Ryder will turn twenty-three in November, but Gretchen and Olivia seem much younger.

"Softball players," says Rhineland. "Gretchen plays first base, and Olivia is a pitcher."

"Go Retrievers," says Olivia. Her brunette hair is shoulder length, curly. She wraps both hands around the drink on the table like it's a precious orb to be examined for secret truths. Her fingers are long, her nails are plain. "I mean, we suck. We played forty-three games last year. Won twelve."

"But Olivia won nine of those," says Rhineland.

"Killer fastball," says Gretchen.

Ryder has a weakness for female athletes. Like Maggie. Does he have a right to think about Maggie? Or does two thousand miles give him license? Permission? He apparently thought that crossing the Canadian border meant different rules.

Pagnozzi doles out more wine. Ryder puts a hand over the top of his empty glass.

"She pitched a hundred thirty-four innings last year," says Rhineland. "And how many K's was it?"

Olivia shrugs. "You want me to talk pitching stats around this guy?" Again with the hand on his arm. This time it lingers. She has a confident laugh.

"She knows how many strikeouts," says Gretchen. "School record."

"Okay, okay. Sheesh. A hundred forty-seven," says Olivia. She smiles at Ryder. Shrugs. "They dragged it out of me."

"She's got a screaming fastball," says Gretchen.

"For women's softball, at least," says Olivia.

"From forty feet," says Rhineland, "it's almost the same thing as a baseball going a hundred miles per hour from sixty feet."

"It's not Eddie Feigner territory," says Olivia.

"A student of the game," says Ryder, impressed.

"Nine hundred and thirty no-hitters," says Olivia. "How can you not?"

"They claim he once threw a softball, what—one oh four or something like that?" says Pagnozzi.

"And some of his pitches came from behind his back, between his legs," says Olivia. She looks wistful. "The man of a thousand motions."

"Feigner only needed a catcher, a shortstop, and a first baseman," says Pagnozzi.

"King Ryder and His Court," says Rhineland. "Try that at Yankee Stadium. For fun."

"No thanks," says Ryder. "I like all seven guys behind me, one behind the plate."

"Exhibition," says Rhineland. "For charity."

"You'd pack the house," says Olivia. This time she bumps a light fist into Ryder's arm.

"In 1967," says Pagnozzi, "Eddie Feigner pitched an exhibition game in Los Angeles, and the other team had Mays, Clemente, Brooks Robinson, McCovey, Maury Wills, and one other."

"Harmon Killebrew," says Olivia. "'Hammerin' Harmon.' At one point, Feigner struck out all six of them in a row. He sat down five future Hall of Famers, and the sixth wasn't too shabby."

"Five?" says Rhineland. "Which one of those isn't Hall of Fame?"

"I know," says Olivia, playing the tease. "Any guesses?"

"It ain't Robinson," says Pagnozzi. "If you don't know that around here, you'll get dunked in the Patapsco."

"Or Mays, Clemente, or McCovey," says Rhineland. "And Killebrew is in the hall; I'm, like, ninety percent sure of that. Maury Wills?"

"Yep," says Olivia. "Hard to believe."

"How the heck do you keep track of all this stuff that happened thirty, forty years before you were born?" Rhineland asks the question that Ryder was wondering.

"My dad. We lived in Wyman Park. Season tickets to the Orioles. He still talks about Memorial Stadium like it was some sort of shrine." Again, the composure. "I grew up with four older brothers. The youngest is five years older than me, and the oldest is twelve years older than me. All baseball nut heads. My second-oldest brother is pitching this year for the Akron RubberDucks. Cleveland Double-A. So, baseball in the blood. When I saw my first game at Camden Yards at age nine? I had a big bag of popcorn, and I discovered you could put your sodas in those holders in the back of the seats? I thought it was the coolest thing ever. Why hadn't Dad told me about that? I mean, the O's sucked back then, but I didn't care."

Olivia is a portrait of poise. The allure is unforced. Ryder realizes he needs to improve in this department.

"Tomboy?" says Rhineland.

"No," says Olivia. "I mean, are you jumping to the clichés of female softball players?"

"No, no, no," says Rhineland. "Sorry."

"I was dolls, dress-up, all of that. But when it came to baseball, it seemed like another thing I cared about. I didn't think baseball was a boy thing. And don't you love it that the Orioles have a female GM today? My dad treated me the same as he did my brothers when it came to that. He thought it was natural to take an interest. Speaking of my dad . . . ?"

Her question ends on a tentative up note.

"Why is everyone looking at me?" says Ryder.

Olivia exchanges a glance with Gretchen, who offers a frowny face, a head shake, and a shrug.

"Okay, it's fan-girl stuff," says Olivia, "but my dad is going to kill me if I don't come home with a photo."

Chapter 13

Ray Gallo knows damn well that, when he's sitting in the front row of the owner's box, triple the size of a regular suite, he will be a target for cutaways to gauge his reactions. He can't be too cocky. He *won't* be too cocky. Sure, he can clap and celebrate with each of the strikeouts to come, but he thinks of all the others who will be watching. He can't be a spectacle of overconfidence.

It's June.

There is a long way to go.

Anything can happen.

Let the crowd roar its approval. Let the crowd be heard in Boston and New York. The crowd can do its thing. He'll be a picture of restraint.

Gallo sips Natty Boh. There is nothing more *of the people* and *by the people* than holding a plastic cup of the city's beer. It's a warm Tuesday night. Every seat in Camden Yards is sold. Gallo's suite is packed—the governor and his horde. The SRO spots near the left field bullpen and above the scoreboard in right field are full. The scalpers have made off with their haul. The neighborhood watering holes were packed before the game and will do decent business after too. The *Baltimore Sun*, the same paper that has sent sportswriter after sportswriter to drag the Orioles down and question every move on the field and off for the past couple of decades, used its editorial space that very morning to celebrate the renewed community pride, attributing the upbeat flavor of the city to the fact that the Orioles are about to sink their teeth into the ankles of the Red Sox and will no doubt soon overtake the Yankees too.

The newspaper concluded that nobody had much hope back in 2014, when the Orioles were squashed four games to zero by the Kansas City Royals, but this year is different. This year the wins are piling up. This year, the paper said, they could "feel" the chemistry on the team. This year there is one player who was changing attitudes and giving the city a reason to hope. The newspaper, the same newspaper that has long drubbed Gallo for his apparent interest in making money and not in chasing championships, was sending him a love letter. They wanted him to forget about all the crap they'd dumped on his head over the years.

Maybe they were buttering him up so when Rex Coburn approached him out in the parking lot before the game, he'd drop his guard and offer a thoughtful response to a question about a crazy plan GM Ford and her team had floated by Frank Ryder. But Gallo never drops his guard in public, prefers to say as few words to reporters as possible, and didn't take the bait.

What the *Baltimore Sun* wants is what everybody else wants: to be part of the inner circle and to claim they were there on the nights when Frank Ryder was pitching.

The mood is pure anticipation. If a power company could tap the electricity thrumming in the stands, they could light the city for a month.

—⁂—

Gallo watches and the crowd roars as his team sprints from the dug-out. Ryder is the last one out of the dugout. He wears number 9. The team wants him to switch with the shortstop, who wears number 1, but Ryder has said it's not a big deal. "Nine *is* one," Ryder says in a somewhat legendary insight played up in a page-one article in the *Sun*.

"The nine of us on the field at any one time. We're all one. It's the same number."

Thinking about it, Gallo laughs.

"What is it?"

"What?" says Gallo.

"You were laughing," says Lisa.

"I was smiling. Inside."

"I heard a laugh. Don't think I don't know the meaning of every oink, whine, and guffaw. After all these years?"

"I doubt it." Gallo gives his wife the deadest of deadpans. "Read this."

She laughs.

Ryder picks the ball from the mound and rubs it in his bare hands, glove tucked under his arm as he stares out at center field.

"You were chuckling at your good fortune." Lisa is younger by fifteen years. Even seated, she is a portrait of youth and fitness, right down to her club soda with lime and the plastic baggies that hold her pistachios, baby carrots, and an organic power bar she'll consider dessert.

"Believe me," says Gallo, "I don't *chuckle*."

Ryder stands behind the rubber. He lifts his cap, replaces it. Tightens it down. He takes a deep breath, scrunches his shoulders up high, and exhales. As hard as it is to imagine, because it's warm-up time, a quiet comes over the crowd.

Twitter anticipated this moment, and here it is. The Orioles' own Twitter feed has played coy, declining to squelch the rumors and feeding the frenzy.

The quiet is reasonable, given forty-seven thousand people. It's no library or funeral home, but Gallo gives them all credit for wanting to play along, and how can Gallo not feel the lump forming in his throat, the whole goddamn city willing to engage in this bit of theatrics, this musical *fuck you* to the opponents. It's whimsical and nasty and presumptuous all at once.

Frank Ryder touches the rubber with his shoe, and it's like he's hit a button. Howling dogs yelp, the big power chords cue the psychedelic organ, and there's the jungle beat, and when the chorus comes around the crowd is right on the money, scream-singing *Hush, hush* as Ryder throws.

The warm-up tosses are easy ones, in Ryder's midrange.

"Don't think I'm overconfident," says Gallo.

"Probably your biggest fear," says Lisa. "To be seen as counting your chickens."

"Or anything. Birds of any kind, including Orioles."

"But you don't have to worry every minute of the day, do you?" Lisa is wearing a simple sleeveless dress that is peach without being *too* orange. The outfit shows off her triceps. "Now is the time to relax and let the game play itself out, right? It's out of your hands."

"Yes and no."

"How is it in your hands? Are you flashing game signals way up here?"

"Grown men—and *women*—are entirely capable of messing up good things."

Gallo is still wrapping his head around Rex Coburn's question about Ford's plan. Gallo had the reporter repeat the question, as if he hadn't heard him right the first time. Gallo declined comment with a stone face.

"It's possible to overmanage, you know?" he says. "Overthink, you know?"

"What's to overthink about Frank Ryder?" says Lisa.

"Precisely."

"How could you ask him to do anything differently?"

"Perhaps you would like to sit with my GM."

"I don't pretend to know baseball," says Lisa. "The ins and outs, I mean. Most runs wins, right?"

"And nothing else should matter."

"But yet, somehow, it does."

"There's way too much overthinking going on, all these cockamamie shifts on defense and everything, so yeah, we are capable of making a mess."

"But you don't need to bring worry to every game, every pitch—do you?"

Gallo says nothing. She is correct, of course. She has always been the one to soften him, or at least try. She is the one who says what others are thinking. Lisa has been his wife now for thirty years, and he still feels as if she was frozen at age twenty-eight, her age when they met. She is sunny, fresh, and easygoing. But going down the path that Lisa suggests means dropping his guard, letting laziness slip in the back door. He got rich by bearing down. He got rich by coupling drive and determination with endless analysis. Nobody could outsell him, nobody would undercut the quality of his products and the stories he would conjure to give them their seductive power.

In baseball, it's three strikes and you're out.

—⁓—

Tampa Bay's leadoff hitter is a scrappy shortstop and longtime Oriole-killer. Tug Lasser is standing in the on-deck circle pretending like he can time Ryder's pitches, as if he has a clue about what he's going to do, but it's all show. Gallo has seen this act before. It's a precious bit of showmanship, and it's meaningless. The entire Tampa Bay team is lined up shoulder to shoulder at the rail of the dugout along third base, no doubt wondering if they can cobble together a last-minute strategy for how to get a bat on the ball. Or, more likely, running calculations for how much their hitting stats will suffer by game's end. Batting averages are down again this year, and more than one sportswriter has calculated how much of the dip can be attributed to Ryder's games. It's not only Ryder game days. When Joe Rhineland takes the mound the day after

Ryder, he feeds on the eagerness of the batters to get their groove back, so he chips around the edges of the plate, inducing even more strikeouts and sending the batting averages further south.

Lasser takes the batter's box with a confident stride. He's a white kid from Arizona known for his hard play. He's been compared to Pete Rose. But there is no chance to show any hustle if you can't get the bat on the ball. Ryder starts him out at 105, right at the knees, and whatever timing Lasser thought he might have perfected in the on-deck circle is all for naught, his swing good for another pitcher or another game or another universe, but not this one. He's late like a clock that didn't get moved ahead come daylight savings. The crowd roars.

Gallo smiles, inside.

It is, in fact, very hard to avoid looking on the bright side and wishing this moment were the last game in September and they were heading into the playoffs with home-field advantage and all their players healthy and hitting on all cylinders.

In the bottom of the second inning, Julio Diaz doubles, steals third, and scores on a deep sacrifice fly. Diaz, with a skinny frame that belies his power, claps his way home until he touches the plate, taps his heart with double fists, and points to the sky with double index fingers, thin gold chain flashing in the light. The run may as well be twenty runs. Or forty. The Rays know it. The crowd knows it.

Gallo stands, knees whining at the effort, and makes a glad-handing round of the box. The governor has found his way to the bar in the back with the good wine and the hard booze. Gallo wouldn't mind a nip or two of bourbon to add some *oomph* to the watery beer. He makes small talk with the slick-haired governor, whose backroom dealings are rumored to make Spiro Agnew's shenanigans look like a schoolboy stealing lunch money. Gallo listens to the governor's fantastical notions for how the season is going to play out. "Does this guy have a brother? Or sister?" asks the governor. "Can you sign him and train him up quick? There's got to be something in the genes."

Six monitors carry the game in the booth. The announcers' comments are buried above the party going on. In between pitches, the camera again finds Ryder's face like it's some sort of medical-school class on dermatology, the shot so close it tracks individual beads of sweat dripping from the tips of Ryder's hair. There is something relaxed about Ryder's gaze tonight. He never had the deer-in-the-headlights look—not for a second—but every trace of the raw rookie is gone. Ryder holds his head high, stares harder, and he is working at an even more confident rhythm, the crowd punctuating each K with thunder.

A cute bartendress asks Gallo for his order. She is blonde and exuberant. She wears a white golf shirt with the cartoon Oriole and his goofy golly-gee smile, which looks neither fierce nor intimidating. Maybe the smiley face logo has been their problem all these years.

Gallo swallows a shot of Knob Creek and gets a cold Natty Boh to chase it. His presence at the bar gives others a chance to come around and make small talk. He is the celebrity guest in his own home. Fawning, frenzied fans whirl about. Ryder this. Ryder that. Ryder. *Ryder. Ryder. Ryder.* Division? League? World Series?

Gallo listens to the ideas and theories and suggestions. Several of his counselors are well buzzed. With the women, he likes to sort through the aroma of sweaty human flesh and pluck a note or two from the fragrance they are wearing. Sandalwood. Bergamot. Jasmine. It's a personal challenge, to notice with his nose and to develop stories about the women and how they might have landed on this scent to call their own.

He listens to the hope. *This is the year.* It's no fun to discourage the hope. It's a weird sensation to see a dominating pitcher who is as good—by light-years—as they said he would be. He knows pitchers. *Goddamn*, he knows pitchers. How goddamn expensive they are. And all the sales bullshit about how the scouts have found some gem in Poughkeepsie or Waterloo. This time, at least so far, the product is as good as the sales job. But how can all the enthusiasts in the box tonight not recognize the perils?

Now, does he want to make a push to the top of the division? Does he want it? The pressure that comes with winning? The spotlight?

"You got three games in your pocket going into the World Series." This is a well-known Baltimore prosecutor, but Gallo can't pull up the name. Gallo smiles, listens. "What are the odds at that point? You gotta win one out of the other four games? Should be a walk in the park."

Gallo is pleasant and easygoing. The huddles morph and shift. He listens to suggestions about players he should pluck away from other teams via trade. He marvels at the ability of others to tell him how to spend his money; would he ever walk into *their* home office and make a few pronouncements about where to invest and how much to risk? The trade activists never name which Orioles to bid goodbye to, unless it's the third-string catcher. Trade pushers forget about the hard part, shipping a player off to a city across the country and disrupting family lives and shattering expectations, not to mention disrupting their personal flow of routines, rent, schools, neighborhoods, friends. Sure, some players ask to find new digs, but for most of the guys it's hard. And who would want to be shipped away from the Frank Ryder craziness?

Even the rhythms of success are taking some getting used to. The buzz, the attention, the fawning, the A-listers wanting access to the locker room. All coupled with a singular and collective expectation, to land in the playoffs and come home with the big trophy.

Gallo decides on one more bourbon before rejoining Lisa. He makes his way to the bar and holds up his thumb and forefinger with a half inch between them. The bartendress is a quick study. She is pouring him another splash, and Gallo recognizes who is also standing at the bar, and for a moment he thinks about slinking away, pretending he didn't order a drink. But the man turns. And grimaces.

"Can I see your ticket, please?" says Gallo.

"Warm greetings backatcha."

"I know you're here for a reason," says Gallo. "Cut to the chase."

"And I thought camaraderie was dead."

"Yeah, as if your band of brothers isn't trying to figure out another way to take a big chunk of flesh out of our hides," says Gallo.

"You've sold every seat tonight, and, let's see, Boog Powell's barbecue tripled the number of beef sandwiches he normally moves, and you're complaining?" Walter Woodson, head of the Major League Baseball Players Association, was a first baseman with the White Sox and Rangers. "That sounds like a sob story. Maybe put out a press release in the morning or call a news conference, tell everyone how rough it's been?"

"Did you come here to piss in the punch bowl? Is that all? I imagine there's some sort of ethical violation happening right this moment."

"Just a friend of the game," says Woodson. "A baseball fan enjoying the night."

"You could be watching the same view from your couch in . . ."

"New York," says Woodson. "Upper East Side."

"They have baseball in New York, too, am I right?"

Woodson was a career .260 hitter. He never played with a team that finished with more wins than losses. Fifteen years, all below average. "I'm feeling the love."

"Good, there's more where that came from."

Cued by a sudden roar like a bomb exploding, Gallo glances at the monitor to watch as a baseball scampers between two fielders in the right-center gap. The ball rolls all the way to the wall in one of the deepest parts of the park, two Tampa Bay outfielders running after it with their backs to home plate. Three Orioles score, and the hitter, Diaz again, ends up on third with a stand-up triple. Diaz points to the dugout with both gun fingers, takes a low-five slap from the third base coach, puts a fist to his chest, and looks up at the night. The crowd goes bananas.

Orioles 4, Rays 0.

"What's it like?" says Woodson. He is wearing a sharp gray suit, blue shirt, no tie. He has a dark complexion and might need to shave twice a day. Gallo always has the feeling Woodson is ready to throw a punch at the slightest provocation. "To be the talk of baseball? Or all of sports, for that matter?"

"It's a hot streak," says Gallo. "A couple of good months."

"Not according to the scribes."

"Whose track record is eclipsed only by writers of horoscopes," says Gallo. "It's June."

"Some would call it late June. Some would be tweaking the lineup, looking to replace the weakest links."

"So why did you call this meeting?"

"Meeting?" says Woodson. "Open bar and forty-seven thousand of your closest friends? My kind of meeting."

"Let's say you didn't wander in because you're doing a national comparison test of ballpark franks."

"You assume I want something?"

"That is the nature of a union, if I'm not mistaken. The status quo sucks. And you get what you want through collective bullying. Oh, sorry, I meant to say *bargaining*." Gallo keeps his voice low. Oddly, there is no huddle of humanity around them. "You wake up wanting, eat lunch wanting, screw your hot girlfriends wanting more, and go to sleep thinking about how you will crusade for your worthy causes the next day, which boils down to wanting more money or less work or, in your dream of dreams, both."

Woodson nods. "Hoo boy. That's a lot to process." He sips his drink. It's not his first. Or maybe even third. "Must be wonderful to care so much about the working conditions of your employees. So you're opposed to free will, most likely, and free agency too? You liked it better when Curt Flood still did what he was told? I can't remember—were you an owner back then too?"

"Why are you here?" says Gallo. "I got a game to watch."

"What's to watch?" says Woodson. "The game is over."

"You're here to fire a warning shot."

"I'm a man of peace."

"Until it's time to strike."

"A peaceful act," says Woodson. "And American as apple pie."

"Pampered millionaires who stay in five-star hotels and drive Ferraris are always such a sympathetic cause. What's your angle?"

"No angle," says Woodson. "Facts. That is, you got one season with this Frank Ryder business."

"You're throwing one of your union members under the team bus?"

"Ryder will be fine," says Woodson. "Long as he hasn't found some new formula for the Canseco milkshakes that doesn't get detected by the random drug tests."

"Frank Ryder?" says Gallo. "About the strongest thing he takes is full-strength whole milk."

"He won't be pitching with quite the same velocity next year," says Woodson. "His arm will feel like he's on vacation. We'll be doing the fans a favor. And the game a favor too. Restoring the balance."

"You're going to artificially limit human capability?"

"Unless his arm breaks or maybe that Little League incident he's trying so hard to forget will finally do its number. And then it will be a case of nature taking its course, and the freak show will be over. You ever talk to him about that? Ask him how he lives with himself? You can't throw like that and think you're normal."

"And you would change the rules for one arm?"

"You don't get it."

"What, exactly, is there to *get*?"

Woodson straightens himself up, holds up a finger. Woodson's eyes struggle to focus. He stares at the top button on Gallo's shirt. "Every single at bat, from Little League to the game being played right here tonight, it's all about hope. It's all about possibility. It's all about whether hard work and discipline can win the day. And your boy has come along and said there is no hope. So what he's doing out there, you know what it is, don't you?"

"Probably not."

"It's un-American. Simple as that."

"You're reading a lot into a game," says Gallo.

"Frank Ryder is the harbinger of doom," says Woodson.

"Give me a break. It's a game. He's one player."

"You gotta snuff out problems when you spot them." Woodson points to the bright-emerald diamond, doesn't turn to look at it. "You gotta attack these issues early."

"And the message to every athlete in the land is get better, but don't get *too much* better?"

"No," Woodson scoffs. "Please."

"Which means you're here about the batters. You're not here about principle or apple pie. The union membership is concerned about how it will look when batting averages dip, when home run totals don't look so gaudy."

Gallo is aware of her arrival a second before the tap on the shoulder. Perhaps his nose has sensed her advance, though Lisa downplays perfume. In that sense, she was always an odd choice as wife. She's fine with a pricey lotion, and she prefers all things rosemary, but that's about it.

"What's keeping you?" Lisa says it in the most nonthreatening, cheery way possible.

Gallo introduces Woodson as if he's bumped into his best buddy from college, turning on the charm and grace. Woodson makes small talk for a minute, says he was about to leave to beat the crowd.

"You saved me," says Gallo when they are back in their seats.

"Union honcho?" says Lisa.

"No different than any other hack out there," says Gallo. "Less work, fatter paychecks. Two-track minds."

"Your favorite."

Bottom of the eighth. The Orioles are up 6–0. The night, right down to the still air and a whole boatload of optimism, is perfect. Too perfect.

"You ask anyone if a team treats their players any better," says Gallo, still ruminating on his verbal bout with Woodson. "Clubhouse food, the best hotels, and I try my hardest when the contracts come up."

"Don't let him rattle you," says Lisa.

Julio Diaz scrapes out a spot in the batter's box. The Orioles' center fielder is a switch-hitter. He stands in from the left side to face a towering Tampa Bay righty with tree-trunk thighs and a beefy gut to go with it. The scoreboard posts his name, Brody Billings, and his headshot. His neck is so thick he could be an offensive lineman in the NFL.

Diaz swings at the first pitch, a no-joke flash of smoke. The scoreboard flashes 102. A wisp of admiration, a collective tincture of sound, rises from the stands. Thousands react as one. It's a gasp of respect.

Someone else with velocity.

"Jesus," says Gallo. "He's like a white Aroldis Chapman."

"Woodson got under your skin," says Lisa. "I can see that."

"They want to cap Ryder. Put up a speed limit."

"How would they do that?" Lisa is incredulous.

"I guess anything over a certain top speed would be a ball. Even if the batter swung and missed, any pitch thrown over that limit would be an automatic ball."

"Doesn't sound right," says Lisa.

"The union has got batting averages to worry about—and the humiliation factor. Big stars being brought to their knees? It doesn't help feed the kinds of stories their agents are trying to sell."

"Frank Ryder is one pitcher," says Lisa.

"There's others out there in the minor leagues, developing their talent. Most will crash and burn. But, yeah, you're singing my song."

Diaz fouls off a curveball on the second pitch. He stares back out at Billings and waits. Lights flood the field from the roof of the B&O Warehouse in right field. Some seats are empty, but not many. The owner's box is gaining wiggle room. A pleasant hum hangs over the field. The game is over, but true fans wait for the bitter end. You never know what you're going to see. If there is a more perfect night, Gallo can't imagine it. That is, other than worrying about what's ahead, the demands and requests from now until September.

And beyond? If the Orioles go deep into the playoffs, success will come with pressure to repeat.

Gallo's gaze comes back to home plate as the third pitch arrives. From this distance and this height, the pitch looks normal. Diaz starts to flail out of the way, but there's a sickening crack.

Diaz falls like a rag doll, his bat tangled up in his own downward tumble. Fans in the lower stands rise to their feet. The trainer races from the dugout, a square black case gripped hard in one hand.

Julio Diaz is sprawled on the dirt across the chalk outline of the batter's box like it's a crude crime scene. He grabs his right wrist. The agony on Diaz' face tells the trainer and the whole world all they need to know.

It's broken.

Chapter 14

The quiet is overwhelming.

Diaz is a portrait in pain. Six weeks to heal, bare minimum. Two to four weeks of rehab. They will be lucky if Diaz, their best hitter, is ready by September. Very lucky.

Will Diaz ever be the same?

Lackland stands next to Ryder on the top step of the dugout. Diaz is figuring how he can move to vertical and slip onto an electric cart.

"You got this?"

Lackland looks Ryder straight in the eye. Lackland hasn't been much use as a pitching coach, but Ryder knows this moment isn't about his arm slot, his grip, or his pacing. This is about tradition. *Baseball polices itself in its own ugly fashion with its own miserable traditions.* At this moment, Diaz is fighting his way through the white-hot pain and abruptly shortened season of this "tradition."

"I'll get tossed," says Ryder.

Even casual fans know Diaz was plunked for clapping his way home on the sac fly in the first inning and overcelebrating the triple in the sixth.

"I don't care." Lackland's gaze is heavy. "You got six runs in your pocket. Get two outs, do what you gotta do. Jaworski is third up for the Rays, so it's righteous kismet right there, eye for an eye, one center fielder for one center fielder. I think the bullpen can cover four measly outs with a cushion that fat."

Diaz moves to the cart, babying his wrist. He's wary of the slightest jolt. Polite applause floats out of the stands as the electric cart rolls off with the wounded. Diaz efforts a smile, his good arm protecting his bad. A thank-you wave is out of the question. To Ryder, applause is a sad consolation for playing by the game's stupidest rule, a rule written by a culture familiar to gangs all over the world.

Lance Tackett jogs out to first base to run for Diaz. This is an *up yours* message to the Rays. Tackett is a speedy utility infielder. He's not there to play for Diaz in the top of the ninth; that will be Jay Everett, their only backup outfielder with some center field experience. Using Tackett sends a signal. The Orioles aren't done scoring, even with a 6–0 bulge.

Tackett swipes second on the first pitch from Billings, whose lumbering move to the plate is a base stealer's dream. The crowd approves.

On the third pitch, shortstop Esteban Ortega punches a seeing-eye single between first and second, bringing Tackett around third in a hot flash. He slides under the tag at home to score the bonus *fuck you, feelgood* run.

Cory Bayless, who all season long has been putting up good offensive numbers and who is making hard plays look easy at third base, stands in at the plate like he could crush a basketball over the fence in the deep center field. He swings much too hard at the first pitch and pops out to end the inning.

Ryder walks to the mound, more than the usual number of his teammates running close by to mumble words of encouragement. They want Ryder to locate the blackness in his heart, but what would be more devastating is nine straight pitches at full velo and let the Rays go to bed tonight wondering if retribution will come during tomorrow afternoon's game or maybe next month in front of the Rays' hometown fans.

Ryder finishes his half-assed warm-up tosses and steps off the mound, watching the ball go around the horn to Ortega, Cruz, and Bayless. When Bayless flips it back, Wyatt is halfway to the mound, catcher's mask tucked under his armpit and his helmet dangling in one hand.

"Wasted visit," says Ryder.

A sour knot gnaws at his guts.

"You got this?" Wyatt's eyes are dead. Eight years, third club. He's an inch or two shorter than Ryder, but his presence is imposing. So is the look in his eye and the tone of voice. He's a bulldog redhead with a thick mustache. "No backing down, now."

"Get two outs and then do what I gotta do." Ryder nods, massages the seams of the ball in both hands.

"Don't dink around," says Wyatt. "Keep it real."

Ryder nods. The rookie-pupil bit is a part he is required to play from time to time. It's amateur-hour stuff. Anyone could pull it off. All you have to do is agree with every scrap of advice being shoveled in your direction and appear otherwise clueless: *I so appreciate the insight.*

Ryder whiffs the first two batters in seven pitches, mixing speeds and spin rates.

Ryder walks off the mound, mops his sweaty forehead with his sleeves, readjusts his cap, watches the ball flick from Bayless to Cruz to Ortega and back into his own glove.

He thinks about scanning the section in the stands where Olivia Key is sitting but doesn't want to be obvious. He can't be obvious, even if it was his idea to have Rhineland set up Olivia and Gretchen with a pair of passes—a request Rhineland fielded without the requisite ribbing. There is talk about the foursome meeting after the game.

Innocent. One drink.

No.

Innocent. One drink?

He'll take all the crap from Lackland and his teammates after the game for not retaliating. He'll just shrug and listen to their shit.

This moment was inevitable. About every week during baseball season, there are dustups and beanballs and taunts. Benches clear, talk shows debate. It wasn't hard for Ryder to anticipate that he would end up in one of these moments, and it was a cinch to decide how he would handle it too.

Billy Jaworski wears a puffy beard. He is a speedy outfielder who makes the highlight reels with his dives and leaps, sacrificing his body at every opportunity. His nickname is "Crash," which is hardly original. He owns a league-leading nineteen home runs and is sitting on a .305 batting average. His stats have taken a hit tonight, however, because he's got three K's to his name already.

Ryder starts with a swooping curve. The pitch looks like it's coming for Jaworski's head but turns at the last moment. Jaworski reels out of harm's way, but the ball misses the strike zone.

Ball one.

It is the first time all night that Ryder has thrown a first-pitch ball. He hates being behind. Ryder screams the second pitch over the inside part of the plate, and Jaworski, maybe smart enough to see if he can work the count to 2–0 in his favor, keeps his bat still. The pitch is a strike. Ryder sees it. Wyatt knows it. Stone and Lackland know it. Jaworski likely knows it too.

But the umpire calls it a ball, prompting heckles and jeers from the dugout and stands.

Now Wyatt gives him the fist. It's a quick flash, like Wyatt is clenching and stretching his fingers, but Ryder gets it. Wyatt wants Jaworski plunked *now*.

When the flash of fist is done, Wyatt puts down the 1, taps his right leg. If Jaworski is going to end up walking, Wyatt's theory goes, then it may as well be a pinch runner on first base, and Jaworski can now take the punishment from the baseball gods, get the teams all fair and square in the pain-and-injury department.

Wyatt would also call for the beanball if there were two strikes instead of two balls, but Ryder has made up his mind. He's not going to play. What are they going to do? Do his teammates love this grisly ritual? Do they enjoy knowing that their season could be over, or their careers, by playing this creepy form of Russian roulette—not knowing if you are the one to be plunked and sacrificed in the name of pride? Will Diaz heal faster or feel better if another bloodied, bruised body is dragged off the field of play?

Ryder ignores Wyatt. He grooves a 108 fastball for strike one.

Wyatt flashes another quick fist, so fast and unassuming that future adjudicators would never be able to determine if it was a signal of any kind.

Ryder ignores Wyatt again and evens the count with another fastball at 105. The pitch is so tempting Jaworski would be a fool not to swing, but he comes up empty, his timing all off.

Ryder wants his complete game.

He wants to finish this inning and pitch the next.

"Come *on*, Frankie," comes a shout from the dugout.

The voice is Stone's.

Encouragement? No. Instructions? Definitely.

Wyatt stands for a moment, staring out at him. He lifts his mask off his face. Glares. Locked jaw, the whole bit. *This ain't your game yet, kid. Feeling a touch of self-interest? Well, get over it, nail this asshole, and show the Rays that the Orioles don't flinch when it comes to a fight. The whole league is watching. Don't let us down.*

No.

Ryder has decided. He'll shrug later when the reporters ask him if it crossed his mind to respond to Diaz' getting hurt. He'll take the cold shoulders of his teammates over being ejected or starting a brawl or hurting a player. Maybe in the all-too-predictable office conversation tonight or tomorrow with Stone or Lackland, he can blame Deon Johnson and his whole psychological "issues" on the fact that he can't throw a fastball at a live human being. He's not going to hurt Jaworski. He's going to send him back to the dugout with another strikeout to his name. That's all.

Wyatt squats in his position. There is no flash of fist. Wyatt shakes his head. Ryder is being scolded. As if it requires monumental effort to extend a digit, Wyatt slowly puts down the 1. The way Wyatt is holding his position, in fact, it's pure petulance. *I ain't your teammate anymore.*

Ryder's windup is good. He allows himself the luxury of feeling good about his decision. He'll need to walk off the mound after Jaworski takes strike three, and he'll keep his head down, find a corner of the dugout where he can sit alone. Maybe Stone will yank him in the ninth anyway, teach him a lesson about insubordination.

Maybe.

The windup is good, the arm slot is good, but even as it leaves his fingertips, Ryder wants to freeze time and pull the pitch back like there might be an invisible yo-yo string that will save the day.

Jaworski waits. He doesn't want to be fooled again. This might be another pitch like the first one, when he looked so ridiculous ducking away from a soft curve. Jaworski's fingers tighten their grip on the bat. He is in full evaluation mode, as if he might pull the trigger. Wyatt moves his glove inside—*well inside.*

Jaworski reads the threat and fears the worst. His body jerks, but like his swing on the previous pitch, he is very late. The ball grinds into his rib cage with a wicked snap.

Jaworski collapses. He goes straight down in a heap as if he is a marionette and one slash of a machete has cut all his strings. The umpire yanks his face mask off. He points at Ryder, recoils his arm, and whirls forward with all the dramatic flair he can muster.

Ejected.

Ryder looks at his guilty hand. *What happened?*

He looks at the Rays' dugout. A half dozen players sprint. Coming for him. Ryder stands his ground, shakes his head. *Fuck!* Ryder's teammates are quicker. And more prepared. Wyatt is right by his side. Teammates fashion a protective huddle around him. Fists fly. Shoves. Names. *Motherfuck* this and *motherfuckin'* that. The bullpens open like a jail break, all the pitchers racing in. Brothers-in-arms. More shoving. Tackling. Punching. Shoving. Shoving. Jostling. Yelling. Accusations. Mostly, shoving.

Umpires chase everyone back to their corners. Jaworski remains on his back. He lies inert, in awkward fashion, his legs twisted around each other. He should be writhing, reeling, showing the pain of it all. But, no. He has fallen with his body lying across the batter's box, his head on the plate.

The Rays' trainer is there, and Jaworski is surrounded by more people—far more people—than routine.

Jaworski's spikes aren't moving. They aren't fucking *moving*. The name-calling subsides. The teams part ways. Ryder can't think. Or focus. His whole system pumps—anger, self-loathing, and confusion. *What the hell happened?* He goes out of body. He's watching himself.

Ryder is escorted off like he's being bounced from a club by his own drunken mates. The fans are quiet, on edge. At the top step of the dugout, Ryder looks again at home plate. One of the Rays' coaches is working to clear some room, move their players back. Ryder stares.

Jaworski's feet refuse to move.

Chapter 15

Ryder studies his right hand.

What in the hell did you do?

There isn't a soul alive who will believe what Ryder says after this. He hates that he's going to join the club of deniers and fakers and bullshit artists. When he tells the truth about this one, everyone will think he's lying.

It will be heard as baseball tongue-in-cheek bullshit when it is, in fact, the truth.

It will be a line he promised to himself that he would never utter aloud.

The clubhouse is quiet. Ryder is alone except for Hawk, one of the clubhouse attendants, who is piling folded towels on shelves by the entry to the showers. Ryder paces, sits, paces again. A pillar in the center of the clubhouse holds four television monitors that point north, south, east, and west. Ryder hears the audio of the buzzing crowd through the monitors—the sound works fine—but the announcers say nothing. The view focuses on the circle gathered at home plate. The angles switch back and forth from a shot overhead and a shot from ground level. And, with no notice, there is Ryder on the screen, the view from the center field camera.

In extreme slo-mo.

Ryder stares, unable to rip himself away. Ryder studies his feet, his hips, his hand, his shoulders. He's looking for something out of place or out of alignment; sees nothing. The video remains free of narration as it starts, until the ball in his grip is at its apex.

"Not that I'm saying Ryder threw intentionally." The voice is Jim Palmer's. "I mean, we've watched this throw from every angle now, and usually you can tell when the pitcher is targeting the body rather than the strike zone. I'm not seeing that here."

Ryder watches the slow windup. His own. When the ball is halfway to the plate, he looks away and looks down.

This is Gary Thorne. "We won't jump to conclusions about anything. I mean, the fact that they're taking this long to even try and get Jaworski off the field of play—obviously it's a case of extreme caution."

"For sure," says Palmer.

"And I don't mean to dredge up bad memories, since you are my broadcasting pal, but didn't Jim Palmer once encounter controversy for a situation like this back in 1976? A few years ago?"

Ryder sits. He realizes his glove remains on his left hand, and he removes it, hurls it across the clubhouse to his locker. It lands in front of the one next to his—which belongs to Diaz.

"Kind of a day I like to forget," says Palmer.

"Not so easy to do."

"Reggie Jackson was an Oriole that year, and he got hit in the face. By Dock Ellis. Funny how these details stay with you. It's all seared in my memory, when some days I can't remember what I ate for lunch."

Ryder stands, paces. He heads to pick up his glove and put it in his locker, where it belongs, but Hawk is a few steps ahead of him and takes care of the chore. Hawk smiles and gives Ryder a congratulatory pat on his shoulder.

"And you were asked to retaliate?" says Thorne.

"It wasn't really a choice," says Palmer. "Earl Weaver wasn't in the habit of giving you choices. And again, I'm not saying Frank Ryder intentionally threw at Billy Jaworski."

"Of course not," says Thorne. "But you said later you didn't want to do it."

"But the key is, I admitted throwing at Mickey Rivers. I mean, it was obvious. I think it took me three or four pitches to wing him in the shoulder. Admitting it got me fined."

"Which was how much?"

Palmer chuckles. "Fifty bucks. I'm sure I would have been fined more by the club if I *didn't* hit Rivers, but, yes, fifty bucks. Cost me the shutout too. Ended up winning the game four to one."

"Okay, there we go." Thorne's voice leaps from chitchat mode to full announcer weight. "Good news right there."

Ryder risks a look at the monitor.

Billy Jaworski is about to be moved to a stretcher, and one of the trainers leans in to tell Jaworski something. A positive sign itself, that Jaworski can hear.

Jaworski raises his right hand, gives a weak wave.

Ryder squelches the urge to cry. The relief is all-consuming. His body shakes. He squeezes his temples with his hand and closes his eyes as the crowd cheers, which has always seemed like a bizarre message to Ryder.

Like, *Yay, great injury.*

Or, *Yay, glad you can kind of sort of move.*

Yay, have an excellent time in the hospital.

For a moment, Ryder ponders a fast change. He wants to head out into the night to his condo, but that would delay the inevitable questions. Disappearing will look weak. His teammates will want to defend him. They will want to strap on their straight faces. They will want to deny that the unwritten rule exists.

Fluke.

Shit happens.

Too bad.

On the monitor, Jaworski is on the cart. To the side, Stone is talking to the umpire. The umpire for this game is a new face, Anthony Carruthers. They are all new to Ryder, of course, but Carruthers' reputation isn't yet established—his tendencies, his flashpoint. Ryder studied up on many of the American League umpires, the veteran ones with strike zone tendencies. Carruthers is baby faced and on the short side.

"Looks like Stone still wants to offer his opinion about the whole matter," says Thorne. "And now here comes the Rays' manager, Krieger, to hear what Stone is complaining about. Whatever Stone is trying to sell is not something Carruthers is buying, based on Stone still carrying on. And, well, now Stone is off to join Frank Ryder in the clubhouse, because *he* just got tossed. It must have been one of those words you don't use around an ump. And now Art Stone has really lost his cool."

Stone jaws toe to toe with Carruthers, who could be lost in a daydream, given the blank look on his face. It's not possible to have less space between the two of them, unless Stone decided to stand on Carruthers' shoes. Stone stabs the air between them like he is deciding which of Carruthers' eyes to poke out first. Lackland plays halfhearted peacemaker, trying to pull Stone off. Carruthers turns and walks away.

The television goes split screen, the new half showing the cart heading to a door where the wall has been opened up in right field. The Rays' trainer remains with Jaworski on the flatbed, a modern stretcher carting dead soldiers off the battlefield.

Ryder takes off his cleats, washes his face, grabs a cold bottle of water, and stalks around the empty clubhouse, not believing he is inside a windowless room of baked-in sweat. All he can see and smell is heat and the Georgia sunshine and the smell of his polyester uniform, and he sees Deon Johnson going down again and again and again.

"Fuck me!"

It's Stone. His hat is pushed back so it's high on his head. His face is red. As if his arrival was not obvious, he bangs a metal locker with the side of his fist. "Fuck that motherfucker Carruthers, who should have tossed Billings right when it happened! None of this warning stuff! Billings taking out Diaz—any ten-year-old could tell that was no mistake."

Ryder says nothing. If Billings had been tossed, it wouldn't have changed the pressure on him to nail Jaworski.

"So, what's with Jaworski?" says Ryder. He can't shake the image of Jaworski going down in a wet-noodle heap.

Stone slams his body down on one of the leather couches set up in a U facing one of the monitors. Ryder joins him on the adjoining couch, glugs some water.

"Got him in the ribs. Maybe one rib, maybe two. Frosty was in there, too, working with their guy." Frosty is Don Forester, the Orioles' trainer. "It was all about Jaworski's chest. He was in a lot of pain, I'm telling you what. Could be the lung is punctured, but of course it's all guesswork."

"Man," says Ryder.

Should he even try saying the words out loud? Maybe practice a bit? *I know it's going to sound funny, but I wasn't really . . .*

To Stone?

"One oh nine?" Stone jumps in. "You didn't think about maybe backing off on the takeout pitch?"

"Speed got away from me," says Ryder. That sounds like an innocuous, harmless lie.

"You okay?" says Stone.

Ryder waits. Shrugs. "I suppose. Yeah."

The fewer words right now, Ryder figures, the better. It was the same for his whole game plan when he knew he'd be drafted. *Fewer words.*

"A no-doubter," says Stone. "I wonder if Jaworski minds being part of a future trivia question—first big-league ballplayer to be plunked by a pitch going a hundred and nine miles per fucking hour. Jesus. A bullet."

Ryder shrugs, chugs some water. "Damn," he says. It's a general statement that covers lots of ground. "Maybe I was coming inside, but that's all. The pitch got away from me."

"Save it for the reporters," says Stone. "Unless . . . ? Are you rehearsing? Is that it?"

"No," says Ryder. "I don't need practice."

"Save it for the appeal. Save your Oscar-worthy stuff for the hearing. They might come down hard, but at the most you'll miss a start." Stone looks like he still needs to punch something. "Aw, hell. I told Lackland he could bring in whoever he wanted to mop up, but Rob Alba?"

Alba got called up from Norfolk a week before to replace another reliever who went on IR for tendinitis. Alba has been up and down a couple of times in the Toronto system but never settled in at the major-league level.

"For one out?" says Ryder. It's so much easier to pretend to talk on the tough side of life, to pretend like he is okay with all of this and that he belongs in the team's good graces, than to say what he is thinking.

"I want a strong head in there," says Stone. "Someone who knows how to finish these boys off. No mercy."

Alba walks the first batter on four pitches, moving Jaworski's replacement runner to second, and gives up a home run on the second pitch to Chip Harmer, a slender left fielder with a smooth swing.

For the Rays, resignation over the looming loss and any worry about Jaworski have evaporated like a drop of water hitting a hot griddle. Now, it's a game. *A chance.*

"Lackland!" Stone shouts as if he can be heard through sixty feet of concrete tunnel. "You gotta be kidding me. Bring in Shorter or Morrison. One little bitty out. Jesus. We need strikes, for crying out loud, not some nervous kid who doesn't understand the situation."

Still nursing a four-run cushion, Alba gives up a single to Hector Santos, the Rays' second baseman, and takes the next hitter to a 3–2 count before inducing a weak dribbler back to the mound. With victory one throw away, Alba scoops up the ball with ease and throws high and way off-line. First baseman Kyle Hancock, who is a lean six two with basketball hops, doesn't even bother to leap. He turns and starts to run after it as it sails over his head. By the time Hancock has reached the ball in foul territory, Santos has scored.

Runners on second and third, two outs.

Alba hands the ball to Lackland. Alba's head is low like a dead man walking, which might be the case.

Doug Pagnozzi jogs in from left field. He appears grim and unfazed. A fireman called to blow out a match. Pagnozzi's first pitch is greeted by a confident swing from Rays catcher Sonny Lucero.

The sound is good—*too good.*

Thorne's voice rises a notch, grows tense. The ball finds the webbing of center fielder Jay Everett's glove as he reaches the warning track on a dead sprint.

Stone slumps back on the leather couch, shakes his head. "Fuckin' Rays," he says.

Pagnozzi walks off the mound. There is a brief on-field celebration, the usual line of handshakes, but the scene has all the festivity of a funeral.

—⁕—

The clock starts.

Ryder is ten minutes from having to pretend like he's not lying, even if the words he will say will be the truth.

I did not mean to throw at Billy Jaworski.

Chapter 16

"You got this?"

Ray Gallo hasn't budged from his seat. The crowd heads to the exits. If this is victory, it comes with a heavy, bummed-out flavor.

"I'm sure you're worried about the same thing as me." Over the phone, it sounds like Alicia Ford is walking.

"Should he even talk to the goddamn press?"

"You can't interfere like that," says Ford. "The writers would murder us. And Ryder would look guilty and—"

"He's a rookie, for crying out loud," says Gallo. "And he's got all those issues."

"I'm aware," says Ford. "We all are. I'll talk to Stone, and I'll get with Ryder after it's over."

"*After* is too late," says Gallo.

Lisa, who held a shuddering hand to her face the entire time they tended to Diaz, and Jaworski, too, remains in her seat. She's a picture of empathy. She hurts too.

"I can't pull him out of there," says Ford. "I can't interrupt the flow of how all this happens in the clubhouse. The questions would come to us—why were we trying to stand in the way, et cetera, et cetera."

"Don't hold back on Diaz' replacement."

"We're putting together a list."

"If you have to give up a few prospects," says Gallo, "I don't care."

"You want a name."

"I want everything we had with Diaz, and I don't want to miss a step. I want a known quantity. I want reliable."

"My thoughts exactly," says Ford.

"And did I hear something about you asking Ryder to pitch more games, start more games—but only a few innings each time?"

Gallo has caught Ford by surprise, which he doesn't mind doing. "It was an idea," says Ford. "A discussion."

"With Ryder?"

"We wanted to get his thoughts."

"Whose idea . . . ?"

"We were exploring ways to maximize his talent, that's all. Looking at everything."

"Well, count on a big-ass story from our boy Rex."

Rex Coburn, *Baltimore Sun*. The guy who wrote the *blink within the blink* business. The same guy who treated Ryder's precious comments about the number nine having the same importance as the number one like some magical insight from a Hindu mystic.

"Dammit," says Ford. "Did he tell you who leaked it?"

"Of course not," says Gallo.

"Did you ask?"

"If I ask about that, it sounds like I know it's legit. It sounds like I knew something, but I know squat. Who was in the room?"

"Just me, Ryder, Stone, and Lackland."

"Then one of them leaked it, or they told somebody else because they thought the idea was crazy, which I have to say I don't disagree," says Gallo. "Unless you're trying to make a name for yourself, trying to get everyone from the *New York Times* to Buster Olney to pick apart your cockamamie scheme."

Ford waits. Finally, "When did you talk to Coburn?"

"Earlier, tonight. Like he knew where I parked and when I come in, he was waiting for me. Even asked me if I had full confidence in my GM."

"And?"

"If you get me a center fielder as good as Diaz and make sure Frank Ryder's head doesn't get twisted into knots by this beanball business tonight, then I'm good."

Gallo gives Ford a moment to reply, but she doesn't seize it.

"You're the one who is going to have to explain that crazy idea with Ryder," says Gallo. "Explain it and then make it go the hell away. You got a guy who put his high school on the map, put little-known Metro State University on the map, and is now helping Baltimore think it belongs on the map, and you want to test a pet theory from some math geek whose most strenuous sport to date is foosball or Ping-Pong? I want pitchers. I want hitters. I want fielders. I want W's. I want all of baseball land to keep talking about the Baltimore Orioles."

Ford clears her throat. She is buying time. "We're on the same page."

Workers hoof the seats, gathering trash to stuff into giant orange trash bags. A pint-size truck sits by first base to assist a grounds-crew guy spraying water on the infield, a giant black hose wrapped around one worker's waist like a python.

Lisa stands, turns around, leans on the railing, and sighs. "Baseball or boxing match? Grueling."

A text beeps as Gallo hangs up. It's Aiko. She was holed up much of the night in the back of the booth, inside, sipping a beer and watching the game—a novel handy for between innings.

Aiko: Worried about Ryder's head?

Gallo: Of course.

Aiko: Me, too.

Chapter 17

"What was your frame of mind when you headed out to pitch the top of the ninth?"

Rex Coburn's mustache obscures his lips. He's got long straight hair and a wrinkled white shirt with a blue tie, the knot low and loose. Purple eyeglasses, big and round, add to the show. He has planted himself on the front edge of the dense scrum of reporters.

"My frame of mind was three outs."

Ryder keeps his gaze down to avoid the piercing lights from the TV cameras, at least six aimed his way. It's an inquisition.

"You didn't intend to hit Jaworski?"

"No," says Ryder. Every time he blinks, Jaworski tumbles lifeless *down, down, down.*

"But your walk ratio is one of the lowest ever recorded, at least for a partial season," says Coburn.

"The pitch got away." It's easy keeping a straight face—*because it's true.*

"You expect your fans to believe that?"

"I wanted the third out and a complete game."

Rex Coburn started writing about sports teams in Baltimore two years after Ryder was born.

"You didn't intend payback for what happened to Julio Diaz?"

"No."

Ryder looks for the ghost. As much as he's been thinking about Deon Johnson, wouldn't this be the time he'd come around? Or maybe *that's* the trick. Thinking about Deon might keep the ghost satisfied that he hasn't been forgotten.

"Didn't your teammates want you to answer?"

Ryder gives the question a couple of seconds to marinate. "You would have to ask them."

"Did you know the pitch that hit Jaworski was at one oh nine?" This is from a female television reporter with long dark hair, a tight black dress, and so much makeup her exterior shell looks as hard as a snail's.

"Yes," says Ryder. "I hope he's okay. Billy and Julio both."

"You were worried?" she asks.

"Of course," says Ryder.

"You seem—*genuinely worried*." She smiles. She has enough teeth for two women.

"Of course," says Ryder. "Julio is my teammate. My friend. I am sure the Rays feel the same way about Jaworski."

"When you saw Jaworski down for so long?" she asks. "What was going through your mind?"

"That I hoped he would be okay," says Ryder.

"Did you think that . . . ?"

Ryder says nothing. He can fill in the blank, but he won't.

"I didn't throw at him."

Back to Coburn. "You're prepared to be suspended?"

"I'll let baseball do what it's got to do."

"Will you appeal if you are suspended?"

"One step at a time," says Ryder.

"But you expect it?"

"Wait and see," says Ryder.

"Do you think this is over?"

"We are playing competitive ball with every team we face." Ryder has learned the art of using lots of words to say as little as possible. "Our focus is on picking up enough wins to take the division in September. We have to play all the teams in our division, and we have to play them all competitively, with an edge."

The comment sounds like a wrap-up, the kind of chunky, full-sentence statement reporters should appreciate.

Ryder waits. He's eager to check on Diaz. A couple of guys are headed to the hospital. Jaworski might be in the same place. There must be some way to find out how Jaworski is doing, even if making a big effort to find out might be viewed as weak or too empathetic. He finds himself imagining Maggie watching him. Many might think they can imagine how he's feeling. She's the only one who will know.

Coburn shakes the mini recorder in his hand, clears his throat. "Can you confirm GM Alicia Ford asked you about starting every other game but pitching only for a few innings—some theory about shortening the game for opponents, reducing the number of innings of offense every other game?"

Ryder blinks. The question has caused a minor stir among the reporters.

"Excuse me?" says Ryder, as if he didn't hear. It's the worst thing he can say since all the reporters heard the question.

"You were asked to start more games. More starts, fewer innings. Nine innings of offense for the Orioles, five or six innings of offense for the teams you face on the days you pitch. Some theory your talent would be better used not using a regular rotation, the whole 'Three R's and pray for a W' business."

Ryder kicks himself for the boozed-up dinner.

"No comment," says Ryder.

It could have been anyone in the front office who got wind of it, decided to leak it.

"But the idea was broached?"

"We meet all the time to discuss strategy."

"But doesn't it sound like it might be frustrating—sort of an incomplete feeling—to only pitch a few innings, to not get the win under your name?"

Ryder gives a toothless grin, stares at Coburn, looks down at his feet, looks back up. "It might be sort of like that," he says. And smiles. And shrugs. And smiles some more. The reporters laugh—everyone is in on the joke. He is being a good boy by not saying too much. He is forced to speak in code, the blah words from a well-worn script. *Say less.* They are welcome to read between the lines or interpret his demeanor if they wish.

Coburn clicks off his recorder, pulls it away.

"That's all," says Ryder. There is a moment in these clusterfucks when Ryder feels the rising panic. There is also a moment when Ryder has had enough.

"One last thing." Back to the TV reporter. She is holding up her phone, showing Ryder her screen. Ryder puts a hand to his forehead to shield against the TV lights.

Olivia Key has an arm around his waist. He's got his arm draped over her shoulder. They are standing much closer than he remembered. Much too close. The photo is so tight on the two of them standing inside the restaurant.

Ryder shrugs.

"You two must have quite a lot to talk about," says the reporter. "And Twitter is having a field day imagining all the possibilities. I mean, two talented pitchers. Does this mean that you're off the market?"

Chapter 18

Maggie: Call me when you can.

Ryder: K.

Maggie: Soon.

Ryder: Crazy here.

Maggie: You okay?

Ryder: We'll see.

Maggie: My heart is with you.

Ryder: TKS.

Maggie: I'll be up.

The right thing to do would be to call her immediately. He wouldn't mind hearing her voice, but the locker room is buzzing and raucous. More than normal.

Ryder: It's nuts here. Call you in the morning.

—m—

"You okay?" says Ford.

"Far as I know," says Ryder. He has showered and dressed but still feels sticky. His hair is damp and heavy. "Better than Diaz. Better than Jaworski."

Alicia Ford is standing, arms folded across her chest. Stone sits in his chair at his desk with his feet up, a can of beer cradled close to his mouth for easy sipping.

"You looked—I don't know—shocked," says Ford.

"I didn't mean to hit him." Ryder is standing too. He doesn't want to draw this out. Olivia is waiting. He texted her after the media scrum, told her he's dealing with reporters. She texted back a thumbs-up and a nervous-face emoji. He reminds himself to take his time checking texts before hitting send. He can't cross wires between Olivia and Maggie. "I know it sounds like a line, but it's not."

"Had it coming," says Stone. "Fuckin' had it coming. And don't tell me he didn't know it."

"If I meant to hit him, I would have kept the pitch way down." *Jaworski's stone feet.* "Under a hundred."

"So, wait." Stone jerks his feet off the table. His swivel chair issues a manic squeal. "I think you are trying to tell us you didn't mean to hit him. For real."

"For real!" Ryder shouts it. The volume feels good. He's been clogging the doorway but now takes a step forward. "I know what you wanted, I know what Wyatt wanted, I know what the team wanted. But I wanted an out. I wanted to finish things off. The pitch got away from me."

"You can't fuckin' do that." Stone slams his beer on the table. His face tightens, goes crimson. He comes around the desk to Ryder, chest to chest and jaw to jaw. "You don't get to decide. It's not your fuckin' call!"

"It's my arm, my hand." Ryder holds up all five fingers, splayed out hard. "It's my pitch, my reputation. I'm not doing this whole bloody-battlefield business."

"Okay," says Ford. "Enough. What does it matter?"

"Matter?" Stone shakes his head, turns around in a tight circle. A bull pawing the dirt. "You can't be serious. It matters because it's war out there, and when one of your soldiers gets shot, you don't take the bullets out of your rifle and slink off into the night. You stand and fight."

"It's bullshit," says Ryder.

"Chicago," says Stone. "The same fuckin' thing. Your precious childhood hero blah blah fuckin' blah. Tim Simons tries to take your head off, and you return the favor with a polite little strikeout. You know what Tim Simons thinks of you?"

"All right," says Ford. "Enough—"

"He thinks you're a coward." Stone goes into a tone like he's reading a story to little kids. The voice is soft, but the eyes are angry. "He thinks you are chickenshit. I don't care if you throw one fifteen. You're in a fantasy land. But this ain't a fantasy. This is the fuckin' major-league version of the game. The spikes spray real dirt at your face. The runners rounding third aren't worried about hurting the catcher's nuts or his fuckin' feelings when they slide in at home. This is the game where somebody comes after you, you better. Go. After. Them."

"Outs," says Ryder. "Outs and wins. Good enough for me."

"And we're supposed to treat you like some sort of fragile glass baby, for crying out loud, because of what happened what, ten years ago? Ten fuckin' long years ago? You could fight two world wars in those ten years and make peace treaties with all your enemies, and for some reason we have to be extra careful around Frank Ryder. Don't talk about it, don't say nothing because maybe his head is balanced on his neck so carefully that a wrong fuckin' word might throw things out of whack and his head might topple off and roll down the street to the fuckin' loony bin."

The room goes still. Ryder's chest pounds.

Stone sits on his desk, grabs his beer, drains the contents, gives the can a crinkly squeeze with one hand.

"You gotta let that dead kid go. It was an accident. It's over. Way, way over. *This* is the way the game is played. *Jesus.* You're worried about Jaworski? Could have been an act out there—playing fucking possum, if you ask me. Making it look worse."

The idea makes Ryder ill. No baseball player would have the where-withal to pull off an act. Jaworski's corpse-like legs were *lifeless.*

"What did you tell the goddamn media?" says Stone.

"That I didn't mean to hit him, which is what I'm supposed to say. Right? They're hearing the lie."

"We'll appeal any suspension," says Ford.

"Do what you gotta do," says Ryder.

He is a soldier getting orders now, not to be consulted. Ryder's head spins. He needs air. He should call Maggie. And he probably better inoculate himself with a story about that photo with Olivia on Twitter, which will likely make the rounds of all social media channels. He needs to call five minutes ago. And still—Jaworski's feet. Maybe a rib cracked, broke a blood vessel. *Glass baby.* Hell. Has he asked anybody, ever, to treat him a certain way?

"They better deal out fines and suspensions fair and square," says Stone. "The whole world is watching."

"For once," says Ford. "And any idea how Rex Coburn found out about our discussion in here the other day?"

Ryder feels a knot in his throat like he swallowed a marble.

"No idea," says Ryder. "Coburn asked me about it a few minutes ago."

"What did you say?" says Ford.

Is Ford sure it's not one of her own staff who leaked it? Maybe the data dudes who came up with the idea thought it deserved more consideration and wanted Rex Coburn or one of the writers to endorse it, too, so the Orioles could be innovators as well? It's bullshit, but still.

"Played clueless." Ryder shrugs. "I didn't say much. I mean, I *think* I didn't say much."

Chapter 19

Olivia is surprised Ryder is willing to be her passenger.

"Precious cargo," she says. "Better drive like a church lady, which I am not, in case you did not know. And only one drink for me."

She names a bar. Butts and Betty's. "It's in Butchers Hill. Place my dad took me for my first official, you know, adult beverage. It was a big deal—that is, it was a big deal for him, not for me. I had the best fake ID you'll ever see."

What he needs to do is call Maggie. He wonders how much he should trust Olivia after she posted the photo of them on Twitter. Ryder pulled up Twitter for himself in the clubhouse after leaving Stone's office, and when he saw the photo he remembered how Olivia had squeezed in tight. Olivia was touchy. Handsy. He appreciated the contact, the near-sideways body hug. She tagged him. Her tweet earned crazy attention, given her beaming face and his wine-soaked smile.

Olivia keeps the mood light. He appreciates this effort. And if it's not an effort, it's a gift how she senses he may not want to jump in talking about Jaworski and the brawl straightaway. She explains why Gretchen peeled off, something about a morning meeting at school. Olivia drives an old Jeep. The ride is rough and clattery. She's got the windows down and she talks to the cars ahead of her, encouraging them to hustle. "Yellow is a shade of green," she says. "Come on now. We got thirst to quench." She laughs at herself, jabs at the brakes when timid drivers ahead don't share her urgency. "No edge," she says. "Loser." And laughs. "Just kidding. I'm a good driver. And an even better drinker. But only one tonight if I'm driving the boy with the golden arm. *Man*, I mean. Excuse me."

That laugh.

At the bar, Olivia slips into a back booth. The night is winding down, but Ryder is buzzed, alert. The waitress, older, shakes her head. And smiles. "Great game tonight," she says. "A bit shaky there at the end, but still. Place was packed in here, watching you. You could have heard a fresh oyster land on a wet sponge in the ninth. We all knew what was coming."

The TV over the bar carries ESPN, replaying Jaworski's last at bat of the season. The video is replaced by a chart highlighting true ribs and false ribs. There's an arrow pointing between rib four and rib five. They already know?

"Serves him right for Julio Diaz," says the waitress. "So there you go."

Olivia gets carded, passes muster. She orders a rum and Coke. Ryder does not get carded. Deference or something.

"Patently unfair," says Olivia, taking note of the discrepancy. She talks with a resonant alto, husky and strong. Her smile alone says sex. Is he reading in too much? "That is some sexist shit right there." She laughs.

Olivia is wearing tight blue jean shorts and a short-sleeve burgundy top with a modest neckline. She owns powerful hands, serious shoulders. She has deep-set eyes, an ever so slightly hawkish nose, and an easy smile behind undecorated lips. Olivia may not be beautiful, but she is seriously good looking.

Gently prodded by Ryder, Olivia says she's working on a degree in psychology and pondering a master's in recreational therapy. Olivia is fascinated by human behavior. "I've got a friend who says, 'Just imagine if we could hear what everyone is thinking all the time. We'd run out of every room screaming.' Think about that, right? It's so true! The public versions of ourselves. Et cetera."

The talk turns to the gritty details of the ninth. They are halfway through their drinks. Olivia sets a restrained pace. Ryder is for sure not going to tell Olivia what was going through his head—at the time, or even now.

Glass baby.

Precious cargo . . .

Ryder is not quite sure why he's here, pretending he's interested and available when he's not. Well, he's interested—*who wouldn't be*—but not available. Or is he? The night in Toronto flashes. Is he proud of how he felt after? *No.* Maggie is two thousand miles away. Doesn't he have the right to . . . *socialize*? Is Maggie another one of those things he carries around, another one of those things he needs to let go? Did he ever promise Maggie anything? *No.* But there is a mountain of unspoken understanding between them. But maybe the universe owes him a warm, naked night with this attractive woman? Owes him for all the stuff he's dealing with?

Ryder met Maggie when they were juniors in high school. Maggie will make a big deal out of their seventh *friendiversary* this coming September. The date marks when they found each other in anatomy class in the third week of their third year in high school. They set a first date for the coming weekend, a movie followed by what is now known as the Single Longest Cheeseburger Dinner Ever Consumed, when they turned a fast-casual meal at Red Robin into a three-hour drawn-out conversation like a fine-dining experience. Neither one of them dared move for fear of breaking the spell.

Olivia asks if Ryder has a special way of getting information about Jaworski's injury. She asks about how his teammates treated him after the game. She wonders aloud about the next time the Orioles face Tampa Bay, how the bad blood will play itself out.

"I mean, tell me if I overstep my boundaries—because I know it's a sensitive area, *obviously*—"

Olivia studies him, waits.

"—but that must have been hard to throw at Jaworski. You of all people, right? This happens on another night, with Rhineland or Wright on the mound, and probably the thought doesn't go through their minds, you know, do what you gotta do."

She waits, studies him.

Is this his chance to prove Stone wrong? Show he can chew on this topic, analyze himself from above, perform his own psychoanalysis in a dispassionate manner without getting all balled up in the emotional baggage? Can his analytical self find a cloud to sit on and observe from on high and describe, in clear terms, the precise nature of Frank Ryder's own personal sack of woe?

Ryder smiles.

"What?" says Olivia.

"It's funny you ask," says Ryder. "Because I was informed earlier today that I need to stop being so protective of, well, *it*."

"Well, *it* was pretty extraordinary," says Olivia. "And if I were you, I wouldn't want to intentionally throw at anyone ever again—not with that arm."

"Not my favorite part of the game," says Ryder.

"For good reason."

"I like to think so. But even without what happened to Deon." The last word is a weak shadow of itself. It's rare to utter the name out loud. Ryder clears his throat. If this is a test run of his ability to wade into this churning stretch of mean surf, he's getting pummeled and soaked. He clears his throat again. He's got his left hand on his glass of beer and his right on the table, and Olivia places her hand on top of his, lets it rest there, and now he really needs to choke back the air, close his eyes, and try another run at articulating his thought. "Even without what happened to Deon Johnson. It's a silly business, throwing at other batters. The game prides itself on beauty, right? Its artistry? That's why it's called *Field of Dreams*."

"Exactly," says Olivia. She's tearing up. She uses the index finger on her free hand to push the wetness back. The other hand remains on Ryder's. He is enjoying every bit of electric feminine contact.

"Baseball begins in the spring," says Ryder. *Jaworski goes down. Jaworski goes down.* "The season of new life. The object of the game is to go home and be *safe*, for crying out loud."

"George Carlin." Olivia moves her hand away from his, gives his forearm a tender squeeze, then stops touching him.

"You're too young," says Ryder.

"So are you, but it's one of my dad's favorite bits. What's he say? Something like 'football has the shotgun and the blitz'"—she says *shotgun* and *blitz* with a deep DJ voice, then goes high—"'and baseball has the sacrifice bunt.'"

Olivia laughs and Ryder follows suit. It's clear Olivia laughs a lot—or as much as possible. Her confidence is intertwined with her sense of ease.

"So they told you to throw at him," says Olivia.

Ryder takes a sip of beer. "Is this part of the investigation?"

"You don't have to tell me," she says. "Four older brothers? Believe me when I say I know a few things about boys, locker-room antics, and secret codes."

"It was pretty clear what the whole team wanted. Expected."

"Culture. Unwritten rules. But you knew that coming in, right?"

"In some ways," says Ryder. "Sure."

"Maybe you think you'll never be in that spot."

"I'd really rather—well . . ."

"Not talk about it?"

"Yeah," says Ryder.

"About Deon?"

"Him too." Ryder tries a smile.

"What next?" says Olivia.

Their drinks are done.

———※———

At Ryder's condo, Olivia finds a parking spot, turns off the Jeep.

"I'll be in touch," says Ryder.

Olivia is a quick study. She slumps in her seat. "One more drink?"

Jaworski.

Glass baby.

Stone.

Rex Coburn.

Maggie . . .

"Another time," says Ryder.

Olivia reaches over for a hug across the bucket seats, and he takes it. Every damn handsy part of it.

Ryder declutches.

"Aw," says Olivia. "Final answer?"

"Yeah," he says. "Afraid so."

———※———

On his rooftop perch, one last bottle of beer in his hand, Ryder checks Twitter for a peek at his reputation.

> @FrankRyder_1 Way to go dude! Standing up for Oriole Nation! #birdland

> @FrankRyder_1 Don't have to look so freakin' scared about it all. #baltimore #orioles Welcome to the big leagues.

@FrankRyder_1 Watchin' Ace Ryder! Bam! Plunk that candy ass Jaworski. Teach those Rays who da boss!

@FrankRyder_1 Woo-hoo, Baltimore Fuckin' Orioles with some Baltimore Fuckin' Backbone! #birdland

There's also a text:

Maggie: I can't sleep, thinking of you. Call me?

Maggie wraps up with an emoji bomb—four hearts, two mini hearts, a mug of beer, five books. And a baseball.

Ryder puts the phone in his lap, takes a sip of beer, tips his head back to the night sky, and watches Billy Jaworski fall and fall and fall.

JULY

When I knocked a guy down, there was no second part to the story.

—Saint Louis Cardinals and Hall of Fame pitcher
Bob Gibson

Chapter 20

"What do you mean he's having trouble throwing strikes?" says Gallo.

Alicia Ford dials up something on her tablet, the goofy Orioles sticker on the back of the darn thing. "Like it sounds," she says.

"I don't see how that's possible."

"It's a glitch."

"A *glitch*?"

Ford's legs are crossed, the top leg wrapped around the other like it's capable of strangulation. Ford asked for the meeting, offered to come out to his office in Towson, but Gallo likes to discuss baseball business in the baseball place. He likes the quiet of the stadium, the view from his office in the B&O Warehouse when the team is on the road. Camden Yards looks enormous. And at peace.

"What the hell?" says Gallo. "Give me a better idea. *Trouble* covers a lot of ground."

She puts the tablet flat on the round table between them. Gallo's sprawling office on the top floor of the warehouse serves as a shrine to the team legacy—every inch of wall space above the dark wainscoting is crammed with framed photos and plaques and pennants, featuring a heavy dose of the late 1960s and early 1970s. McNally, the two Robinsons, Powell, Palmer, Murray, the overlooked heroes like Pat Dobson and Tito Landrum, and of course Ripken—a whole section devoted to Ripken. They all are watching and waiting for the rebirth of a winning franchise.

Ford's video is frozen. Frank Ryder stands in what looks like an underground, bunker-like chute. There are places inside Camden Yards Ray Gallo will never see. That's okay.

Aiko, who has been working on her phone at Gallo's desk, a well-maintained Hekman with an expansive walnut top, stands up and parks herself behind Gallo's shoulder.

"I mean, I'm no shrink," says Gallo. "But wouldn't it be better to let him keep his routine with the team, get him used to other parks?"

The Orioles are starting the fourth stop of a death march slog—Twins, White Sox, Blue Jays, and Rays. The trip ends with the four-day All-Star break.

"We deliberated," says Ford. "We started out there too. But as you'll see, and I think for good reason, we wanted as few people around as possible."

"You're scaring me," says Gallo.

Ford's entire look is dejected. She adds, "We didn't want him to be dragging this around with him all over the country."

"This?" says Gallo.

On the screen, a catcher squats. He's behind dense black netting suitable for mosquito protection on safari.

"Who's that?" says Gallo.

"Dennis Rosedale," says Ford. "Backup catcher from Norfolk. Good bat, shaky D. Brought him up for this session since Wyatt is on the road. Rosedale and a pitching coach from Norfolk, Harvey Bing. Bing has got all sorts of tricks to get pitchers back on track."

"Rosedale doesn't look comfortable," says Gallo.

Ford says nothing, touches the screen to make the video run.

The shot zooms out. Frank Ryder stands on an indoor practice mound, a fat wedge covered in fake neon-green turf topped with the slab of white rubber. Ryder is wearing a plain black T-shirt, and inside a giant circle are the words RETRIEVER NATION surrounding the smaller letters, UMBC. He's wearing sweatpants—or . . . *leggings*? Gallo isn't quite sure what you'd call them, but they fit well. They are the ubiquitous charcoal that has infested American male gyms and locker rooms since forever. It's strange to see Ryder out of uniform. He's wearing a baseball cap Gallo doesn't recognize. There is no sign Ryder is an Oriole, which is disheartening. Shouldn't you be an Oriole 24-7? Maybe the players get sick of the grinning logo too.

An enormous basket, enough baseballs crammed in there to meet the baseball-loving needs of the entire Dominican Republic for a whole year, stands next to the faux mound. Ryder's demeanor is downcast. He looks—*lost*.

Rosedale pulls his mask down. Ryder goes through his motion. The ball leaves Ryder's hand. Rosedale comes out of his crouch and stabs the air to the left, about where the head of a right-handed batter might be if the batter existed. Rosedale plucks the pitch from the air, but his lurch is so sudden it throws him off balance, and he spins into the netting and gets tangled in its darkness.

Rosedale collects himself and tosses the ball back.

"May I see it again?" says Aiko.

"What are you?" says Gallo. "A glutton for punishment?"

"Please," says Aiko.

Ford hits the backward-arrow replay symbol, fiddles with something, walks away to look out the window this time. "I've seen it plenty," she says. "This time is in slo-mo."

The video runs again, but it takes ten times as long for Rosedale to entomb himself in the black shroud.

"His energy is very low," says Aiko. "I don't see the fire."

"We would agree with that assessment," says Ford.

"Mother*fuck*," says Gallo, a hollow, sick hardness making itself at home in his guts. "When did this start?"

"Well, the start against the Angels after the Rays were here? You'll remember it wasn't his strongest outing."

"Yeah, but he won."

"Four hits," says Ford.

"He won!"

"Two walks."

"There were rumblings and whisperings for sure," says Gallo. "Doesn't a phenom get to have an off day?"

"And the suspension was announced after that game, and he appealed."

"I remember," says Gallo. "Like yesterday."

"And the appeal took three days, but he was throwing a side session between starts, and it was a disaster. Out of the blue."

Ryder's suspension was one of the most controversial penalties ever doled out by MLB for on-field issues. Joe Torre, who handles discipline for on-field incidents for MLB, had cited the speed of the pitch and the extent of the injury, two fractured ribs and a punctured lung, to justify the harsh terms. Frank Ryder has clearly demonstrated his ability to control the speed of his pitches, read the official statement from MLB. The intent to harm cannot be ignored in determining the appropriate length of suspension.

The announcement came one day after Ford had pulled off a trade, with Gallo's approval. Utility infielder Lance Tackett and two potent pitching prospects from Triple-A Norfolk were shipped to the Philadelphia Phillies for center fielder Steve Penny, who has added some thump to the offense and who covers as much ground as Diaz did on defense. *Almost.* Still, the Orioles have reverted to the mean, winning as many games as they've lost since Ryder started serving his time, while the Red Sox and Yankees have both put together two winning weeks. The Orioles are four games back of the Yankees, six behind the Sox.

The whole city is waiting for the suspension to lift. In fact, as the sports columnists have made clear, the whole city is hanging on the team's ability to avoid a return to mediocrity, given this blow to their lineup. With Ryder gone, opponents smell blood. The sixteen-day punishment, announced after the failed appeal, means Ryder will miss three starts.

"The video goes on like this?"

"He throws a strike now and then," says Ford.

"Jesus."

"Yeah."

"His speed?"

"High nineties," says Ford.

Gallo pushes his chair back, stands up. He crosses to the window and stares out at downtown, wonders how fast the writers and the leaders and the fans will throw in the towel when they hear this news. He can only be angry with fate and mystery and the weird, wild depths of how some people are wired. Or not wired.

It was too good to be true.

"All his pitches?" says Gallo.

"His changeup hits the strike zone—that's about it."

"And you've been doing what—?"

Gallo keeps staring out.

"Working with him."

"And what have you tried?"

"Everything," says Ford. "Gave him a few days away from it—no pitching at all. We looked at video from Metro State. We showed him video from his games earlier this year. The thing is, nothing *looks* that different."

"His head?"

"He's a scared puppy."

Gallo returns to his chair. He shakes his head, sits down, pushes his chair farther back from the table, crosses his legs, thinks about another season going up in smoke. He reminds himself to never again get eager or anxious or excited unless it's mid-September and a scrappy bunch of nobodies is closing in on ninety-plus wins.

"His *arm*?"

"He claims his arm is normal. The same."

"What's Lackland say? Stone?"

"Obviously, they are traveling with the team. They talk to him on Skype, text, phone—all of that. Lackland has been giving him drills."

"How about Tewksbury?" says Gallo. "That guy has turned into some kind of baseball head game guru or baseball whisperer, whatever you want to call it, the second coming of Harvey Dorfman. What about him?"

"Bob Tewksbury is back with the Red Sox," says Ford. "Working on *their* heads."

"Then I hate him," says Gallo. "What about the All-Star Game?"

"Tell me about it," says Ford.

"If you're the American League manager, you let Ryder go three or four innings, even if it is the All-Star Game and even if you're supposed to use as many players as possible," says Gallo. "Am I right?"

"You're right."

"The media is bonkers over the All-Star Game."

"I know."

"You're not going to let him go out there—like this?"

"Not an option," says Ford.

"And when do you announce he won't be there?"

"Soon."

"And what story are you going to concoct?"

"Our best idea is a blister on the finger of his throwing hand. Stick a bandage on there, buy some time."

Gallo feels like he's falling. He's always been paranoid about fast starts to the season. He's always been wary of winning streaks. There have been days this year when things were going so well Gallo's built-in paranoia seemed to evaporate. The writers liked the "gutsy" trade. Gallo got praise for going "all in" on the season. They talk about his "checkbook" like it's theirs and like they presume they can tell if he believes in winning or if he's another cautious owner who is fine with mediocrity.

"It's the commissioner," says Gallo. "It's not Torre. It's Morris—you don't think Joe Torre decided this one all on his lonesome, do you? I can feel Morris' hand on this one, squeezing my you-know-what. He pretends he's King Solomon, but you know he believes Frank Ryder isn't good for the game. Julio Diaz is out for the season, like Jaworski, but Ryder gets sixteen days and Billings gets ten because he hit Diaz with a ninety-four? Give me a break. Question now is how long can we keep this quiet, and can he get better, like, say, tomorrow? Tomorrow would be good."

"We can keep it quiet for a few days," says Ford.

"You couldn't keep a strategy meeting quiet," says Gallo. "And you don't think this catcher kid from Norfolk hasn't bragged to his whole team? Said what he saw?"

"We had him sign papers," says Ford.

"And when do you announce about the All-Star Game?"

"Today—we think today. The sooner, the better."

"So there's no chance of a miracle cure?" says Gallo. "He wakes up tomorrow and shakes it off? The heebie-jeebies are kaput?"

Ford considers the idea for a respectful second. Or two. "Probably not."

"All because of the goddamn suspension?"

"It's not the punishment," says Aiko, sitting at Gallo's desk. She pauses her double-thumb attack on her phone's minuscule keyboard. "It's the crime."

"Crime?" says Gallo. "What crime?"

"In his mind," says Aiko. "He is punishing himself. Did you watch the interviews with Ryder about throwing at Jaworski?"

"Of course," says Ford. "He said what every pitcher says."

"But he meant it," says Aiko.

Ford is mystified. "How do you know that?"

"You watch his eyes," says Aiko. "Feel it when he talks. Feel *him*. Ryder did not mean to hurt Billy Jaworski. He didn't even want to scare him, but he felt the pressure to do it. Peer pressure. Baseball pressure. He was worried. Scared. He was no Osamu Higashio."

"What the heck?" says Gallo.

Aiko turns her phone around to show them all the screen, as if they can read it from across the room. She waves the device in her tiny palm. "When I was in Japan, we traveled out to Tokorozawa, not too far from Tokyo, to watch the Saitama Seibu Lions play the Chunichi Dragons. Osamu Higashio was one of the Lions' legendary pitchers. Late last century. Hall of Fame. He was a country boy. Rougher and more blunt than other, sophisticated Japanese pitchers. He hit a hundred sixty-five batters in his career—and never apologized for it. He was once attacked on the mound by a batter but stayed in the game after the brawl and got the win. He never changed his method. He thought the inside part of the plate belonged to him as much as the middle of the plate and outside. While other pitchers believed you didn't scare batters. And I quote—"

Aiko studies her phone, scrolls, shakes her head, scrolls some more.

"In the words of Osamu Higashio." Aiko clears her throat. "'Throwing the ball close to the batter puts fear in the batter. It is considered a virtue not to scare the batter because it might lead to violence, and that is not good in Japan. But I have a family to take care of. Without winning I cannot enjoy a good living. If I didn't throw inside, I would not be able to be a winner.'"

"So—in other words—no pretending?" says Gallo. "Batters need to know you're going to work inside; why say anything else?"

"It's knowing who you are," says Aiko. "You watch Ryder? Somebody needs to put him back together again."

Aiko puts her phone down with a clatter on the desk, like some sort of exclamation point to her diagnosis.

Gallo looks at Ford to get her reaction. Ford is standing, arms crossed and mouth ajar.

"Osamu Higashio," says Gallo out loud to fill the void.

"O*sa*mu," says Aiko, correcting his emphasis to place it on the second syllable. "Depending on how you write it in kanji, it can mean *reign* or *discipline* or *logic*. Take your pick."

Chapter 21

"Blister?" says Maggie. "You've never had blisters."

The coverup is worse than anything else so far.

"I know."

Ryder paces in his cold living room, cradling his phone on speaker in his "good" hand. Outside, the harbor is gray. The skies have threatened to rain all day. Ryder wants the cleanse. He needs a flood.

"Then it'll only be a few days, right?" she says. "A week at most, given all the medical staff they have, right? Specialists? *Hand* specialists? Blister specialists? Frank Ryder specialists?"

"You're the only one of those."

It sounds like a line. Has everything he's ever said sounded like a line?

"Once upon a time, maybe that was true," says Maggie. "Cover of *Time* now too? And you don't really believe the *Sports Illustrated* jinx stuff, do you?"

Jinxes? No. Ghosts? Yes.

"No," says Ryder, studying the perfect skin on the index finger of his "bad" hand.

"So you'll be back in action in a few days or a week, and you got lots of games left to pitch and a ton of strikeouts to add to your collection."

Staying in Baltimore, not being with the team, he feels like the kid from a large family who accidentally got left behind at the rest stop.

Except he can't imagine the embarrassment of having others see the current, messed-up state of his vaunted arm. Ryder debated whether to bring Maggie in on the ruse. But doing so might crack open the room where he is storing all his feints and deceptions, Olivia the obvious one among them.

"Every blister is different," says Ryder. "From what I've been told."

"Hey, Frank—come on, give me some confidence. *Dude.*" Maggie likes making fun of what she calls Boys Who Talk Bro. "Don't sound so unsure."

"I start throwing again, the blister might come back."

The real story might eventually come out. It's unlikely to stay under wraps, given the Norfolk catcher and Coach Bing and how word leaks out. There is video too. There is *always* video. What if someone leaks the clip? Posts it?

Jesus.

"I'm sure they've dealt with this before, but maybe not with a guy who throws like you?"

"Let's talk about something else."

"Tell me how your head is doing," says Maggie. "Forget about the blister—that'll heal. All blisters heal. They can't help themselves. It's the head I care about."

"I'm okay."

"Said with conviction."

"I've never been here before."

"The suspension?"

"That was no fun. And now this."

"I feel like there's something you're not telling me," says Maggie. "Yeah, it's a blister. Yeah, you got suspended. Too bad about the All-Star Game, but it actually comes at a good time, right? All the teams are off for, what, three days at least? I'm still hearing the hangdog."

Ryder sighs. "Yeah," he says. "I hear him howling too."

Ryder slips on his prop bandage. It's a fat one for dramatic effect. For *obviousness*. He pulls on an oversize hoodie to hide, like a boxer coming into the ring, and goes out to jog and sweat. He runs to Patterson Park, goes twice around, and heads back, walking the last few blocks with his hands clasped on his head.

Still, no rain.

In his condo, he stretches, does push-ups until he feels the hot burn in his shoulders, showers, and texts Olivia.

—៣—

"Baseball Factory Field? As the kids say, WTF?"

They are sitting in the third base dugout in the empty UMBC stadium, as spiffy a college field as Ryder has ever seen. Olivia has brought sandwiches and a four-pack of red wine in cans.

"It's a player-development company. They poured beaucoup bucks into the field renovation," says Olivia. "Yeah, baseball factory."

The *factory* aspect? There is nothing automatic about the training process. It's counter to everything Ryder knows. Ryder's brother, Josh? *Not* so automatic.

"You don't play here," says Ryder.

She passes him a sandwich, turkey on a soft sesame roll, and cracks two cans.

"The softball field is next door."

The UMBC campus is reminiscent of Metro State—all in a somewhat defined area near downtown. Ryder appreciates the change of scenery. And the scenery. Olivia wears tight-fitting purple yoga shorts and a white tank top. Running shoes. She smells like lemon.

"That finger okay?"

"It'll heal," says Ryder.

His arm? That's another story. He hasn't had one good night of sleep since the Angels game, when he gave up four hits and his arm

153

was balky and foreshadowing its disobedience. There's a busted circuit somewhere, and as much as he has racked his brain and tried all the drills prescribed by all his coaches, he can't find the breaker.

"Must be tough not being with your guys after all those weeks and weeks."

"Sucks," says Ryder. "Really sucks."

"It's not like it costs the team much more to bring you along," says Olivia. "Right?"

"True."

In the outfield grass, six players are throwing, loosening up.

"Your replacement, the kid up from Triple-A? So far he's not making anyone forget about you."

"All I know is they want me to find a miracle fix for blisters. If one exists."

It's weird to feel more shame for having told the truth about Jaworski than it is to sit here and tell a lie about his goddamn finger.

"I think the whole city agrees with the idea of finding that miracle. *ASAP.* You want to throw?" From the big green bag that produced the food and drinks, Olivia plucks out two gloves and a softball. She holds the ball in front of Ryder's face, twists it around. "Think you can get your hand around *that?*"

"Well, I'd love to see your stuff," says Ryder.

"Hey!" she says. "Watch yourself, sailor." She laughs.

"I can't throw," says Ryder. "Doctor's orders. But I could catch, roll it back."

Olivia paces off forty-three feet, shows Ryder where to crouch.

"If you're bringing the heat, I'll need a mask," says Ryder.

"I'll try to check myself," she says. "And if I understand it correctly, that might be something you have to learn to do. Dial it down, right? Didn't I hear some chatter, that's one of the options out there?"

"Don't make me hurl," says Ryder.

They are alone on the field along the third base line. There are no bases, no chalk line. Olivia's white calves flash in the near dusk. Her pitches arrive with a healthy zip.

"Drive, drag, snap, release," says Olivia. "And keep a stiff front leg. Want to try?"

She throws another pitch.

"That mean old doctor," says Ryder. "You know."

"Underhand? It's not an issue. A couple of my grips, I'm only using my ring and middle finger. The index is along for the ride." She comes close to demonstrate. "That's just one of the grips. For my screwball and my rising fastball. Index finger doesn't do a thing except hang on."

Olivia adjusts his fingers with her own. She's got strong hands. Her nails are trimmed. No polish. She shows him how to place the tips of his fingers not too far across the seams, jogs back to her spot.

Ryder throws, worried as hell about making a fool out of himself. At least with a new motion to learn, he'll have an excuse.

"Strike," she calls.

She's the most fetching catcher Ryder has ever had for a target. He wants this to last all night. She goes to her knees, sits on her heels.

"Ball," she calls. "Just outside."

"Strike."

"Strike."

"Strike."

The underhand motion comes easy. Ryder feels nothing in his elbow. The windmill action is easy on his body, and, much to his surprise, the ball is going where he wants it to go.

Is he cured? Has his wiring snapped back together? He doubts it. So much else is different—the ball, the distance. And, without a batter standing in the box, no terror ripping at his guts.

Olivia gives a little head bob to suggest Ryder look around. Behind him, the six players from the outfield stand in a loose huddle. They are steps away. Four Black guys, one white, one Hispanic. One of the Black guys is holding up his phone. It's clear he's been holding up his phone for God knows how long. *Video.*

Video everywhere.

"Fuckin' A," says the kid with the phone. "The one and only."

Olivia comes out of her crouch to come stand next to him. To pose. A few of the other guys dig out their phones. The light isn't great, but it's enough. Ryder is helpless to stop them. He says nothing. He tries to keep Olivia at a safe distance, but why? He wants to know—*why*? Doesn't he deserve something, something to soothe his pain? Did he promise Maggie he'd never stand next to a woman in public?

He can't be a jerk.

A light drizzle falls. Olivia leads him back to the dugout for a few more bites of sandwich. Ryder misses company. Female company. This particular fork in the road was predictable. On the rocket ride from Metro State to the major leagues, there were one zillion unknowns. What would the road be like? How would it feel to know you could buy fancy dinners, fancy things? Expensive shit? How hard was the travel? And what would happen to his relationship with Maggie? What about *distractions*? How did baseball players manage—on the road for weeks at a time? What were the salves? The comforts? The escapes?

In the end, he found, the biggest challenge was getting decent sleep. New hotel rooms, new time zones, feeling beaten up by all the flying— nothing about life on the road was conducive to rest.

Drizzle turns to gentle rain ticking on the dugout roof. They each crack a second can of wine.

The inside of the dugout is dry, but the rain adds a mild chill, and Ryder gives her the only thing he brought with him, a brown-and-gold windbreaker with the big Spartan logo.

Olivia studies it. "I need to know what I'm getting into. So to speak. What's TJ?"

"Thomas Jefferson High School," says Ryder.

"In Denver? I mean—the city itself?"

"In a suburban-looking part of it, but yeah."

"All four years there?"

"Yeah," says Ryder.

"What about before that?"

"After the deal—"

Why doesn't he say, *After I killed Deon Johnson?* Is that what Stone wants him to do, get to a point in his life where it's all matter of fact, la-di-da?

"—we were homeschooled while my parents looked around for a new place, and we moved to Colorado."

"We?"

"My parents, my brother, and me," says Ryder. "Twin brother. People forget Josh was the catcher. That day."

"I knew that. I mean, I read that at some point."

"It's okay," says Ryder.

"And you started pitching again? In Denver?"

"No," says Ryder. "Not for TJ, anyway."

"Then where?" Olivia's words are tender.

"Just not right away. My parents made a deal with me and Josh that we could do what we wanted athletically except, well, no team sports, except for stuff like swimming or track."

"How did that sit with you?"

"It made sense on paper, I suppose. But I couldn't stop thinking about baseball."

"You went behind their back?"

"Sort of," says Ryder. "My first two years at TJ, I ran track, but I worked on my pitching. Late at night. In my room. All the exercises, studied grips and motions, watched games on my phone. Sometimes Josh and I would sneak off to throw in a park."

"Hard habit to break," says Olivia. "Once baseball gets in your blood."

"Tell me."

"But nobody at school knew—your story?"

"New kids every year, big school. I was a new kid from out of state. No baggage. A year had gone by." Ryder smiles for himself. Sadness floods in from every corner too. "I wouldn't be here today except for what happened next."

Olivia waits. Ryder needs a moment, takes a sip of wine.

"One day I left the gym after a good workout. I had this coach, Coach Rush. Scott Rush. Dude made the Olympic team for javelin, but then the US boycotted the games in Russia. Great guy, helluva coach. I was drained every day. I loved it."

"Sweat comas," says Olivia. "A certain kind of high."

"Exactly. So I drifted down to watch our team."

"The Spartans!" She laughs.

"You got a thing about that?"

"Only it's funny how we rip down all these statues from the Civil War, which I'm fine with, while the ancient Greeks knew more than a little about slavery. They relegated certain people to the underclass and the under-*under* class. Sound familiar? And we adopt the Spartans as mascots as easily as Red Sox or Blue Jays."

Ryder gives Olivia a sideways look in the darkness, puts a hand on her shoulder. "Is there any chance you're taking this too seriously?"

"Not me." She laughs. "Never."

Somewhere in the distance, the *whoop-whoop* of a siren. One burst and it's gone.

"Go on," says Olivia.

"I go out to watch the game, and one of my guys is at bat. Chris Ellroy. Big chest, easy swing. Anyway, he comes to the plate and hits a home run. I'm the only guy out there behind the fence, just watching, and the ball comes my way, so I run and catch it."

"Bare hands?"

"It kind of floated to me, no big deal," says Ryder. "And I threw it back in."

"Let me guess. All the way to home plate."

"On the fly," says Ryder.

"The jig was up."

"To say the least."

"Except for the problem with your parents."

"You got it."

"But the first thing you had to do was explain to the coach why you hadn't gone out for the team."

"Coach Bullard, the baseball coach, said he understood. I mean, once I explained it, which wasn't easy to do and not something I wanted to get around the school."

"And then?"

"Coach Rush and Coach Bullard must have talked, and they asked me if they could meet with my parents. I said okay but didn't think it would do any good."

"What do you think they told your parents?"

"Coach Rush told me later. They urged my parents not to let this *thing*, this *incident*, this *whatever it is*, prevent me from doing something I enjoyed."

"Your parents bought it."

"They swallowed hard," says Ryder. "They knew I would soon be making my own decisions."

"And now?"

"I think they're worried, but more than happy for me too."

"Do they come to games?"

"Sports were never their thing."

Ryder should be flat-out fatigued, but he doesn't feel it.

"And what about the girlfriend?"

Ryder nearly spits out a swallow of wine.

"Who?" says Ryder.

"She was in one of those newspaper profiles. You know, reporter visits phenom's high school. Reporter catches girlfriend at home after she's come back from a ten-mile run, and reporter tries to pry into girlfriend's insights to see if she can discover what gives Frank Ryder his drive, his talent?"

"They wrote about her?" Wouldn't Maggie have mentioned something? A mountain of crap has been printed about him. Ryder can't begin to imagine reading it all.

"I like to know what I'm getting into—or not getting into," says Olivia. "Eyes open."

Ryder smiles. "We're . . . in touch."

It's true. And noncommittal.

"Does *she* come to games?"

"Maybe not after seeing that photo on Twitter," he says.

Olivia sighs. "I am sorry."

"It's fine."

Maybe taking Olivia to bed would be the capper on a few miserable weeks—nearly killing Jaworski, having his head ripped off by Stone, getting suspended, lying about having anything to do with the ill-conceived pitching-rotation strategy reaching reporters, and having his arm go haywire.

It's not like he and Maggie have a deal. But he and Maggie have a deal. It's an unwritten rule.

Still.

He's only ever been with Maggie, with the exception of that night in Toronto that must have happened to a different rookie Frank Ryder with the Baltimore Orioles. So he can't say he's *only* ever been with Maggie. But it's close to that. And Toronto, he realizes now, is more about how lucky he got, given how careless he'd been. Maggie is the opposite of careless. She made Ryder wait until they were seniors in high school. On their first *friendiversary*. Every detail of the first time was planned, but the lack of spontaneity did precisely nothing to dampen his enthusiasm.

Is this what goes with the sports-god lifestyle—easy access? Many choices? Do the *Olivias* of the world come with the territory? Do they pop out of the woodwork? Ryder has a hunch that most such encounters, for most of his teammates, involve little talk. It's a signal. A look. Shouldn't he take what's given? Doesn't he deserve some *company*?

"You got your hands full," she says. "Ruining the game of baseball and saving Baltimore all at the same time. Taking hope away from every batter on the planet while at the same time breathing new life into a whole city. Tall orders. You got enough to worry about."

Olivia laughs. Ryder efforts a laugh to go with it, but it's lame.

"Come on," says Olivia, standing up. She drains her wine.

Ryder stands, too, and she gives him a hug. The hug comes with hips and chests and there is a near-instant reaction, a spotlight going off in a dark room.

Her arms wrap his chest. She is not shy.

Ryder puts his hand and fingers—from the unbandaged hand—on the small of her back.

She works a warm hand under his shirt, straight up his breastbone. Maybe it's a healing hand.

He wants to get all tangled up in her hair and her limbs. Her grip.

You're a star . . .

Not right now.

You got this.

Then why the uncertainty?

She wants *to come up to my place. It must be easy.*

Make a move.

"I think you've got your hands full," says Olivia.

"No," says Ryder. "I—"

She pulls him back down to the dugout bench in their dark hovel, takes his bad right hand in both of hers.

"Not just in Baltimore. Across the country, too, every time you walk on the mound. Every time now you have to worry about some weak-hitting second baseman macho jerk testing you—crowding the inside of the plate, showing he's not afraid of letting one of your fastballs tattoo his body."

"I don't really think that's what's going on."

Of course it is.

Olivia sits up straight, turns to face him. She kisses the scant patch of bare skin on the tip of his bandaged index finger.

"And let's not forget there is someone in Denver waiting for you. I can't ignore that fact."

"She's—"

Maggie is what? Not an actual person?

He can't complete the thought.

He's going home alone.

Chapter 22

There are more than a few days when Frank Ryder wishes he didn't have long hair. It's hard to go incognito. The best he can do is aviator sunglasses and diversionary headgear, such as the UMBC baseball cap Olivia dropped off with the UMBC T-shirt, the UMBC flip-flops, the UMBC travel mug, and the UMBC bobblehead figurine—a brown dog—as a package of gifts before his departure. "Go Retrievers," said her note. "Have a good trip. Olivia."

It's been two days of texts since the dugout scene. Cutesy stuff. Teasing. Double entendres. She could be one of the guys, except for that body. The last text was from her. It arrived on his way to the airport:

> Frank, I feel like there's something hidden, too. There is a lot going on in that head of yours and I think some of it is dark. Somewhat dark. I think it's dragging you down. I can feel it. It's ingrained in you. I think it ripples below the surface of everything you do. And it's, in a word, worrisome. I've been around lots of athletes—all my life. It's almost like I get a sense that you feel unworthy, that you've been living a lie. I can't see myself getting wrapped up in it—and I know for damn sure I'm not capable enough to deal with it. You know what it is. I think you need to go back to the very roots of it—and sort it out step by step, wound by wound, and blow by blow.

Ryder hasn't flown commercial in months. A TSA agent brings up the Tampa Bay Rays. "Underrated," he says. "The team to watch."

In his seat in first class, Ryder pulls down the shade, yanks his cap down over his sunglasses, plugs in his white earbuds with the white cord visible against his black UMBC T-shirt, and slumps down. He's got Olivia's "Songs of Summer" playlist cued up on his Spotify app, and he lets Dua Lipa and Imagine Dragons try to distract him.

Boarding takes forever. Nobody is in a rush. Is he? Ryder pretends to sleep. He wonders if he shouldn't pop an Ambien, even if he might be groggy when he arrives. So what? The seat next to him is vacant, vacant, *please-stay-empty* for the longest time. Maybe he's lucky. Maybe an empty seat will be a sign. Maybe things are going to start turning around for him—turning around and looking up—and suddenly he feels the weight and the presence of the seat filling up.

Ryder keeps his eyes closed. He shifts and puts his head back harder against the seat, and there is a hand on his arm, and it's his new seatmate letting him know the flight attendant is asking if he wants a cocktail or coffee. There is a big wall of thunderstorms over Pennsylvania, and their departure is delayed. Ryder waves off the drink, but before he can get his earbuds back in, his seatmate gives him a soft elbow bump, says, "My wife is going to kill me."

Ryder smiles.

"I mean, I'm a fan. Lifelong Orioles fan." The guy is at least fifty, maybe sixty. A proud paunch strains the buttons on a white oxford shirt. A red tie falls straight down from a tight knot, takes a sudden turn up and around his bowling-ball belly. "But my *wife*. She is the real nutcase when it comes to the O's. She once got an autograph from Cal Ripken, and I really think it's up there in the top ten moments of her life. If autographs were orgasms, know what I'm saying?"

Ryder offers a partial smile. Each set of fingers cradles an earbud. He can hear the distant, snappy rhythms of Monáe's "Make Me Feel." He should shove the buds back into place and keep to himself, but he can't bring himself to slam the door.

"You got a blister? Is that right?"

"Yeah." Ryder wiggles the digit and its fraudulent gauze wrap.

"Pickle juice?" says the guy. "Maybe some pickle juice from Pickles Pub? You ever been there?"

"No." Ryder is as matter of fact as he can muster. Disinterested.

"They got this thing called a Crabby Patty, which is a hamburger topped with crab dip and cheddar cheese. I mean—seriously now. Crazy flavor." The guy has a crewcut and bulbous jowls. "You gotta hit Pickles Pub before a game and sometimes after. What about the juice?"

Ryder waits a moment, to ease the pace. He might be a Crabby Patty if the flight is going to be like this. "Old wives' tale," he says.

"What do they prescribe these days?"

"Betadine soak and give it time."

"You puncture that sucker? Though you know, I guess the advice on it goes both ways—puncture it so the good skin underneath can start to take over its job, dermis becomes the epidermis, that sort of thing. Or let the top layer heal all on its own? You believe in picking scabs?"

The guy looks at Ryder like he's a doctor and should have the wisdom handy, but the truth is Ryder doesn't have a blister and has never had a blister but thinks what he needs is for someone to come along and rip away the bruised skin all over his body, uncover his old self and his old arm—all of it's in there, waiting to be freed.

"I do what they tell me." Ryder shows the guy the earbuds. He wants to reach up and pull down an imaginary blackout curtain between them, but shouldn't the earbuds alone be a clue?

"Shame about the All-Star Game."

Ryder decides if the guy tries to introduce himself, he will show the guy the Ambien and force the guy to watch while Ryder takes the pill. Maybe two. Since Jaworski, sleeping pills have been mandatory. A couple of beers and sleeping pills. A couple of beers, a shot of bourbon, and sleeping pills.

"Yeah," says Ryder.

"I heard tickets in Detroit dropped, like, two hundred bucks when the news went out you weren't pitching."

Ryder smiles, tucks the earbuds into place, slumps back in his seat, and closes his eyes behind his sunglasses. He shrugs and mutters, "What can you do?"

Maggie plays it cool at baggage claim, except a casual arm around his waist. She wears teal running shorts, a loose white short-sleeve top, and dark-purple New Balance running shoes, no socks. Summer sun has sprinkled light freckles under her eyes. Maggie's dark hair scrapes her shoulders, and the strap holding a small black purse tightens her pullover top, accentuating her thin, fit frame. Maggie is calm all the way to the garage. He climbs into the shotgun seat of her Subaru, and she reaches for him. She purrs and kisses and hugs and grabs. Her car is parked on one of the lower decks inside, out of the direct sun, but the car is nonetheless warm, and Ryder gets Maggie to flip on the electronics so they can lower the windows for air. Ryder gets the bizarre sensation Baltimore doesn't exist. Perhaps on the other side of a backward airplane ride is a twilight zone of mysteries, and *maybe* his arm will work fine out here. Maggie's kisses are desire. He needs control here, too, but it's a whole different kind.

"Luckiest blister ever." Maggie is driving out Peña Boulevard toward downtown Denver, two hands on the wheel.

"Hell, yeah," says Ryder.

"Poor Detroit. Lucky me."

The AC blasts. Maggie's tan legs catch the sun. Kacey Musgraves sings "High Horse" off one of Maggie's mixes. He reminds himself to delete Olivia's from his Spotify app.

"What's the plan?" he asks.

"Do we need one?"

"Not especially."

"Then I'm your girl."

"Isn't planning your middle name?"

"I might have a couple of ideas." She gives him a dead stare. Raises her eyebrows. "Gotta check your head first, mister."

Ryder shrugs. "If you think that's a good place to start."

Maggie lives in a basement apartment in an old Queen Anne in Curtis Park. Her rent is due for another big bump, and she's worried about making ends meet. She waits tables at night and takes classes during the day—only a partial academic load because of how much money she needs to earn. Light trickles in from a high window well in the bedroom, where there is room for a rock-hard, queen-size bed and a few feet of space to scooch around it.

Ryder hopes they might soon be tumbling around on the bed, but Maggie wants to go for a run.

Ryder has brought shoes for this purpose. Maggie sets an easy pace. They run shoulder to shoulder on her route through the city to the path along the South Platte River and to Cherry Creek and along the bike path back to downtown before heading north. Maggie says little. The run is part meditation. The pace is relaxed. Her strides are long, and she runs up on the balls of her feet. She has run two marathons but doesn't enjoy the organization of it, sees too many weekend warriors in true pain. Ryder's legs work fine. They function as normal, including the occasional complaint about all the concrete. Unlike his disobedient arm, one leg doesn't suddenly go wonky and yank Ryder into the street to dodge traffic.

They finish as dusk begins to fall. Ryder has put distance between himself and the Orioles and whatever the fuck has happened to his arm—perhaps a few days away and a change of scenery is what he needs. Would it be possible to not think about it? Would it be possible to not think about it if you impaled yourself on a metal fencepost, straight through the solar plexus?

Maggie's "shower" is a tub with a curtain and a handheld silver snake with a nozzle. The bathroom provides enough room to stand and turn around. He studies the fingers on his right hand. They are all 100 percent normal. His hand is normal. His arm is normal. He leaves the finger unbandaged. He dresses in her bedroom—shorts, sandals, a new T-shirt—and checks the score of the game on his phone. He expects a gallon of guilty, but it's even worse because his team is getting shelled, 9–0, and it's the eighth inning in Tampa Bay, and he can imagine the players in the Rays dugout thinking the Orioles had their shot at the season and now, on the last game before the All-Star break, it's all falling apart.

In the pint-size galley kitchen, Maggie hands Ryder a pitcher of ice water and a bottle of red wine. She carries a tray and leads him out to an expansive front porch with an open view of the street. Whenever the renters in the first-floor unit are gone, Maggie appropriates the outdoor space.

Maggie doles out ladles full of icy, tomato-rich gazpacho topped with chunks of avocado. She slices sourdough bread and coats them edge to edge with globs of butter.

"What's with UMBC?" she says. "New sponsor?"

"Part of the disguise," says Ryder. "You'll notice not one person spotted me on the run."

"Very clever," says Maggie. "And your finger is all better? Couple hours in the dry Denver air and you're all healed up?"

Maggie misses nothing.

"Not a blister issue," says Ryder.

"I figured."

"You did?"

"I knew something was up."

"Something?"

"You've been pretty quiet," says Maggie. "And then a side trip out here? Your team in Florida?"

"Team's decision, not mine."

"I peeked at the score while you were in the shower—you know the Orioles game is *Sunday Night Baseball* tonight, right? Your favorite, Jessica Mendoza, talking all about you. I wonder how many times they played the clip of you and Billy Jaworski?"

"Too many." He's a doubly disloyal cheater. One, sitting in Denver when he should be with his team. Two, the platonic but nonetheless intimate moments with Olivia. Ryder knows what he would have done if Olivia's light had been any shade of green.

He should be watching the game against the Rays. The fucking Rays. Every pitch is something he should study for future reference. He should be watching for sparks and flare-ups.

"The woman in the photo?" says Maggie. The bowls of soup sit empty. They are working on the second half of the bottle.

"What photo?"

Ryder scrambles for a plan of what to say.

"The restaurant one," says Maggie. "Softball pitcher?"

A flash of prickles flares down Ryder's legs. He swallows. Knows he can't hesitate. "You should see the selfie craziness I get into. Everybody wants a piece."

"And then she pops up on a baseball field somewhere, each of you with a couple of baseball gloves? *She* is the UMBC connection."

This is a statement, not an accusation. Ryder should know not to try to slip anything past Maggie.

"She is a friend of Rhineland's," says Ryder. "Showed up at this one dinner. Pitcher to pitcher, she wanted a photo."

"And came bearing gifts?"

If there is one thing Maggie can't stand, it's a liar. Did Ryder even think to clear his phone of texts? There are dozens and dozens. One that references the tender hug in the dugout. Maggie isn't a snoop, but still.

"She dropped off the shirt later," says Ryder. "A token or whatever."

"So you showed her some pitching, what, *techniques*? I thought you weren't supposed to be throwing with that blister, even if it's a fake, huh? What?"

"You see, underhand . . ."

There is no explaining. Ryder backs off.

"You must not read her blog."

"Blog?"

"Yes," says Maggie. "Her Instagram links to her blog. She is a psychology major, right?"

It wouldn't be good to know such details. "I'm not sure."

"She doesn't name you. But she goes on and on about a guy who, in her words, is '*breaking* the game of baseball.' The same guy who is 'overcoming a major childhood trauma.'"

Maggie lets this sink in. Should he feel betrayed by Olivia? Again? Or is this a price he is paying for doing what he does, for being who he is? How many others will try to slice off a piece of him, keep it for themselves?

"Wonder who she means? Know anyone? She was writing about your parents' decision to go along with your high school coaches when they found out you could pitch." Maggie is a shadow. "It's a well-done piece of writing, very academic. I guess keeping her blog is something required by her course. *Key Observations*, it's called. Get it? Olivia *Key*?"

"Maggie, I—"

"It must have taken a lot of conversation to get to that point, to go into all those issues."

"She is a talker."

"And I guess so are you." Maggie sips her wine. Stares off. Sips again. "You told her stuff you have a hard time talking about with *me*."

Ryder, stuck in a brutal loop of recriminations and self-loathing over his disobedient arm, not to mention how routine lust for Olivia blinded him on the trust issue, didn't prepare for this.

Maggie pinches her nose high up, between her eyes.

Ryder can hear the tears.

Ryder's phone chimes. The caller ID is a glowing green flash in the darkness, the chirpy ringtone a jolt in their quiet cave. It's his agent, Mickey Staller. Ryder puts the phone on vibrate, thanks his not-so-lucky stars (what the hell, a *blog*?) it wasn't Olivia calling to try and check in. It could still happen. He pockets the phone.

"You're not taking that?" says Maggie.

"He can wait."

"I can't keep you from socializing," she says. "From having friends."

"Olivia and I are not a thing."

Even Ryder doesn't think the statement sounds convincing. It's another nonlie that sounds like a lie. Like the last nonlie: *I did not mean to hit him.*

"You go days without calling."

"There's never anything new to say. And I know you follow my games. It's the same thing followed by the same thing."

"Sometimes it's nice to hear your voice."

"It's like I'm in a movable frat house in a college where they got green-ass freshmen like me and grizzled veterans like Pagnozzi. It's guys, guys, guys—everywhere you turn is guys and bare asses and sweat and inside jokes. Like being on a submarine on a six-month assignment, not allowed to surface and interact with the real world."

"All the more reason?"

"I'm sorry I hurt you." Would he trade Maggie for an obedient arm? "I'll do better. I mean *try and.*"

Silence festers.

"So missing the All-Star Game isn't a blister thing? I read pitchers were complaining about the seams? Some of these new balls?"

Ryder lays it all out. He goes moment by moment, starting with Julio Diaz. He overloads the detail. He tries to explain how it felt to pitch—that is, *not pitch*—under the watchful eye of the Norfolk coach, Bing.

Maggie waits when he finishes, takes it in. "I didn't know that was possible."

"It's rare," says Ryder.

"So the blister is a ruse to help you avoid making a mess at the All-Star Game?"

"It wouldn't be pretty."

"And the fix is what?"

"I honestly don't know." Ryder gives a brief rundown of the Rick Ankiel saga. "The problem never went away, but he managed it. Dude was a fearless piece of work, how hard he fought to recover."

"It's a hiccup, maybe," says Maggie. "A glitch."

Ryder's phone vibrates in his pocket, and he plucks it out to give it a peek—Staller again. There's a voice mail message, too, probably from the first time Staller called.

Maggie tells Ryder to return the call while she cleans up. She leaves Ryder with a full glass of wine and disappears in the dark.

When Ryder dials back, Staller is amped. It takes a minute for Ryder to get the essence, but it's something Rex Coburn is tweeting about and there is a link to an online story and Ryder needs to check it out pronto and Staller needs to know if the rumor is true—that the blister business is bullshit and that Frank Ryder, in fact, has a "bad case of the fucking yips," and the coaches are stymied trying to figure out what the hell might have happened to their star who was bringing all the hope.

"Is it true?" says Staller.

Ryder pictures Staller in his lounge chair by an outdoor pool in Beverly Hills, smoking a cigar and sipping a scotch. Ryder doesn't know if Staller has a pool or smokes cigars or lives in Beverly Hills, but he has seen Staller with a tumbler of scotch and knows he lives in LA. Staller is a short bald guy with the ever-present five-o'clock shadow.

"I'm giving it a day or two."

"Jesus H.," says Staller.

"I'll figure it out."

"You will? How's the arm feel?"

"Fine." *Better* than normal, in fact, with all the rest. "Absolutely fine."

"What are you doing?"

"Doing?" says Ryder.

"Doing about it," says Staller. "You can't just wait and hope. If the arm is fine, it's a head thing—is that it? Who are you talking to?"

"I'm in Denver."

"Denver? What the hell? What the hell am I supposed to tell Rex fucking Coburn?"

"You don't have to tell him anything," says Ryder. "Don't call him back."

"They are going to figure it out. Something has leaked, and holy shit they are going to cancel all the bets in Vegas and reset the line if you're not starting the All-Star Game for the AL. Am I correct?"

"Not my business."

"It sure as hell is." Ryder puts his phone on speaker, lets Staller scream into the darkness. "*Everything* is your business. Every moment of how you handle this thing, whatever it is, matters. Your attitude. Your public statements, your willingness to do the work and get better. All those future GMs who want to sign you after your time with the Orioles is up? They are watching every move you make. And that includes whether Ray Gallo and Alicia Ford will go way out on a limb and lock you up for a decade or more. You got it? Because we will make Ray Gallo crawl all the way out on that branch. We will make him hang upside down like a monkey until every penny has fallen from his precious-ass pockets, and we will make sure you will be an Oriole forever. And if he doesn't lock you up, he's up against a dozen other teams with pockets so deep they look like pockets on a clown's pants compared to that tight little change-slot thingy in a new pair of jeans. So everything counts. Are you a team player? A good clubhouse guy? Do you hide when the going gets rough? Do you piss off the fans or sign autographs until your fingers are blue?"

"Okay," says Ryder.

"And that's true for the endorsements too. You think Nationwide and Gatorade and Domino's don't think about the whole Frank Ryder story—what you represent? Do you know how many calls I get every day with requests for endorsement deals? Do you know how uncreative you have to be to come up with a tagline to be read by the pitcher who throws the fastest ball on the planet? A *ketchup* company thought it would be hilarious if you would demonstrate how *slow* their ketchup comes out of the bottle—but they thought they could get you for a song because you're so young. Give me a break. Every breath you take is getting evaluated, every statement you make."

"Got it," says Ryder.

"Don't *get* it," says Staller. "Decide. Decide what *you* are going to do. The Orioles don't matter. Yeah, of course they *matter*, but this is your life, your career, your injury, and you get to tell the story of what's going on and how you're going to get back out there and dominate. I don't care if it takes all the shrinks in New York and Los Angeles put together, you are getting back out there."

"Got it," says Ryder and regrets his lame response, the awful echo of himself.

Ryder hangs up, takes a few long glugs of his wine, and goes down to find Maggie in the final stages of restoring order to her tiny kitchen. There is no more wine. She only keeps a bottle at a time. It's a clutter issue as much as anything. Ryder offers to retrieve another bottle. He takes a Lyft, loads up a box with eight bottles of good cabernet and a bottle of good brandy at a liquor store on Colfax Avenue. He comes back to Maggie accusing him of trying to buy his way back into her good favor. She's not happy. She thinks Ryder is showing off his cash and his freedom. He's "flaunting it" and "going overboard." Ryder tries again to apologize, for the Olivia infraction and the fresh offense too. Unless he was planning to stay for a week, and she knows he is not, he should not have bought so much wine.

"Sounds like you've got bigger problems than little old me," says Maggie. "I don't mean for it all to sound so bitter. But when I see you, I don't think of the big star, I see the guy I met in science class. *That* guy. The student. The easygoing kid who cared about his grades and worked his butt off in school."

"Easygoing?"

They are back on the porch. Ryder has opened a new bottle, and she gives in to another glass. "I know you were still dealing with Deon Johnson before you started pitching again," she says. "But back then, he didn't haunt your every move."

"He was there."

"I'm sure he was."

"So what do I do?"

"You keep working at it," she says. "When you wanted to throw faster and when you worked at having impeccable control, you studied it from every angle, every possible aspect. Wipe the slate clean, study the components. You need to spray yourself with a neuralyzer. You know? You break it down, look at it all over again. Right?"

Maggie yawns.

"Right," says Ryder.

"I'll be sound asleep in twenty minutes," she announces. "Totally up to you how you want to use them."

Back in her bedroom, the clothes come off. Maggie is skinny, slight. She is also unabashed. Normally, she is a playful lover. Normally, she likes to draw it out. Talk a bit, screw a bit.

Not tonight. Tonight, Maggie is down to business. *Places to go, things to see, sleep I don't want to miss.* It's not unloving, but it's more goal oriented than what he's used to. She's verbal, directive. More than she's ever been. Ryder likes it.

Ryder hopes there are healing powers in her dark bedroom. Maggie finishes. She falls asleep from one breath to the next, which must be some sort of cruel message she's sending him, too, about her busy but centered world.

—⁂—

Ryder waits a long fifteen minutes and unwraps himself from her body. He sneaks his way back to the kitchen. He finds a wineglass in a cupboard, figuring good brandy deserves something better than plastic. Out on the porch, he falls into a dull trance watching the cars on Seventeenth Avenue. Traffic is light. Soothing. Ryder savors the tangy tingle of the booze. He waits to feel his head slump or the alcohol to take over, but it feels like he's on his first drink.

He checks his phone for the scores. The Orioles have lost, 10–2. It's a rough way to go into the All-Star break and a bad omen for the second half of the season.

It's possible the arm will click itself back into gear tomorrow, right? Or it's possible he's 100 percent screwed. He blames Stone. He blames Lackland. He blames Billings for hurting Diaz. He blames Olivia for being so goddamn tempting.

He blames himself. He replays the first side session, the first one after the suspension was locked in and when the appeals were over. He pictures the first pitch. He thought the errant throw was some sort of wacky joke, maybe because he knew he wasn't *really* practicing between starts. Maybe his internal clock was off, given it would be weeks before he would need to crank up the intensity again.

He focused more on the second pitch, tried to pretend it mattered, which it did, but the second one skipped off the dirt about five feet in front of the plate. Of course, Ryder did what pitchers do. He kicked the rubber. He checked his cleats. He took off his cap and put it back on. He rolled his shoulders, adjusted his uniform, and fired again. This ball was dead center over the plate and about five feet above where it needed to be.

The next six pitches weren't any better. Lackland shut him down for the day. Two days later, Ryder tried again. This time, indoors. Different mound, different setting, different light. Lackland was with the team on their road trip, so they brought in pitching guru Harvey Bing from Norfolk and a catcher named Rosedale.

Ryder started with easy tosses, playing catch. No issues. But when Ryder went into his motion, it was as if he'd lost control of every bit of connective tissue between his brain and his fingertips. His body moved in the right sequence, but the coordination was a joke, and, really, he had no idea when the ball would leave his fingertips, which of course played a big role in the ball's trajectory and final destination. The release point was a joke.

Bing's fix-it skills were legendary, Ryder was told. He was the kind of coach who knows essential mechanics but gets inside each player's head, too, to understand what makes them tick. Bing's pupils always emerged from his training with a trademark calmness and a presence on the mound that was uniformly chill.

Bing wanted to talk. Ryder? Not so much. Ryder didn't want to get into a long explanation—again, again—of everything. Ryder wanted Bing to put him through the right sequence of practice drills or adjust his arm slot or release point, and when Bing took him to an office to chat, Ryder found himself petulant and resistant to Bing's attempted probing about Jaworski and about Ryder's thought process during the game against the Rays. Ryder knew he wasn't mean or disrespectful, but he didn't engage in the attempted headshrinking chat and begged off, asking Bing when he should try throwing again. "When you're ready," said Bing like some sort of Yoda. "You'll know."

And back to Maggie. *Wipe the slate clean.* Easier said, right? Easier said than done? Unless it's a movie. *You're a rumor, recognizable only as déjà vu and dismissed just as quickly. You don't exist—you were never even born.*

Wouldn't that be nice?

Every slurp of brandy brings hope he will soon feel nothing. Better, he might go all the way numb. *Hell.* Maybe he needs a long break. Maybe he needs a bong with his brandy. Maybe he needs a lobotomy, have his hard drive wiped. Maggie called it a *clean slate.* The genius who figured out the buttons you pushed to erase all the extraneous crazy junk bouncing around in the human head? That person should win the Nobel Prize for Science. Every treatment would seem cheap at a million dollars, right? Where the hell could Ryder buy one of those?

Ryder chases each stupid thought with a fresh sip. Around and around. Olivia and Maggie. Stone. Lackland. Ryder wonders if it's possible the brain might eat its owner alive if it's forced to think the same thought one too many times.

———

Ryder wakes slumped and contorted in the chair. In the split second between sleep and consciousness, he jerks his body to attention. For a moment, he is uncertain of his surroundings. The wineglass he'd been holding slips from his grasp and shatters on the deck with a convincing clarion crackle. He reaches down, gropes with his fingers in the dark. He finds the stem, but it's lighter than it should be. The bowl has been smashed. The top of the stem is mean and sharp. Ryder lightly rests his hand on the jagged points, then lets the weight of his arm add pressure to the pain, which feels real and good in its own way.

Ryder's head throbs and his neck aches. The harder he presses on the sharp stem, the middle of his palm begging for a puncture, the less he recognizes the other complaints.

But no.

He has no idea of the time, but he needs a broom and a dustpan.

When he snakes himself back around sleeping Maggie, he's worried that his head will return to its tired, old, wide-awake groove.

Chapter 23

"You want a meeting?" says Gallo. "Stop on over to my place of business. Camden Yards. My hunch is you know it. But I can give you the address if you need it."

Gallo shakes his head, rolls his eyes. Aiko shrugs.

"You got me on speakerphone?"

"Yes, I got you on speakerphone, and we are all alone, if you're worried about that."

Aiko smiles.

"Give me a break."

"Two ears are better than one," says Gallo.

"What if you've got a roomful over there?"

"Then choose your words wisely."

"Well, in that case, please don't think anything about your governor calling at this particular moment of time. I am merely calling with a note of encouragement."

"Right." Gallo pictures Governor Rick Pembrose and his silver, shiny coif. Pembrose must keep a tanning bed routine. He's probably got a plastic surgeon on speed dial. He is half matinee idol, half back-alley thug. "You call every year at the All-Star break."

"Only on years when the Orioles have won more games than they've lost," says Pembrose. "So have we got big problems, little problems, what?"

"We've got to win more games," says Gallo. "As always."

"I mean with our boy."

"Boy?"

Aiko shakes her head, covers her eyes with a tiny hand.

"With Frank."

"What are you getting at, exactly?"

"What I'm getting at is the story that's splattered on page one of the morning birdcage liner."

Gallo ponders a photo on his wall of Hall of Famer Mike Mussina in full windup mode. "Certainly you, of all people, should know the newspaper is not a fountain of accuracy."

"Coburn's sources sound solid," says Pembrose.

"It's sports. They can get away with that shit."

"And Twitter has lit up."

"Twitter will light up over burnt toast that looks like Jesus."

Pembrose says nothing, as if he might be doing a Twitter search for the crispy bread in question. Finally: "Just tell me if the window is closing?"

"Window?"

"Window to win," says Pembrose. "Of course nobody thought this year was our window to win until that kid came along, right? You can't honestly say you thought you were going to be better than any other team in the division until that kid showed up. And he gave us a window to win."

"Us?"

"Yeah, *us*. You know damn well the city, the whole damn state, is all in, hanging on every game. Look at your goddamn attendance, for crying out loud. Check your beer sales too. Yeah, it's *us*."

"Nobody wanted this rough patch," says Gallo.

"But what about Ryder? Is it a blister issue or a head case issue? You know Vegas is going crazy with this, right?"

Rick Pembrose's shady past and his corrupt ties to contractors and developers have filled more than a few newspaper articles too.

"So now we understand what this call is all about," says Gallo. "Now we are past the preliminaries."

"A little straight talk from the Orioles wouldn't hurt. Don't you sense an obligation to be transparent?"

"So you wouldn't mind a little, what do you call it, *tip*? Say, if that came before we go all transparent?"

Gallo can imagine the vast network of friends, pols, and fellow gamblers who would receive a signal from Pembrose should Gallo decide to pretend he's buddies with this weasel.

"You're going to have to say what's up in a day or so anyway," says Pembrose. "Soon as you come off the All-Star break, you'll have to declare if Ryder is in the rotation or not."

"We will?"

Gallo hates it when others try to tell him what to do.

"You can't fucking hide Frank Ryder!"

"I guess we've got nothing more to discuss."

"You've got people out here dying to know."

Pembrose sounds desperate.

"By *people* you mean gamblers?"

"It's whether we've still got that window. If the window is slamming shut, we have to know."

"Noted," says Gallo. "Is this how you spend your days, calling around to various Maryland enterprises to share your thoughts and insights?"

"You don't seem to get it."

"Are you betting on the whole season? Or individual games?"

"People out here have rolled the dice on you guys. They loved the trade for Steve Penny after Diaz went down. Alicia Ford is gutsy. Dare I say ballsy?"

I pulled that trigger, Gallo wants to say. Aiko shakes her head.

"Your stock went up," says Pembrose. "Now it's like Blue Monday and Black Friday all at once over here, everybody throwing in the towel. Another season lost and the guy, it turns out, is healthy except for a bad case of the goddamn yips, and all the hardworking people of the city and the state—the road crews, the lawyers, the fishermen, the cops, even some of our less than upstanding citizens—saw a season of hope and maybe the start of a long run that would put Baltimore back up there with Boston and New York and LA and Saint Louis. You know? A real *baseball* town. You gave us three months of happiness and a feeling like we could respect ourselves again. And now? All those people out there busting their hump every day? They think to themselves as they are driving a trash truck or pulling crabs out the Chesapeake at o'dawn thirty trying to keep their families in Wheaties, and all this guy has to do is throw a baseball and he's got *mental issues*? What the hell? You better fix it, Gallo. The window to win is now."

Chapter 24

Ryder wakes in Maggie's bed. He tries to remember coming back inside but can't recall leaving the porch—nothing. His hand tingles from sleeping on it wrong. He clenches his fingers, stirs the blood.

A note on the kitchen table:

Nuke coffee if it's gone cold. I'm really glad we had time together yesterday. Call before you leave town? M.

It's noon. The coffee is room temperature. Ryder zaps a cup in the microwave, showers, pops three Advil, puts on fresh clothes. Jeans, a lime-green polo shirt.

Ryder orders a Lyft, waits on the curb, and texts Maggie:

If you dragged me off the porch last night, thank you. In fact, thanks for everything. By that, I mean everything.

Ryder stares at the phone. He expects a reassuring reply—a heart emoji or heart eyes or even a thumbs-up, which would probably feel as good as a *fuck you*. At least it would be something. While he's waiting for his ride, his phone finally pings.

I probably sounded like I've got all the answers, Frank. I don't. Sorry if I came across too harsh. Let's talk before you leave?

—⁓—

The Lyft driver wears long hair in a tight ponytail. He looks to be pushing sixty. He starts to tell Ryder about how long he drove a "real cab" before switching over to the rideshares. Ryder replies to probes with a series of blunt replies designed to dampen any enthusiasm for full-blown chatter. "Visiting a friend." "East Coast." "Used to live here—yeah." "Not where I grew up, no."

"You look so familiar," says the driver.

"One of those faces," says Ryder.

The driver works his way down Colorado Boulevard to the University Hills neighborhood with all the hustle of a Sunday drive in the country. He treats yellow lights like red, makes room on the road for others.

Ryder's phone screams, and he checks the caller ID. It's Marty Ash—the *Denver Post* prep sportswriter who covered him at Thomas Jefferson High School. Ash is older and a straight shooter. He always treated Ryder like a grown-up. Still, it's a risky time to shoot the breeze. He doesn't answer.

The Prius air conditioner fights the heat but fails. Ryder sweats. His head throbs. He curses himself for thinking he could escape unharmed from pounding down so much brandy on top of everything else. He cracks one of the courtesy bottles of water and pops three more Advil.

Ryder keeps his Twitter and Instagram notifications turned off, but he peeks to see how he's faring. It's like being back in high school but knowing every single word is being said about you—in every hallway, classroom, and both locker rooms.

@FrankRyder_1 Blister? Pop it, suck it, get on with it. We need home field advantage in the World Series for the A.L. A blister? Really? #getoverit #healfast

@FrankRyder_1 Tell us what's real, man. If @Rex_ Coburn is right—if you're going all Rick Ankiel on us— we better know yesterday. Blister? Or is your head a mess? Got bets to figure out, dude. Like, come clean dude. #headcase #uhoh

@FrankRyder_1 Take care of that little ouchie. Oriole Nation needs you back in the second half. Dogfight to the finish! #birdland

@FrankRyder_1 Look, F the first finger. You don't need it. Thumb and the other three, you'll be throwing 105. Come on, man. #comeonman #buckup #dontfuckup

@FrankRyder_1 Where the hell are you? You can't give us all that early-season flash and then just disappear like a woo-woo ghost. #ghosted #herewegoagain #ryderheadcase

@FrankRyder_1 The Orioles suck. Straight down the dumper in the second half, no question. Revert to the mean! The Orioles CANNOT help themselves. A little hope comes along and the Orioles find a way to . . . Fuck. It. Up. #nohope #goingankiel

Ryder's mother answers the door in shock. It was a long shot she would be home and not at school running a summer program or at the downtown offices helping on a curriculum committee of one sort or another. Her hug means business. It is triple the length of a normal hug. Karen Ryder holds both of his hands like she's never letting go. She steps back to look at him and tells him his hair is getting way too wild.

Ryder's mom is trim and unfussy. She keeps her hair short. It's been gray for years—a proud gray. The hair color is the sole clue to her age—she is lean and bright eyed with an easy smile. She explains she was out in the vegetable garden, and she gives him a hard time about the lack of notice. She tells him Adam explained about blisters being a problem for pitchers. She questions Ryder about the big All-Star Game. The questions keep coming, and she leads him to the kitchen. Did he fly in this morning? Last night? Does he plan to see Maggie? How long is he staying?

"They spent five minutes on the *Today Show* this morning talking about your finger, Frank Ryder. Five minutes! About *your* finger. They talked to a high school kid from Texas who throws one oh four on a pretty regular basis, but I guess he only has one pitch. But what high school kid can hit one oh four? Right? Anyway, they asked this kid about you, and of course you are his idol, and he was really disappointed you wouldn't be pitching in Detroit. Bad timing, right?"

"Pretty much."

She apologizes for the lack of lunch options. She suggests they could go out, but Ryder wants to stay under the radar and soak up the deep familiarity of the house, its essence a salve. She makes him a turkey-and-cheddar sandwich with brown mustard, and she heats up some homemade chicken soup.

"And then I guess the gamblers are going crazy—as if we're supposed to care about them? Now they're favoring the National League, when before your injury, if you call a blister an *injury*, that is, the

American League was supposed to clean up, have I got that right? The terminology?"

"You're doing fine."

Ryder's parents don't follow professional sports. His father rails against the absurd salaries. He dreams of schools full of kids who come to class without the distraction of worshipping celebrity athletes, singers, and actors. Ryder's mother brags about having found one of the few guys on the planet who doesn't spend his Sundays watching football. Swimming at the Y and long summer hikes are their priorities.

"Well, I'm repeating what I heard."

Ryder wraps the fingers of his left hand around the Kabuki-theater bandage on his right index. When he left Maggie's, he decided he wouldn't drag his parents into the real reasons for his absence with the team.

"Well, you're in good hands, so to speak, I'm sure."

She quarters a pear to go with his lunch, and she sits down, too, with iced tea and a plate of sliced tomatoes and cucumbers. Ryder could use a Coke to help with his fuzzy head, but he knows better than to ask in *this* house. Despite her upbringing in the suburbs of Atlanta, home to corporate HQ of Coca-Cola and premiere fried-food capital of the South, Karen Sobel was health conscious beginning in college, long before she was a Ryder. She wants to live to be one hundred, but it's not something she proclaims widely. She understands luck. As the mother of a kid who accidentally killed another kid, what mother wouldn't?

Ryder helps himself to a glass from the cupboard. Ice from the freezer. Water from the tap. The process is familiar and quaint. It's one he repeated a thousand times as a kid without thinking. A rush of sentimentality pokes a wistful flavor through the hangover. He is grateful this simple routine exists. The drinking glass is the same. The ice cubes. The house. The view through the square window over the sink to the backyard is a portrait of life and activity. White business shirts and two blue-striped towels hang on a line. Thick green ivy covers all the fences.

One half of the backyard is a well-tended patch of grass. The other half is Karen's garden. She is keen on tomatoes, beets, and colored carrots. It's as if this is a museum diorama and he's inside the exhibit, a picturesque peek into the ordinary life of twenty-first-century city dwellers, at least those with a few resources and a solid work ethic.

"Dad at work?"

"He's going to kill me for being the lucky one who was home, and then of course he's going to get on your case for dropping in unannounced, but Dad is at a conference in San Diego."

Ryder eats and fields questions. It's like a one-on-one with Jessica Mendoza, but different areas of concern. Yes, he's talked to Josh. Yes, he saw Maggie. Yes, she's doing fine. Yes, he thought about swinging by the high school to see Coach Rush, but it's the dead of summer and what are the odds? Yes, his Baltimore home is fine, if you like an indifferent white room in the sky. Yes, he's eating well and sleeping well.

Ryder is digging himself a hole. He can't seem to help it. At some point, he'll have to come clean. He doesn't have the energy to lay it all out.

"You sure you're sleeping okay? You look like you could use a big bowl of spaghetti every night for about three weeks straight. Bread and real butter, the whole bit."

"I won't deny it's a grind. I mean, I'm still wide eyed wherever we go, but I gotta say the second half of the season looks long." Uttering the complaint sounds disingenuous to its core, given the size of the checks deposited in his bank account, on top of the signing bonus and the endorsement deals. "I guess it's something you get used to."

"But it's better when you're winning."

"Which, right now, we're not."

"But the goal is to play *meaningful baseball*—that's a phrase I picked up—come September?"

"I'm impressed."

"But isn't every game meaningful? The ones in April and May count as much as the ones in September as you try to get into the playoffs, right?"

"True."

After Ryder started pitching at TJ, his parents didn't even ask much about it until it came time to decide on college.

"So if you treat every game all year like *meaningful baseball*"—she raises her eyebrows, ponders her thought for a moment—"then you won't have to worry come September."

"A lofty observation. You should be a coach."

"Seems obvious." She shrugs. It's legitimate, as if every team must be crazy for not trying harder.

"In April, you think you have plenty of time to make up for your mistakes. For the losses."

"So you're giving yourself an excuse. An excuse to lose."

"It's not an excuse. It's a matter of fact that if you win six out of ten games, over and over, you're doing good." In fact, Ryder hates this way of thinking about it. "You win six out of ten, you're in the playoffs."

"So why not seven out of ten? Or eight?"

"Nobody is trying to lose."

"But if you head out for every game in April as if it's a must-win in September, no problem—right?"

"Hell," says Ryder. "Forget coach. I'm promoting you all the way to manager."

"That will be the day—the first woman manager."

"You've been watching a lot of baseball," says Ryder. "Obviously."

"Only your games. You've got a woman GM, right?"

"Correct."

"First one, right?"

"Again, correct."

"So why can't you have a woman in the dugout deciding when to bunt or call for the hit and run? Why can't a woman walk out there on the mound and tell a pitcher he's done for the day? What's the big difference?"

Well, there is the clubhouse and all the jockstraps. But with all the female reporters running around, it's not exactly like *Lord of the*

Flies in there. "Good question," he says, deciding not to mention that the Yankees have already installed a female as manager for one of their minor-league teams. The game is changing all the time.

"They would have better instincts too," says his mom. "Right? Better intuition about when a pitcher is losing it? They could read a pitcher. Am I right?"

"Some of the managers and coaches are pretty good about that too. But it would give a whole new flavor to the game."

"Another glass ceiling," she says. "Waiting to be shattered."

During the year in Alpharetta, before they moved to Colorado, Karen Ryder went through the motions of homeschooling and running the house and family, but the effort was buried within a cloak of sadness and pain. His parents, looking back, kept up appearances. The move to Colorado allowed Adam and Karen Ryder to breathe new air, think new thoughts. It took time, but soon Ryder realized how the year in Atlanta after the incident was nothing more than a family trying to find its way in the world again.

—◊—

Ryder helps with the dishes. She won't let him do them alone. In the bathroom, he splashes cold water on his face to scare away the lingering leftovers of his callous hangover.

"Do you want coffee?" she shouts down the hall.

"I'll be there in a minute, Mom," he says.

Ryder slips into his old bedroom for a quick peek. It's unchanged. José Altuve is still there, in his ready stance at the plate. The tough-as-nails Altuve's bat is cocked up with his hands by his ear, waiting for another pitch. He's been holding the same position for years.

As a high school kid throwing imaginary heat and wicked sliders in this bedroom, Ryder struck out petrified Altuve a thousand times. All backward K's! The star Astro never swung at one single pitch.

Now, with an arm that's developed a mind of its own, Ryder doubts even the imaginary pitches would find the zone, especially since Altuve is five foot six.

It's easy to see the ratty spot in the carpet where he placed a small metal box to give himself a mound—of sorts. The worn brown box sits on a shelf in the closet. Ryder pulls it down and secures it in its old indentation, the box sliding into its familiar groove like a smooth key in an oiled lock.

The brown box is wide and flat and four inches high. Ryder used the box to work on his balance. The box worked for practicing the first half of his windup. If Ryder exerted too much pressure—forward or sideways—the box would slide on the carpet. Late at night, long before the ban was lifted on Ryder playing sports again, Ryder would lift his left leg to replicate the beginning of the simulated windup, his left knee tucked up by his chest. He would hold the pose for a count of three, his right calf shaking and his right quad screaming for relief. When he started with the drill, the unsteadiness began with the first few reps. After a few weeks, the unsteadiness waited to appear on the twentieth rep. A few weeks later, the thirtieth rep. And a few weeks later, it was gone. The exercise was prescribed by Coach Rush to go with all the balancing work and upper-body workouts in the weight room at high school.

Now Ryder stands on the box and notices how much more he towers over Altuve, a mere ten feet away.

Ryder's old bed looks juvenile and confining compared to the king-size acre of mattress in his condo and the ones in the hotel rooms too. He pictures himself under the covers—watching YouTube videos of Jacob deGrom, Justin Verlander, Chris Sale, Max Scherzer, Aroldis Chapman, Jordan Hicks. Chapman and Hicks and the others were hittable. Nobody cried "unfair." They were spectacles and their pitches were crazy fast, but nobody thought it was the end-times.

Ryder had practiced all their motions and grips. He practiced his fist-pumping move after a strikeout—particularly the third-out strike-out, and even better the third-out strikeout when a backdoor slider fooled them and they didn't even think about swinging. You could give a shout and pump your fist like an obnoxious gladiator, or you could walk off the mound without the histrionics—so he practiced that too.

Look down, start walking.

Buh-bye. Straight face.

Not a glimmer of gloat.

Gee, I really can't say how sorry I am that you didn't get a bat on the ball.

It was in this room, and with Josh's encouragement, that Ryder planned to get better and stronger in every aspect of what a pitcher needed. If you could learn addition, his old theory went, you could learn algebra or quantum mechanics. It was in this room where he told his brother about the day he had been "caught" throwing back the home run ball at TJ and how his coaches now wanted to have "a word" with Ryder's parents. And it was in this room where Adam and Karen Ryder relented and went along with his coaches' suggestion to not keep a kid with so much raw talent and internal motivation out of the game.

"Frank?"

It's not the first time she has called his name—only the first time he's really heard it. And now he recalls a doorbell too.

Ryder puts the box back on the closet shelf, walks down the bedroom hall, and thinks how easy it would be to slip out the sliding glass door off the kitchen nook and make his way through the backyard and off down the alley. What he would *really* like to do is to lay on the lounge chair, inhale the scents wafting from the garden, sip his way through a pitcher of iced coffee, and read a healthy chunk of *Dune*.

The front door is open wide. His mother props open the screen door with one arm. The visitor remains outside.

His mother smiles and turns to him. Says, "Here he is." His mother pops her eyebrows up and shrugs. The look suggests this is none of her business.

"Frank," says the man.

"Mr. Ash," says Ryder.

He has always been Mr. Ash. High school seniors don't call reporters by their first names. Nothing changed when Ryder did interviews at Metro State and another one the day after his first big-league appearance during the expanded-roster month the previous September.

"I heard you were in town," says Ash.

"Really?" says Ryder.

"One airport sighting yesterday, something went up on Twitter about that; a Lyft driver this morning gave me a tip, and I thought I would come out and see if the man of the hour was home visiting. Thought I might grab a quick interview."

The Lyft driver? A nosy media tipster?

"Forgive me, but it wasn't hard to look up the family home address, given I knew the TJ neighborhood and your folks are pretty well involved in the public schools. Right?"

"Good to see you," says Ryder, for the polite factor. Ryder rubs the bandage on his right index finger with his thumb to make sure it's still there. The bandage remains damp from the cold water he splashed on his face.

Ash steps inside at his mother's urging. She suggests they all sit down in the living room. She asks if Ash would like an iced tea, as if Ash is welcome company.

"I'm sorry," says Ryder. "Not today."

Despite the heat, Ash wears gray slacks, a blue shirt that looks like it's on day two or three, and a black tie.

Ash slips a pen off the notebook as if he didn't hear. "Why not? A few minutes, that's all. Your fans want to know how you're doing."

Ash is medium height. Patches of his nose and cheeks bloom with intricate vessels like skinny violet worms. Ryder wonders about the toll of being a near-retirement adult who has spent all his life around teenage hopes and dreams.

"Thanks," says Ryder. "Like I said—"

"Look," says Ash. "I won't touch the controversy or the rumors."

"I'm not *touching* or talking about anything."

Ryder's head whirls. Isn't this some sort of flagrant foul, to come here unannounced?

"I see you've got a bandage on your finger."

"I gotta go," says Ryder.

"You want to show me the blister?"

"No," says Ryder. Jesus, he thinks, the gall.

"I'm sure you've got more Band-Aids." Ash holds up his phone. "One photo. Your finger."

Ryder shakes his head, tightens his mouth.

Ash starts to write something down, stops.

"You can't mention this," says Ryder.

"I certainly can."

"And say what?"

"That you were here."

"No." He points to Ash's notebook with his bandage. "No notes. I didn't agree to this."

Ash ignores him. "I'm looking at you. Frank Ryder came home to Denver. It's a fact. We're friends, remember?"

"I don't."

"I was the first one to write you up."

"Somebody else would have done it."

"Frank—" Ryder has forgotten his mother is right there.

"You were quiet," says Ash. "Humble. Focused on the game."

"Good," says Ryder.

"You don't think I helped put you on the radar?" says Ash. "You know scouts read my stuff, right? College scouts, pro scouts. There's speculation about how truthful the Orioles are being with your . . . *injury*."

The nonquestion says it all.

"We're done," says Ryder.

"How do you *feel* about missing the All-Star Game? Did you think about maybe being there with your American League teammates to support them? For morale?"

Ryder says nothing.

"You owe it to your fans," says Ash.

"I don't owe anybody anything." The declaration comes out much louder than he thought it would.

"I don't think he's here to hurt you, Frank." His mother sounds sincere. Sincere and clueless.

"You don't think your fans deserve to know the truth about your condition?"

"This"—Ryder holds up the pretend bandage on the pretend wound—"is not a condition. It's a blister. It will heal."

"And as for the rumors?"

Ryder steps down out of the house and closes the gap between himself and Ash. Ash is slump shouldered and slight. He holds up his free palm like he's stopping traffic.

"Frank!" says his mother.

"Do you print rumors?"

"There were credible sources," says Ash. "I know Rex Coburn. He's big time in the baseball writers association. He's a good reporter."

"Rumors," says Ryder. "You said it yourself. Don't tell me they are rumors one second and nuggets of truth the next."

"So, you're denying the rumors?"

"We were done five minutes ago," says Ryder.

"You can't sit on the blister story for long." Ash tucks the pen into his shirt pocket. He hasn't scratched one note. "People know how long they take to heal."

"There is no story," says Ryder. "We didn't talk."

"Yes we did." Ash plucks something from his pocket. It's small—smaller than a phone—and black. A recorder. "Got every little word."

Chapter 25

"I object to this whole emergency meeting—plain and simple." The red on Jimmy Wharton's neck and cheeks pulses under his white cowboy hat, which looks even more out of place, somehow, in an air-conditioned hotel conference room in Detroit. "Anyone who doesn't think we take this straight to the Rules Committee and clean up this mess before the first pitcher reports to spring training next February is out of their cotton-pickin' minds!"

"A quick caution to not use racist jargon in public," says Brawley. "Or in here, for that matter. You know?"

"*Racist?* What in hell are you talking about?"

Brawley sighs, like it's too tiring to have to explain it. "Let's all just chill out a little bit."

"Chill out?" says Wharton. "Can you see where all of this is going? We can send a message now, *right* now. The Frank Ryders of the world are interesting, in a freak show kind of way, but if we give even the slightest suggestion that these warp speeds are okay in our game, then we can sit back and watch the revenues crash."

"Jesus H.!" Tampa Bay Rays owner Carl Quintana smacks the table with the palm of his hand. "That is some seriously dangerous ammunition out there now on the mound. Why the hell are we even having this discussion? Did you watch Jaworski go down? Out for the season, and for all we know it could be longer."

Gallo shoves his chair back, jumps to his feet, points at Quintana. "You have some—"

"Sit down!" says Ziegler. "Yeah, yeah—Julio Diaz is out for the year too. Tit for tat."

"One oh nine!" Quintana sits up straight, points a finger straight back at Gallo. "Might have killed him if it was one twelve or one fifteen. *Killed him.* Imagine what *that* would have done to your boy's head. And horrified every single person who was there as witness."

"Sit down," says Ziegler. "This isn't going to get personal."

"Of course it's personal," says Gallo. "It's about you doing anything you can to keep my guy off the field."

"Looks like he's taking that issue into his own hands."

The crack, uttered in a moment of calm and loud enough for the whole room to hear, is followed by a nervous laugh from a cluster down at the end of the table.

"Who said that?" says Gallo.

"Hey, guys, come on." It's Commissioner Morris. He whacks a water glass with a metal pen like he's at a wedding, about to give a toast. "We need to help our fans think about the future of the game. They know the spectacle of it now, but can you really let this go, unanswered, in the way we structure our game?"

"So you're taking sides," says Gallo. "Plain as day."

"It's a question," says the commissioner. "You either let things slide—you lay back and let all of nature take its course—or you realize that we're in charge. We get to choose."

"And sometimes it's a mess," says Rafferty. "Like the DH."

"Nothing we can't fix," says Morris. The room has calmed down, but Gallo still wants a piece of Quintana, later, out in the halls of the Book Cadillac.

"Have you seen all the biomechanical stuff they're working on at MIT?" This is Jerry Hyde, way down at the end of the table. "Exoskeletons? It's like a robot wrapped around a human, and it's designed to work the body part, whatever part it is, to make it stronger or quicker—they can dial in whatever is needed. They had a thing on HBO with Bryant Gumbel. Say a guy lost his leg? Think he's done? No. He's better. Now he can climb El Capitan better than a guy with feet and toes because of the attachments they can put on with a goddamn Allen wrench. Pentagon is dumping boatloads of money into it because, well, imagine the soldiers they could get out of it. So they use the same technology around a healthy leg or a healthy arm, helps it train and focus. The Terminator? It's happening. Now."

"It would help to know if he's going to pitch again this year."

"Aw, jeez," says Gallo. "First it's Tampa Bay all going crazy over here and now the Red Sox are snooping around for intel."

"It's possible the whole Jaworski incident means, perhaps, that he'll never pitch again." Fergus Rowley's green tortoiseshell glasses, round and oversize, are slumped down on his sloop nose. He looks cool in his blue-striped seersucker suit, white shirt, and no tie. "Blister or head case, either way."

"Twitter is convinced," says Ziegler. "And the denials from you guys have been nonexistent."

"It's a *blister*." Gallo holds up both hands, palms up, like a priest at mass.

"Seems like there has to be something behind that story," says Rowley.

"Read my lips." Gallo doesn't understand how a pitcher's motions can appear fine and normal and yet the result is out of control, like a gun with multiple chambers and none of them shooting straight. "It's a blister."

"In that case, he'll be back," says Rowley. "And the issue is on the table, and I concur with Commissioner Morris that we should hash this out. Slap on a speed limit, move the mound back. Something so the game retains a reasonable modicum of fairness."

"This was a trap," says Gallo. "An ambush!"

"Hey," says Hyde. "We want Ryder healthy in late July. Orioles are in Seattle for four games, and the ticket sales are good, you know, fans hoping they picked the right game of the rotation to see this guy and what he can do."

"We'll be there," says Gallo.

"One more thing," says Rowley.

"The oracle speaks," says Gallo.

"Make it quick," says the commissioner.

"Today's buzz could easily be tomorrow's boredom," says Rowley. "Could be a yawn after a few rounds of flash and sparkle, do you know what I mean? By August or September, except maybe in Baltimore, the Frank Ryder games could be a nonthing. What's the point of going to a game if there is, in fact, *no game*?"

Chapter 26

Ryder spots Coach Rush's old red VW bus in the parking lot and thanks his Lyft driver for the ride.

It's midsummer and there are few people around, but Ryder avoids the front door and circles around the outside of the building to avoid a long walk through the inside hallways and to sidestep any protracted conversations with teachers and staff who would fawn and gawk.

He doesn't need that. Doesn't deserve it.

The back door to the weight room is propped open by a twenty-pound barbell. Ryder stands in the doorway for a moment. He listens to the gentle clacking of the machines, the occasional *ping* and clatter as weights settle back in the rack after a set. The weight room's peculiar aromas waft his way—sweaty floor mats, the sour-salty smells of teenagers. The room is bustling with activity and purpose. For every weight machine, there's a balance drill and a stretching exercise too.

Ryder's location outside the weight room overlooks the main ball field at the base of a long slope down from the school. It's dead summer, so the white striping is all gone and there are no bases, but the mound is in place, and even without the chalk marks, Ryder appreciates the simple balanced geometry of the playing field, how home plate marks a beginning and an end. There are five players on the field getting in some extra practice. One pitcher. One catcher. One batter. One shortstop. One outfielder. The balls come off the aluminum bat with a ringing, pleasing ping, and Ryder listens for a moment to see how the metallic sounds from the weight room match up from the ones floating up from the field.

It's now the pitcher's turn to hit, and everyone rotates—batter to catcher, catcher to outfield, outfield to shortstop, shortstop to pitcher, pitcher to batter. Each batter gets ten swings. When the new pitcher comes to the mound, it's easy to see that this guy is varsity-level good. His motion is smooth. He throws with certainty, as if human beings were built with this precise length to their arms and this exact length to their legs and with shoulder joints and knee joints that were all fashioned for this critical function—to throw a baseball off a pitcher's mound toward a target sixty feet away.

When the next batter is done, the pitcher moves in for his turn at bat. He whacks a ball to deep center. The outfielder runs out of room. The ball lands in almost the exact spot where Ryder caught the home run, the ball that he tossed back to home plate on the fly that put him in an Orioles uniform and in the mess he is in today.

The outfielder approaches the fence on his way to retrieve the home run ball. Maybe it's the heat or that the outfielder appears to be on the hefty side, but it's an arduous journey up and over the chain link. He scrambles back to the playing field with an equal amount of awkward effort and hurls the ball back toward the infield, only to watch the next ball sail over his head and, again, over the fence.

"Hey!" the kid shouts back toward home plate. "Fuck you!"

The others all laugh.

Ryder laughs too.

—⚌—

"The last person I expected to see today." Coach Rush is sixty-nine years old but, to Ryder, hasn't changed a lick. "Or maybe ever again."

"You know I would stop by in the off-season," says Ryder. "Come on."

"Thought maybe you'd move your folks to Baltimore, never have to come back."

"My parents?" says Ryder. "The same parents I'm thinking of? You know them. Heck, my dad is at a conference in San Diego today—for school. For work. No breaks for that guy."

"Just giving you a hard time." Coach Rush's face is long. His eyes are blue. He doesn't smile much. His exterior is unexcitable. There are times he is talking that you think he's looking straight through you. "Some parents might relax if there's that much money now in the family."

Coach Scott Rush hands Ryder a bottle of cold water from a mini fridge on the floor. The room is windowless and hot, and the air is close. The cinder block walls, the scratched-up old desk, and the bright fluorescent light give Ryder the flavor of an interview room in a cop shop. At least, the ones on TV.

Behind Coach Rush's desk is a pocket library of books on technique, from high jump to hurdles, along with DVDs of Olympic Games highlights and sports documentaries, unchanged since Ryder was last here. A tiny plug-in radio plays the classical music station. Coach Rush is a Mozart freak. An old javelin stands in the corner, and Ryder can't believe it hasn't been banned from the high school grounds as a potential lethal weapon. Ryder daydreams about shagging Coach Rush's practice tosses out on the field. Maybe he could catch a javelin with his throat and give Marty Ash something to write about. The autopsy could reveal to the universe that *there was no blister.*

Coach Rush's strength and conditioning programs, along with his *ethic*, are unwavering. He doesn't play to the testosterone-pumping stereotypes. No AC/DC blasts. Girls are not only welcome; they are recruited. He never plays favorites. He's known to ignore the overachievers who arrive in high school having been given the equivalent of a private education when it comes to sports, the kids whose parents paid for summer skills camps and signed them up for traveling teams to tournaments out of state. Coach Rush watches out for the kids who haven't had teams or coaching. Street kids. He hates athletic fees, a hurdle some families can't clear and a barrier, sometimes, for kids who might need the opportunity the most. More than once Coach Rush has gone to the school board meetings in downtown Denver to plead for the elimination of all athletic fees. It's a plea that gets routinely ignored.

Coach Rush explains about the grant he wrote and won from a foundation for the four-week summer training work, and Ryder quizzes him about what it took to apply.

"How's that blister?"

Ryder yanks off the simple bandage, holds up his finger for inspection.

"Then how come you're not in Detroit?"

"You haven't heard the rumors?"

"Where would *I* hear a rumor?" says Coach Rush. "I watch the ten o'clock news and I scan the morning paper, thin as it is."

Don't bother reading tomorrow's Denver Post, Ryder wants to say. The Marty Ash story is going to be brutal. Ryder should call Ash and apologize. He should call to try and soften whatever he might write. But that would mean answering the same questions.

For Rush, Ryder lays everything out, from Billy Jaworski to Rick Ankiel. The account is anchored with one key phrase: "I can't throw a strike to save my life." Ryder mentions the smooth-throwing pitcher on the ball field outside and how he doubts he could throw high school batting practice and keep it in the zone.

"Nick Worley—he puts in his practice time up here." Coach Rush points to the weight room. "First one here, last one to leave. Strength and balance, both. He can run all day too. Nicest kid ever."

"Smooth style," says Ryder.

"I watched the Jaworski stuff and the so-called brawl it provoked." Coach Rush was never much of a natural talker. His herky-jerky leaps from topic to topic are well known.

"And."

"And if I were to hazard a guess, you didn't mean to throw at him."

"How could you—"

Ryder leaves the question hanging.

"Everything went south after that?"

"I went out to pitch a side session. During the suspension," says Ryder. "And—"

And what?

"So what do you want from me?" Coach Rush's gaze is matter of fact, but it could be saying, *What the hell are you doing here?*

"I need to start over," says Ryder.

Coach Rush shakes his head. "Start over? *You?*"

"Rebuild."

"You think you're some kind of computer—you can wipe the memory drive?"

"I'd be fine with that."

All his memories? Deon too? Bring it on.

"Computers are machines. Linear. You don't want that."

"I need a new head, brain—something."

"You want me to watch you pitch?"

"If you can call it pitching."

"I'm not the baseball coach. I'm straight-ahead physical education. A generalist."

"I know."

"You worried about Jaworski?"

"Of course."

"You hated hurting him."

Ryder shrugs. "Yeah."

"You didn't feel like it was your job to deliver the payback?"

"I wanted to strike him out."

"So?"

"So I thought maybe my old coach might have seen something," says Ryder. "Tell me what to work on."

"You don't want some yahoo high school coach giving you advice—I can guarantee that. And your pitching coach doesn't want me mucking around with your arm slot or your release point or any of that either. I wouldn't even know where to begin. You think he knows what he's doing?"

"He must," says Ryder.

Coach Rush shakes his head. "You don't want me telling you something different, something that will pull you in the opposite direction, something that might run counter to the ideas he's trying to get across."

"Like a big idea?"

"Big or little. It's certainly not a physical adjustment."

That's not good news. There are few things going on with a pitching motion compared to the billion or more random-shit, free-floating notions bouncing through Ryder's head on any given day.

"I can only tell you one thing," says Coach Rush.

"One is good."

"But you can't hang on this, you know? Don't squeeze it too hard, don't think it's something more than what it is?"

First *glass baby*, treating something like it's too precious. Now he's being cautioned against gripping something too hard.

"Okay."

Ryder takes a drink of water. The air in Coach Rush's office is sticky and still.

"This goes back to watching the Jaworski business."

"Sure."

"You know they replayed that one a whole bunch of times out here?"

"I can only imagine."

"You know they interviewed the baseball coach here at TJ after that—because you never hit a batter in a game in two seasons here. Not one."

"I know."

"You walked plenty, but you never hit a batter."

"Proud of that," says Ryder. "For all sorts of reasons."

"You were like that kid out there—Nick Worley. The kid you saw pitching."

"Seriously?"

Coach Rush shakes his head. He waits. Ryder shrugs.

"All I can tell you is what I saw during that game against Tampa Bay," says Coach Rush. "*That* face didn't know where it was. *That* guy didn't have his feet on the ground. You could have been wearing snow-shoes out there. It looked to me like your mind was bouncing all over the place."

"You saw that—on the tape?"

"You can't pitch with a busy head." Barbells clatter. Coach Rush waits. Stares. Ryder can't recall the last easy-thinking day. "Why did you want to throw so fast? Why did you work so hard on one random skill that is useful for one purpose—throwing one certain type of ball a certain distance from a certain kind of mound? You must have thought it was important for some reason. What was in it for you?"

Chapter 27

Ryder catches the last nonstop out of DIA to Birmingham. He pulls his hoodie over his head against the aggressive AC in first class, and slumps against the window.

It's midnight in Birmingham when he lands. The muggy air coats him in a fine sheen of sweat. Ryder asks a regular cab driver for a recommendation on a place to stay. It's past 1:00 a.m. when he checks in at the Redmont Hotel. They seem happy to have him, but it's a weeknight, so the rooftop bar is closed. Ryder orders himself three tequilas and a ham sandwich from room service. ESPN is replaying the highlights from the Home Run Derby in Detroit. It's Aaron Judge's year. Ryder's mug fills the screen behind the anchor, and they switch to a reporter on the field in Detroit talking about a *Denver Post* story claiming Ryder was defiant and agitated when confronted about the true nature of his injury.

The anchor thanks the reporter and gives the camera a shrug. "Is it a blister?"

The anchor is a longtime figure known for his flashy sports jackets and signature bow tie.

This is a replay of an earlier *SportsCenter*—it's 3:00 a.m. in Detroit.

"Clearly there is something wrong with the phenom Frank Ryder, and perhaps this little brush that baseball had with its own immortality—a brief glimpse into a future where the game is rendered dysfunctional and only salvaged by a radical rule change or two—was only a near miss. However, we know there are other Frank Ryders on the way. Frank might be the first, but he won't be the last. Now, with his injury, perhaps the second half of the season will return baseball to normal and not one where nine out of every ten stories involve Frank Ryder's undeniable dominance over the best hitters money can buy. Yes, Frank Ryder showed us what's possible with the human body. Yes, Frank Ryder was—or *is*—entertaining. He is a freak, and I mean that in the kindest way possible. Mozart was a freak. Symphony number one at age eight? Give me a break. And so was Arthur Rimbaud. Yes, a poet can be a freak. And Arthur Rimbaud was about Frank Ryder's age today when he started writing one of his most famous works, *A Season in Hell*. This is a sports show and not a book club, but we all took English 101 for a reason. That poem, among other topics, posed a question that is central to all of us about the nature of hope and testing the limits of human existence. It's considered a masterpiece, and Rimbaud was nineteen years old when he started writing it. Of course, music and poetry are art and not spectator sports. Of course, nobody wants to see Frank Ryder's career end like this. Of course true fans of the game would love it if Ryder was in Detroit to show us how he can perform in that kind of limelight. If it's a blister, great. Let's get Frank Ryder back out on the mound and wrestle with the question of how baseball is going to answer the existential question that he poses every time he throws a fastball a hundred and ten miles per hour. If there's something else going on, then we can assume that right now Frank Ryder is the one whose season has truly, well, gone to hell."

Ryder boxes with sleep. Over and over he drifts halfway there, only to be yanked back by a weird image or stray comment from the day.

Ryder can't believe the last bed he slept in was Maggie's. The strangest notion of all, and it won't let go, is that Deon Johnson was there in Denver and somehow Ryder failed to notice. Ryder realizes he wouldn't mind if Deon came around for a chat. He has this nagging sensation that Deon is trying to grab his attention.

Ryder's mind grinds. Shards and scraps fire his way from Maggie, his mother, Marty Ash, Coach Rush, and the ESPN commentator. The *Denver Post* story, which Ryder pulled up after listening to the insights from the pompous little asswipe on ESPN, is brutal. Ryder struggled to down a few bites of sandwich, but he downed the tequilas like liquid candy. Maybe he should go a few nights without sleeping before trying to throw again—maybe he needs to empty his tank, and try to thrive on the outer limits of sleep deprivation, so his mind will forget and his body will unfuck itself.

—⚏—

"What the absolute hell are you doing here?"

"Came to see you, of course. And you better be in the starting lineup."

"I'll tell Omar."

"Who?"

"Omar Vizquel. Our manager. Eleven Gold Gloves. You know him."

"Jesus. Of course."

"Jackson Generals tonight," says Josh. "But you must have checked the schedule if you came to Birmingham."

"Maybe."

It was a fifty-fifty chance, right?

"You guessed?" says Josh. They are sitting in Marconi Park with giant coffees and sausage biscuits from Urban Standard. The stop at the coffee shop cost Ryder one gushing selfie with a tall blonde barista named Marie. Josh is a regular, and Marie already knew about Josh's famous brother. She couldn't wait to post the shot on Instagram. "You didn't look? I could have been in Jacksonville or Nashville. Hell, anywhere."

"Lucky," says Ryder.

"And you'd rather sit in Regions Field than watch the All-Star Game?"

"As long as I can get a ticket."

Josh is wearing sandals, long white athletic shorts with the UAB logo, and a gray T-shirt with the word BLAZERS above a fire-breathing dragon. "Not often I have a reason to do that, but I'll get you a good seat."

"Who's pitching?"

It's going to be hard to sit and watch somebody throw with command over the ball, Double-A level or not. Ryder plans to bask in the self-loathing—ruining Jaworski's season, pretending he was available to Olivia, playing rich guy around Maggie, misleading Maggie, using a stupid bandage to dupe everyone, including his own innocent mom.

"Nate Zavala," says Josh. "Good fastball and decent curve—still working on his slider. Changeup is good but, you know, down here we're all working out some sort of issue. You came straight here from—?"

Ryder lays everything out. He's boiled the story down to a few big brushstrokes. How much detail do you need to say your arm doesn't do what it's told? Or that you're hoping to dupe America, not to mention baseball fans worldwide, with a fake story about a tender patch on your index finger? Ryder wonders if talking about his problem gives the glitch more credibility, a better root system in his brain.

Josh listens in pain. His brow furrows, his mouth opens. For a moment, at least, he stops eating. He stares back at Ryder. "The rumors," he says.

"Somebody leaked it," says Ryder.

"And Mom's call."

"She *called*?"

"Said you didn't seem to be yourself."

"I don't need reporters hounding me at home," says Ryder. "That's all."

"So the big issue is you don't have much time to come clean?"

Josh is at least twenty pounds heavier than Ryder, with a wide chest and a bull neck. His hair is military short, which goes with his whole rule-mongering ways. Josh always needs to know how he is being evaluated, wants to make sure it's a fair process. He broods on problems. Ryder only played chess with Josh if they used a timer.

"I've got a few days. Is that what you mean by *much time*?"

"When's your next start?"

The tequila hangover has a vicious streak to it. Ryder avoided taking any pills to attack it, however, and stared himself down in the mirror as punishment. Ryder's mantra for the day is *Get your shit together.*

"Stone hasn't listed his starters for the weekend, but I think it's fair to say I'd go Friday night if I didn't throw more than thirty pitches tonight in Detroit—where, in case you did not notice, I will not be."

"Jesus," says Josh, the weight of it all dawning on him. "How are you going to, you know, come clean?"

"What if I don't have to?"

"You're saying it's going to fix itself?"

"It *unfixed* itself, didn't it?" As far as speedy recoveries go, it's his best hope. "One day to the next. It snapped. So it can snap back."

"How can you not be more worried?"

Ryder gives his brother an aggrieved, pinched-face look. "Seriously? I feel like I'm trapped in an underwater cave at night with five sips of air remaining."

"You shouldn't be sitting here."

"Where should I be sitting? Or do you want me to try and yank the park bench off its bolts and smash it to bits with my bare hands?"

"You aren't pissed off."

"You mean pissed off enough—to *your* liking?"

"You should be starting the All-Star Game tonight."

"I'm reminded of that every five minutes on ESPN."

"I mean, if I was you, I'd be throwing every day and I'd be talking to all those mental-skills guys—they've got to have some way to rewire your head."

Ryder takes a last bite of sausage biscuit, washes it down with coffee. It's so tasty that if he must start over, he'll request a trade to the White Sox organization to play Double-A ball with his brother and the Barons.

"You think panic will help?"

"Not panic," says Josh. "Urgency. Why don't we throw?"

"Throw?"

Ryder says it like he's never heard the word.

"You and me in the park right here. Got your glove?"

Ryder can't remember the last time he didn't have it with him. The glove isn't to blame. It can't be punished or exiled, much as he wishes he had some inanimate object to scold. "Of course."

"Right here. Or we can find a spot in Railroad Park, next to Regions." Josh points toward downtown. Ryder glances at the modest skyline. Birmingham is to Atlanta what Baltimore is to New York. "Casual. *Real* casual, just toss the ball."

Ryder can't picture it. "It's not the same."

"You mean without the big windup and the crazy-ass speeds?"

"Of course. It's a different deal. We're not kids."

"But we're playing a kids' game," says Josh. "All I'm saying is keep it simple, break it down. You know? Take it back to basics."

"And if my arm won't even let me do that?"

"That ain't going to happen."

"No," says Ryder. "Thanks, but no."

"What are you going to do—*wait it out*?"

Ryder is hoping he'll *feel* something, an internal click of approval when his body releases itself back to him.

"If I can't throw today, it's like I moved the starting line again," says Ryder.

"And what the hell does that even mean? You're either working on your problem or you're ignoring it. Ignoring the hell out of it."

Doesn't talking about it with Maggie count? Doesn't dragging the lake with Coach Rush count?

For the hell of it, Ryder concentrates on his toes inside his Nikes. This is a trick of meditation, to focus all your attention on one extremity or joint. Ryder presses his feet down on the concrete pad where the park bench is fastened. He tries, for a moment, to acknowledge where he is and what he's doing and why he's here.

"I'm not ignoring it," says Ryder.

"Then let's throw," says Josh.

"And I said that ain't the deal."

Ryder has no doubt he can handle a casual game of toss.

Right?

"So show me," says Josh.

"There's no point."

"Jesus," says Josh. "You are one stubborn son of a bitch."

"Stubborn is underrated."

"And helps keep you stuck when it's time to try something new. You're banking on hope. How will you even know when to try it again?"

"I'll know."

"*How?* How, how, how, how? Let's say you decide to try tomorrow. It doesn't go so well, and then you wait even longer until the next time you try."

This is Josh Logic. It's also Josh's worry hole. He can troubleshoot problems for hours.

"It's not going to be like that," says Ryder.

"Because you'll know." The line oozes sarcasm.

"Sure."

"I'm sure Michael Jordan would take the same approach."

"Don't switch sports on me." Ryder finds basketball wacky and unorganized.

"*Baseball,*" says Josh. "Jordan played for the Birmingham Barons. Hit something like .200 his first season down here but didn't give up and went straight to the Arizona League to keep on working at his whole game, everything. The guy goes back to the NBA because of the baseball strike—"

"And gets three more titles as a Bull," says Ryder. "Second three-peat."

"After they retired his number too," says Josh. "He switched to the number forty-five because they had *retired* the twenty-three. And forty-five was the number he wore down here—with the lowly Birmingham Barons. So he wore it as a Chicago Bull too. Just another baseball player working on his game. In fact, the only reason he even tried baseball?"

Ryder shrugs. "I'm not a Jordan nut."

"You should be. His focus? His dedication? Did you know he bought a fancy bus for the Barons out of his own pocket?"

"He could afford it," says Ryder. "And don't forget Jordan was a big-time gambler. Why did he play baseball?"

"Because baseball was his father's dream for Michael—not basketball. His father was murdered, couple of lowlife carjackers after a Lexus, three months before Jordan announces his retirement from the Bulls. And Michael wanted to fulfill that baseball dream."

"Good for him," says Ryder.

"He worked at his game. Hours and hours out taking BP, hands all tore up."

"Doesn't really help me, does it?"

"There's the arrogance we all love. Does Maggie let you get away with this kind of shit?"

"I'm not *getting away* with anything." In fact, Maggie would call him on it too. Ryder crumples up the empty biscuit bag. He stands and gives the paper ball a toss toward a plain metal trash bin lined with a green plastic bag. The projectile wobbles in the air and dinks off the side of the bin.

"Basketball was never your thing," says Josh. "Don't count that miss."

"I'll count what I want to count," says Ryder.

"Good." Josh stands, too, walks his coffee cup to the trash and drops it in. "Keep living in your own world. Frank Ryder's misery room. You act like you were the only one there."

"Bullshit."

"Yeah, you do," says Josh. "And you don't even think about the fact that I had a role."

"What *role?*"

Josh jerks his thumb. "Calling for the pitch inside."

"Nothing to do with it."

Josh shakes his head. "Fuck *you.* Or maybe you think you're the one who gets to decide who else gets to deal out the guilt cards? Is that it? You love having this big heavy burden on your shoulders, don't you?"

"Not exactly," says Ryder. "Not at all."

"Yeah, sure." Josh's mouth tightens. He shakes his head. "Gives you a reason to carry around this hard exterior, that inscrutable woe-is-me bullshit—which, by the way, is pretty hard to take, given your contract and your sprawling condo in the sky in Baltimore, and, Maggie or no Maggie, we all know the girls who must come around and throw themselves at your feet."

"It's not like that."

"Bullshit."

"If there are temptations in Birmingham, there are temptations in Baltimore."

"Maybe." Ryder flashes on an image from a file he'd like to forget. Labeled *Toronto*. "But—"

"Then *get some*. Enjoy the fuck out of your endless waterfall of cash. Own it. Balls out. I bet you don't even know *how* to enjoy it. You put on a fancy suit, and it probably makes your skin crawl, if I know you. You probably hate your fancy digs too."

"Fuck off." Ryder is toe to toe with Josh, wishes they were somewhere he could raise his voice without attracting interference. It might feel good to come uncorked. "I offered you a big-ass chunk of the signing bonus."

"Because I didn't take it means, what? I don't get to speak my mind?"

"I think the envy is obvious."

Josh shakes his head. Offers a forced smile. "Then think again."

"You like seeing me here. You like seeing me out of sorts."

"Not one scrap of truth to any of that. I'm playing *baseball*. Yeah, the money down here ain't much. But I'm working on my game, man. I've got good friends on the team. I've got a few irons in the fire as far as girlfriends go. I get nicely laid once or twice a week. We keep it real. We go out for pizza, see movies. I play video games with guy friends and my girlfriends. We go bowling. I take my dirty clothes to Suds n Duds. Once a week. I come out to a game or practice, and ninety-nine percent of the pressure I feel is because I want it there—to get better. I'm not the focus of an entire fucking sport. So why the absolute hell did you come here if you wanted to make me feel like shit?"

Ryder, in fact, isn't sure. "I had time. I wanted to see somebody I knew, I guess."

"You guess? Come on, Frank. What the hell are you doing? You think you're never going to run into problems if you pitch for another twelve, fifteen years?"

"No."

"Then you better come up with a plan to face your first real problem—yes, first real problem, because Deon Johnson was an accident, and we all know it was an accident. So either you're going to come up with a plan, or you're going to dig down in your foxhole of misery a little deeper and cover yourself up even more. Why? Because you're not even going to let someone help you figure this shit out."

Is this why Ryder came to Birmingham? To have his brother slap him around?

"You got all that money and you think it's not a physical thing, because otherwise you'd be throwing the ball with me right now, like we used to do when we'd sneak out to the park before you got quote-unquote *discovered* at TJ. Back when the parents didn't want either of us playing baseball—and don't forget, that applied to me too. Right? I was under the same orders from the parents, and don't forget I liked baseball as much as you did. You think you like baseball *more*? Is that it? I'd like to see you like baseball when it comes without all the pampering. So you got money and you're sitting here hoping your arm heals itself through, what, some sort of mystical bullshit intervention?" Josh walks away, shakes his head, turns back around. "Anyway, you got all this money, so go hire a shrink who can shrink you good and shrink you fast because, dude, time is really running away from you. Right now."

Chapter 28

Ryder jogs in the Alabama afternoon heat, punching his way through the hazy humidity. A thirty-minute loop from the hotel leaves him drenched. He rows for a half hour on a machine in the hotel's cell-like fitness center. He works his way around a busy bundle of machinery with pullies and weights, punishing his arms and legs. The air inside is cool. Cool and lifeless. The room is cramped. Ryder sweats alone.

After a shower in his room, Ryder checks his email for details on check-in and hotel information in Atlanta.

Of all the places for the All-Star Game.

He replies to a text from Lackland.

Ryder: Have not thrown.

Lackland: Feeling better?

Ryder: The break is good.

Lackland: Where are you?

Ryder: Does it matter? Visiting my brother.

Lackland: You hearing all this chatter about you?

Ryder: Probably not ALL.

Lackland: That's good.

Ryder: Yeah.

Lackland: You going to watch tonight?

Ryder: The Birmingham Barons, yes.

Lackland: Michael Jordan's old team!

Ryder: I'm aware.

Lackland: See you in Atlanta. Get to the ballpark around 11 a.m. and we'll see what we got.

Ryder: Throw, you mean.

The response takes five minutes to come through.

Lackland: Unless you're wanting to switch positions?

―⁘―

The Birmingham Barons struggle with every phase of the game.

Ryder's seat is ten rows up behind the Barons' on-deck circle, so he has a good view of Nick Zavala's very average work. Even Ryder thinks he would have been able to smack one of Zavala's pitches, but in the minor leagues the DH is universal unless both teams are affiliates of the National League. The Barons are American League.

Nate Zavala throws strikes. Control is no problem. He is a big moose of a pitcher with one stoic expression. Zavala's pitches arrive in the strike zone like gifts. There is no tease or tact. He throws afraid. Zavala is yanked with one out in the top of the third inning, and Josh stands out on the mound with Omar Vizquel, waiting for the new guy to walk in from the bullpen. Vizquel is a definite Hall of Fame candidate, given his years of sure-footed defense with Seattle and Cleveland. But here he is in Birmingham, pouring out his baseball soul. Vizquel needs to stop the bleeding. The Barons are down 7–1. A quiet crowd, given no reason to agitate itself and induce more sweat, has switched to full church mode.

Josh's mask sits on top of his head. He wipes his brow on his sleeve. On the walk back to home plate, with the formal butt-whack greeting of the new pitcher complete, Josh stares at the ground in front of him. So far, Josh has yet to look Ryder's way. Even in the on-deck circle during his one at bat so far, Josh could have turned around and given Ryder a head bob or something to acknowledge their brotherliness, their pitcher-catcher bond, but nothing.

Ryder: Are we good?

Waits.
Waits.

Maggie: Hope so!

Ryder: I know I wasn't at my best.

Maggie: Don't be afraid to ask for help.

Ryder: Ask who?

Maggie: Or take it if it comes. Are you still in town?

Ryder: Visiting my brother in Alabama.

Maggie: You were going to call before you left. Remember?

Ryder: Sorry.

Maggie: Dollars to donuts it's not a physical thing. I gotta run ...

—☶—

The fans start coming Ryder's way in the bottom of the fifth. The first is a young girl. She can't be more than ten years old. Her lips are smudged blue from cotton candy. Her auburn hair is in braids. In one hand, she grips a sparkling white baseball like it's the last toy on earth. In the other, a black Sharpie. He asks her name. "Brenda," she says. A whisper. Ryder signs the ball. This girl is the canary in the coal mine. She has come to check if it's Frank Ryder and not some random dude with a bandage on his finger. She is also there to gauge Ryder's reaction—will he mind being bothered? Ryder asks for a high five before he hands the ball back, as sure a signal he can imagine to anyone watching. The girl beams like nobody's business. She scampers off with her prize. He is not a monster.

They come in polite groups, at the inning breaks, and Ryder is glad his seat is on the aisle. Programs, T-shirts, baseballs, and random scraps of paper all get signed, and Ryder wonders how they will feel when they learn they were fawning over a guy who is a fraud. The autograph hunters don't bother him—they are a fine distraction, in fact, from thinking about Friday morning, and now, of course, he wishes he had taken his brother's advice and at least thrown a little casual toss. Would there be a more forgiving throwing partner on the planet? And all Ryder did was piss him off.

Josh strokes a double in the bottom of the sixth, throws out a would-be baseball stealer in the seventh, and gets a seeing-eye single in the eighth. Tonight, Josh is the Barons' highlight reel. The Barons lose, 9–2.

Ryder checks the All-Star Game score on his phone. The National League won in ten innings, 2–1. Ryder glances at the box score. He knows the second run was plated in the top of the tenth. The other run sits, like a perfect matching bookend to all those zeros, in the top of the first.

The message from Detroit is clear. Had Ryder been pitching, the National League would have lost. Had Ryder been pitching, whatever American League team reaches the World Series would have gotten four home games, not three. It's a huge advantage.

And Ryder, fake wounded digit and all, is to blame.

Chapter 29

The ride from downtown Detroit to the Jet Linx terminal at the Oakland County International Airport is slow and long. To add to Gallo's woes, there is a delay in their scheduled departure. The explanation is a rare morning thunderstorm in Baltimore. A doozy. They need to wait an hour and let it clear.

Gallo is ushered to a waiting room that's set up like an all-American generic outer office, an oversize waiting room. He settles into a chestnut armchair. Aiko brings coffee and perches on the edge of a matching armchair, which is big enough for Aiko triplets.

Aiko holds up her phone to show Gallo a photo of a smiling young boy. The boy holds an autographed baseball up for the camera. The boy is rubbing shoulders with a seated Frank Ryder, who has his baseball cap on backward and is grinning like a drunk kid at a frat party.

"Birmingham," says Aiko, shaking her head. "On Instagram. Hashtag blisternoblister. Trending on Twitter too."

Gallo calls Ford.

"The latest?" says Gallo. "Any good news for me. For *us*?"

"No."

Gallo shakes his head for Aiko, who has been treating the Ryder issue like her own personal failing, like she wants to reach inside Ryder's head and massage the cerebellum.

"I don't like that," says Gallo. "You wouldn't believe how I was getting pressed up here, about the rumors."

"Lackland talked to Ryder yesterday," says Ford. As if that explains anything.

"Let me guess. He was in Birmingham."

Ford is unimpressed. "As of last night, that was no secret. His brother plays there. The Birmingham Barons."

"Why is he goofing around in the stands of a minor-league park when he should be doing something?"

"Lackland says Ryder thinks he'll be fine."

"They talked?"

"Well," says Ford. "Texted."

"This is based on text?"

"Yes."

"You can't go on text." Gallo grabs the back of his neck, a sudden throb of pain. "The Baltimore Orioles cannot roll into Atlanta with this cloud over our head. The whole world knows we better get on *Baseball Tonight* and let the cameras zoom in on Frank Ryder's blistered-up index finger—and it better look damaged and tender—or else he better be out there pitching one of those three games."

"I know," says Ford. "Believe me."

"But what are we *doing* about it?"

"We've got the best mental-skills guys on speed dial."

"That sounds like a process," says Gallo. "Sounds like weeks. Or months."

Ford ignores him. "But Frank Ryder has to be willing to work on that side of it, you know? It's a two-way street."

Gallo says goodbye and hangs up. Finger-pointing will do no good.

"Dragon," says Aiko.

"What, now?" says Gallo.

"Don't think I know something about Buddha because I'm Asian. I'm as American as a hot dog."

"Okay." He teases her with an eye roll, but he likes her stray thoughts, what she brings to the table. "I'm all ears."

"Just dragon. Not the creatures, just *dragon*. During our trip to Japan, we visited an old wooden temple near Kyoto and learned about a Zen monk from the thirteenth century. He wrote about dragon. The No-Gate Gateway. Dragon is the force of change. We tend to ignore it, avoid it."

"Dragon," says Gallo.

"Not the beast," says Aiko. "We have to recognize the mountains are moving. All the time. We are part of a life force. Dragon is the embodiment of the ten thousand things. It's contact with that essence."

"How about your grip on a baseball?"

"Frank Ryder is stuck," says Aiko. "He is focused on himself, not aware of his connectedness to everything around him."

Gallo waits. Is there more? "So what does a pitching coach tell him to do?"

"It's not a *do* thing. It's a recognition."

"You feel this, do you? Dragon?"

"I'm studying it. Reading about it."

"So let's get some articles together—books, whatever. Send him a reading list."

"It's not *reading*. It's an openness to the world, awareness that your place in everything is transforming all around us all the time. Constant change."

Gallo isn't sure how it connects. He wants a prescription. A drug. A tincture. A potion. Voodoo. Hypnosis. He wants Frank Ryder to walk back to the spot in the road where the bright light snapped off, to see if he can trigger it to come back on.

"Frank Ryder needs to understand his own walking," says Aiko. "If he doubts the mountains are walking, he does not understand his own walking."

"I don't know what I'm supposed to do with this," says Gallo.

"Do with what?"

Gallo is so lost in his thoughts—and trying to picture this non-dragon *dragon*—that he fails to catch the approach of Tommy Rafferty.

"Good Christ," says Gallo. "Isn't this airport about halfway to Chicago? Why not drive?"

Rafferty ignores him. "Don't want to interrupt anything."

Rafferty wheels a chair over, makes himself comfortable. He's wearing gray slacks and a blue shirt. He is marathon-runner gaunt and preternaturally young. "Feeling good?" he asks Gallo.

"Never better," says Gallo. "It's impossible to feel any better than I do at this moment in time."

"You got what you wanted."

"They'll get their way eventually. The clampdown. Whatever." Gallo wants to throw in a taunt, something about the World Series, but checks himself.

"Maybe."

"Might depend on how you do—and how your boy does, after he comes back from his injury."

Gallo detects a slight note of sarcasm on the word *injury*, decides not to bite. "Yep," he says.

"And if he's back to being Frank Ryder of April, May, and the first big chunk of June, then I guess all the pressure shifts to you."

"You'll recall that I don't hit. Or field." Talk of trading players bugs Gallo. As if they are pieces of a puzzle, not people with lives and families. Gallo still hasn't met Steve Penny—and needs to do so. "You're doling out advice? Is that a good idea?"

Rafferty ignores him. "Did you see the article in FanGraphs—the trends of even your best players in the second half of the season? It's not pretty. You're going to need some talent to support your freak—and I mean that in the most complimentary way possible."

Chapter 30

Ryder's Lyft driver is college age. She's got a fat anatomy textbook flopped open on the front seat of her old green Malibu. She studies at Atlanta Technical College, with the goal of becoming a medical assistant. She is cheerful, drives with care, and does not seem to recognize him in any way, shape, or form. Her skin is creamy copper. Her dark Ray-Bans remind Ryder way too much of Agent J—Will Smith—in *Men in Black*.

"I'm thinking of going to California after I get my degree." Her name is Asia. "I'm scared of earthquakes, but the pay is better."

"Family here?"

Ryder's phone dings—a text from Lackland:

Check in when you can. Need to hear.

It's the third such message. What Ryder wants is a text from Maggie.

"Parents and two sisters," she says. "Older sisters. They're staying here, but I feel like I have to change things up. I've gotta choose my own place to live, know what I mean? I want to drive that, not let my parents decide where I make my home. Getting born is an accident, right? I mean, at least, it's not a choice. My sisters don't get it, but that's okay."

It's ten a.m. Ryder took the first morning flight from Birmingham, dumped his stuff in a hotel room at the Omni, and booked his Lyft.

He could have stayed in his room and pretended Friday morning might never come—the first Friday in the history of Fridays to never arrive. But he can't come to Atlanta and not go see.

Ryder: Checking in.

Maggie: From where?

Ryder: ATL

Maggie: The arm?

Ryder: Still attached. Last I checked.

Maggie: Unless you're texting with one thumb.

Ryder: I see two.

Maggie: Good. Have you thrown?

Ryder: No. I have a feeling I know how it'll go.

Maggie: I'm not sure how I can help.

By telling me we're okay? That might help.

Ryder: Can we talk later?

Maggie: Of course. Text me first.

The morning air in Georgia is heavy. It's eighty degrees, heading to ninety. The AC in Asia's Malibu is not up to the challenge. Ryder's blue polo shirt is grafted to his back, a new, damp outer skin. He wears a gray Barons cap with the Old English fancy-lettering *B*, the same style cap Michael Jordan preferred. He's got on a pair of light-tan slacks and brown sandals, no socks. He wishes he'd brought a cold water or two from the mini bar, or a cold beer or two with a tequila shooter.

Traffic clogs their way. "Doesn't matter anymore what direction you're going or what time of day," says Asia.

"California is not exactly known for its open roads," says Ryder. Like he's the expert. Ryder fingers his bandage. "*Southern* California is one big traffic jam. All day. All night."

She looks around at him in wonder. "You been there?"

"Couple times," says Ryder, trying to turn it down now. "Oakland. Anaheim." Back when he was a functioning athlete.

Ryder wonders if parting with a fat chunk of cash might form some sort of bargain that the universe will recognize as secular forgiveness. What if Ryder gives Asia enough cash for a down payment on a modest bungalow in Santa Monica, and the universe gives him back his arm? How's *that* for a deal? He'd skip to the "other amount" on her Lyft tip and leave her $50K. What the hell. Yes? Why shouldn't a hardworking student win the lottery? Why shouldn't he be able to find a simple path to a hassle-free Friday morning? How should he inform the universe of this plan? Or does the universe track such deals all on its own?

"I want to be near the water," says Asia. "I want to sit on a cliff and look out at the ocean, watch the sun drop down and get swallowed up. That's all I ask."

—⁓—

Atlanta sprawl has engulfed Alpharetta. It's been that way since Ryder was a kid, but there are new office buildings and developments he doesn't recognize. The trees don't seem so imposing, as if they have been discouraged. He and Asia are on the highway, crawling along.

Ryder imagines the twisty single-lane roads winding through the pines past brick ranch houses from a vanished world—crappy carports with banged-up metal garbage cans and rusting tools, their roofs strewn with dead pine needles, smack dab up against new communities where the palatial houses hide behind horsey white fences with imperial gates and the HOA cleans the streets, picks up trash, and arms security guards to protect their massive mansions. Sprawl displaces hardscrabble work.

The big shopping center isn't a shopping center but its own mini city. There is no actual need to leave. It's called Avalon, of all things, and Ryder wonders if Asia might want to detour through its streets so Ryder can keep an eye out for outsize swords jammed into giant stones. Perhaps the universe has drawn him back here to demonstrate he is the one true king.

Find that stone.

Whatever consumer wonderland is Avalon isn't visible as they exit Highway 19. Asia heads east. She is following the directive of the map app on her phone, mounted on her dash. They wind east on Webb Bridge Parkway, past the Alpharetta International Academy and through Georgia pines and high-end residential enclaves and country estates that whisper, *You might be welcome* but, well, maybe not.

Pedestrians are not encouraged on the one-way road that leads through the manicured woods.

Webb Bridge Park is a place apart. No kid will ride their bike here. This place was built for moms with monster SUVs or minivans piled with offspring. Fields A, B, C, and D cluster around the low-slung stone building in the center of the clutch of diamonds.

"This won't take long," says Ryder. "Any chance you could wait?"

"I have class in ninety minutes," says Asia. "How long?"

How long can it take? He needs to check this box, offer one last heartfelt apology, and get back to not thinking about Friday morning.

"Fifteen minutes, tops," says Ryder. "Keep the meter running."

"I am never late to class." Asia means business. "Lettin' you know."

"Deal."

Halfway up the tree-lined pathway, passing two empty baseball fields on either side of him, the pleasant summer ping of an aluminum bat rings out from Field A. It's the only field in use and, of course, it's the one he needs to stare down. It's not a game but another one of those makeshift practice sessions, like the one he watched back at TJ. This time there are four players—pitcher, hitter, catcher, and one fielder who is playing a deep shortstop or a shallow left field. On an adjacent field, a class of elderly tai chi devotees moves slowly and precisely through their forms.

Ryder finds a spot in the shade by the bleachers to stand, wishing for a cold water. The four ballplayers are all in shorts, T-shirts, and ball caps. The pitcher is a lanky kid with decent velocity. His pitches are grooved. He's got a routine. They are high school kids. They play with poise, but they are loose. When they switch roles, the pitcher doesn't rotate. The catcher calls balls and strikes. Ryder imagines implementing that idea at the big-league level. Laughs at his own fantasy. Why did nobody think of this before? In the early days of the sport, the pitcher was seen only as the person who put the ball in play—and hitters were once allowed to ask for pitches to be thrown in a certain way and to a certain spot. Pitchers were nobodies.

Ryder sits on the fourth row of covered aluminum bleachers. The seat is hard and hot. The full fifteen minutes will be punishment, if he can endure it that long.

Ryder stares at the mound. He wonders if the rubber is the same rubber from that day. He wonders if the dirt is the same dirt, if the home plate is the same too. He swallows hard. His vision goes blurry. He wipes his eyes on his short sleeves. It's only a brief revolt, Ryder tells himself. He regains composure, inhales deep, straightens his back. He thinks he has regained the moment but can't look up. He can't look at where it happened. He is light headed and clueless about what he's doing. Or what he's supposed to do.

Ryder listens.

The smack of ball in glove. There is no other sound like it. Something so final. A catcher's mitt emits a heavier, happier sound than a fielder's glove as the ball *thumps* home.

"Ball," says the catcher. He's bored. And tired.

Again, the smack of ball in glove. "Strike," says the catcher. "Right in your sweet spot."

Ping! Ryder looks up. The ball is coming at him, a soft liner with a gentle curve to it. Ryder stands, lurches to his left, and misses catching the ball with his bare hands. The ball pinballs under the bleachers and disappears. One of the kids shouts, "Sorry, mister!"

Ryder snakes down into the gap between the benches. He drops to the ground in the cave-like space and spots the ball. He threads himself back out around the rear of the bleachers into the harsh sunlight. The catcher pounds his mitt. Ryder's index finger strokes the nicks and dings on the ball. Ryder hasn't touched a worn ball in how long? He's spoiled with freshness and new things.

Ryder puts the ball behind him. Peers in for a sign. The catcher shrugs. The catcher turns to the pitcher, shrugs again, looks back at Ryder, and punches the heart of his glove one more time with his bare fist.

It's the universal sign for *Hurry up, motherfucker.*

Ryder winds. He feels the rhythm. His grip is funky thanks to the bandage. He throws the ball to the catcher on a rope. The catcher flinches. He braces himself. The ball zips in with that same pleasing smack, but it arrived with twice the juice of anything he's caught so far today or maybe ever. "Thanks!" yells the catcher, who adds a thank-you wave with his mitt. The catcher is proud of himself for having stood his ground, for not letting his knees buckle. Ryder and the catcher are bonded now. All it took was one throw.

Ryder climbs back to his spot. He can't leave quite yet. He hasn't said what he needs to say, and besides, now he's got a role to play. He's useful. *Goddamn* useful.

And he's not alone.

"Whatever you say, don't say this is the last place you expected to find me—because that would be weird."

Deon is sitting, two rows up, in the top row. He is wearing school clothes—dress shoes, khakis, and a dark-purple polo shirt. He's got one arm resting on his big black backpack. Ryder puts his hands out to the side, palms up.

"Jesus Christ, you are hard to follow," says Deon. "Denver, I figured as much. Birmingham threw me a curveball, so to speak, right there. I didn't see that one coming. So I decided to come here and wait."

Ryder climbs the last step, sits down on the same bench as Deon. Today there is no powder-blue batting helmet. Deon's hair is trimmed tight and sharp. His left ear is round and perfect, the size of a half dollar. His face and forehead are free of sweat, as if he's channeled a cool breeze from the Rocky Mountains.

Ryder shakes his head. He wonders if he's light headed. Did he have breakfast? When was the last time he ate? What was the last thing he said to Josh? Anything? How did he get here? Is this Atlanta? Fifteen minutes—how long has it been? What was her name? Asia, Asia, Asia. Asia had business cards in a dangling plastic sleeve on the console next to the cup holder full of mints, and Ryder should have taken one so he could text her now and say, *Please wait.* Ryder can't imagine if it's been an hour or five minutes. And way down at the end of time, will it matter that he didn't say goodbye to his brother? No text. Nothing. He didn't knock back a beer with Josh after the game, only went to find a dark bar by himself after the game to hide. Will he get punished for that too? Where is *that* scoreboard? And is tomorrow Friday or—

Wait.

Friday morning.

His mind respools the last minute. He punches play.

That toss. When he threw the ball back to the catcher . . .

He remembers the catcher being spooked, wary at what was coming. He remembers the sizzling succulent sound—the ball's stitching cutting the soggy morning air. Is it still morning? Which one?

And the catcher's mitt didn't move. The ball arrived chest high, dead center.

That smack . . .

Ryder closes his eyes, squeezes them tight, puts his head down between his knees.

"What the hell are you doing here?" he says to Deon.

Ryder always imagined himself alone at this moment, maybe crawling out to the mound on all fours.

"Seems like this is right about where I'm supposed to be," says Deon, "since all the shit happened right here."

The throw to the catcher was a *throw*. It wasn't a *pitch*. It was closer to ninety feet than sixty. There was no batter. No windup. He's not off the hook, he's not off the hook, he's not off the fucking hook.

Ryder looks over. Deon is straight faced. Now he's wearing the powder-blue helmet. Where was he keeping the helmet?

Ryder is still thinking about his throw. Should he ask to borrow a glove? Toss a few off the mound and see what's what?

That mound?

A shudder seizes Ryder's spine. He can think of no worse mound if he's going to test his misbehaving arm.

"Let me ask you something." Deon's tone is so la-di-da. Ryder studies Deon's forehead for a blemish or scar. The skin is as polished and smooth as a billiard ball. "Do you think you get to move through life like you're the one, the *only* one, whose presence doesn't impact others?"

An aluminum *ping!* pulls Ryder's attention back to the boys. The ball heads for home run territory. The hitter hotdogs it around the bases, arms up in victory and then flapping, palms up, encouraging an invisible crowd to roar louder.

"I don't understand the question."

"You think you're separate."

"I'm not following," says Ryder.

"Let me put it this way. You think you're special because of one thing you do well. One thing. And it's a strange thing. I mean, stop and think about it. Very specialized and very particular, wouldn't you say? That thing will help you do zero other things. Won't help you put out fires. Or build houses. Or solve equations. Or diagnose a disease. Or paint. Or write. Or teach." Deon pops his eyebrows up like he's waiting for an answer. "Can you think of anything?"

"I know baseball is a game. If that's what you're getting at."

"And don't tell me Frank Ryder doesn't know he's the best of the best."

"Okay."

"And lives inside some kind of bubble."

Ryder is tempted to tell Deon to cut to the chase but doesn't want to tell a ghost that Asia's clock is ticking. That doesn't seem fair.

"And you never accepted the fact that life inside that bubble has consequences on the outside."

"I threw the pitch!" says Ryder. "I killed *you*. Of course I know."

"And you hate yourself for *not* being blamed."

Ryder feels like he's been punched.

"It gets worse," says Deon.

"It can't."

Ryder knows Deon is right. He wishes a thousand long accusatory fingers had been pointed at him. But no. His parents wrapped him in a fuzzy warm cocoon. Blame didn't exist. Blame wasn't allowed. *Blame* wasn't discussed.

"Yes," says Deon. "It gets much worse."

"Not now." The year of homeschooling, the cross-country flight to Colorado. Ryder broke zero rocks, did no time. Yes, it was an accident.

"You've been avoiding this one."

There was the memorial service too. His father went. Frank Ryder was kept at home. As if what he'd done hadn't happened.

Ryder wonders if he can conjure the blame, let it do its job of squeezing the pain out of every pore. He needs to give himself over to the guilt, let it sow a thousand boils and blisters on every inch of his body until he is a writhing mass of white-hot pain.

"I think that's it." Ryder senses a brightness, a lightness. It's the recognition of a path forward. "The blame. I missed a step."

"You don't realize exactly how connected we are," says Deon. "What about all the things that happened to you? What about all the things you've done to the game and all the things you've done *for* the game?"

"What about them?"

Ryder is focused on the fix, the cure, about drenching himself in a fountain of fault.

"You have refused to consider the idea that all this fame and glory would never have come along, that you wouldn't have driven yourself as hard, you wouldn't have focused as much and buried your own self-loathing, if you hadn't killed me." Deon rolls his head around. His eyes too. "Am I right?"

—⁓—

Ryder has no idea how long he's been sitting. He's stewing in a pool of sweat. Alone. The four ballplayers are huddled around a red cooler. Each of the players holds a sports drink with not-from-nature colors. Ryder hobbles down the bleachers, which clang and squeak with every step. He's desperate for shade. It's very possible Asia is sitting in her classroom in Atlanta.

Once his feet are back on soil, he gives a final glance to the cluster of ballplayers. The catcher looks over. He finishes a swig of the drink, its electric-aqua glow like a secret elixir. The catcher gives a little head-bob acknowledgment, his black mask parked on top of his head.

Respect.

Chapter 31

"He'll panic," says Ford. "It'll feel like we're ganging up on him."

"It doesn't have to be an intimidating moment," says Gallo. "I want everyone in Atlanta we can bring in—I'll pay their highest daily rate for the whole weekend. Whatever it takes. I want the best sports psychologist we can find. I want a fresh voice or a fresh coach or two to study his motion. The shrink side of things doesn't need to be a baseball guy. This isn't about the game. It's about performance. It's about clearing your head, it's about—"

What is it about? If Gallo knew, he'd fix it. He doesn't know. As much as he appreciated Aiko's Zen morsels, it feels as if somebody out there knows the cure. Maybe he needs a brain surgeon like Sanjay Gupta. Maybe Mike Mussina can fly in and see what's wrong with Ryder's arm slot. They need drills, workarounds, *techniques*.

"Are you only trying to send a message?" says Ford.

"What do you mean *only*?" Gallo's jet is taxiing after a harrowing flight. They circled way around to avoid a thunderstorm. Gallo is not a fan of lightning. It's raining as they land at Martin State Airport. The sky is an angry black. "I mean that I want us to be ready with every available resource in Atlanta, a team of experts. Maybe they can get down there tonight or tomorrow, start coming up with a game plan of how to attack this thing."

The pause before Ford's response tells Gallo everything he needs to know.

"I'm sure this is not a technical adjustment," she says. "And I'm not sure it's about getting Frank to think about new ideas. With all due respect, I can't imagine anyone who knows more about the thoughts running through his head than Frank Ryder."

"The whole season is on the line in Atlanta."

"I'm aware."

"The whole season," says Gallo. "If Ryder isn't Ryder, we have no shot of taking two out of three. The Braves are good."

"Agreed," says Ford.

"And if Ryder doesn't pitch, it's a PR shitstorm."

Gallo's jet stops with a sudden brake. The plane rocks and settles. Rain lashes the wing and Gallo's window.

"For sure."

"And if Ryder doesn't pitch, and pitch well, it's going to be a long season."

"I won't be needing my plans," says Ford.

At a fundamental level, he distrusts player swaps. The whole concept is rooted in data. He believes in old-school team chemistry, teammates who pick each other up. "You know I hate big trades."

"If we have a shot, we better take it."

"The team was right there before Ryder's suspension."

"Two key pieces is all we need," says Ford. "There are teams selling in late July."

"Which is why we can't leave it to chance in Atlanta," says Gallo. "We can't hope that Ryder shows up, you know, self-cured. What are the odds of that?"

"I don't disagree. The more in the room, however, the more people who can talk."

"Have them sign an NDA," says Gallo. "We don't care if the story gets out later, as long as Ryder is back on the mound doing his thing. We need people there."

"Complete strangers?" says Ford. "If I'm Frank Ryder, I'd think my team is freaking out."

"*Of course* I'm freaking out. Shouldn't someone be freaking out?"

"If he's not better. I don't think we're looking at an instant fix. It's something impacted, like a wisdom tooth burrowing sideways instead of up."

"Sounds like you're throwing in the towel."

"It might be more about finding someone he trusts," says Ford. "The opposite of the technicians, the scientists, the shrinks, the fixers."

"You got an idea?"

"His girlfriend? Maybe?"

"That's what I'm trying to get away from. *Maybes.* It's not any old city, of course."

"I know," says Ford.

"It's very possible—"

Gallo stops, realizes something: they flew to the wrong city for this operation.

"What is it?" says Ford.

"It's very possible Atlanta is messing with his head."

Chapter 32

"How long has it been?"

"Nineteen minutes flat," says Asia. "You had one more minute before my grace period ran out of grace. You were cutting it close, let's say that."

Grace.

Ryder digs in a soft-sided cooler behind Asia's seat. She is backing up and pulling out. She is on a mission. Ryder plucks out a cold bottle, glugs water.

"You okay?" Asia's sunglasses fill the rearview mirror. Ryder can't tell where her eyes are looking.

"Yeah," says Ryder. "Ended up throwing the ball around with a couple guys up there."

"Little too hot for me to think about sweating like that. On a day like this?"

"Seriously."

"Drop you back at the Omni, right?"

"Give me a second."

Ryder pulls out his phone. It wobbles in his left hand. He rips off his stupid bandage because the wrap is frayed and grimy and the phone screen doesn't recognize the foreign substance. Doesn't recognize *him*.

His fingers shake like he's got palsy.

Deon Johnson + Atlanta + Little League.

The answer pops right up—a link about the funeral.

"Westview Cemetery?" says Ryder.

Asia ponders it, running calculations in her head. On the website is Deon's photo—the same photo—of him looking off to the side.

"It's ginormous," says Asia. "Something like, I don't know, last I heard? More than a hundred twenty-five thousand people buried there. They got a mausoleum for ten thousand tombs. Ten thousand!"

Does he want to wade into all that death?

"West of town, as the name implies," says Asia. "A bit out of the way, but saves me from going through downtown, which might be a nightmare. I think we can make it."

—⁂—

The cemetery is, well, dead. Ryder follows signs to a stone building with a stubby tower. Two older men staff the semicool office near the entrance. Ryder holds up the phone screen, as if that is question enough. A trim older Black man jots down the memorial ID number, all nine digits, and consults a map. He is wearing a straw hat, glasses, and white dress shirt. He writes down a plot number and a row on a slip of paper like he's done this a million times. "Right there across from Serpentine Garden," says the man. "You be careful out there. This heat."

The sky is hazy white. The air is so heavy Ryder wants to wring it out in his hands. Trees droop. The road undulates like a kiddie roller coaster. Ryder sizzles in the long, stifling stretches between patches of shade.

Can he conjure the blame? Can he summon the guilt, fill himself to the brim with fault and all the anguish that will come with it? How long will it take?

A sea of markers dots a hillside to Ryder's left; a dark stand of pine trees towers over the road to his right. He slogs up a rise and comes to a flat section, the giant abbey and its mausoleum now in view looking European and ornate.

Tears mingle with the sweat on Ryder's cheeks. Maybe he can find a shovel and start digging. Maybe Deon is down there with his backpack and he needs to be freed. Maybe all these ghost visits have been Deon saying, *Come get me.* Maybe he can sleep under the trees until dark and come out at midnight and start clawing the dirt with his hands, burrow down. It's possible the marker won't be enough proof that Deon's ghost is a ghost.

The map shows him Serpentine Garden and, across the road, the plot where Deon is buried. Ryder finds the row and starts looking at the markers, though his vision is fuzzy. A buzz hangs in the air—buzzing cicadas or a diesel motor idling off in the distance. The sound and the hazy heat press down.

And there is the simple gray stone. It lies flat with the groomed grass.

DEON JOHNSON
A BELOVED SON
BLESSED ARE THE PURE IN HEART

Ryder sinks to his knees. He touches the gold lettering on the black rectangular plaque. The sole design extravagance is a bouquet of engraved daffodils, embedded in a corner. Permanent flowers.

There are two blank stone markers next to Deon's before the labeled stones pick up again. How does it feel to lose a child and go the rest of your life knowing you will join your son in this precise spot, knowing the rest of your life the exact bit of dirt you'll occupy when the time comes?

Ryder sits on the grass with his arms around his knees and his head down, waiting for the weight to come down so he can let it build, like a dam holding back a river, and if his plan is good, he can open the spillway and scream or cry or curse or all three.

It won't come. There is heavy sadness, but it's not much beyond where his mind might take him when he's got his guard down, when he's trying to sleep or standing in the shower and thinking about what being dead really means or when he thinks about Deon playing first base and trying to catch the ball, unaware he'll be gone in a few minutes' time. Or when he thinks about Deon's father bellowing at his son, unaware that he's watching his son's last-ever scene.

Or when he thinks that if one molecular thing had been different about the innings and the pitches and the throws that preceded Deon's turn at the plate. If a double had been a single. If a ground ball had been a home run. Then Deon might have been spared because of how fate writes its scripts. If any double had been a single and if any ground ball had been a home run, after all, doesn't it make sense that Deon would have come to the plate at a different point in time, that the ball would have wound up in Ryder's grip in a different way that would mean a good pitch instead of a bad one?

Ryder has gone around and around with such thoughts, and, now, as he sits here in the heat, at Deon's grave, it's no worse.

Ryder hates that it's no worse.

Chapter 33

Ryder's room at the Omni looks out over the Atlanta Braves' ball field. He stares down from his tenth-floor room across right-center field to the mound where he is supposed to pitch. The stadium is lifeless. The grass is a hazy, mushy green.

A text from Stone told him all he needs to know.

> You start Saturday. Two extra days to heal. Hope you are doing better. Friday morning be ready to throw 20 pitches. 25 tops.

A check online turns up a Buster Olney tweet about Ryder's delayed return. Wright starts Friday, Ryder Saturday. Rhineland goes Sunday, an ESPN game.

Ryder is exhausted. It's midafternoon. Sitting idle in his hotel room will drive him crazy. The morning felt like a week, but he needs to keep moving. Somehow. Some way. He tries to convince himself he left Birmingham that morning. He must have broken some law of physics to be where he is now, to have seen all he has seen in a day. He feels like he's been through the wringer, but he wants to run through it again on a setting that will leave him flattened or knocked out. Something isn't finished.

Ryder unrolls his yoga mat. He goes through the motions. Planks. Lunges. Dead bugs. Ryder stands for scapular wall slides and, back on the floor, grabs his foam roller for the quadruped reach throughs. There is no need to thank his body: not this time. Ryder tries a few warm-up tosses—no ball, no glove, no real target. It's ridiculous. Ryder is outside himself, looking in.

Ryder checks his phone. He has no idea of Maggie's schedule, but she picks right up.

"You were supposed to text first."

"I am sorry," says Ryder. "I forgot."

"I'm heading into class—in five minutes." She is in a busy area, outside. "What's up?"

"I don't know," says Ryder.

"That's not good."

"I went to the ballpark where it happened. I went to his grave. I should be feeling something I'm not."

"And what's that?"

This is Maggie's logical side. Analyze, discuss, develop solutions.

"I think I never felt the blame."

It wasn't as hard to say as Ryder thought it might be.

"You can't be serious," says Maggie.

Ryder is back at the window, staring down at the waiting mound. "Dead," he says.

"You carry Deon around like a load of cinder blocks on your back," says Maggie. "It was an *accident*. Is there blame to be assigned?"

"Some form of responsibility," says Ryder. "My parents—"

"You want therapy now? On the phone? Your parents did nothing but protect you."

"Too much," says Ryder. "They kept me at home for a year and then moved me four big-ass states away."

"You were *twelve*."

"Old enough."

"They didn't think you should be subjected to all the looks or others wondering how you were dealing with it."

"It wasn't discussed."

"It was *instinct*," says Maggie.

"There's a piece missing."

An idea flashes—and it scares him to his core. The idea is obvious, but he would rather try pitching again.

How the hell would he find them? Last name Johnson? In a city the size of Atlanta? And what's to say *they* didn't move as well? Change of scenery. Escape from landmarks and locations that trigger memories of their son.

He explains the idea to Maggie in a tentative way, in case she spots a flaw in his reasoning.

"But how do I find them?"

"Really?" says Maggie.

"Really what?"

"Google, for one. Maybe they did an interview—you know, later. If not, hire somebody. Finding people isn't hard. And then—" She stops. "I have kind of a crazy idea."

"Spit it out."

"Ask your folks. Your mom."

"My *mother*?"

"I had a flash," says Maggie. "That's all."

—⚬—

Ryder orders a cheeseburger, a salad, and two iced teas from room service. He lies on the bed and stares at the ceiling while he waits for the food. Knocking on the door of Deon's parents is the worst idea he's ever heard.

Or the best.

There's a text from Orioles media director Brett Matters:

Lots of requests, as always. Rex Coburn, for one. His preference is Thursday but officially you're still on break. You don't have to do exclusives, unless the network requests one. They will. Friday afternoon is fine if you want me to set a time for all the reporters at once, since you're not pitching until Saturday. You are the only story in Atlanta, apparently. You owe nobody anything, especially Coburn. Don't let him corner you. He'll be moving in for the kill.

And a text from Stone:

Wouldn't hurt to put the old guy's mind at ease, you know. How ya doing? There are some folks up the food chain who would appreciate some information.

And Maggie:

When you find Deon's folks, maybe call over there first? Just a thought.

And Olivia:

With you all the way. If you ever need someone to talk to, okay? Remember drive, drag, snap, release. There's an order to everything.

—ᴍ—

The cheeseburger comes on a plate painted like a baseball. Ryder takes a bite, adds all the extra mustard, and eats half.

For the hell of it, Ryder punches in **Deon Johnson + Buckhead** in the browser app on his phone. He scans a few articles, shoving aside all the paragraphs that talk about the pitcher or the pitcher's identity or why the pitcher isn't being named. His eyes get used to the rhythm of the news stories. He is looking for something longer, more detailed, or perhaps a follow-up story a year later. He goes back to the search and punches in **Deon Johnson + parents + Webb Bridge Park**.

This time a link comes up, and it's a sports story about the Buckhead Braves Little League team and how, the year following the loss of their teammate, the team went on to win the state championship.

> "We dedicated the entire season to the memory of Deon Johnson," said Coach Randy Braun. "We felt his can-do spirit with every practice and every game. And, while they could not be here today, we will be making a special trip, as a team, to present the trophy to Deon's parents."

> Cedric and Gail Johnson, who lost their only son more than a year ago, and who only issued a brief statement after the incident thanking the community for all their support but who have politely turned down all requests for interviews, live in nearby Mozley Park.

Ryder punches in **Johnson + Mozley Park**, but the internet returns no individual names at all. Mozley Park is a neighborhood. It's *Atlanta*.

Ryder goes to Whitepages.com, punches in **Cedric Johnson + Atlanta**, and gets forty-two results—Cedric Lamont, Cedric Lanard, Cedric S., Cedric B, but no Johnson.

He doesn't know what he'd do if he finds the right one anyway. Lyft over and bang on the door? Lyft over and hope his words work when someone answers the door? Lyft over, sit across the street, and wait for someone to come and go? Scare the hell out of them out there on the sidewalk? What would be the first, possible words he would say? That is, if his mouth agrees to work under so much pressure?

The Orioles offered basic media training for rookies. He needs something like that now, to rehearse his message and stick to it.

How will "I'm sorry" sound?

Ryder looks at the article again about the Buckhead Braves winning the state trophy the following year and wonders when Coach Randy Braun took over for Cedric Johnson. Before today, Ryder never had a reason to learn the name of Deon's dad. Why would he? Again, that bubble. It was like his parents whisked him off to a hermetically sealed, emotion-proof room. His parents pretended the incident didn't happen. By the time the fall rolled around, it was understood that Frank and Josh Ryder would be homeschooled. Understood, but never explained. The cause and effect went unstated. Maybe his parents assumed they would get the connection. Or maybe his parents avoided any conversation that might lead to discussing or mentioning Deon Johnson's death in any way.

It was as if it didn't happen.

Seeing the name *Cedric Johnson* is surreal. Ryder flashes on Deon's father. Ryder might not have known Cedric's name, but he never forgot how Deon's father acted, showing up with the Buckhead team and their spiffy uniforms and their black vans, acting like they owned the field at Webb Bridge Park. The scene brings Ryder back to Deon—Deon's *ghost*—and his search for a bucket of blame.

Bucket, pool, ocean—Ryder wants to strap on concrete blocks and sink to the bottom, where it's black and bleak.

His mother answers on the first ring. After the chatty preliminaries, she says, "Okay, Frank, why are you calling?"

"I can't call to say hello?"

Ryder paces in his hotel room—door to window and back.

"Not if you were here a minute ago."

"A few days."

Ryder isn't sure.

"It's not like you to call."

"I'm in Atlanta."

"You *and* your finger."

"Yes," says Ryder.

"Is it better?"

"We'll see."

"Whole world is waiting," she says. "And watching."

"The baseball world."

"It's in the *regular* news too," she says. "What do you need?"

"An address, if you've got it," says Ryder. "Address or telephone number."

"Of course," she says. "Who are you looking for?"

"Deon's parents."

There is a pause. Ryder waits. As tough as it was to say those two words to his mother, to suggest that he might be interested in closing a loop that's been open for ten years, it also feels good. Scary, in a way, but good.

"What for?" *Which means she's got it.* "What are you thinking of doing? I know it weighs heavy on you, Frank, but—"

But what? He is not going to counter her. Or argue.

"Because you're in Atlanta?" Her voice has gone tentative and meek. This is the electric third rail of the Ryder clan. *Do not touch.* "You want to *visit*? What makes you think that's a good idea? What about what *they* might want?"

"At least it will be their choice," says Ryder. "If I call them first."

"They might be embarrassed."

"Embarrassed?"

How is that the issue?

"They aren't very well off."

This doesn't compute with the story in Ryder's head. "I thought Buckhead was a rich part of town."

"They don't live in Buckhead."

Ryder stops at the window, stares out at the expansive green field. The empty stadium looks sad and lonely, even drenched in the hazy Georgia sun.

"You mean now?"

"Never."

"An old news story I found mentioned Mozley Park."

"Is that Atlanta?" she says.

"Yes. Did you go there? Before we left?"

"That was a long time ago," she says.

"But you did."

His mother struggles for words. This conversation is a flashback she doesn't want. The silence is his answer.

"You've stayed in touch?"

"Not *in touch*. Well, we met with them a few months after—" She needs time to compose herself or recall—or both. "We met once."

"And said what?"

"How sorry we were, of course. To tell them you were sorry too."

So his parents thought they were speaking for him, closing the loop on his behalf?

"And what did they say?"

"They said what people say. Polite things. Understanding things. It was all very civilized. And since then, holiday cards every year. I wouldn't say they were Christmas cards, but we send ours at that time of year, to let them know we would never forget. And we won't."

"And they wrote to you too?"

"Ours goes out first, and a week later or so we get one back from them—you can tell it's Gail's handwriting."

"What does she say?"

"It's always short. *We appreciate your kindness* or something along those lines."

This ongoing interaction is something Ryder never imagined. Ryder gives his parents credit. They might have fled Georgia to give him a fresh start and to go to school with a clean reputation, but they didn't abandon the connection with Deon's parents.

"How did Deon end up on the Buckhead team?"

More silence. Ryder fights his own emotions. That first meeting—should his parents have brought him along? Why didn't they? What would twelve-year-old Frank Ryder have been able to say?

"Why now, Frank?"

"Does there have to be a reason?"

"You are bringing all this back up," she says. "All the feelings. You know how absolutely awful we felt."

"I'm curious," says Ryder. "How he wound up on the Buckhead team."

"You know, some people thought the league should have stopped you from pitching—long before it happened."

"That's not what I'm interested in right now."

"Your father might remember this part better than me," she says.

"Give me what you recall."

She sighs.

"They needed a coach. I guess Deon's father was a big sports guy. Baseball crazy. Like you." Ryder hears a smile. There might be tears too. "He offered to help on the condition that Deon could get a spot on the team—something like that."

"Was that a big secret?"

"It was controversial, I guess, with the Buckhead folks—bringing in this poor kid. But we also found out later, rumor mill stuff, that they didn't like Cedric's style. He didn't create a very nurturing environment—put it that way."

"The opposite of you two."

"Yes, parents who think sports are okay if you keep them in their perspective, with a sense about their role in the world, wind up with two sons who play professional baseball. Nurturing? I don't know. It's all good. You're both fine sons and good people. That counts for something."

"You did good, Mom," says Ryder. "What was the last address you had for Deon's folks?"

Chapter 34

"I'm not inclined to trade Cory Bayless."

"Eighth year in the league," says Ford. She is ready. "Every single year so far he has started the year with a bang and each month is progressively less productive at the plate. If we played eighty games each year instead of a hundred sixty-two, he'd be all the buzz."

"He is a star," says Gallo. "One of our best hitters. And a fan favorite. Hey, he's not Brooks Robinson out there at third, but who is? He's damn good. You think this Triple-A kid won't get a case of oatmeal knees when we tell him he's taking over third base at the big-league level smack in the middle of a hunt for the division title?"

Ford is smart enough to not reply quickly. "Bayless is going to be a free agent at the end of next year; Cincinnati is desperate for a good third baseman since their guy Brash tore his ACL, and we get Quinn Martin in exchange. Sixth year. Prime of his career. Total workhorse. Eats innings for lunch and dinner. A lefty—it'll give us a good mix."

Ford is also smart enough to not dive into all his stats. There are acronyms and gobbledygook now that Gallo can't grasp. Even WAR, wins above replacement, remains a concept he can't quite get a grip on. Forget about UZR and the others.

"What's *wrong* with Quinn Martin?"

They are sitting in Gallo's suite at the Waldorf Astoria in Buckhead with Aiko and Stone and Lackland too. Breakfast dishes clutter the coffee table. Gallo is operating off a rough night of sleep. He's cranky. He's worried that by the end of the weekend, the Orioles will be an afterthought, a cute historical curiosity. Frank Ryder will be a footnote in the record books. The Orioles will go back to their job as doormats of the division.

Ford shrugs, looks around. "There's nothing wrong with Martin that we can see."

"Come on," says Gallo.

"Seriously." Ford is wearing a soft purple top with black jeans. Glasses. A fresh, even shorter haircut. All business. She could be a loan officer at a bank, except she dreams baseball, not money.

"You know better than me—we're happy to throw Bayless overboard because we see a weakness. Cincinnati wouldn't put Quinn Martin on the block if he was solid gold, would they?"

"His numbers are knockout," says Ford.

"Good clubhouse guy?"

Gallo admires Ford's proposal. It's the right thing to do, to bring options. She has never done anything other than bring baseball insights and ideas to the table.

"We've done all our due diligence. The answer is yes."

"You're not looking hard enough."

Ford is the only one who grabbed a hard-back chair. Gallo likes that. Lackland and Stone are sunk deep in a white couch. Aiko is propped at the edge of a comfy chair, leaving so much open space on the seat behind her that a Great Dane might be able to sprawl out and take a nap.

"I'm trying to improve the team," says Ford. "Improve our chances. Especially if Frank's situation isn't—what would you call it? *Resolved*, I guess."

"A journeyman like Quinn Martin isn't going to replace a guy who could win fifteen or maybe seventeen more games in the last ten weeks of the season. So why bail on a guy like Bayless in mid-July?"

Ford looks around for help, decides to back down.

"He's got a wife, two little kids," says Gallo. "You're making them move and hunt for houses in a strange city? And don't forget, Bayless expects to be here for the ride, the ride to the finish with Frank Ryder, and he's in a good place on the field with Ortega. And Mario Cruz. The Triple-A guy—?"

"Stenson," says Ford. "Neal Stenson. Hitting .328 right now, eighteen home runs. Lots of pop in his bat."

"You don't know how he's going to react—first time he's in New York? Yankee Stadium? We got six more games in the Bronx, five more in Fenway? Am I right? That's a whole different deal than going into Toledo to play the Mud Hens. I'd rather have Cory Bayless' experience, I'll tell you that right now."

Gallo glances around to read the room. Aiko, who is working on a yogurt and a fruit cup, clears her throat. "We are avoiding the real issue," she says.

"Quinn Martin is insurance," says Lackland. "Pitching insurance."

"So you're in on this?" says Gallo.

"I told her you don't get that kind of talent every day. He's under the radar." Lackland has already powered his way through a ham omelet with grits on the side. "I know it's not an easy call."

Stone and Lackland both look tired and worried. Preoccupied.

"Is *any* insurance really going to mean a thing?" says Gallo. "We're kidding ourselves, right? One thing got us here. Has anybody heard anything?"

Lackland and Stone exchange a glance. Ford shakes her head. "These off days belong to them," says Ford.

"And we're back to hoping."

"We've got Bob Tewksbury here," says Ford. "Waiting and available. Best mental-skills coach in the game."

"What did you tell him?" says Gallo.

"I kept it vague. But he can read between the lines."

"Isn't that a conflict with his current team?"

Ford smiles. "Not if he's not getting paid."

"Not getting *paid*?" says Gallo. "Why in the hell would he do that?"

"He said he didn't want to see it end like this."

"It?"

"He knows why he's here," says Ford. "Happy to help if he's needed."

"You never mentioned Frank's name?"

Gallo can't believe it.

"No," says Ford.

"But he knows?"

Ford looks around the room. "Without question."

"The whole country," says Aiko. "The whole country knows what's going on."

Chapter 35

The Johnson house is white but eager for a coat of paint. It sits near the middle of the block. Compared to the two on either side, the Johnson house is the neatest. The grass, suffering for the most part, is evenly clipped.

It's 9:00 a.m. This is Ryder's third trip to Mozley Park. Right after he got the address from his mother, he took a quick shower and grabbed a Lyft. On the first trip, his heart tried to stop him the whole ride out. He steeled himself to knock on the door. No answer. He retreated to his room, ordered room service, tried to eat, and promised himself he would go out to the ballpark and give his pitches everything he had come Friday morning if he connected with Gail and Cedric Johnson. If he says everything he's got to say. And if he says how he would trade everything to bring Deon back. Every win, every pitch, every strikeout, every bit of attention. A million times over—he believes that with all his heart. On the second trip, he found himself calm, as if rehearsal had paid off. But his knock was greeted by the same dull nothing. There were a few more people around the neighborhood, but the Johnson house did not stir.

Now, in the morning, his heart is back to asserting itself. One pale-yellow light is visible through vertical blinds in the front window. It's the first sign he has seen of human activity. It's enough that he tells his driver not to wait. Ryder takes the three concrete steps to their door with his head up. He wears tan slacks, brown dress shoes, and a white short-sleeve shirt. It's the most respectful look he could put together.

Ryder knocks. The response is the muffled sound of a human stirring. It's a sound Ryder can't specify. It is subtle and yet unmistakable. Thirty seconds pass. It could be an hour.

The door opens with a crisp clack.

She is medium height. Her face is wide. For a split second, her expression is unchanged. Neutral. The next, a faint sparkle of recognition. She stands up taller.

"Well," she says. She swings the door open all the way. "We don't get too many superheroes in this neck of the woods." She stands back and waves like a traffic cop, getting him to hurry up.

"Mrs. Johnson, I—"

What?

"Wait," she says. The word is like a pardon all by itself. "Come in."

She leads him through a tidy living room to a kitchen with green wood cabinets and white appliances past their prime. A rectangle of light from a small window covers the cream-colored top of a four-seat kitchen table. Gail Johnson pulls out one of the red chairs, and it glides on the worn tile floor.

"Iced tea? Coffee?"

"Just water," says Ryder, taking the seat.

"With lots of ice," she says. "Good Lord, this July."

The inside of the house is close—and sticky. Ryder smells bacon and toast.

Gail Johnson is wearing a dark-blue uniform, like a doctor's scrubs but with a patch on her left chest that reads **Arbor Glen** in white script. Her hair is dappled gray. She keeps it short. Simple stud earrings, gold dots, are the lone visible decoration. Ryder puts her at five foot four. Her head is bowling-ball round. She is by no means overweight, but she is sturdy. Her steps in the small space are purposeful. She breaks a plastic ice tray from the freezer into a square plastic tub, scoops ice with a glass, and turns on the tap in the sink for what little water will fill the space that remains.

Was this a glass Deon used? Is this where Deon sat?

She plunks the glass down on the table for Ryder. She finds her own drink, but only chips of ice remain. Her glass oozes beads of sweat.

"Thank you," says Ryder. Wouldn't it be easier, he thinks, if she asked him questions? It would be great if the questions were posed so he could answer "yes" or "no" and not have to form complete sentences. "I appreciate a few minutes, if that's all we've got."

Gail Johnson finds her phone on the counter, holds it up. The phone is out of place in a kitchen that belongs in a retro photograph. "We got a good fifteen minutes," she says. "Not exactly the kind of job where you want to be late. Meals come with their own clock."

"Meals?" says Ryder.

"I'm a kitchen supervisor at a senior center. Assisted living. Lunch at eleven thirty, and the folks start lining up a half hour before that. Thank God for my wonderful crew." Gail Johnson presses her palms together in front of her chest, looks up. "I got lunch and dinner duty today, so we have a few minutes. A few."

"I don't know where to begin," says Ryder.

The moment blurs. She sits down opposite him at the table, says nothing.

"I didn't want you to think I forgot," says Ryder.

She nods. Sighs. Nods some more. "Thank you," she says.

"I think about Deon every day."

Seen him too. Here and there. He has quite the vocabulary—tell you what.

It's not a good idea to mention the sightings.

"You have made quite the splash," she says. She says it again, softer. "Quite the splash." Shakes her head.

"The attention doesn't mean I forgot."

"Who knew? Right? Well, some people knew. You knew."

"I'm not sure what—"

"That you had a reputation. The pitcher no team wanted to face. Did you know that?"

"Kind of."

"I remember Cedric saying—"

The memory is too strong. She stands up, plucks four tissues from a box on the counter, and returns to her seat. She presses both hands to her face, the tissues tangled in her fingers. She takes a minute to compose herself.

"I remember Cedric saying that facing Frank Ryder, back then, that the best thing was to swing and hope." The tears come. "Hope for the best."

The last four words come out in a whisper.

"I wanted you to know he's still on my mind."

"The last time I saw Deon, he was going out that front door." She points through the kitchen wall. "And Cedric was saying it over and over—*Swing and hope, swing and hope*. Over and over. *Better to go down swinging than looking*." She smiles at the sad memory. "I guess not much has changed, has it?"

"No, ma'am."

"And Cedric coming in that same door, alone. He went to the hospital with Deon, even though it was too late. It's what you do, right? Anyway, he could have called from the hospital, but he didn't want to tell me on the phone. You know, I thought maybe it was a long game and maybe Cedric took Deon out for an ice cream or something after. Maybe to celebrate. It seemed like forever, and Cedric comes in alone and he was the saddest man I've ever seen. It took me a long time, I mean a long time, to understand what he was trying to tell me, but I think I knew the second I saw him come through that door. Sometimes a mother just knows."

"I need you to know I wish I had come to the service." Ryder wonders if he could pick up his glass of water without giving away a telltale tremble. "So I could tell you I was sorry. So I could tell you and your husband. And all Deon's friends too."

"You ask me, your parents were trying to protect you. I can't say we expected you to be there. But I have to admit." She turns to look at Ryder. "It wasn't easy at first—when Cedric first spotted your name on the list of prospects. Of course we knew you were in Colorado."

"Yes," says Ryder. "My parents' choice, of course."

"Because your mom sent cards every year—she told us you had moved. Good Lord, I can't even imagine a state like that, all those mountains. So Cedric started following you at college. He'd tell me every time you pitched how well you were doing." Gail Johnson stares like she's got x-ray vision. She doesn't blink. "Every game, I'd get a little report, and, you know, it made us feel good in a way. Somehow. I think it helped me more than Cedric. And the reporters did all those stories when it was clear you would be the number one, what's the word—?"

"Pick, you mean?" says Ryder. "Pick in the draft?"

"Yes, pick. You got *picked*. Chosen. The top dog. And Cedric tells me the money they were offering you to sign. A bonus just to *sign*. Pick, sign, go to the bank. Haven't even reported for work yet, am I right?"

This topic, in this house, makes Ryder squirm. But perhaps it's part of his penance. "Yes, ma'am."

"You were good," she says. "You must have worked hard. And you are really good now."

Ryder doesn't deserve to have Deon's mother be so gracious. *Understanding.*

A lump tightens Ryder's throat. "I never know what to say."

"I know Cedric and I talked about the fact that *you* never said much about it," she says. "We took that as a sign of respect."

Ryder takes a moment to imagine how this might be the case. "And all they wanted was how it all made me *feel*, as if there is some way to describe it. But there isn't much to say."

"There's not, is there?"

"Nothing that sounds real," says Ryder.

"No," she says. "It's just words."

"You know I would do anything—*anything*—if I could go back and change it."

"We know," she says.

"I'm relieved you don't hate me."

"Hate you?"

"Or blame me."

"It was an *accident*."

Ryder nods, says nothing. The word *accident* is not forgiveness. Saying it changes nothing. The word should be a gift, but it causes pain.

"There were times I thought about asking your mother to send you a note from me," says Gail. "I tried writing it once or twice. I could never get it quite the way I wanted. Maybe it's better in person like this."

Ryder shakes his head, shrugs.

"Now you have two lives to live."

"Two?" says Ryder.

"Live the life you were going to live," she says. "And live another life for Deon. But stop carrying him around. He is gone. He is most definitely gone."

Gail Johnson beams a wide, full smile—the same one she'd give if Deon magically appeared in the kitchen door right now, backpack and all, wanting a peanut butter sandwich. She is crying through the smile, but it's mostly smile. Ryder nods his head up and down. It's all he can manage. Tears rush in where there should be words. Ryder's chest shudders. He clasps his hands together over his knees and hangs his head.

"And you know it's fine to talk about him, to talk about what happened," she says. "Help other people understand. Accidents are accidents. We didn't choose to be born into a world where you don't get to control your own fate. We're just here. Accidents are a *part* of this world. Part of the bargain."

Ryder is still thinking about the two-lives idea. He's struggling to keep up with her.

"Think you're going to hide?" she says. "They got earthquakes and tornadoes for that, or an airplane can fall out of the sky. You might be in the airplane. You might be ironing a shirt in the house it hits. Either way. We must deal with what's *here*. The world we got."

Ryder isn't sure he could form a coherent reply if they paid him ten million dollars on the spot. The tears flow from a newfound wellspring deep inside. He sobs.

"I know," she says. "That's the one thing I could never get Cedric to understand."

Ryder wipes his face once with his palms and again with the sleeves on his shirt. He's got a bad vibe about the question he wants to ask.

Gail Johnson is lost in her thoughts. She looks defiant, but with no meanness attached to it. Undaunted.

"And Cedric?" he says.

There it is. He's put it out there. Ryder needs to know.

She takes a sip from her now-iceless iced tea. She sighs. She smiles that fearless smile again. "Can I show you something?"

She leads him through the living room and down a narrow hallway. Wood floors creak. The light is dim. The walls look yellow. There are two doors near each other at the end of the hall. One door is wide open to a modest bedroom. There's a bed, a dresser, and a small cross on an otherwise bare, pale-blue wall. Gail Johnson opens the door that's closed. She waves Ryder to go in first, reaches around to the switch. The room fills with light.

The air is stale, like a musty attic. A bright-blue bedspread features a dense coating of stars and outsize planets. Saturn. Jupiter. Earth. A white telescope sits on a black tripod next to a closet door. Three sets of bookshelves are jammed full. A small wooden desk by the bed is home to an old-fashioned desk blotter and a green banker's lamp. In the middle of the desk is a full-size book open to a page about President Kennedy.

"Cedric found this set of encyclopedias at a garage sale for twenty dollars," says Gail. "For Christmas. Deon was happier than if you'd brought him a whole box of puppies. He loved to read. He loved looking at pictures too. We were thinking about getting him a phone, but I'm not sure it would have mattered. He could sit in this room for hours. Some on the internet at school, but mostly books."

"Astronomy?" says Ryder. "I mean, obviously. Right?"

"*Anything* to do with rockets and space. His dream was to have Cedric drive him down to Florida. Cape Canaveral. You could tell him Disney World was right there, but he didn't care. Science, math. He loved school. He loved teachers."

Ryder squats down. There are books about astronomy, a set of books on the planets, some on life sciences. One row is filled with the Harry Potter titles. Most are titles he doesn't recognize. They have a bent toward fantasy. Ryder lets it sink in—twelve-year-old Deon Johnson was a better reader before he died than Ryder is today.

"Deon bargained and pushed and did all sorts of chores, and finally Cedric gave in and the two of them went down one Friday. Five hundred miles. They spent all day Saturday around the Kennedy Space Center. Took a bus tour. All of that. Deon had saved up for a T-shirt, and he also bought this."

Gail Johnson reaches across Deon's desk and plucks a black necklace from where it's hanging off a pushpin on a bulletin board. At the end of the necklace is one of those flattened, elongated pennies with a small image of an astronaut on the moon, saluting the American flag.

"He wore it every day."

Gail Johnson dangles it in front of him, and Ryder fingers the embossed image.

"Every day," she repeats.

Ryder stands up. Gail is sitting on the bed. She is stroking the spread. She is smoothing wrinkles that aren't there.

"Cedric died," says Gail. She shakes her head, tips it back, stares at the ceiling. She comes back, stares off. Her eyes tighten in the face of an invisible wind. "Seven weeks ago, as a matter of fact. Seven weeks ago and a day, but his last three weeks he wasn't here. Not really. The last game he watched of yours was in Chicago—the one where you hit for the first time? He was worried for you. Of course he hated anything to do with players getting hit by pitches, but he watched all your games. He was torturing himself, but he'd been doing that for years. Years and years. Well, ever since."

Ryder shakes his head. He can't believe he never imagined a ripple effect. Of course, other than causing a mountain of sadness. Tears jet down his cheeks. He does nothing to stop them.

"Cedric worked hard. He was a car mechanic. He was good too. So he'd have a beer every night. Maybe two. I'd join him now and then. Weekends, maybe a glass of brandy." Gail stops stroking the bed. She stares at Saturn, starts stroking again. "After Deon died, Cedric started *drinking*. I mean, hard. He got ugly. He lost one job. Another. And he stopped eating too. And then his liver started to fail."

Ryder slumps to the carpet, sits back against the desk. It's now that he spots the backpack by the door. It's *the* backpack. The black one. The pack is fat and full. It's heavy with books. He doesn't need to look. Somehow, it's more solid evidence of Deon's death than the tombstone itself.

"He wouldn't even be buried next to his son," says Gail. "There was no relief, no rattling it loose. He insisted on cremation, what little was left of him when he finally died."

"Because of me," says Ryder.

"No." A whisper. "Don't think that for one precious second. Cedric blamed *himself*."

Ryder shakes his head, trying to picture all the pain he caused. The floor rolls like they're at sea.

"Look at this room," says Gail. "Do you see one sports poster? Anything? Cedric pushed Deon. Pushed him and pushed him. Told him that in order to be a man, a *complete* man, you had to be on a team, get yourself into shape. Cedric hated that Deon carried an extra ten pounds or something like that. Ten pounds at twelve years old? Big deal, I said. Cedric gave Deon a hard time about that. A real hard time. You can be a good person with ten extra pounds, or fifty for that matter. But Cedric believed every kid, boys especially, needed to play sports."

She pauses, shakes her head.

"Deon even had a plan for that," she says. "He knew that come college he'd get in shape, start working out to become an astronaut. He knew the *precise* physical requirements, and he would get on top of those issues when the time came."

The tears can't be stopped. Ryder doesn't try.

"That day, Deon did not want to go. He knew he wouldn't get to play. All the other kids were better baseball players. But Cedric wasn't having it. Cedric thought he could change Deon by yelling at him, screaming at him to 'put on your goddamn uniform and get in the goddamn car and just try harder to enjoy the game, learn how to play it right and play it well.'"

Ryder weeps. "I am so sorry," he says. "So sorry."

Gail Johnson is lost in her thoughts. She studies him through wet eyes.

Ryder shakes his head, waiting.

"I know," she says. "*Everyone* knows you're sorry. We can see how you carry yourself. We all see how you talk, how you think."

"But do you forgive me?" says Ryder. It's the question he's been meaning to ask since forever.

Gail Johnson nods her head. She puts a hand up to cover her eyes. Her fingers are nicked and worn. "Of course," she says. "But it's on one—oh, what do the lawyers call it? Stipulation."

Ryder's throat is a knot. His eyes burn and flood at the same time. "Name it."

"That you don't think I'm in charge of your feelings."

Ryder sighs, steels himself, tries to find level ground.

"Got it."

"Because I'm not."

"I understand," says Ryder. "Completely."

"You're a good man, Frank Ryder. Your mother is a good mother. The notes she writes every year—she takes time to say something different every year. I feel her heart. I feel your heart too. And now I can *see* it."

Ryder shakes his head, struggles for a breath.

"I'm a Christian," says Gail. "I believe, in my bones, about forgiveness. Its power. And I forgive you. You have suffered for years, and now it's time to live your life in full. No more guilt. I am Deon's mother, and I think of him every single day with all the love God has given me in my heart. That's for me and me alone—so you leave Deon to me. And God."

Ryder's body shudders. Something drains out of him. Something fills him up.

"I have one minor request," she says.

Ryder nods. It works better than trying to form words.

"You will be in the World Series," she says. "I know it and I feel it. When you make the last pitch to win it all, say to yourself, 'This one is for Deon.' That will take care of it all."

Chapter 36

Gallo stands in a tight huddle with Stone, Ford, and Aiko Tanaka. The massive indoor practice room, artificial turf covering the floor from wall to wall, is divided by flowing curtains of black netting that define batting cages and pitching chutes. Each of the smaller areas is accompanied by a white observation platform that is four steps above the turf. The platform is intended for one or two people, not four. The indoor air is dead, much too still.

Gallo is tense—and, despite the expansive room, claustrophobic.

A distant door opens. Gallo turns at the sound. The door closes with a raucous bang. Coming toward them are Ryder and Wyatt. Gallo hopes he can pick up a signal from the pair, but curtains of black netting make it hard to discern much in the way of body language. The twosome are inscrutable. Ryder wears long blue shorts, a plain orange Oriole T-shirt, and black cleats. Wyatt is dressed in his full catcher-gear regalia, mask up on his head, but he's dressed like a chill college jock—dark sweatpants and gray T-shirt.

It's 9:00 a.m.

"Jesus," says Lackland.

"Jesus H.," says Gallo.

"Good Lord," says Ford.

"Well said," says Stone.

Aiko stands with her arms folded across her chest. She is sharp and cool, in a dark-blue skirt and a green blouse. She's in heels but still so tiny she could pass for a high school freshman. "It is what it is," she says.

"How is that helpful?" says Gallo.

"It's not *helpful*." Aiko smiles. "It's fact."

"Jesus," says Lackland.

Ryder is first through an invisible gap in the netting. Wyatt follows him in, gives Ryder a tap on the butt with his catcher's mitt, and heads to home plate—a stark pentagon, no batter's box or diamond to go with it. Without its normal accoutrements, the plate appears even smaller.

"He claims he's fine," says Stone.

"Has he thrown at all in the last few days? Week?" says Lackland.

"He doesn't seem worried," says Stone. "That's all I know."

"I'm a wreck and he's la-di-da?" says Gallo.

"He said something clicked," says Stone. "Said he did drills in his hotel room last night, and everything felt good."

"We got Tewksbury on speed dial just in case," says Ford. "He could be here in ten minutes."

"And if it's something mechanical?" says Gallo. "Physical?"

"It ain't that," says Lackland. "Guaran-fuckin'-teed."

Ryder stands in front of the mound. Wyatt stands about eight feet in from home plate. They toss the ball for a minute.

Wyatt steps back after each third throw. Soon, he's behind the plate, and Ryder inches up the mound, backward. With each throw, he does a partial windup. He's getting the feel of the distance.

There is something so pure and clean about the way Ryder throws, the sheer sweet soulful rhythm of it. Gallo gets a little lump in his throat. Frank Ryder's motion *is* a thing of beauty. It's rhythm and melody together. The air cries as the ball carves its path. Each throw is punctuated by the pleasing pop of ball into glove, a gunshot snap. The sound echoes in the giant hall.

Wyatt squats, pulls his face mask down. Even without a batter and no chance for a foul tip, there is no point in taking a risk.

Lackland digs out his Pocket Radar. He holds it up where they can all glance over. Gallo tells himself he doesn't need numbers to know if Frank Ryder is back, but the confirmation doesn't hurt.

Eighty-five.

Ryder's tosses appear effortless. He lands comfortably after each throw, catches the return from Wyatt, climbs back up the mound, taps the rubber with his foot, and begins all over again.

Toss, *pop*, catch, climb, tap.

Wyatt is a statue. The pitches aren't strikes. They are strikes within strikes. Pitcher and catcher are connected on a blurry white filament, an indoor jet contrail of white light.

Ninety-five.

Ford turns and gives Gallo a hopeful look. She shakes her head. Her eyes sparkle.

One hundred.

Nothing changes in Ryder's motion or routine.

Lackland leaves the radar gun with Ford. He steps down to the artificial turf. He walks around behind Ryder and stands halfway up the mound behind him. The extra person in Ryder's orbit, on *his* mound, doesn't change his focus.

The ball's arrival in Wyatt's glove is accompanied by a new note on the scale. It's more tenor, more staccato. It's a cleaner sound and even snappier.

One hundred and five.

Ford presses her hands together, palm to palm, under her chin.

Still, Wyatt's only motion is the minor bit of rocking he needs to toss the ball back to Ryder. By the time Ryder starts his windup again, Wyatt's target is set. It doesn't move until the ball whacks it again. Ryder could hit the middle of a beer cup if it was nailed to the top of a two-by-four.

One hundred and eight.

"That's eighteen," shouts Stone.

"I know," Ryder shouts back.

"He's limited to twenty-five," says Stone for the remaining three on the platform.

The weight lifts. The Orioles have a narrow window to win. It's this year. It's the few months that remain. The crackdown is coming.

There are eleven weeks and two days left in the schedule. There is time. Catching the Red Sox and the Yankees will be a grind. It will require focus and teamwork.

Toss, *pop*, catch, climb, tap.

One hundred and nine.

Frank Ryder lights the way.

Chapter 37

"*You* sound different," says Maggie.

"Different . . . *better?*"

"Definitely. And you're sure everything is going to be fine?"

Ryder stands at the window in his hotel room. The view of the field and diamond provokes no churning acid or bleak worries.

"Yes."

"You found them, then? Talked to them?"

"The mom," says Ryder. "Gail. I'll tell you the story of Deon's dad soon. Real soon."

"Okay," says Maggie. "How about now?"

"I want to talk about us."

The pause is obvious.

"Really?"

"I do," says Ryder. "I want to talk about the off-season."

"Frank Ryder is looking ahead?"

She's dubious. And right. This *is* a rarity.

"I want to talk about us getting a respectable place to live together in Denver. Nothing out of control. Just something a few steps better than what you've got now. And I want to talk about the fact that I don't want to take our relationship for granted. Nobody really knows how long a career lasts in baseball. I want *us* there when my baseball days are over."

"Frank, where is all this coming from now? There's no rush."

Frank feels a tingly flash of sadness and longing mixed with something like joy. *Weird.* He wants Maggie on the next flight to Atlanta.

"Maybe." Ryder is due back at the ball field in an hour. He's eager to be with his team. "Maybe there's no rush. Not exactly. But I've got some ideas, and I want your reaction. They might be crazy thoughts, but they're not going away."

"Brand-new thoughts? Like since your talk with—"

"Sort of new." Are all the new thoughts since yesterday? He feels like he's been sitting in solitary confinement and has only now realized the door was never locked. "And maybe they've been there all along. It's about finding something that matters."

"*You* matter, Frank," says Maggie. "You've practically launched a national conversation about getting better, about focusing on improvements, about human potential. And think what you're doing for Baltimore."

"How?" says Ryder. "How is one guy throwing a baseball *doing* something for a city? Anything?"

"Come on, Frank, you know. You know very well."

"But ending up in Baltimore was so random. If I was a year younger, it could have been Detroit. Or Kansas City."

"Then it would have been Detroit or Kansas City. It's not. But, Frank?"

"What?"

"You've had a rough stretch. I saw you, remember? You were eating yourself alive. And the whole world was wondering if you were telling the truth or not. I can't imagine. And now you're back to even keel, great. You say you are; I believe you are. Good. But give yourself some time to catch your breath. Don't worry about me, where I live. Go back to doing your thing. Let them all see the fun and loose side of Frank Ryder. And enjoy it. You got a lot of games left."

"I hear you. I think. And I appreciate it. All I know is these ideas in my head," says Ryder. "New ideas."

"Baseball ideas?"

"No. And maybe they're nothing. I don't know. I feel jazzed."

"Not baseball?" says Maggie. "There's a headline right there. Baseball is practically your religion."

"I know," says Ryder. "And I'm starting to have my doubts."

Chapter 38

"Thanks for doing this."

As reporters go, Buster Olney is unassuming. No airs.

"Sure," says Ryder. They are sitting in the dugout. It's three hours until game time.

"Your skipper says you're ready to go."

"Hope so."

"Art Stone didn't want you to start the game last night, the first game after the break, and yet your Orioles went out and put together a nice win on the road to start the second half of the season. What did you see?"

"Good pitching from Wright. Challenged the hitters. And Cory Bayless' clutch hit in the eighth, heads-up base running so he could get to third and score on the long sac fly from Penny. Good team win. Someone always steps up."

"Does your clubhouse believe you can overtake the Red Sox, challenge the Yankees for the division?"

"One hundred percent."

"With the lineup as is?"

Olney knows hundreds of famous ballplayers; perhaps he knows what Ryder is feeling. Should Ryder cough it all up, lay himself bare? Ask for advice?

"We have loads of talent," says Ryder. "We wouldn't be in this position if we didn't."

"And what's your mindset going into tonight? After so long a break?"

"No different," says Ryder.

"The arm?"

"I feel ready."

"What was going on?" says Olney. "There were rumors that it was something other than a blister."

"Rumors." Ryder shrugs.

"And this all started, as we know, with that incident in the game against Tampa Bay. All that business with the unwritten rules of baseball."

"That's a big book," says Ryder.

"Yes," says Olney. "As our fellow announcer Tim Kurkjian likes to remind us, it's a long one. Do you think about that situation very much? What will you do if you're faced with the same decision again?"

There is no point in trying to sell the same old line. There is no point in trying to prove his intentions were good.

"It is hard to sit here and say what I would do," says Ryder. "What I know is I'm part of a good team. We watch out for each other."

"That's code."

"It's true."

"That's code for status quo. Leave the game the way it is."

"Would I prefer baseball players not take the slightest offense and turn it into a situation where you could hurt somebody?" says Ryder. "Yes."

"You of all people," says Olney. "Of all pitchers."

Ryder nods. "Yes."

"Do you think those unwritten rules need to be eradicated, somehow, from the game?"

"I think we need kids to keep coming to the park to watch the game," says Ryder. "Not see their favorite players taken off the field on a cart."

"What *does* go through your mind out there?"

Buster Olney's style is so matter of fact. His eyes are eager in a youthful way.

"Well, you hope there's nothing in your head," says Ryder. "The better you are in the moment, finding the zone, feeling your cleats on the rubber, seeing the catcher's mitt—and executing the way you're supposed to, trusting in all your practice—the better off your throws."

"But it sneaks in from time to time. Right?"

"Sure. I'm human."

"And you're famous for not talking about it."

"There is not much to be said. Or added." He is sober and clear about all of this. "Describing the grief all over again doesn't change how sorry I've felt since that day, that moment. And getting me to feel emotional about it—and that doesn't take much—overlooks Deon Johnson."

"And do you guard against it, somehow?"

Ryder looks across the field. He counts the rows of windows in the Omni until he finds his hotel floor, thinking how good it felt to sit in his room and stare out at the field all afternoon knowing he had turned the corner, knowing in his bones he was healed.

"I don't guard against it," says Ryder. "I own it."

AUGUST

To me, baseball has always been a reflection of life. Like life, it adjusts. It survives everything.

—*Pittsburgh Pirates and Hall of Fame outfielder*
Willie Stargell

Chapter 39

Ryder feels his toes in his cleats; he senses the cleats on the rubber. The tap, the start. The right leg goes to work. He builds power in the leg, doesn't force it, lets the energy flow from his core to his arm to his hand, and by the time Ryder is dialed in on his hand and its tight grip on the seams, he is picking out Wyatt's glove and aiming for the center-center. He lets it flow.

Ryder doesn't see Frazier. He doesn't see Rosten. He doesn't see J. C. Dooley. Frazier is out on a weak dribbler back to the mound. Rosten fans in four pitches, Dooley in five.

Every matchup a story. What story is the batter telling himself? Counter it. Flow against it. Do the unexpected. Throw three curves in a row. Curveball away, fastball in, cutter away, cutter away again. Get them to chase. Get them off their heels. Make them nervous. Tease them, tantalize them, make the slider do silly things. Ryder mixes speeds from 91 to 108. He has yet to show them 110. Maybe he won't. They are waiting for it, guarding against it.

Pitching in Fenway Park is like pitching in half a ballpark. The Green Monster is the architectural equivalent of a pitcher's bad dream.

But after six full innings, not one Red Sox hitter has reached base. Two hitters have made enough contact to loft meaningless pop-ups, one to center and one to left.

In the seventh, hotshot shortstop Alex Estrada flails. He's a swing-and-hope guy. The Red Sox aren't going to counter the three runs the

Orioles have put up, of course, unless they get their bats off their shoulders and start making contact. Estrada is late on a swing for pitch one, swings a full second early on pitch two, swats uselessly at high cheese on pitch three, and walks back to the dugout shaking his head.

The crowd buzzes. It's the hum of humanity. It's restlessness. It's wonder. It's 37,700 squirming fans who have agreed through some sort of telepathic communion to react as one. There is a certain sound from the chatter of this many people. Perhaps they are discussing which one of their precious Red Sox hitters will break the spell. Perhaps they are discussing whether the Orioles can catch the Yankees. An Oriole win tonight, after all, will put the Red Sox in third and leave them looking up the standings at Baltimore and New York. Perhaps they are chatting about work or relationships or their plans for Labor Day weekend on Cape Cod. Ryder can't hear words. The occasional "Beer here!" rises above, but otherwise it's a low rumble. The shape of the park might change, the air in his lungs might be different, but that collective conversational buzz is the same from town to town to town. Ryder feeds on it. The city doesn't matter. The ball field doesn't matter. He is where he belongs. He is doing what he wants to do. And something feels different.

He catches the return ball from Wyatt and peers in for the signal. John Fanger takes two quick strikes, lunges at the third pitch, and taps a weak grounder back to the mound. Mark Sanchez wants to go down swinging. Ryder gives him a full-throttle 110. The crowd issues a collective gasp, a mix of fear and awe. All of Sanchez' between-pitch maneuvering with his bat, helmet, crotch, and practice swings does nothing to delay the inevitable. Pearce, the left fielder, goes down in four pitches. Took it like a man.

"Bye-bye, you precious little fucking Red Sox," says Wyatt between innings in the dugout. "Your glory days are over."

They are seated next to each other in the dugout. Ryder takes a towel to his forehead, the back of his neck. The mood in the Oriole dugout is workmanlike, steady.

"They've got their rings," says Ryder.

"Our turn," says Wyatt. "Our turn at last."

It's okay to show a touch of cockiness: enough to call it swagger. But when it comes to interviews, the teamwide mantra is *One game at a time*. There will be no predictions about overtaking the Yankees. The focus is on the next at bat, the next ball coming your way. Execute the play. What's next? Execute the play. What's next? Execute the play. There will be no dreams of *Oriole*-tober.

The Orioles look older, wiser, smarter. Steve Penny taught them to believe that grown men getting to play baseball are the luckiest damn men on the planet. He told the team there are more people working as dentists in New York City today than have ever played professional baseball in the history of the game, to be damn grateful about the sport and the contracts, and to play each pitch with pride. And joy.

Steve Penny has given the Orioles a new chin-up, heads-up mojo. More backbone. All the W's help. Of course. But it's Penny who has persuaded batters to forget about the umpires—to go up battling pitchers and hunting for hittable pitches. Steve Penny is from the Mike Trout school of athletic demeanor—every minute onstage establishes your reputation. Penny is big shouldered, square jawed. He would make for a good marine. He doesn't like whiners. He doesn't believe that taking a baseball bat to the Gatorade jug does a lick of good. Penny's mood has rubbed off. It's amazing how one player can tweak the chemistry in the clubhouse. *Win like you expect to.*

There is also plenty of motivation to battle on behalf of Julio Diaz, who has shed the cast and is beginning rehab and might be ready for the spring. *Might.* The blown-up x-ray of Diaz' fractured wrist is on the bulletin board in their locker at Camden Yards. It's by the tunnel that leads to the dugout.

Ryder treats the eighth and the ninth innings like the first and the second. His arm flies. The routines are good. June and July never happened.

An idea is brewing in Ryder's head. It has to do with November and December. And everything to do with the new spaces in his head.

Chapter 40

"No soda," says Ryder. "No insurance companies either. No shoes. I'd do the baseball cards."

"Upper Deck," says Staller. "Like *this* place. Jesus, Frank Ryder, what a view."

They are at his Baltimore condo. Ryder has moved the meeting to the rooftop.

"Upper Deck is fine," says Ryder. "Naturally."

"They are way more than baseball cards. You know that."

"Yep, hockey and NBA. Games." Maggie helped him think through his approach on these options. *Remember,* she said, *any commercial you make will last forever.* It was easy to figure there would be plenty to choose from. "That's okay."

"I got a mortgage company," says Staller.

"What do I know about mortgages?"

"They had this idea that your pitch, so to speak, would be how fast they approve borrowers."

"Lame," says Ryder. "Sorry. And I just want a few."

"You could have a dozen."

"And look like a fruitcake," says Ryder. "I don't want to spread myself too thin."

"Nobody would blame you."

Staller has no idea about what he's said. He is short and pudgy. He last played baseball in high school, as a shortstop, but didn't make his college team, somewhere in California. That was thirty pounds ago. "Nobody would think twice about getting what you deserve. It's part of the deal."

Mickey Staller's agency, the Staller Group, represents more than 120 big-league ball players. Beyond contracts, they want to manage all of Ryder's finances, legal work, publicity, and life-skills coaching too.

"I want companies I believe in," says Ryder. "Something *smart*. No clothes, no beer."

"Shoes," says Staller. "Best money."

"And they are really all the same."

"Unless *you* say so." Staller sips a gin on ice. A fine breeze, like a gentle tap on the shoulder, is coming off the harbor. This meeting was at Staller's insistence. "That's the point. And now that you've caught the Red Sox, now that you've won every one of your starts since the All-Star break, even more so."

"No shoes. No gear."

"You're leaving a lot of money on the table."

"And maintaining a smidge of pride."

"Because careers are short," says Staller. "Because the owners make more money than God. You have to take advantage. You have a brief window of time on the baseball stage, unless you're telling me that elbow and that shoulder aren't turning into caramel taffy before you're, say, thirty-five."

Ryder isn't thinking that far ahead. He is thinking about the next start, at home versus the Yankees, the following night. Aaron Judge. Stanton. Gregorius. There's a four-game gap to close in order to catch the Yanks, who have gone on a tear.

"No shoes," says Ryder. "No athletic gear."

"You would clean up on a shoe deal."

"That's okay."

"You're trying to send a message?"

"No," says Ryder.

"Pizza?"

"No."

"Personal care?" says Staller. "I mean, with your hair. The shampoo people might figure out something."

"*My* unruly hair? No."

This whole conversation is curious and strange—to randomly decide on what products you claim to love.

"You gotta go after the companies with the deep pockets," says Staller. "Look at Peyton Manning. Look at LeBron. Look at Phil Mickelson. They are set for life. We are talking about no worries. Ever. Their *kids* will never worry about money. And all their grandkids too. Speaking of Peyton Manning."

"What?"

"You could use a lighter touch. In public."

"Touch?"

"Persona," says Staller. "You gotta loosen up."

"Did Maggie call you?"

"Everybody is waiting."

"How so, *waiting*?"

"Well, wondering if there's another side," says Staller. "A fun-loving side. Get on YouTube and watch a few old Peyton Manning skits from *SNL*. Have some fun. Next time when one of your guys gets a walk-off hit or home run, maybe you're the one there with the bucket of Gatorade or the pie tin with shaving cream. Show 'em you're a great teammate. On national TV."

"I can try." It might seem forced at first, and the game-day mindset will never change, but Staller is right. Maggie too.

"A few smiles wouldn't kill you. The more charm, the more we can charge."

"No shampoo," says Ryder. "What about a college? Or an online school? Aren't there some good online schools? Legit folks doing good work? Or charter schools doing good things in cities?"

"Here we go," says Staller.

"What?"

"You're talking peanuts."

"Seriously?"

"A private school or private college might take you," says Staller. "They might be thrilled. But, again, so damn serious. Heavy. Put the world to sleep. You want to go with one of those companies with fat margins."

"I'd rather do three that I believe in than one that I don't."

"So baseball cards and what else?"

"I don't know." Ryder watches a motorboat making its way across the harbor. It's as small as a water bug. "Not sure about how to decide. And I'm starting to think about the Yankees."

"You have to do more than trading cards."

"That's the part I don't get," says Ryder. "The *have to* part."

SEPTEMBER

Love is the most important thing in the world, but baseball is pretty good, too.

—New York Yankees and Hall of Fame catcher
Yogi Berra

Chapter 41

The school is clean and bright. The sea of faces is Black. The students at Lockerman Bundy Elementary School sport a uniform—white shirts, of any variety, dark or navy pants or skirts. Martha Greer, his taxi driver from earlier in the summer, explains the common logo on all the shirts. "It's college and career readiness," she says. "We start talking about college in kindergarten."

Ryder would rather not stand and talk down to the third graders, so he sits on a chair at the front of a classroom. The students read prepared questions from notebooks. What does he eat? Where does he live? What is his favorite thing about Baltimore? Why does he pitch so fast? The classroom buzzes. Ryder turns the questions around. What do *they* eat? What are *their* favorite things about the city? He ignores the question about where he lives. He gets them to guess about why he likes to pitch so fast. "Because the ball becomes invisible," says one girl. She has long black braids, small glasses that look uncomfortable. "That's what my daddy says. *Invisible.*"

"Could you tell the class about getting better? About practicing?" This is the teacher, Alice Kempton. She wears an oversize white T-shirt with a drawing of the Lockerman Bundy mascot, a friendly-looking bear. The bear is smiling. Miss Kempton is not. She has a strict vibe. "How did you train? Some of these kids don't see how hard you have to work."

"I didn't see it as work," says Ryder. "That's because I *love* the game. I am talking about deep, deep love for the game."

The morning goes okay. The kids are fine. He talks to them about picking one thing and getting better at it—it doesn't matter what it is. Ryder doesn't know what he's telling them—he's not even sure it's a good idea to be so focused on one thing, even if it sounds good on the surface. What does he know about these kids? Their lives? Sue Woodward, one of the Orioles' media-relations team, studies something on her phone. She's heard all these bromides before. Ryder's only request was no media today.

Ryder is a break in their routine. He thanks Martha Greer and the school principal outside in the warm morning sun. Group photos, a few selfies with individual teachers. Ryder slides into one of the team's tanklike SUVs. Ryder realizes he has spent the whole morning thinking ahead to what's next.

It's a five-minute drive to the church. Ryder follows Woodward down steps to an expansive brick patio that extends off the garden-level community room in the rear of the modest building. The inside room comes complete with sofas, comfy chairs, a Ping-Pong table, a pool table, foosball, and a small library with books and magazines. No TV. No computers. The space looks like the living room for a family of forty.

"You counsel them?" says Ryder.

"That's a strong word," says Woodward. She is six feet tall with long auburn hair. She is not yet thirty. She is freshness and polish. "Mostly, I listen. I get them to talk, and then I listen."

The kids arrive together. There are four. All teenagers. Two girls, two boys. One of the girls is Black, the other is white. One of the boys is white, the other a blend of Black and brown.

Lisa, Melva, Jamal, Eduardo.

Woodward gets brisk hugs. Ryder gets tentative handshakes, no eye contact. They sit on heavy metal chairs in a circle on the patio, shaded by the church and three giant oaks. The shade is welcome but not critical. It's one of those perfect-temperature days. The air is still. Woodward offers up cold canned sodas.

The ice doesn't break without effort. The four are reticent and skeptical at first, as if they have signed a pact. Ryder plays nosy reporter, trying to come up with questions to prod them along. But he doesn't want to come across as pushy. Or impatient.

They all go to the same school.

"Are you all friends?" says Ryder. He's been trying to crack their code or gain an ounce of trust for about fifteen minutes.

"Not *really*," says Jamal. He is skinny. His eyes are heavy and his gaze is blank. "Just through this deal here."

"Here?" says Ryder.

"The church deal," says Jamal. "Getting together to talk."

"Does it help?"

"Some."

"It's not like we come every week either." Melva keeps her hair cut short over one side of her head; the rest is three inches of Afro. She wears a black T-shirt with three white block letters: B L M. She's at least thirty pounds overweight, and she sits in the chair leaning forward like she wants to leave. "This isn't a regular thing."

"It's a big school," says Lisa. "Eight hundred or something kids in there?"

"Mine was something like two thousand," says Ryder.

"Was it crazyville, though?"

This is Eduardo. He's wearing a Baltimore Ravens jersey, 52. Ray Lewis' number, the number Lewis picked because that's how many cards are in a deck. Eduardo is a big kid, worthy of a football offensive line. He wears glasses. One forearm is well tattooed.

"Probably not," says Ryder.

"You had teachers in your school getting attacked?" Lisa has long stringy hair, which allows for a perpetual search for split ends. She is gaunt and skinny like a long-distance runner.

"No," says Ryder.

"We got TV news there once a week," says Lisa.

"For?" says Ryder.

"Cops," says Jamal. "Ambulances. And the reporters are right behind."

Ryder trusts Jamal as the group's straightest shooter. Maybe.

"Always the cops," says Lisa. "You can't breathe."

"So what brought you here?" says Ryder. "To this group?"

The four exchange a glance, say nothing.

Ryder tries another tack. "Why did you agree to talk to me?"

"More like—what the heck are you doing here?" says Jamal. "Talking to us?"

"Why?" says Ryder.

"Because you are fuckin' Frank Ryder," says Eduardo.

"Aren't you pitching—tonight?" says Jamal.

"Tomorrow. Yankees are in town. It's a long way off."

"My dad says you got a golden arm. Says you're going to be the richest athlete on the planet, and Mars and Jupiter too." Melva forces a laugh. "Is that right?"

"I'm here because I want to find out what you guys might want."

"Us?" says Jamal. "Us here?"

"I mean, in general."

"What's in general?" says Melva.

"For kids in schools like yours."

"It ain't *my* school," says Lisa.

There is no further explanation. Even at his most lonely and isolated when he first arrived in Denver, Ryder never hated or distrusted Thomas Jefferson High School. He knew that if he made an effort to step out of his baseball bubble, and to stop marinating in the endless sadness over Deon Johnson, he would have found a home. And he did.

"I'm thinking of starting a program," says Ryder.

"A *program*," says Jamal. He's the most skeptical of the foursome. "Ain't that something you do to a computer?"

Ryder kicks himself for his lack of tact or touch. He should have prepared. He assumed they would gush information and ideas. They might get chatty if he dangles the big idea, but Ryder doesn't want to come across like a rich dude with money to burn.

"We got more *programs* than you can count," says Melva. "Doesn't change a thing about coming to school not worried about everything else."

"What 'everything else'?"

"Everything other than school," says Eduardo. He shrugs. "Everything other than learning."

"Like getting shot," says Lisa. "Like girls getting attacked. Like a student flipping out. Like a teacher going berserk. Like somebody showing you a big-ass knife on your way home. Like getting groped or told you're a whore. Or a cop stopping you to check you over and make your day miserable for being a city kid while Black—and, yeah, you're right, I'm white, but I see it all the fuckin' time."

Melva gives Lisa a little fist bump.

"That school is a trip to nowhere," says Eduardo. "We all know it. *They* probably know it too. But they pretend like we're all going to fuckin' Johns Hopkins."

"Nothing *real* about it," says Jamal. "Except when there's blood. That's real. Other than that? When they start talking about college *entrance* exams? All I can think of is some big door three stories high and all the pointy heads behind there—maybe if you walk straight and mind your business they will open that door a crack and share some of their precious fucking knowledge. *Entrance.* Like some sort of king and queen waiting on a throne."

The kids he saw earlier in the day at Lockerman Bundy—the fantasy of college for every kid will set them up for failure, later on, when some of them realize they have other ideas about how they want to live their lives, when they realize they don't want to deal with the debt and the pressures of another institution that makes them feel *lesser than*.

"So that's what I need to know," says Ryder. "What do you need? Let's say you had six weeks to get away from all of this. Six weeks to get out of the pressure cooker and go do something else? And think about other things, without worrying about whether you're going to make it through the day?"

He might have been depressed, off and on, when he was in high school, Ryder realizes, but he has no idea what city kids face day to day.

"Away from here?" Melva has perked up. "I went to the ocean once. North Point State Park. Sometimes when I'm trying to sleep, I think of my toes in the water and the sand, looking out to sea. I could see for miles. No sirens. So calm. That *sound* of water lapping on the beach. I fell sound asleep on the beach."

"So—open space," says Ryder. "Lakes. Ocean. Fresh air?"

"Can't swim," says Eduardo. "Scared of water."

"Away from the city," says Ryder. "Somewhere."

"Away from *here*," says Eduardo.

"Why the hell don't you *know*?" says Jamal.

"Know what?" says Ryder.

"What might be good—what we might want?" says Lisa.

"You were right here, right?" Jamal sits up, points to himself and swishes his finger at the three others. "I mean, a couple of years ago? Right?"

"Denver is not Baltimore," says Ryder.

"I doubt that." Melva laughs. It's a brief, dry laugh. She shakes her head. "Had an uncle who lived out there told me the school he went to looked like it was surrounded by nice houses, but a kid was knifed and killed in the cafeteria. Said that city had a way of hiding the poor kids, glossing over everything."

"Here's the deal," says Ryder. He takes his time. Melva is right. Ryder wants to say something about how he was lucky to have parents who supported him, even if they didn't back his precise dream. He wants to say something about the fact that back then—*a minute ago, a century ago?*—he didn't care about these issues. "I'm not comparing my deal to what you're going through, okay? But I was in my own tunnel. For most of high school. Again, a different type of deal. But I wasn't happy. Not really. I kept to myself. Not all the time, but for long stretches. The thoughts in my head weren't helping me out, you know?"

"If you're talking about kids taking their own lives, we got plenty of that too." Lisa is matter of fact. "Plenty of that going around."

Melva holds up a finger. "Boy," she says. Another finger: "White." Another finger: "Athlete." Her thumb juts out: "Crazy talented athlete."

Ryder says nothing.

"You were *greased*," says Melva. "The whole system was watching out for you. Even if you didn't know it. Or feel it."

"At TJ," says Ryder, "they didn't know I could pitch until the end of my junior year."

Ryder hears the lame defensiveness immediately. Melva is right on all counts. By the way he looked, the high school version of Frank Ryder was normal. Back then, he was the default student the system was built to serve. And he was treated that way.

"Talk to me about what it would take to make it all seem more optimistic," says Ryder. "Positive. Better. Like you had a ray of hope. Do you know what I mean?"

"Six weeks away from here?" says Jamal. "But we gotta come back to the same old shit? What's the point?"

"Help me with the first part. Help me with what happens during the six weeks, then we'll figure out the next."

The four look at each other. Jamal is the ringleader, in a good way. Approval goes through him. They are a unit. Jamal nods. The mood shifts. The space between them opens up.

And the ideas begin to trickle out. And then flow.

Chapter 42

"You like it?" says Ryder.

"Yes," says Gallo. "Why don't we get it rolling here, first? In Baltimore?" says Gallo. "Proof-of-concept kind of thing? Then we'll work up a presentation. I'll make the big ask at the national."

Frank Ryder is a portrait in calm. It's the morning after another Frank Ryder one-hitter, a 1–0 win over the Yankees. The Yankees have let dread slip into their locker room. Gallo is keenly aware of the infectious nature of dread. It's vicious and self-fulfilling.

The Orioles, conversely, are loose. The mornings are brighter. The staff around Camden Yards is kinder. The coffee tastes better. Drivers are more patient. Riots and Freddie Gray and the scandal with the mayor and her self-dealing? Baltimore is moving on. The harbor looks spiffier; the streets look cleaner. Real estate agents answer the phone with enthusiasm. Gallo gets texts and phone calls from people he hasn't heard from in years. The Orioles sit two games off the division lead.

And Frank Ryder's got philanthropy on the brain.

"We need kids from all over," says Ryder. "Lots of them. Thirty teams, maybe four kids per team. Two boys, two girls. For starters. Small at first."

Gallo scratches his neck, tries to think how best to respond. Aiko gives a *What's not to love?* look, eyes open wide and a mini shrug. Alicia Ford smiles like she woke from a relaxing nap.

"These big national campaigns are years in the planning," says Gallo. "That whole 'Let the kids play' bit a few years back? There's a long runway before launch."

"Doesn't have to be a big splash," says Ryder. "And it doesn't have to replace anything. And never will we say this is the answer."

"No," says Gallo.

"The key comes down to listening," says Ryder. "Nothing top down. We give these kids a six-week chance to explore whatever they want. We start every day by listening to them. We might have a few options at first but nothing mandatory. If they want to help out around the farm or the camp or whatever we want to call it, fine. Some kid might want to learn to garden, another to cook, another might want to stay up late and study the stars. Right? Kid focused to the nth degree."

"Sports?" says Aiko.

"Sure," says Ryder. "Depending on equipment and facilities. And the number of kids, after we grow it a bit, in each spot."

"Arts?" says Ford. "You've seen how they've gutted arts programs in public schools?"

"You bet," says Ryder. "Put a band together. Or sketch and paint all day. Or writing—anything."

Gallo wonders what he did to deserve this. He demurred on a trade. He hired a solid general manager and has paid her well. If not for chalking up the fewest wins in the season before the draft when Frank Ryder became available, this could be Pittsburgh's moment or the Texas Rangers' path to glory. Now, it's easy to see how Frank Ryder's presence changes the arc of the team's destiny for years or a decade to come. The sheer interest and willingness to play for winners changes the entire dynamic. Gallo figures he can only take credit for hiring good people and sticking with them even through the occasional bonehead idea.

"This is only a start," says Ryder. "I want to see a mental health movement for teens around the country. I want to be part of a major push. I've been there."

Gallo quietly admits to himself that he's rarely seen a rookie ballplayer, a kid really, look so grounded and sure. He's got a quiet authority. He owns the room.

"I know what kids with troubles go through," says Ryder. "I'm the lucky one—don't get me wrong on that score. But there are too many kids carrying burdens that they don't deserve to have. As a nation, this is something worth fixing. But our idea is only one approach. We need a powerful team effort with top experts and major benefactors working on lots of solutions. I want to be part of this. As you can probably tell."

"The community is going to love this, Frank. Tangible benefits, right now, to kids in need."

Reflected glory, thinks Gallo, is a silly thing. The idea that a city and its fans feel better about themselves based on the success or failure of highly paid and well-pampered athletes who for the most part don't give a shit about all the working stiffs and middle-class families that make it possible for them to play a game for a living. Like most professional sports franchises, the Orioles send out players for hospital visits and community service projects, but the city would probably trade all those feel-good visits for one fresh World Series trophy.

"What I'm not suggesting is that this is an answer to poverty or urban troubles," says Ryder. "It's about tuning in to each kid. I mean seriously tuning in. It's about letting them prioritize. Of course we'll get a sense of what they want before they come out for the six weeks, but then we will tweak and tweak. It's about the specific kids who get involved. It's about keeping their hopes alive. Making them see what's possible. That's all. Hope."

"We know a thing or two about hope," says Gallo, starting to ponder exactly how they'll be able to afford Frank Ryder when his initial contract is up. "Don't we?"

"We'll get it running first," says Ryder. "We'll make it successful, and *then* they can milk it for whatever PR feel-good stuff they want. Maybe it's all on the down low, in fact. That's even better. I've got someone looking for places in Colorado. Out east of Denver—easy shuttle ride from DIA. Farm country. Wholesome, simple. And make it the Orioles' idea, if you want. The less it's about me, given everything, all the better."

"Colorado?" says Gallo. "It would *have* to be your deal."

"Well, the MLB's, then."

"It's real," says Aiko. "And it focuses on our connections to each other."

"What do we need to get the ball rolling?" says Ryder. "You gotta believe MLB could use something with real kids."

"For sure." What Gallo knows about Baltimore is what he reads in the newspapers. For the past decade, you could smell the decline. But the league hasn't done a good job supporting youth baseball, which should be their wellspring for future talent and future fans. "I can feel out some of the other owners first, you know, soften them up and get them behind the plan so I'm not going in cold. Or alone."

"Speaking of which," says Ryder.

"You can't ask me," says Gallo.

"*What* am I going to ask you?"

"If I think they're going to try to slow you down."

"Bingo," says Ryder. "But it's not just me."

"Yes, it is," says Gallo.

"It's the game," says Ryder. "The whole idea of an arbitrary pitch-speed ceiling."

Gallo shrugs, holds his shoulders up. "It's brutal. If the vote was today, it would be damn close."

Ryder shakes his head. "Does public opinion matter?"

"Not if they think attendance would take a nosedive. Attendance and ratings. One camp says we can't go down this road, that we'd be opening the floodgates to an imbalanced game. You know there are others coming right behind you, right? If the fans stop watching, the ratings drop and you may as well be siphoning money straight from their bank accounts, because that's how all the owners will feel."

"And when we win the World Series?" says Ryder.

"Loving the confidence," says Ford.

"Me too," says Gallo.

"Me three," says Aiko. And laughs. "It's going to happen."

"And when we win, that would make it easier for them to change the rules?"

"Probably," says Gallo.

"And because it's Baltimore," says Ryder.

One of the joys of the season has been breaking up the vaunted hierarchy of storied franchises. The Red Sox, Yankees, Cubs, Cardinals, and Dodgers have way too much power over the other teams. Gallo feels like the Orioles are the new neighbor in town, rattling the windows with a boom box, hosting noisy parties, and guzzling unpretentious beer.

"Some like to tell themselves it's a theoretical matter," says Gallo. "It's not. Every one of those owners? If the shoe was on the other foot? Believe me, if you were a Yankee? Ziegler would be throwing fits if anyone mentioned anything about restraining you."

"And beanballs? Any discussion of that?"

Gallo sighs. "The unwritten rules still rule."

"So a batter flips his bat like he's king of the world after hitting a monster home run, right? And the next time up he pays the price by getting drilled. Might break a wrist, like Diaz, or bust up an ankle or crack a rib. Right?"

"I think we all know," says Gallo.

"Pitcher might get suspended, miss a start. Or two," says Ryder.

"Right."

"But if a pitcher strikes out the side and storms off the mound grunting and pumping himself up over his own talent, pretending like he slayed a dragon, why can't a batter go out there with a bat and smash his kneecaps with one good swing? What's the difference?"

"There is none," says Aiko. "It's the very definition of double standard."

"There is so much I love about this game," says Ryder. "But that whole deal, if you ask me, is one fucked-up mess right there."

Chapter 43

In his second start of September, back at home in a packed Camden Yards, Frank Ryder throws with carefree ease. Every fresh batter presents his own unique puzzle. Each batter triggers a game plan in Ryder's mind. Each batter is separate, and yet each batter is connected to the one before and the one after.

Ryder gets sharper by the pitch, by the inning. His pitches appear to gather steam as they come into the zone. They waffle, flutter, dive, and rise. Ryder keeps his gaze riveted on Wyatt's glove as he moves it around the zone. Ryder focuses on the next pitch he's going to throw. He doesn't fear random thoughts.

The fifth is an "immaculate inning." Nine pitches—all strikes. Three batters up, three batters down. Of the nine pitches, batters swing at two.

Ryder ends up with a no-hitter. The Orioles win 6–0.

After the game, the music pumps. The vibe is loose. The reporters take double the time. Ryder fields all the questions with patience. Behind the reporters, teammates fake yawns and point to imaginary watches on their wrists. Ryder tries like hell not to laugh.

⁓

"What I know is it's more complicated than it looks," says Maggie. Ryder sits on the rooftop, alone. They have been talking for a half hour.

"Acreage, sure. But water rights, that's the big one. Access—how are the roads? County or private. Improvements—the quality of the houses and barns and all of that. Public land nearby. Or not."

"We need it within ninety minutes of DIA," says Ryder. "I don't want them getting off a flight and being bored on the drive out. An hour east would be great."

"And a river," says Maggie.

"That's in my dreams."

"And why shouldn't you get what you want?"

Because I already have everything I want.

"Well, what would be perfect is an abandoned summer camp with two dozen cabins and a big ranch house that isn't a complete fixer-upper."

"I'm on it," says Maggie. "By that I mean I'm in regular touch with the agent who is sending me links to various listings. She hasn't found the right spot yet."

In the discussions to date, Maggie's involvement will be meaningful in the summers once the programs are running. Nothing is going to distract her, however, from finishing her master's degree.

"You can do it, too, you know," says Maggie. "Put all your wish criteria into one of those real estate websites? Like Zillow?"

"*All* of my wish criteria?" says Ryder.

—∞—

On the road against the Dodgers, with the Orioles one game back of the Yankees, Frank Ryder steps up on the mound at Chavez Ravine thinking about Sandy Koufax—his records, his domination, his personal integrity, his quirky aloofness, his ability to be himself in a game that wants to swallow players whole and assimilate them like soldiers. The Yankee Clipper made a fortune peddling Mr. Coffee. Sandy Koufax spent most of his life declining endorsements. Frank Ryder feels, given

Gail Johnson and the new way forward, like he's already cashed a big fat check.

The ballpark is jammed. It's a late-arriving crowd, as always, but Ryder takes a moment before throwing the first pitch of the third inning to take them in. He likes spotting people—*individual* people and *individual* kids—and thinking what it took for them to decide to be here, tonight.

Santa Ana winds bake Los Angeles. Ryder savors the warmth. Steve Penny blasts a three-run moon shot in the sixth, bringing home the two men on base, Cruz and Wyatt. The three high-five each other at home plate, and they walk together back to the dugout like three guys who helped a friend load a truck. Ryder is among those whooping as the trio comes down the steps. The celebration is brief.

Back to work.

The three runs are two more than Ryder needs. It's Ryder's second shutout of the month. On the field, Ryder is stopped by the ESPN crew to do the postgame interview with "Boog" Sciambi.

Ryder smiles. He smiles for Maggie and he smiles to let his folks know—*all is good.* He smiles for Deon. He smiles for Gail Johnson too.

"It was an honor to pitch on the same mound as Sandy Koufax." Ryder's mind goes to the flattened penny on his chest. "Don Drysdale, Don Sutton, Orel Hershiser, and Fernando Valenzuela too."

Ryder dabs his face with a towel. Sweat drips from his hair, his eyebrows, and down his back.

"And you had to go and get a hit in your first at bat?" says Sciambi. "A double? Just to rub it in?"

"Lucky," says Ryder. "But I enjoy the chance to get up there."

"If you had a chance to tell the owners one thing about their deliberations this winter, about the rules, what would the advice be?"

Sciambi grins. His eyes are sincere. Part of the business about live television is quick replies.

"Don't focus on me," says Ryder. "Focus on the safety of all the players. Send a message. Baseball can control this if it wants to do so."

"You mean more than a slap on the wrist for throwing at a player— *that's* what you mean, right?"

"Make a good pitcher sit on the sideline for a whole month or something, you hurt the whole team with that kind of punishment," says Ryder. "The beanballs would end pretty quick."

"But it seems like baseball is talking only about you," says Sciambi. "The no-hitter against Texas, the performance tonight. Everybody has an opinion. What do you think of having started so much talk about the future of the game? About penalizing pitchers for exceeding some kind of arbitrary speed limit?"

On the morning before Ryder's start, the *Los Angeles Times* felt the need to weigh in on the issue. "Major League Baseball cannot let this linger," the newspaper concluded. "Balance must be restored. The game banned dead balls for safety reasons. The game lowered the mound in 1969 to give hitters a better chance. Spitballs were forbidden too. In the 1990s, when it was obvious to all, MLB finally went after the scourge of performance-enhancing drugs. The game has continuously recalibrated itself. Now comes a new challenge in the form of Frank Ryder. The game must respond again."

Sciambi's foam microphone is shoved at Ryder's mouth. Ryder can smell the plasticky electronics.

"I don't think I'm the big issue," says Ryder. "I'm one pitcher on thirty teams, one pitcher out of three hundred pitchers on those thirty teams. How much harm can I do?"

—⁓—

In Detroit for three games on the way home, Ryder isn't scheduled to start. He spends the first game in the dugout, the second two in the bullpen, where he can hide from the peering camera.

In the ninth inning of the third game, the Orioles within one game of the Yankees, the Orioles hold a one-run lead into the ninth inning. The Tigers get a man on second. The bullpen phone jangles.

Lackland.

Is Ryder willing?

There is a man on second and third by the time Ryder is warm. At least, warm enough.

Still no outs.

Ryder treats the ninth like a side session. He needs eleven pitches to quell the uprising. He doesn't throw anything harder than 105.

And the Yankees lose—to Boston, no less.

On the plane home, it's late. Ryder sits by the window. He likes to watch the stars or the moon on the nights when it's clear. Ryder believes the moon only gets the loving attention as a sliver or when it's full—the wobbly, oddball shapes and sizes go underappreciated.

"You know, that's the other option," says Stone, making himself at home in the open seat next to Ryder.

"What's that?" says Ryder.

"Your laid-back style today gave me the idea."

"Laid back?"

"The kids call it 'chill,' I suppose," says Stone.

"I'm listening."

"Police yourself," says Stone. "Decide on your own to throw one oh three to one oh four. That's ample firepower for winning."

"You mean, hold back *on purpose?*"

"Take the issue off the table. Voluntarily." Stone is drinking beer from a can. "Flash a one oh nine every now and then just for grins, but don't give them a reason to come after you."

"*Holding back* doesn't sound like competing."

At 103, there is still time for a batter to think. And act.

"We measure our effort all the time," says Stone. "No pitcher throws as hard as they can on every single pitch. No batter swings as hard as they can with every swing."

"Neither do I."

"Exactly. So bring your average speed down."

"By ten percent?"

Far below, a vast sheet of clouds is lit by the moon, like the earth has been wrapped in Marshmallow Fluff.

"Say you're protecting your arm for the long haul," says Stone. "Which, by the way, would hardly be a terrible idea. Say you have a feeling for how many bullets are loaded up in that thing and tell 'em you have to dial it back a notch, not push your luck."

"It sounds wrong."

"In fact, you don't need to *say* or announce anything," says Stone. "Just do it. And maybe preserve yourself in the process too. Which means you get a few more years out of that arm, end up with even more cash in the bank by the time you need to figure out what's next. You know, after baseball."

—⁓—

"TIED FOR FIRST PLACE!" screams the page-one headline the morning after the team flies home. There isn't a local or national news or sports show that hasn't put in a request for Frank Ryder's time. Ryder talks on the phone with the team's media staff—he tells *60 Minutes* to wait for the off-season, if they don't mind, and sends HBO's Bryant Gumbel the same message. At least Gumbel wants to focus on the unwritten rules, the whole culture of retribution. Ryder keeps to routines, sticks close to his teammates, and decides for now he will avoid all commentary about the game and its decrees. The Sciambi interview is being played in a steady rotation on the sports talk shows, the morning national news shows too. Ryder wants to concentrate on winning games.

In his third start of September, against the Blue Jays, Ryder begins like it's a normal game, but in the bottom of the second he thinks he'll give Stone's idea a whirl. Maybe his arm will send him an upbeat message. Maybe his arm will approve. Maybe they'll stop talking about adjusting the game. Maybe owners and the media and even the players association will focus only on the beanball business. For once.

Ryder walks the first batter of the second inning—on five pitches. There is nothing off or strange about his windup or follow-through, but something is not clicking right. The fastest of the five pitches is 103, and Wyatt needs to stand up and stick his arm in the air to prevent the pitch from sailing all the way to the backstop. It's Ryder's first walk since early in the game against Texas.

Return of the yips?

No.

He should be able to throw strikes at 104 all day long. Ryder walks off the mound, plays with the rosin bag, rolls his shoulders, climbs back up to the rubber, peers in. Wyatt wants the 1.

The next pitch is center cut, belt high, and Ryder is saying *Thank you* to the pitch and its accuracy when he hears the solid, deep sound of wood whacking ball and a white blur comes screaming back at his face. Ryder buckles at the knees, hears a buzzing whir whiz past his ear, and lands awkwardly on his hip in the dirt as a collective gasp goes up from the crowd.

Ryder climbs to his feet, dusts the dirt off his pants, waves the trainer back to the dugout.

Wyatt wastes a mound visit. "Something wrong?"

"No," says Ryder.

"My hand's not on fire. What gives?"

"Stone had this idea."

"It's a dumb one," says Wyatt. "Forget about it."

"It's just that—"

"Don't leave a tool on the table," says Wyatt. *Jee-zus.*

Ryder fans the next three batters on thirteen pitches. All go down swinging. The Blue Jays manage three hits through the remainder of the game. The Orioles spend the rest of the game sullying the reputations of six Blue Jay pitchers. Oriole fans remain raucous as Ryder does the postgame interview on the field, wishing he could decline and scramble into the dugout to be with his teammates. Cruz had three doubles. Why don't they talk to him? The on-field interviews are a trap. After an 11–0 romp, victors don't say, "No comment." Victors are expected to explain their ability to vanquish a foe, even if you say the same thing every time. Ryder wants to disappear in the clubhouse but has no real choice.

"You had that one bobble in the second inning," says the reporter. She is TV polished. She seems to be staring at Ryder's chin. "And then you came roaring back. How did you make the adjustment?"

"It was a great team win tonight," says Ryder. "No pitcher can stand here and smile without an offense that gives him a cushion. Tonight, a big one."

"From the third inning on, however, the radar gun said your last six innings were the hardest, fastest six innings of pitches you have thrown this year," she says. "You know, cumulatively. You weren't giving in after those walks in the second and the hit that nearly took your head off. You were still okay? Mentally?"

The microphone moves from her mouth to his. The motion is the question mark. *Your turn! Please chime in now.*

"Good win for us," says Ryder. *Of course the line drive was frightening.* But it's not something you reveal. "We know it's not over yet."

Ryder turns down requests from his teammates to head out for late-night beers and watch the Yankees, who are on the road against Oakland. The Yankees are losing, 4–2 in the fourth. It's possible the Orioles wake up, alone, in first place. Ryder wants his rooftop. He wants to be away from the questions and the noise and the speculation. He wouldn't mind a long chat with Maggie. And get his mind wrapped around everything else.

—∿—

Ryder's fourth start of September is the first game of a road series. It's the last series of the regular season.

In the Bronx.

The math is simple.

If the Orioles can win two of three, they skip the Wild Card Game and go straight to the playoffs.

If the Orioles win one game only, they will be forced to play the Wild Card Game—a winner-take-all, one-game battle to decide who advances to the Division Series.

Ryder's regular turn falls on the Friday-night game, and that's not a bad thing, in part because, in theory, Ryder would be rested for game one of the playoffs the following Tuesday night.

If they get there.

Whether it's the Yankees they'll be facing or whether it's the sheer possibility that the season might soon be over, Ryder senses a sudden tightness among his teammates. It's a mix of fate and fear. It's normal. And Ryder hates it. It's almost as if they are practicing what they'll say when the door is slammed on their playoff plans.

Stone looks worried too. And Ford. And Lackland. It's as if the weight of *now* is too much to bear.

They are in Ford's hotel room, at Ryder's request, fifteen minutes before the bus is due to leave for Yankee Stadium.

"It's a fine gesture," says Ford. Ryder gets the feeling that the three of them have been here for hours. The room is thick with dark juju. "In fact, it's fabulous on your part to step forward and suggest this, Frank."

In his gut and in his arm, Ryder knows he'd be fine pitching the first three innings of all three games.

"It was *your* idea," says Ryder.

"Way back in June," says Ford.

"When we could have given it a trial run," says Stone.

"It could still work," says Ryder. "A psychological edge too. It would put the Yankees back on their heels."

"Appreciated," says Ford. "Seriously. It's much appreciated. It's obvious how much you want the team to win."

Ryder shrugs. "It would be like a strategic curveball—a whopper."

"Sure," says Ford.

"What else would be the point to all of this, the first hundred fifty-nine games? And can you imagine the letdown if we don't get to the Division Series?"

"And then what about the first game of the playoffs?" says Lackland.

"The proverbial bridge," says Ryder. "We cross when we get there. And we have to get there."

Ford looks at Stone. He shakes his head. Ford looks at Lackland. "Call me forever *no* on this one," he says. "Forever and the day after it too."

———

In the ninth inning of the Friday game, the score is 0–0. Ryder glugs a Gatorade in the dugout, tells himself he could go another three or four innings if needed. He's at ninety-nine pitches with fourteen strikeouts. His groove is good.

Leading off the top of the ninth, Cory Bayless smashes a double, and, two outs later, Esteban Ortega follows with a drag bunt up the first base line to put runners at first and third.

Steve Penny, showing zero indication he's aware of the pressure, strokes a soft single to center field, and Bayless jogs home with the first run of the game. Ryder joins the gaggle at the dugout steps that greets Bayless, who gets high-fived and backslapped like the return of a long-lost son.

There is a sense of order to the moment. *We deserve this. We earned this. We are better than them.*

The story fits like a tailored suit—scrappy, longtime loser team from a troubled city defeats team of legends and glory representing America's business and cultural capital. Ryder is sure a writer somewhere is plucking out the whole "destiny" chestnut, as if any deity cared about a game being played by rich adult boy-men.

Wyatt sends a ball deep to center field that looks like it could be a three-run bomb, but Yankees center fielder Mike Temple stands in the deepest part of the park and puts his back to the wall, and the ball settles in his chest-high glove like he's been playing catch.

All the Orioles need is three outs. All Ryder needs is three outs.

The crowd buzzes. Ryder tells himself to embrace the moment. The situation hasn't altered the physics of the game. The situation hasn't diminished Ryder's skills. Nor has it turned the batters into men with keener senses, better insight.

Ryder stands on the mound. Relaxed. His mind sits for a moment with his toes. His mind sits for another moment with the fingers in his glove, the fingers on the ball. He inhales, exhales. He touches the top button on his jersey like he's got an itch. He presses Deon's flattened penny to the skin on his chest.

Ryder throws his warm-up pitches thinking of a warm spring day in Denver. For a moment, he erases the stadium and all the fans from his head. He finds a boy in the upper deck, in the front row above third base. The boy is wearing an Orioles cap.

Ryder smiles to himself.

Wyatt goes into his crouch, flashes the signal.

Wyatt wants the 1.

Funny, thinks Ryder.

So do I.

OCTOBER

Just take the ball and throw it where you want to. Throw strikes. Home plate don't move.

—Negro League, Major League Baseball, and Hall of Fame pitcher Satchel Paige, who threw his last professional pitch two weeks shy of his sixtieth birthday

Chapter 44

"I am calling to wish you luck."

"So I can only assume you are making the same call to owners of playoff teams in your own league?"

"Of course not," says Tommy Rafferty. "But if we get there, and I hope we do, I hope we're playing the Orioles."

"So you *want* Frank Ryder?"

"The Orioles," says Rafferty.

"Ryder will start three games. Right?" says Gallo. "That is, if that seventh game is even needed."

"October," says Rafferty. "The winds blow in strange ways. Ask Kershaw. Ask David Price."

"Frank *Ryder*." It's a chamber of commerce afternoon in Baltimore. Camden Yards is stuffed to the gills. Game one. "Perhaps you have encountered an item or two about his first full year in the major leagues. Perhaps you are watching the game right now and you'll notice the goose egg for the Mariners under the H on the scoreboard."

"The whole country is watching."

"And you really want your boys to face those fastballs?"

The Orioles are up, 2–0, courtesy of a 440-foot blast to dead center field by Cory Bayless. The home run has the announcers listing the longest home runs in Camden Yards history, including Darryl Strawberry's and the time Ken Griffey Jr. hit the warehouse during the Home Run

Derby. The fact that it's Bayless who hit the home run gives Gallo a quiet jolt of pride.

It's the fifth inning. Frank Ryder appears to be on cruise control. On the monitor in Gallo's box, where Gallo takes his seat far from the relentless sunshine, close-ups of Frank Ryder show a man working at an easy rhythm. He could be laying bricks. He could be sorting mail. He is, in fact, teaching a class. The hardest hit so far in the game against Ryder has been a routine grounder to short.

"The Cubs want to play the best team in the American League," says Rafferty. "When the time comes."

"How do you beat Frank Ryder?" says Gallo. "I'm all ears."

"Things change in October," says Rafferty. "Summer is a memory. And maybe your boy runs out of gas. Or he gets a touch of the Julys."

"Oh." Gallo fakes surprise. "So you believe all that crap that Ryder was having issues?"

"October is rarely a seamless extension of the regular season," says Rafferty. "Frank Ryder can't start every game, and since the National League won the All-Star Game—because of that July issue for Ryder—the series starts here in Wrigley Field."

"If the Cubs make it that far."

"Yes, *if*," says Rafferty. "You might be counting your chickens, but we are not."

Winning all three series is widely viewed as a lock. Las Vegas thinks so. The mayor is cocky. The governor too. ESPN says the Orioles are the favorite. The *Baltimore Sun*. Aiko. Gallo's wife.

The quiet doubter is Alicia Ford. She doesn't buy into the big sweep of positive juju. She's been downplaying it. In fact, the closer you get to the team and its players, the more the confidence becomes elusive. The players are all going with the *It's just another game* mantra.

"Well," says Rafferty, "back to the reason I called—to wish you good luck and make a suggestion."

When it comes to Frank Ryder, everyone's got ideas.

"Put together a PR campaign," says Rafferty. "Get the public behind you. Get the fans to demand that they leave the game alone. Get the sportswriters behind you. Play offense."

"Endorsements, you mean. Backers. Make it political."

"Yes. Ask baseball stars to write columns. Hall of Famers. Organize a big news conference and include all the legends you can muster. Get Sandy Koufax to speak up—that would be a headline right there. Hold the news conference at Cooperstown. Or hold it on the pitcher's mound at Camden Yards. Get politicians there. Heck, have some fans. Let 'em speak. Figure out a way to win social media."

Gallo has seen the polling data. Fans like baseball games to last about three hours. Fans prefer baseball games that include a few home runs. There is nothing more exciting than a bottom-of-the-ninth comeback win. More than anything, they want hope. They want *surprise*.

Frank Ryder doesn't allow for those possibilities. He snuffs out hope. He murders surprise.

Rafferty isn't done. "You take a million out of the playoff bounty and hand it over to a PR firm, let 'em go crazy. You'd be protecting your boy. You'd be protecting your investment. Well, you haven't paid him much more than the signing bonus, and that was a whopper, but Ryder's payday is coming. If they try to put the brakes on your boy, what's he worth? The whole equation changes. Find yourself a billionaire who wants to do something good for the game. Or find yourself a billionaire who wants to support Frank Ryder as some badge of honor. And you better step on it."

"What the hell does that mean?"

"Commissioner Morris is calling a meeting. He doesn't want it to drag out. Drag on. *Drag*—you know, period."

Lapdog commissioner Morris . . .

"When?"

"Between game five and six of the World Series. In the city wherever those games are going to get played. Either on the travel day or the morning before game six."

"Did anyone tell him it's possible there's no game five, in which case there would be no game six or day *between* the two?"

"Take it easy, Ray."

"Easy?" says Gallo. "The hell I will. The commissioner's a useless fuzzball bootlicking buffoon. He's doing the bidding of the big boys, who always get their way. And how the hell do you know all this shit all the time—it sounds like you've got some inside track, some mole."

"No," says Rafferty. "Just making it a point to be in the loop."

"Fucking loop. We're a *league*. There shouldn't be any goddamn loops."

"I think we both know better."

"He's going to influence the outcome of the World Series."

"The commissioner doesn't see how a conversation about the future changes the way a ball gets thrown or hit in the present."

"It's messing with their heads. With Frank Ryder's head."

"He wants to send a message while baseball fans are all paying attention—he wants them all to know the league is dealing with this head-on."

"Then why doesn't the namby-pamby little piece of shit come out and say something like that, rather than slinking around behind the scenes playing politics with his goddamn loops? I can hear New York and Boston laughing up their sleeves if he goes through with this. *They* know the meeting has a ninety-nine percent chance of messing around with Ryder's head."

"That's why you need to fight back. You need America on your side. You need fans standing up and saying it's un-American. We didn't go three-quarters of the way to the moon and turn around; we went to the goddamn moon and kicked up some goddamn moon dust. Nobody is going to care if someone runs a marathon in ninety minutes or swims one hundred meters in eight seconds. You have to get your campaign organized, win the hearts of the fans, and show up at the meeting with America lined up at your back."

—⁓—

Will a PR campaign make a difference with the Cal Zieglers of the world, who grumbled to the media after the Yankees were dismissed from the playoffs by none other than the upstart Orioles? Will a PR campaign change one mind among demigod owners who believe all is within their control?

On the field, Frank Ryder fires another pitch. The hapless Mariner at the plate flails at the air. His swing is so exuberant he loses his balance. He crumples to the dirt and lands in a seated position, his legs crossed. He looks comfortable, as if he's just sat down to read a book in the park.

Wyatt heads to the dugout. The umpire drifts away. Frank Ryder hops across the chalk baseline, head down.

The batter sits, alone. He taps home plate with his bat three times.

It must feel good, thinks Gallo, to let the bat touch something.

Chapter 45

The TV network interviews Ryder at length, given that it's the American League Championship Series. Given that it's a series against Tampa Bay. Given that it's game one. In Baltimore. Given that the winner of four games will go to the World Series.

Special lighting, two cameras. Ryder doesn't even recognize the room. He endures the extended probe by concentrating on what lies ahead and by knowing that every word and inflection at this point will make the next step that much easier. He needs to lighten up. He will always need to lighten up. It's something he can learn, and it will be a good new skill no matter what he's doing. There is a sweet spot between perfunctory commentary and complete ingratiation.

It doesn't hurt to practice. Same as everything else. He's been working at the relationship with Maggie too. Regular calls. Listening. Refining their plan. Asking about her day. Listening more. And recognizing that on the other end of the line is a young woman who has every right to expect honesty out of him.

—⁓—

There is talk of Ryder starting three games in the ALCS and, if they make it, three more games in the World Series. There is "talk," that is, among the sportscasters who are trying to guess how Stone will call it. That is, if Stone is in charge. With a commodity like Frank Ryder, the decision-making might run to Ford and the data team, and it's possible Gallo gets to weigh in too.

The camps are split. Some believe you take full advantage of the freak. Some believe you don't overwork such a young talent. *You might ruin him for life.*

Ryder is aware of the other story line, the one having to do with the alleged "bitter rivalry."

Game one of the ALCS is more than a simple matter of Orioles versus Rays.

It's Frank Ryder versus Brody Billings.

It's the pitcher who shattered the ribs and ruined the season for Billy Jaworski versus the pitcher who shattered the wrist and ruined the season for Julio Diaz.

Even though neither pitcher is on the field at the same time, given the DH rule in the American League, the story line is set. It doesn't hurt that Brody Billings, who had been a reliever when he plunked Diaz, worked his way into the starting rotation before the Rays' stretch run.

The June clip of Billy Jaworski getting nailed is replayed ad nauseum, back to back with Julio Diaz writhing in pain. In case the players have forgotten about the incident back in June, the reporters want everyone involved to treat the October game one of the ALCS as if the June brawl happened yesterday.

Ryder is getting used to watching the coverage now. He's getting better at seeing himself on the television in all the highlight shows. Even the local news mentions the Orioles way up in the rundown alongside the politics and blood. Ryder is getting better at watching himself because he realizes the person they are talking about is two dimensional. The Frank Ryder they are talking about is nothing more than his stats. The Frank Ryder they are talking about is a concept, a "conundrum" for the league to "figure out." Ryder heard the word on Fox Sports the morning after his no-hitter against the Mariners in game one of the Division Series. *Conundrum.*

Frank Ryder is one thing. An arm. Half the TV analysts want to compare him to other famous burnouts; the other half believe he has a ticket to the Hall of Fame. None of the reporters believe in today. In *this game.* In *now.* The volume of words wasted on useless forecasting is mind boggling.

The reporters are hyperfocused on the brewing rivalry. The reporters want round two. They want repercussions. They wouldn't mind a benches-clearing dustup. They want feistiness. They want attitude and emotion.

Ryder gives them cool.

He pitches with a blank face. He is a million miles away. He stares at Wyatt's glove. He hears the crowd, but it's white noise. The buzz is a baseline din, a roiling hum. He could be throwing in the park with his brother. With one batter, he tattoos a pattern like a capital *U* across the strike zone. With the next, it's a capital *A*, minus the crossbar. Ryder works one batter up the ladder. The next, nothing above the knees. One pitch does a jitterbug. The next, a slow waltz. Each batter stands alone. Curve for a strike. Curve for a ball. Slider for a swinging strike. Two-seam fastball at 108. *Buh-bye.*

Ryder takes them one at a time. Moment by moment. Three batters in a row try bunting. Ryder has seen it before. Squaring up the round barrel on a ball moving at 105 is not an easy task. The first batter pops up a foul that's snagged by Wyatt; the next two go down on foul tips on their third strike. All strikeouts are humiliating, but it's weak to walk back to your dugout having made negligible contact with the ball, to watch it tick harmlessly off your lumber. It's not a manly moment.

In the dugout, nobody says a word about the no-hitter in progress. It's bad luck to mention it. To Ryder, it's silly. Are the fates really watching a baseball game? Will a comment alter the form and function of Ryder's arm? His ability to locate? How can one vocalization by the wrong person in the dugout change the outcome and final stat sheet of one game?

Ryder plays along.

It's what you do.

In the bottom of the seventh, Brody Billings walks Ortega. The fourth called ball earns sharp barks at the umpire from the Rays' manager and a disdainful glare, never advisable, from Brody Billings. Ortega races to second on the next pitch. As Ortega skids in, he tangles with the second baseman. Ortega adds an extra *something* to his arrival that pushes the second baseman, a moment after applying the tag, over on his back. The second baseman gets up, protesting the "safe" call like a petulant child. He hobbles in pain from Ortega's hard slide.

Intentional? Who can say?

The Rays' manager calls for a review of the tag by the invisible Star Chamber referees in New York. Three umpires don headphones like they have a temporary gig at NASA. They stand and stare. After an agonizing wait, the Camden Yards keyboardist doodling the theme from *Jeopardy!*, word comes back. *Safe.* The Rays' manager throws a fit, comes close to getting tossed. The crowd roars back at his red-faced rant. They want him thrown to the lions.

The mood in the dugout is good but controlled. "Even keel," says Steve Penny. "We got work to do."

Ortega moves to third on a long fly ball to right. Then Cory Bayless hits a routine grounder to short. It's routine except Ortega takes off on contact. With one out, it isn't the prudent thing to do. But Stone signaled for it. He wants to force the Rays to defend home plate. Ortega's dash is a surprise to the Rays' shortstop, who bobbles the ball and throws late to home.

Orioles up 1–0.

Except for the walk, Brody Billings has given up one measly hit, back in the third, to Steve Penny. Billings is on fire. He's got eleven strikeouts. He doesn't look like he's losing any steam, but given who he's pitching against, endurance isn't the issue.

After the bottom of the eighth, Ryder walks off the mound, head down. Easy stroll. The crowd cheers, but Ryder doesn't look up. He sits, starts to think about the next batter he'll face.

"Desperation time." Stone says this to anyone who will listen. "You watch."

"They don't dare," says Wyatt.

"They're dirty," says Stone. "Dirty and pissed off. All that sabermetrics crap goes right out the window now."

The Rays waste no time. At least, Brody Billings wastes no time. Mario Cruz leads off. On the first pitch, he hops like he's jumping rope to avoid getting hit on the foot. The ball skips past the outstretched glove of the Rays' catcher, bangs the backstop, and ricochets toward the Orioles' dugout. The umpire flips up his mask, points at Billings, the Rays' dugout, and the Orioles' dugout too.

Warnings all around.

"Hey, not us!" shouts Stone, but he's got no heart in it. Stone knows. Ryder fears the worst.

Three pitches later, Cruz takes a pitch off his butt. Cruz winces, arches his back, slams his bat, and glares at Billings. He takes two steps toward the mound, stops. The benches clear. Cruz is no fighter. He's a gentle kid from Santo Domingo, but he's giving the mean look everything he's got.

Up on the field with the scrum, players from both sides hurling creative epithets, Ryder hangs back. There are no blows. This is a nonfight. Cruz, a full fifty pounds lighter than Billings, is restrained by Bayless.

Billings gets tossed.

The Rays' manager, who is required by the unwritten rules to throw a fit over Billings' harsh punishment, is sent packing too.

The crowd goes bonkers.

When the game resumes, the Rays bring in a rifle-arm lefty who strands Cruz at first base.

Nobody says a word as the Orioles take the field for the top of the ninth.

For Ryder, the walk to the mound is heavy and heavyhearted.

Flashes of Billy Jaworski's still feet.

Flashes of Webb Bridge Park.

Flashes of Deon.

Flashes of Ryder's pitch worming its way under the bill of the blue batting helmet.

Ryder puts his cleat on the rubber for his warm-up tosses and knows what he needs to do.

Chapter 46

"Never crossed your mind?"

Tonight Rex Coburn's eyeglasses are Day-Glo orange. White shirt, neon-green tie. *Look at me.*

"What?" Ryder says it with a straight face.

"To get back for plunking Cruz."

"No need to put a runner on first base."

"So it did cross your mind."

"At that point, we still had four games to win," says Ryder. "Now it's three."

For the ALCS, players answer questions in a media briefing room, one interviewee at a time. Ryder sits at a table in front of a screen full of MLB logos. The table-as-buffer helps, but there are so many reporters Ryder wants to run. He is dressed and ready to bolt. His mouth dries up. His heart flickers in an odd fashion, and, for a moment, his head goes light.

Coburn stands off to the side, but near the front. He doesn't like Ryder's answer. He pushes his glasses back up tighter on his nose.

"So you're leaving the job to Kevin Wright?"

Ryder waits. Thinks. Shrugs. "I think the next game is the next game. Kevin will pitch how he wants to pitch."

"You're saying you don't mind Mario Cruz getting hit."

"I'm saying we've got three more games to win." He doesn't look at Coburn. He stares out at the throng and the lights. "They've got four."

"Back-to-back no-hitters?" This from a local TV reporter in the front row. "Can you talk a little bit about what's going through your mind in the eighth and the ninth, knowing you're about to set a record that will never be broken?"

Ryder stares down at the table, pushes out a little smile. "I go one batter to the next," says Ryder. "That's all. I try to get the next batter out the same as I did the last and leave it at that. If nobody gets on base, there's no complications. Who wants complications?"

The room laughs. Ryder beams, looks around. Coburn isn't one of those laughing.

"And," says Ryder. But he's not ready for what he wants to say. He looks up. He scratches a nonitch on his cheek. "And all records get broken. Baseball isn't going away. Look at the changes in the game since I was a kid. Did we ever think we'd see a two-way player like Shohei Ohtani? Pitchers aren't supposed to hit like that. And hitters aren't supposed to pitch like that. But there you go. Who knows who's coming down the pike? Or what?"

"One walk tonight," says a voice, ignoring his point.

Ryder puts his hand up over his eyes to shield the lights and to see if he can spot the female behind the nonquestion. She is seated near the front. Black skirt, yellow top.

"Sorry," says Ryder, dead serious.

The room laughs again.

"What happened?" she says.

"I threw ball four."

It's a full-on comedy show now.

"Were you upset about that?"

An invisible garotte throttles Ryder's attempt at a response. He wants to leave. "Upset?" It comes out dry and consonant heavy.

"Mad at yourself," she says.

"No."

"Care to expand on that a little?"

"What more is there to say?" says Ryder.

"But you were pitching out of the stretch."

"Same goal—get the next guy out."

They want paragraphs.

He is good for phrases—verbal shrapnel.

He can't imagine how he'll get through the day when he tells them about his plans.

Will they make any sense to anyone but him?

Chapter 47

Speed is the new coin, the new handle, the new reference point. A TV reporter stands outside a Baltimore hospital to introduce a story about the new most popular name for boys. *Frank.* And girls. *Frankie.* Black, brown, white, or whatever—it doesn't matter.

There's Ryder as a given name too. It's as unisex a name as names come.

Ryder Jones. Ryder Johnson. Ryder Brown.

It works.

A TV reporter interviews a homeowner who painted his house orange with black trim, complete with a Baltimore Oriole logo, the grinning version, on his garage door. The homeowner is fighting with his HOA—no outdoor signage, wrong colors.

Reporters are dispatched to spend a day with college girl Maggie, "Frank Ryder's down-to-earth" beauty with the whole "girl next door" schtick.

Reporters interview the parents and come away underwhelmed. How could a kid with such freak-level sports talent sprout in such a house where sports weren't celebrated? Hell, even encouraged? It makes no sense.

Reporters quiz Coach Rush about his training techniques and philosophy, but they come away with random musings on life. The interviews sound like a chat with Yoda. Or a yogi.

They sniff around Metro State looking for the secret sauce Frank Ryder must have sipped. They talk with his teachers in Alpharetta and Denver. Everybody remembers Frank. Or claims to.

—⚡—

They track down Josh Ryder in Denver. He's got a full-time job at Costco eight hours a day, hits the gym for three hours a day—working on his swing, his footwork, his framing. He'll be back in Birmingham in February. Josh Ryder has turned up on the Bleacher Report list of top fifty baseball prospects, but not on the lists from *Baseball America* or MLB. They try to get Josh to reveal what was special about Frank, but Josh doesn't lay claim to an explanation. "The only difference between Frank and any other pitcher out there is that Frank didn't believe okay was good enough. He analyzed everything. And every single time he practiced, he practiced for a reason—not to go through the motions but to work on something specific. A grip. His rate of spin. His release point. He took a video of every practice and watched that too. He did it with intensity, and he did it to understand. He didn't do anything that someone else couldn't do."

They try to track down Gail Johnson. Certainly she will be angry or bitter or at the very least she'll cry for them, on camera. They are greeted at her home in Mozley Park by a note that's been laminated and taped by the doorbell: **NO MEDIA. Have a great day!**

More than a couple of reporters have done their stand-ups in Westview Cemetery next to Deon Johnson's grave.

They might not have an interview with Gail Johnson, but there are school chums who remember Deon and all of Deon's dreams. There is no way to check, is there, if they were there that day at Webb Bridge Park? An earnest account is all that matters.

—⚡—

Chicago Cub confidence is tepid—at best—but it is the World Series and, well, *maybe*? A fluke? The fates? The Mets had never been to the playoffs before 1969, yet they toppled the Orioles, who had won 109 games that year. The Royals took down the mighty Cardinals in 1985 with only one true star in their lineup. George Brett seemed to make everyone play better around him. The Red Sox were down three games to the Yankees during the 2004 ALCS—they were *losing* game four in the ninth inning, in fact—and came back to win the fourth game and the next three too.

Maybe?

Just maybe?

On paper it's a cakewalk for the Orioles if Frank Ryder can pitch three games—games one, four, and seven.

On paper it doesn't seem likely the Cubs can or will win all the other games.

Chicago sportscasters reach for straws. They reach for reasons to believe. They feed fans what they want—*hope*. Even the hopeless can be seduced, however briefly, into discarding logic. They can be encouraged to dream, even if it's for a few minutes. Sports anchors give it their best shot. Their pep talks are monologues of comfort against tribulation. They grasp and reach because they are required to lift the spirits of the faithful. *Believe.* It's part of the job description. Anything is possible. Gamblers, too, are seduced by the odds. Millions are thrown down on that faintest glimmer of hope, a sparkle of gold in a lost mine.

There is one problem with the Orioles' attempt to win it all. Frank Ryder can start three games—*if his arm is up to it*—but he can't start four. And he'll have to pitch two of his three starts on the road, thanks to the National League winning the All-Star Game, if it comes down to a game seven.

It's true that Joe Rhineland and Kevin Wright pitched well down the stretch and have held their own, for sure, in the playoffs to date. It's true that some of Frank Ryder's focus and discipline, even a touch of his cool demeanor, has rubbed off on the rest of the Orioles' pitching staff. It's true that the Steve Penny pickup, hailed as Alicia Ford's genius move of the season, has given the Orioles' clubhouse a "veteran presence," as they say. The Orioles look like they belong.

But still, no human being has won three World Series games since Mickey Lolich did it in 1968.

So all the Cubs need is to win the other four games, when Frank Ryder is resting his howitzer. When Frank Ryder can't hurt them. When Frank Ryder is a nonfactor.

There is hope.

But there's not.

Not after Frank Ryder pitched games one and four in the ALCS and made it look easy. The Orioles swept their series with smooth fielding, good hitting. Defense and offense clicked together as one.

Meanwhile, the Cubs took seven games to get past the dreaded Dodgers. The Cubs are bedraggled. They have that look in their eyes. *What's the point?* Long odds for the Cubs or not, game one is the Ticket. Scalpers manage more action than Wall Street. Some are chumps—they have unwittingly sold to other scalpers, who jack the price again.

Hotels are packed. There is no logic to this because Wrigley Field is so damn small, but among those who hop Learjets or Gulfstreams and head to Chicago, there isn't one who doesn't have a connection that might pay off or a favor that they might call in. And, if it doesn't pan out, there is always the energy around the game itself. Restaurants roar. Bars buzz. Excitement loosens wallets, turns the sullen giddy. The full feed again. The tipsy order another round. In concept and theory, Frank Ryder may be trouble for the future of baseball, but everybody wants to say they were there when it all went down.

For the forty-eight hours before the first pitch, the party around Wrigley Field begins in the late morning and ends an hour before dawn.

Even with his Dodgers in the dustbin, Will Ferrell wants to bear witness.

Jimmy Fallon decides on a week's worth of shows in the Second City. His Yankees got flattened and humiliated by the orange and black, but Fallon wants a seat.

Mark Wahlberg flies in on behalf of Red Sox Nation, and Jerry "Mr. Met" Seinfeld is compelled to show up.

Ex-president Barack Obama, a South Side guy and a White Sox fan, opens a speech in Detroit with a few comments on the importance of the underdog in American history and the American psyche. "The challenge is to fight. If the defense comes up with a new wrinkle, the offense needs to rethink. Revise. And respond. When the chips are down, you must fight harder, think harder, and dig deeper. If America had a middle name, it would be *outsmart*, and of course belief and conviction have always played a role."

Obama, the man connected to the word *hope* like nobody else in the twenty-first century, gives one of his trademark pauses. He takes in the room. It's the Church of God by Faith, One Hundredth General Assembly.

"And then other times you toss your cards on the table, take your lumps, and skedaddle the heck away. Sorry, Cubbies, you won't look so cute and cuddly after Frank Ryder is finished with you."

The room roars with laughter. If Obama isn't offering succor to the weak and downtrodden?

It's over.

Chapter 48

Frank Ryder claws the dirt with his cleats and stares in at Luke Wyatt.

Ryder sees leather. *Round* brown leather and the dark hole at the center, the hole where his throws will land, unsullied.

Ryder stands straight, both feet on the rubber. His right hand is buried inside his glove, where he grips the ball.

For a long moment, he is still.

Leadoff hitter Kurt Costa doesn't like the ball inside. But he's got a knack for the big moment.

Ryder focuses on the spots where he'll nibble and toil. The location isn't an issue because Frank Ryder is rested. His arm is good.

The October night is a peach. It is game one of the World Series, and there have been days of hoopla and buildup and silly questions about everything from his diet to his love life, but nothing has changed in the distance or the equation or the question Frank Ryder is about to ask when he throws the ball.

Can you hit my stuff?

Right down the lineup, the answer is no.

Of course not.

It will be the same question and the same answer for twenty-seven batters, unless he walks one or two because he's nibbling too hard, being too careful.

A week and a day—the end is not far off. The one wrinkle is rain. A storm might delay the series, but the opening two games in Chicago won't be a problem. Tonight is relatively warm for October in Chicago. It's a Tuesday. Some fans wear jackets and sweatshirts, but there are plenty of tough guys in T-shirts. Tomorrow is supposed to be the same. Ryder has heard nothing about storms along the Atlantic coast for games three, four, and five over the upcoming weekend. If all goes well, it's very possible they won't come back to Chicago. And that means the alleged meeting of owners to decide on the Frank Ryder Issue will happen after the series, not during. Ryder has heard the rumors. He assumes they are true.

Whoa.

Ryder catches himself.

His mind should not be wandering or wondering about tomorrow or the next day. All that counts is now.

Now. Now. Now.

The issue for Frank Ryder at this moment is to snuff out hope. The Cubs' batters are likely thinking positive thoughts—or trying. Cubs manager Ben Lucas thinks he's got something up his sleeve, maybe some form of psychological warfare. Cubs fans have a hope, at least for a few more minutes.

Frank Ryder's job is to take that hope and light it on fire, like a match to hydrogen, one batter at a time.

Ryder is minister at his own funeral—the funeral of the celebrity version of himself, at least—and it feels right. That none of the fans know it? That Ben Lucas doesn't know it? That Buster Olney doesn't know it, or Jim Palmer? No matter. It's the moment. It is very hard, make that *impossible*, to pretend this is another game in May or June. The buildup, the pregame introductions, the mood in the clubhouse, and the masses of fans staring at him—Frank Ryder can't pretend it's anything other than what it is.

Luke Wyatt flashes the 1. It's the worst-kept secret in the history of competitive sports, but he calls for it anyway to get in the groove. Wyatt's target is steady, tucked down tight by Costa's knees.

Ryder goes into his motion. His body remembers. His feet, his legs, his hips, his torso, his arm, his bones, his fingers all say, *We got this.* Frank Ryder goes into the zone. For the rest of the night, he will cocoon himself in a mental headspace of *now.* For the rest of the night, he will forget about *next.*

At the top of his arc, a microsecond before the release point, Ryder sees that Kurt Costa wants to play. He is starting to swing. Costa thinks he can outthink physics or outsmart the fact-based essence of science— one truth building on the next about why the world hangs together the way it does, one truth building on the next why the game of baseball works the way it does and works so well because of the proportions and distances and the utter simplicity of it too.

The swing is good. It's beefy. It's serious. It means business.

But it's late.

The ball whacks Wyatt's glove one tick before Costa's bat moves through the zone.

Whack—

—whiff.

Inside, Ryder smiles. He catches the return throw from Wyatt and peers in again.

Kurt Costa is not smiling.

—⚏—

The postgame quizzing takes forever. How often can you say, "One batter at a time"? How often can you say, "My arm felt good"?

Ryder works his best to expound and to smile. "They are a good team—look at their record," says Ryder. "A mighty fine team. I knew my job was to focus."

"How did you feel out there? The pressure?"

"We're all feeling the pressure." It sounds like something most people would say—right? "It comes with the territory. Pressure comes from all the fans back home in Baltimore. Pressure comes from all these lights."

Ryder shields his eyes with his hands, looks around. He gives a face like he's seen a monster, and the reporters all laugh. They want to feel close to him. And, like a monster, they want to jab sharp spears in his tender spots.

"And you don't think it's that big a deal? Being the first since Don Larsen to throw a World Series no-hitter? That was 1956."

"I had my good stuff tonight," says Ryder.

"And the two walks?"

"But not perfect stuff. I'd say those were lack of focus." *Nibbling too much.* "The thing about pitching is there is nobody to blame but yourself."

"The umpire."

"You go down that road, you already lost," says Ryder. "Umpire might be your best friend on the next pitch."

"Two walks from a perfect game," says a female reporter. There is no question.

"Room for improvement." Ryder delivers this answer with his best smile, provoking a ripple of laughter among the media.

She goes on: "Does the fact that the owners are meeting bother you? During the series?"

"No," says Ryder. "Do I wish they would wait until after the series? Sure. But if a bunch of guys talking in a room affected how I throw the ball, that'd be weird."

"You could be down to your last game or two when you can throw with everything you've got."

Ryder shrugs, looks up. Thinks. "Only if the series lasts that long."

—m—

The clubhouse is suppressed giddiness. The win is electric. A happy, zippy buzz crackles through the room.

Ryder feels it. You can't *not* feel it. One World Series win is like a month of wins in August. On the road? Add all the September wins too. On the road and a no-hitter? It's too good. It's sublime. Surreal.

The Orioles . . . ?

The Orioles.

Smiles. Laughs. Music. High fives. Low fives. Fist pumps. Jokes. Replays. Ribbing. Looseness. Ease.

"Good game."

Steve Penny is dressing next to Ryder. His wrists are taped. He wears a black wrap on his left knee, a white one on his right ankle. He smells like Old Spice and muscle cream.

"Thanks," says Ryder.

"As in, amazing game."

"It was fun."

"You're playing it so cool."

"Not champagne time yet."

"If this is what one World Series win feels like, I can't imagine grabbing the whole shebang," says Penny.

"One game at a time," says Ryder.

"Don't you ever cut yourself some slack?" Penny says it in a casual way. *Just fooling with you.* "Like your rope is tied to a whale way down deep in the dark water."

Ryder laughs. "Colorful," he says. "As soon as we win three more games, you will soon be observing the most relaxed man on the planet."

Ryder sits at his locker, dressed. He's got his head down, waiting for the call to the team bus. His phone is jammed with texts. Josh. Both parents. Coach Rush.

Olivia: Just wow.

Ryder: Thanks.

Olivia: No darkness. Playing with reporters like a cat toying with a mouse. A whole house of mouses.

Ryder: Not disrespectful?

Olivia: Hardly. The whole country is eating it up.

Ryder: Good I guess.

Olivia: I'd like to see you.

Ryder: Kind of a crazy time. Maybe after the season?

Jessica Mendoza: Can we get you on with Buster tomorrow morning?

Ryder: Sure.

Mendoza: Can we talk about the owners' meeting?

Ryder: Sure. You positive it's happening?

Ryder believes the meeting, and all the background chatter about him, is unnecessary noise. It's a messy distraction. The discussion about rules makes the game look malleable, changeable, and human.

The game should appear like a gift from the gods. Not perfect. But close.

Mendoza: Our sources are good.

Ryder: Why can't they just wait?

Mendoza: Say that on the podcast?

Ryder: Gotta stick to my world. That whole hypothetical business? Not much to say.

Aiko: You found Dragon.

Maggie: Damn. Just day-um! Call me later?

Ryder: You bet.

Chapter 49

In the morning, Ryder rides the elevator to the top floor of the team hotel. He didn't head out and toss back beers with the boys. He spent the evening avoiding sports shows, overtipping room service delivery for a late-night cheeseburger, and laughing on the phone with Maggie. There is an ease to their chatting now, a flow.

Aiko greets Ryder at Room 4201 with a double-handed handshake and a big, wide smile, leads him down a hall to an expansive corner suite. Giant windows overlook the Loop in one direction and wide chunks of a calm Lake Michigan, lit by a mellow morning sun, in the other.

Three men are inside. Ray Gallo greets him with a smile and firm handshake. The other two are introduced. One is Aiko's father, Ethan Turner. He is pushing seventy. He is trim and fit and spry. Aiko mentions her father's title at the Jet Propulsion Lab and something to do with Mars.

The second man needs no introduction, but Aiko utters the words in case Ryder is clueless.

"Sal Ricci."

Movie star. Academy Awards. Tough guy on screen. The new De Niro. His breakout movie was a remake of *The Wanderers*, about gangs in Boston. It was said to be based on Ricci's youth on the streets, though the story was drawn from a novel.

"Another Red Sox diehard here," says Ricci. "But a pleasure to meet you. The enemy of my enemy is my friend. It was great to see the Yankees sent home for a long winter."

"You're welcome."

Ryder's nerves flutter. He wishes he could make small talk about some of Ricci's movies. Ricci's clothes are dark and sleek.

"And it's great to have the Orioles back in the heat of the division," says Ricci. "Old rivals, of course."

"Of course," says Ryder.

There's a well-stocked breakfast buffet with blueberry pancakes, scrambled eggs, sausages, orange juice, and coffee. An open bottle of champagne sits in a bucket of ice. Ryder helps himself to a plate of food and coffee. The others follow and settle back into fat, comfy chairs and a wide, welcoming couch.

A *Chicago Tribune* on the marble coffee table screams a headline: THE WHIFFY CITY.

"One bit of advice—take it or leave it," says Ricci. His jaw is crooked, the skin on his cheeks pocked and rough. He wears his hair short. He leads with intense eyes.

"Fire away," says Ryder.

Maggie is not going to believe this.

"Watch the media. Your story is your story." Ricci speaks deathbed slow, with certainty. "Nobody else controls your story. Choose your path. Protect yourself. Don't give them everything. Why? Because you owe them nothing."

"I'm starting to figure that out."

"I mean, you gotta talk about the game," says Ricci. "The game is the game. Beyond that, zip."

"They always seem genuinely curious."

"It's a trick," says Ricci. "Don't fall for it."

The talk turns to Ryder's plan. He spells out the rough outline, though nobody in the room knows how far Ryder plans to take it.

"You're talking to a convicted felon," says Ricci. "I was eighteen. Got tried and convicted as an adult. A couple years ago I tried to go after a pardon in Massachusetts, and the district attorney came after me—how would it look for a white guy with money to get a pardon? Did I think my *celebrity* and all that allowed me a shortcut?"

Ricci holds Ryder's gaze, shakes his head.

"I did some bad stuff as a kid," says Ricci. "Stupid stuff. Me and my buddies. My *locos*. It was my stupid days. My *high school sucks* phase. We hurt people because they weren't one of us. We made trouble because we were angry—but we didn't know why we were angry or what we were mad about."

Ricci sits up straight, swallows hard. If he's acting, it's damn good stuff. Remorse fills the room.

"Lucky we were stopped," says Ricci. "Lucky there were others around."

"Aiko called me," says Turner. He is sitting next to Ricci, and he slaps the movie star's shoulder. "Our family contributes to Mr. Ricci's foundation."

"Generously," says Ricci. "Very."

"And the foundation?" says Ryder.

"Focuses on the inner city," says Ricci. "Kids who don't know better. Kids who hear *no* a thousand times a day. Kids who don't recognize there are opportunities out there. Aiko called her father, and Mr. Turner called me when he heard of your idea, which sounds fantastic. They're ideas at this point?"

"Everything is a plan until the ball leaves your hand," says Ryder. "Right?"

"Of course," says Ricci. "But, even as a plan, our foundation would like to hear what you're thinking. There would be no downside in working alongside the biggest name in professional sports—and clearly someone who will be holding that title for many, many years to come."

Gallo and Aiko follow Ryder back down the elevator and all the way to the hall outside his room. Ryder can't believe the sheer size of the commitment from the foundation, albeit tentative. Ryder needs to write some proposals, develop a budget, detail some of the logistics. Ricci made it sound like a done deal.

Ryder thanks Aiko with a warm hug. There is a tear in her eye. "You're a good man," she says.

"Where would I be without friends?" says Ryder.

Gallo switches topics to the meeting that looms over all of baseball. Gallo wants to make sure Ryder isn't "troubled" by it. He wants Ryder to not worry about the meeting, to focus on the games, and "ignore the sideshow."

It's hardly a sideshow. It's a circus.

"Here's the thing," says Gallo. "I want you in that room."

"Me?"

"I'm working on it," says Gallo. "I want the union man there; I want the umpires represented too."

"What am I going to say?"

"You're going to plead your case."

"Like a criminal?"

"Your point of view," says Gallo.

"What's to say?" says Ryder. "Everything has been said."

"They are all worried about the precedent."

Ryder remembers looking up that phrase in high school, certain it would be spelled a *fate* accompli.

"You gotta tell them they are cutting the heart out of the very spirit of America," says Gallo. "That they need to think about the message they are sending to every kid out there who is working to get better—at anything."

"And they don't know that already?"

"These clowns?" says Gallo. "They think baseball is a toy for their endless tinkering. They don't think like you and me."

Chapter 50

Any brief suspense in game four is over after the first few innings, when the Orioles chase Tim Simons from the mound in the third inning with a barrage of singles and doubles. With Ryder on the mound, one run would have been enough.

Ryder gives up a hit in the fifth inning. He gifts Chris Bachman a ninety-nine-mile-per-hour pitch down the middle. Bachman does what Ryder wants him to do. He strokes it into left field. Bachman arrives at first base pumping his fists at his teammates back in the dugout, exhorting them as if he's jabbed the first spear in the dragon's eye.

Ryder strikes out the next three batters with ten pitches.

"You put that one on a platter for Bachman," says Stone between innings.

"Yeah," says Ryder.

"Why?"

Ryder wonders if the reason will sound arrogant, says it anyway. "I want everyone behind me to relax."

"Holy hell, Frank." Stone shakes his head. "Stop overthinking everything. What, you don't think your players are good enough to back you up?"

In the postgame news conference, after the Orioles square the series at two games each, Ryder shrugs off Bachman's hit. "We needed to tie the series back up. I was focused on the W."

"Are you going to be good for game seven if it comes to that?"

"I'd start again tomorrow if they want me to." It's the way he feels, but Ryder realizes how it might come across. "That's not my *preferred* option." Ryder holds up his arm, wobbles it like a wet noodle. "Just saying."

The room laughs.

Ryder laughs too.

Outside, about to climb into a cab, he notices a young couple in matching UMBC sweatshirts and nonmatching Oriole caps—one the simple orange *O's* on black, the other old school, with the batting bird—before he registers the woman's face.

Olivia.

"Frank—"

Ryder feels a burst of heat in his chest, an internal alarm.

Olivia comes in for a lightning hug. "I want you to meet John," she says. "Fellow Retriever, as you can see. John Bishop. First base." Olivia laughs. "We just wanted to say great game."

They are all sorts of clingy with each other—arm in arm, shoulder to shoulder, hip to hip. Her new guy has got a good three inches over Olivia, who melts into his embrace.

"Thanks," says Ryder.

"Wanted to see you in person," says Olivia.

"Means a lot." Ryder gets an idea. "I've got to come see the Retrievers in action. You know. Next season. How about a quick photo?"

Ryder's selfie game is weak, but he knows the rough idea. He holds his phone with his arm extended, makes sure that Olivia and John are entwined in each other's clutches. Their matching smiles are ample evidence. The double-vision UMBC letters seal the deal. And if that's not already enough, there's a visible gap between Ryder and this randy, handsy couple.

In the cab, Ryder posts the photo to Twitter.

> Ran into a couple of passionate fans after the game.
> Go Retrievers! Go Orioles! And thank you, Baltimore!
> Oriole fans rock!

He's never used so many exclamation points in his life, but it feels good.

In case there's any lingering question, he thinks of a few hashtags that might work.

> #bringingithome #noquestionnow

He copies the photo and message for Instagram too. It's designed for one person only. Ryder doesn't want Maggie to miss it.

—∞—

Ryder finds a seat in the bullpen for game five. Kevin Wright pitches a scoreless no-hitter into the eighth inning, but the Orioles' bats are quiet. A lone moment of hope comes in the fifth. Cory Bayless reaches second on a single and an error, but second base is the end of the line.

With two outs in the top of the eighth, Kurt Costa connects. Even in the bullpen, the sound is different. It's the crack of authority. O's left fielder Lanny Wilson takes four halfhearted steps toward the fence and stops. *You don't give up on any ball,* the old mantra goes. That's even more true in the World Series. But sometimes you know. The ball lands in the Orioles' dugout, rattles around, and comes to rest at Ryder's feet. Ryder kicks the ball away, stands up to go lean on the fence, and watches Wright strike out Mateo Torres on three pitches.

Wright is pissed. Ryder is pissed. The air goes out of the stadium, other than the smattering of Cubs fans who have paid top dollar to mix their blue caps and shirts into the sea of orange and black. The fans sit on their hands in the bottom of the eighth. The O's offense gives the fans no reason to shake off their growing fear. Penny strikes out, Wilson grounds out to first, and Bayless pops out to third.

Weak, lame, sad.

Wright finishes what he started in the ninth. It's his last game of the season, no matter what. Why not wring him out? Stone can save a few bullpen bullets for game six. The Orioles go quietly in the bottom of the ninth too.

Cubs three games, O's two.

The fans have resigned themselves to the traditional loser role.

Ryder feels them as one.

We didn't deserve it after all.

Reporters want to know if Ryder will start game six. If the Orioles lose game six and therefore lose the series, what was the point of the season? What was the point of *Frank Ryder*? Reporters believe the owners will do something to clamp down on the "warp speed" pitching before the next season, so why not ensure you can make it to game seven by having Frank Ryder go on two days' rest?

Frank Ryder said he was good on zero days' rest, right?

He *did* say that, right?

Was he joking?

Reporters nod knowingly as Stone dismisses all such fantasies. Stone is emphatic at Camden Yards as the final reporter is whisked out of the clubhouse. He's emphatic at the airport. He's emphatic when they land in Chicago on the off day, when all the media attention will shift from the ball fields to the power meeting among men—*all* men—at the Fairmont.

Ryder echoes Stone.

"We're going with the pitching rotation that got us here," he says.

In a million different ways.

"We have to win two games, one way or the other," he says.

In a million different ways.

"What do I think? It doesn't matter what I think. I get told what day the mound is mine. That's all."

Ryder answers the questions, the ad nauseum questions, in a quasi-zombie state. He has found a new place in his head where he goes when he's surrounded by reporters. He slows things down. He listens to the question. Ponders. Answers. He goes for vanilla. Polite, heartfelt, vanilla. He isn't *there*. He tells himself to treat every question like a gem, to respect a reporter's job, to feed the media machine.

How do you let reporters see inside a pitcher's head? What's really going on?

You don't.

Do these reporters realize what's about to happen, in a few short weeks?

They don't.

Do these reporters know of the elaborate plan to sneak Ryder into the meeting?

Of course not.

"Do you think you're capable of pitching at slower speeds?" asks one.

"Yes," says Ryder. "Of course."

"You could still be throwing very fast pitches, nearly unhittable."

"Yes," says Ryder. "True."

"But would the game interest you as much? Would you be as eager to pitch if they say you can't pitch above a certain speed?"

"I'll always love the game."

"What about this big meeting tomorrow? Does it toy with your head that they're fooling around with the rules while the World Series is still running its course?"

It's childish theatrics . . .

It's ridiculously overdramatic . . .

"No."

"But do you feel as if your fate is out of your control?"

"Isn't that the question we all ask ourselves every single day?" says Ryder.

Chapter 51

Twenty-six hours before first pitch for game six, Ryder is escorted from his hotel by a representative from MLB. She is tall with short hair. All business. A tad nervous. She doesn't say much. She leads Ryder to the hotel service elevator.

Ryder pulls on a knit hat—Chicago Bears—and oversize sunglasses. He zips up a light-green windbreaker. The elevator clunks its way down to an underground parking area with the laundry trucks and loading docks. They climb into an idling minivan. There's an older man behind the wheel who says nothing. The van's side windows are tinted like a limo's. The van is a few years old and needs a wash. It's perfect.

The trip to the Fairmont takes only a few minutes. They pass the front of the hotel, where news trucks are jammed together like there's been a mass shooting. Reporters primp for their live shots outside. It's not hard to imagine MLB has a room for the postmeeting briefing, where all the World Series media, hundreds of them, will be gathered inside.

Ryder is hustled in a rear door for employees. They head down a flight of stairs. They hike long subterranean corridors before heading up another flight of stairs to a kitchen. Ryder peers out through oval windows in a pair of swinging doors that leads out to a giant meeting room.

In the middle of the room is an open square of tables. They are all covered in white. The room is windowless with high ceilings and a large chandelier, the sole touch of glitz in the workmanlike space. Ryder spots Ray Gallo standing in a huddle of men with Cubs owner Tommy Rafferty. There's one guy in a cowboy hat, a couple of guys in full suits, but most wear casual attire. Gallo shakes his head. His arms are crossed.

Ryder's imminent arrival must have triggered a signal because Commissioner Morris lifts his water glass and whacks it with a spoon five times to get everyone to take their seats.

Suddenly Ryder realizes this will be An Entrance. He wriggles out of the jacket, stuffs the Bears cap in the empty sleeve, and removes the sunglasses. Underneath, he's wearing blue jeans, generic sneakers, and a black polo shirt with the tiny smiley face Orioles logo.

Commissioner Morris starts speaking, the words low and muffled through the door. Ryder waits. He feels as if walking a tightrope over the Grand Canyon would require less concentration than covering the ten yards of open carpet between the door and the table with some reasonable degree of aplomb.

Ryder spots an empty seat next to Gallo, and as Ryder's heart tries to wriggle up his throat to escape, the commissioner points to the doors, and suddenly it's too late. He's through the doors.

The grumbling is automatic. Predictable. "For Chrissake." "Jesus H." Someone claps. And a laugh.

Ryder treats the jeers the same as if they were coming from an enemy dugout. What's the difference? They want to see him chopped down to size. They want to see him humiliated, chased from his perch.

Gallo stands, pulls the empty chair back for him. He greets Ryder with a handshake, leans in close.

"It's their way of saying they're big shots, that's all."

Ryder's seat is the last one on the corner. He sits and looks around the room, stares back. Chin up. He imagines each of these guys in the batter's box and thinks about what he would do to carve them up.

Players union honcho Walter Woodson offers a handshake. Ryder takes it, smiles. Ray Gallo already walked him through the nonowners in attendance—and warned Ryder that Woodson would be arguing for the batters, who comprise the union's bread and butter. Woodson might claim to be fighting for family entertainment, but his goal is to protect batting averages and splashy home run records.

Next to Woodson is Lou Kozlowski, head of the umpires association. He's got two other umpires sitting next to him. "Hi, kid," says Kozlowski. "Welcome to God only knows."

—∾—

Ryder listens. The chatter rises and falls.

The owners squabble over stepping around the normal procedures of the Rules Committee. One argues that the process needs to be respected "at our great peril," like it's war and not just a game.

Commissioner Morris is as effective at keeping order as a rookie teacher trying to break up a lunchroom food fight among thirty kids on a sugar high. These are his bosses. You don't scream at your bosses.

Ryder's name isn't mentioned. It's as if he's not in the room. He's a theory. He's a mental-skills challenge. He's a cipher. *A ghost.*

Gallo listens, shakes his head. Kozlowski, the umpires' guy, rolls his glazed-over eyes for Ryder. Woodson tries to gain footing in the room—and fails.

Ryder sits, waiting.

"Aw, for crying out loud, what is the point?" Cal Ziegler. "The longer we sit in here, jerking around, the worse it gets. We should be in and out. Twenty minutes. Maybe thirty. We're sending a message by how long we're dragging this out."

Someone suggests the umpires should weigh in.

For a moment, the room settles. Finally, some "What to do?" meat.

Kozlowski says he's sampled opinions from umpires in both leagues. It's not a scientific survey, he says, but one theme is pervasive. "Meaning no disrespect to the only ballplayer in the room, but there's a balance to the game that needs to be maintained. We can do our jobs either way, but to us we're in the business of entertainment—and that means action, and action means putting the ball in play. It's pretty simple."

"Hear, hear," says the Rangers' Jimmy Wharton, putting a hand to the tip of his cowboy hat and saluting Kozlowski. "We're putting on a show. Like I've been saying."

"*And* hyperpitches are too dangerous, *and* they're boring as hell."

"That's Quintana—Tampa Bay," mutters Gallo to Ryder. "Big surprise, right?"

"Okay, the umpires are clear, and we know where the union comes down." The Red Sox owner. Ryder knows this guy. He looks more like an art critic than anything to do with sports. He's wearing round blue glasses and a green bow tie. "And again," he goes on, "with all due respect to the only baseball player in the room, we really don't have a hard time imagining what *he* is going to say, do we? So let's decide on something and be done with it, feed the media, and let everyone get back to the World Series. The statisticians can use a whole bunch of asterisks for the pitching records Frank Ryder set this year, and we move on. We walk out of here united and reassure all the ticket buyers for next year that they will hear the lovely sound of a bat on a ball when they come to the ball game. How hard can this be?"

"Except it's artificial."

It's Ryder's voice.

He pushes back his chair.

Stands.

Fear is the mind-killer. From *Dune*. From Maggie.

He can't come all this way and not have his say.

"Whatever miles-per-hour number you have in mind—it's artificial."

The room goes quiet.

"You would pluck a number from the sky, and for the first time in the history of this beautiful, primarily American game—all due respect, as you say, to baseball players around the world and especially in Japan—you would be asking athletes to purposefully *underperform*."

Ryder looks around the room, goes for direct eye contact with at least one owner on each side of the table. The silence is delicious, empowering.

"You would be asking athletes to *not* do their best. Can you seriously go out there with a straight face and say you run a sport, but in this one single case you're asking someone to only bring their B game? Leave the A game at the door? *That's* what you stand for?"

Ryder moves around behind his chair, pushes it in, thinks of all the practice time, from his bedroom to Thomas Jefferson High School to Metro and with the Orioles too. All the work. All the analysis.

"That idea boggles my mind, to think you would clamp down on *potential*."

Ryder shrugs.

"Did you tell Nolan Ryan he couldn't throw another no-hitter? Did you tell Sandy Koufax he could only toss five devastating curveballs per game? Did you step in then? Why not stop a no-hitter before the ninth inning and say, 'You know, we really want some balls in play today'? Why not? Why not set fifteen strikeouts as the maximum number any pitcher can get in one game? What's the difference?"

Ryder shakes his head. A minute ago he was sitting in his teacher-prep classes at Metro State. A minute ago he could have grabbed a sandwich at the Intermission Cafe and eaten in peace. A minute ago he was another Division II pitcher working on his form. He wasn't ready for *Sports Illustrated*, *Time* magazine, paparazzi like flies, and a public image he can't control.

"I don't get it. I don't think the kids will get it. What kind of a message is that? The beauty in baseball is the balance. The beauty in baseball starts with the battle between a pitcher and a hitter. It's mental. It's physical. And now you're talking about telling pitchers they would get *penalized* for throwing too fast? Like I've said, it's unnatural. It runs counter to essential pitcher DNA."

The room is dead quiet.

"This battle between pitcher and hitter. It's been going on for a century and a half. Sandlots. Stickball. Little League. Minor-league teams from Birmingham to Norfolk. Yankee Stadium, Fenway Park, and Wrigley Field tomorrow night. You'd be interfering with that natural ebb and flow, that decades-long battle between all pitchers and all hitters? You really want to do that?"

Ryder smiles.

"And speaking of tomorrow night." The smile is powered by a strong hunch. "Game six will not be the last this year. Mark my words. There will be a game seven. I have it on good authority the Orioles will win it all."

"Noted," says Rafferty. "I'll be sure to pass the word along."

He laughs. A few other owners join in, but the laugh gets no traction.

The laugh fizzles and dies.

Chapter 52

Ryder takes a seat in the dugout for game six. The game is tense from the first pitch. It's delicious. Chris Bachman smacks a two-run home run to center field in the bottom of the second inning. The resulting cheer is as if the Cubs faithful have witnessed a stake pounded into a beating heart. Joe Rhineland settles down. He doesn't allow another runner to reach base until the sixth, when he gives up a walk and induces two easy grounders. The first one is a double play.

In the top of the seventh, Cory Bayless doubles and reaches third on an Esteban Ortega bunt. Steve Penny lifts a fly ball high to left.

Bayless stands at third, his right leg jammed against the base. Waiting. Bayless stares at left fielder Stan Foley, who takes two steps running before the ball lands in his glove.

The throw is on the money. It takes one hop ten feet from home plate and zips into the waiting glove of Cubs catcher Barrett, who sweep-tags the shin of Bayless.

The umpire barks a boisterous "Out!"

Stone signals for an official review.

The replay shows Bayless' shoe digging a furrow in the dirt before it hits home plate, and it's possible, barely possible, that Bayless' shoe hit the edge of home plate a microsecond before the tag. If Bayless wore a smaller size shoe . . . it's that close. Another angle shows the tag, but Bayless' foot is obscured by the catcher's shoulder. The gods of logic and the remote umpires put two and two together, and, after a long wait, the umpires remove their headsets and signal "safe."

It's 2–1, Cubs.

Boos rain down. Bayless gets chest-bumped and high-fived in the dugout like he hit a grand slam.

On the next pitch, when fans are settling back into their seats, Luke Wyatt launches a towering ball that clears the outfield bleachers and bounces hard on Waveland Avenue. He rounds the bases like he's a bored Barry Bonds, but this is only his sixth home run all year. His arrival in the dugout is the signal that Stone was right, that Oriole Nation can relax, that the Cubs are beatable, that the whole country will get to watch Frank Ryder again tomorrow night.

It's 2–2.

For Cubs fans, tonight could be a party or pure heartache.

If it's a party, it will last through tomorrow.

If it's heartache, it will be two nights of pain. For the Cubs, it's tonight or never.

In the bottom of the seventh, two singles put Cubs on first and third. No outs. The crowd fires up. Ryder's stomach burns.

It could all be over soon.

All that practice, all that work . . .

Ryder finds a spot alone. He tightens his jaw against the rising sensation of loss, hopes the cameras have other places to pry. Head down, he walks down the stairs toward the locker room underneath. At the bottom of the stairs is a bright-white cinder block passageway with four sharp television screens, each carrying a different view of the game. The screens are brighter than the view with the naked eye a few steps up the stairs.

This could be it.

Right here.

You should be with your team. A hit here and only six outs stand in the way of what's next.

Ryder's guts lurch. His thoughts clash.

The game doesn't want you.

This is the game you love.

Rhineland induces a dribbler back to the mound. He picks the ball up, stares down the runner at third, stares some more, and turns to throw the ball to first. The ball squirts out of his grip like a slippery ice cube. By the time he picks it up, the bases are loaded.

The cheers are deafening, complete with a dose of humiliation.

No outs.

Rhineland's jaw tightens.

"Frank!"

The shout rattles down the stairwell.

Lackland.

Ryder bounds back up the stairs.

"Bullpen," says Lackland.

Ryder grabs his glove.

Stone walks to the mound like a Sunday stroll, head down. Ryder sprints out to a cascade of boos.

Ryder runs across right field for the bullpen door with the one-way glass.

Now is now . . .

The assignment feels good.

The door opens as Ryder arrives. A ball drops into his glove.

Ryder throws.

Half tosses at first, eight of them.

Rhineland gets the next batter to pop out.

One out, bases loaded.

Ryder throws when Rhineland is not—two pitches between every one of his teammate's. Rhineland gets Torres to a 3–2 count. Torres fouls off the next two pitches. The second foul is a screaming line drive that touches down an inch from being fair way up the left field line.

The fans roar. And sigh. The camera zooms in on the distinct dent in the dark dirt, a mini crater of *almost*.

Rhineland takes a small walk-around. He is gassed.

Ryder watches the television feed in the bullpen. The cameras find a stoic Bill Murray. Next, a grandma in her Cubs sweatshirt. Next, three topless drunk guys in the bleachers, their flabby chests a collective message board: FLY. THE. W.

The phone rings. The bullpen coach answers, shoots Ryder a questioning look. Ryder gives the thumbs-up. He'll get eight more practice tosses from the live mound.

Ryder runs—fast.

This is the game you love.

Chapter 53

Gallo's suite is packed. The governor. The mayor. The mayor's buddies. Corporate types. Wives and girlfriends. Everybody wanted in. There were ten requests for every spot Gallo controlled.

"Jesus," says Gallo.

"I know," says Aiko.

"Midbatter? In the middle of a goddamn count?" says Gallo. "When was the last time you saw that?"

"Long time."

"My heart's a wreck."

In fact, Gallo hasn't been feeling all that good since Ricci and the meeting with Aiko's dad. There was something about Ryder. Something too easy. Too eager? Too comfortable? Again at the owners' meeting— Ryder was too cool. The meeting yesterday was a mess and a joke, though somehow the pact has held. No leaks. So far. The commissioner told a disappointed media that the decision, one way or the other, would be announced after the series ends. Another hour's worth of mind-numbing regurgitation was needed to reach that conclusion after Frank Ryder's brief speech and somewhat dramatic and very public exit straight out of the meeting room's main doors.

"When was the last time Frank Ryder threw a pitch with the bases loaded?" says Gallo.

"High school?" says Aiko.

"Little League?"

Aiko laughs. "Maybe. But remember. The baseball doesn't know there is pressure. The game doesn't know there's pressure."

What Gallo knows now, sitting in his suite at Wrigley Field with the windows open to the cool night air, is that he wants to win. He *needs* to win. He needs Baltimore to win—the city *and* the team. It's not as if a team can help the city clean up its act. But Ray Gallo knows the power of a good story, how the impact of a small ingredient boosts self-confidence, pride, and poise. Look good, feel good. A World Series trophy would go a long, long way.

Now, his so-called guests don't matter. They all vanish. Gallo is deep into the game, imagining Stone's choices and what's stirring in the mind of Cubs manager Ben Lucas too. It has been so long since Ray Gallo has felt this *worried*. Good worried. Childlike worried. It's giddiness mixed with horror. It's the knife edge. It's spine tingling. Gallo wants the same thing again next year and the year after that and for years to come.

We all want happy endings.

But part of this bargain is you must prepare to lose.

"He wasn't in the bullpen very long," says Aiko. "Even Frank Ryder—" She lets the thought go unfinished.

—needs time to warm up.

Ryder is on his third warm-up toss on the mound. He's not flashing much speed, but his control looks pinpoint. Wyatt is a rock.

"So let's say Ryder holds them here, wriggles out of this inning," says Gallo. "Then we have to score. *Soon.* Top of the eighth would be good. We don't want to drag Ryder into extra innings. He'll be spent before game seven rolls around."

"One pitch," says Aiko. "One pitch at a time. It will all come down to Frank Ryder's ability to think, to find himself so relied upon, and get his head right. You know, he was probably all about tomorrow. And now tomorrow is up to him. All he has to do is feel the moment."

"Yeah, sure," says Gallo. "And strike out Mateo fucking Torres."

Chapter 54

Ryder keeps a grim face, as the moment requires, but he could laugh.

This real enough for you now?

You wanted more of a say, right? Was that it?

Mateo Torres waits in the box.

Wyatt breaks out of his crouch and comes out for a chat.

"Jesus, really?" says Ryder.

Wyatt wants to review the signals with men on base.

"Yeah, yeah," says Ryder.

"And I needed a moment," says Wyatt. "Are we going to mess around?"

"There's no *room* to mess around. Hey, nice homer, by the way. No homer, I'm not here."

Wyatt thinks. "Good point." He jogs back.

Ryder finds a switch. If he thinks about what's next, this moment doesn't matter. If he has no *reason* to be tense, except maybe all of Baltimore hoping to slip out of this noose, he can relax and let his body do its thing.

The game matters.

But, of course, *not really.*

—⚋—

Ryder doesn't look at the three Cubs on base. He won't acknowledge their existence, but he senses their presence.

It's crowded.

He's not used to so much . . . *traffic.*

Not out here.

Wyatt flashes the 1.

Torres is going to swing. Torres might think *that's* a secret, but it's not. Torres flexes. He wants to take a healthy hack.

Ryder's motion looks like any of his best pitches, but it's all about the mismatch between what Torres expects and what's being delivered. Torres is done swinging, his bat wrapped around behind him, when the ball turtles up to the plate, dead center.

Fans groan.

Bases loaded, two out.

Tim Barrett. Ryder gives him 107 on the inside of the plate, 110 at the top of the zone, and 108 away. Good morning, good afternoon, good night.

Ryder walks off the mound. He's got one thought.

Bring on tomorrow.

—◊—

After a fruitless O's top of the eighth, Chris Bachman reaches first on an attempted bunt. Wyatt's throw to first skips wide. Bachman ends up at second.

Nobody out. Chicago fans bellow. Hope rises. A dink bunt and an errant throw are not good reason to get excited, a fact Ryder demonstrates by fanning the next three batters in quick order.

In the bottom of the ninth, Kurt Costa swings and misses on strike three, but the ball is low. Wyatt can't corral it. Costa reaches first ahead of Wyatt's throw. Costa steals second, which isn't attempted often, given the speed at which Ryder's pitches reach the catcher's mitt. Wyatt's throw is high, and by the time Ortega comes down with it, the umpire calls safe. The call goes in for review. From what Ryder can see, it could go either way. It's good someone knows. Or *pretends* that there is certainty. There are no do-overs in baseball. There might be indecision, but there is always a decision. In the end.

The Cubs win the review. Cub fans believe their cheers will give Costa a magic carpet ride to third. But, no. Inside, Ryder smiles. A quick thought of Maggie for a reality check, a quick reminder of the basic issue at hand—sixty feet, six inches. *Hit this.*

If you can.

Ryder strikes out the next three batters, leaves Costa on the field looking dejected, waiting for someone to bring him his glove.

—⁊⁊⁊—

In the bottom of the twelfth, the temperature dipping and the clock closing in on midnight, Ryder's first three pitches are a touch off—two inside, one outside. The crowd wants this to be Ryder's breaking point. Ryder takes three more pitches to retire Chris Bachman and nine more pitches to retire the side.

"You're up third," says Stone.

Ryder nods. "You can't pull me now. You'll still need me in the bottom of the frame."

"And if we have a chance to score, I've got to take it."

Ryder nods. "I'm your chance."

Ortega starts the top of the thirteenth by whacking a sharp, full-barreled hit to right field. Wyatt follows with a bloop that drops in behind the shortstop. Standing in the on-deck circle, Ryder looks back into the dugout. Stone is a statue.

Ryder hears his name announced.

And inscrutable Ben Lucas strolls out of the dugout, keeps his head down until he's on the lip of the mound, and gives the signal.

New pitcher.

It's not a secret. Cubs fans have been schooled by the media. Well, Cubs fans don't get schooled by anyone. The cheers can only be for one guy.

"Now pitching for the Chicago Cubs . . ."

Tim Simons.

Simon Says.

The sight of him walking in, warming up, brings it all back—Ryder's bedroom, the posters on the wall, his metal box mound, the hours of practice. Ryder smells his shag rug and sweaty boy clothes. If anything, tonight, Simons' giant jaw looks bigger. More clenched.

Ryder watches Simons from the on-deck circle. This time there will be no knock-down throws. The Cubs can't allow another base runner, can't afford to let this game get out of hand.

Simons can touch ninety-five, but he will work in the low nineties. *Slow enough.*

Ryder steps into the batter's box and assumes the pose of a normal hitter for a brief second before squaring around to face Simons and to hold his bat in the bunt position.

The first pitch comes in low. Ryder tries to get his bat down and *tries* to bunt. Gets nothing.

Strike one.

The second pitch comes in high, way too high, and Ryder lets it go. Ball one.

A walk is as good as a bunt . . . or better.

Does Simons seem wild? Is he feeling . . . pressure?

The third pitch comes in dead center, waist high, but the ball has movement on it, and Ryder gets a tick of the bat on the ball, which goes foul.

Strike two.

The crowd, of course, loves it.

Ryder steps out of the box, inhales the fresh night air, and looks at the analog clock that tops the old scoreboard in dead center field.

It's 12:20 a.m.

It's already tomorrow.

Ryder steps back into the box, squares up again. Chris Bachman creeps in from third, Costa from first.

Simons shows his high leg kick, hides the ball in his grip. Simons' pitches are as much about the prelude as the melody. There's a furious whirl of hands and knees up high, all accompanied by a stern grimace. And Ryder gets a flash of insight.

This pitch *will* be retaliation.

For making Torres look so foolish an hour ago.

That changeup.

Despite the furious kick and all the flailing around on the mound, this ball will come in easy.

Ryder's job is patience.

And timing.

In the middle of Simons' three-act motion, Ryder shifts to an upright stance. Sure enough, it's a floater. It might be doing eighty. Ryder keeps his head down. He keeps his stroke simple. He swings thinking *easy*. Thinking *contact*.

The sound is good; the feel in his hands is better.

Bachman lays out, airborne with his glove extended. The ball scampers into left field.

Ortega, jets for feet, rounds third. The crowd reaction tells Ortega he's got an easy lope to home.

3–2, Orioles.

The floodgates open. The Orioles pummel Simons for four more hits, including two doubles, and two walks.

The Orioles head out to the field with a five-run cushion.

It's four more runs than Ryder needs.

Chapter 55

"You weren't expecting to pitch tonight?"

"Absolutely not."

"You pitched six-plus innings tonight. You're not going to feel it in game seven?"

"I didn't say I wouldn't feel it." Ryder smiles.

"You'll be one hundred percent?"

"I'll *give* one hundred percent."

"Have you ever pitched so many innings one day to the next?"

The lights are bright. Ryder stares at a spot. "No." Smiles.

"But you're confident."

"I feel fine tonight," says Ryder. "And glad that we have a chance tomorrow."

"Your first hit in the major leagues."

Ryder waits. "Is that a question?" The room laughs.

"Care to comment?"

"Had a hunch. And when the NL goes to the designated hitter, the fans will be deprived of seeing pitchers like me quaking in their boots at the plate. A real loss."

The room laughs harder.

"And you have no idea what the owners decided?"

"I left before it was over. As you know."

The footage of Ryder leaving the room—and his statement that the meeting was still in progress—has been played ad nauseum.

"Did Gallo tell you after? You were the only player in the room."

"No," says Ryder. "I haven't seen him since."

"There's a rumor going around that you guaranteed a game seven during the meeting. Is that true?"

"I don't recall saying any such thing," says Ryder.

"Would you like to know the decision before tomorrow? It could be your last game pitching, you know, with complete freedom."

"One day at a time," says Ryder.

Chapter 56

Ryder rides the bus to the hotel. It's not quite business as usual among his teammates. Wyatt is getting a fair amount of grief, as is Ortega. The mood is fatigue mixed with pure excitement. Adrenaline. The game lasted five hours and twenty-eight minutes. There isn't a player among them who didn't want to walk right off the field in their uniforms, skip the postgame bullshit, and head to the hotel.

Ryder's phone signals a text. It's from a number he doesn't recognize.

Two minutes of your time at the hotel. I'll be in the bar. BTW, I got your number from a mutual friend.

Ryder stands in the hotel lobby, deciding. His room screams for him. His bed. He might not sleep for a few hours, but it would be good to be alone.

More than a few players drift into the bar. Most will head to their rooms and order food and drinks from room service and try to unwind.

Curiosity wins.

Tim Simons is sitting on his stool, his back to the bar. He is not alone. Steve Penny and Cory Bayless, a minute ahead of Ryder, are trading laughs. Penny played with Simons, for a season and a half, as an Atlanta Brave.

"There he is," says Simons.

Penny and Bayless stand back to make room. Ryder shakes Simons' hand. *Is this real? Do players do this?*

Simons Says . . . smiles. The smile rearranges his face. The bearer of bad news is childlike, easygoing. His eyes light up. "I wanted to say one thing to you," he says. "If that's okay."

"You know I grew up in Atlanta," says Ryder.

"It's not a secret," says Simons.

"You were my—"

"No time for that crap here," says Simons. "We are ballplayers. And mercenaries. Our loyalty can be bought. And anyway, my hero as a kid was Mike Mussina. An Oriole. Go figure."

Ryder tries a laugh. "Okay."

What the absolute hell?

"I came to say one thing." Simons is sipping brown liquor over ice. Penny and Bayless order beers, and Ryder joins them. Simons tells the bartender the drinks are all on his tab.

"One message," says Simons. "Probably nobody has to tell you this, but you are the future of baseball. You will throw for years and years. Don't let anyone cramp your style. Fight like hell if they try to change the rules. Let those goddamn hitters"—without looking at them, Simons points to Bayless and Penny—"let them figure it out. They *will* figure it out. No sport looks like it did forty years ago, sixty years ago. You are changing the game. Yeah, we both know there are others like you on the way. That's evolution. The game evolves. Us humans evolve. Goddamn good thing, I say. Show them all the potential of pitchers to improve, to dominate. They think they can mess with you because you're Baltimore. Don't let them."

Tim Simons holds out his hand, palm down, fingers splayed. It's an enormous hand. He wraps those same fingers in a fist and pumps it right in front of his chest.

"If they mess with the rules," says Simons, "you need to know there isn't a pitcher alive that doesn't have your back. Throw a stink—a big one. You could have a hundred big-league pitchers standing behind you at a news conference, got it?"

Ryder nods. "Yeah," he says.

"Your career is just getting out of the gate. Don't let them jerk you around, okay?"

Chapter 57

"Well, if he goes out there—and I do believe he will take the ball—this is like Kirk Gibson, torn hamstring and all, hitting a home run in game one back in 1988." Jim Palmer is being interviewed on one of the morning news shows.

Ryder doesn't watch these kinds of shows, but he is making an exception. Today is special. He wants to savor it, slow it down. The drama factor is ridiculous. So are some of the crazed fans they have interviewed in Chicago and back home in Baltimore.

Palmer looks worried. "I mean, if he even goes out there and can even give four or five innings, after last night? It would be one of the greatest pitching or sports performances of all time. If he takes the mound, it will be up there with Willis Reed hobbling back on the court in game seven of the NBA finals in 1970 or Tiger Woods winning the US Open with a torn ACL. There have been other examples, I'm sure. But pitchers? That arm needs rest. Time to recover. He won games one and four, played the key role and won the game last night, and the idea of going out to pitch nine innings—and I'm here to tell you, Frank Ryder expects to pitch all nine innings—makes my arm hurt. Just *thinking* about it."

"He could end up with four wins in the World Series?" The anchor is as serious as 9/11. *Lighten up, dude.* "Never been done."

"*Three* hasn't been done since 1956."

"The Orioles *could* shut him down," says the anchor. "He got them to game seven. They could save Frank Ryder's arm for next season, make sure he doesn't do anything to hurt himself, and take their chances with Joe Rhineland or Kevin Wright—who at least have had more rest. Or cobble together a fleet of pitchers and do the 'opener' approach that Tampa Bay is famous for."

Jim Palmer smiles. "I don't think you know Frank Ryder."

Ryder flips over to ESPN.

" . . . get comfortable is the main thing." It's Kurt Costa, looking confident. It's a postgame clip from the previous night. "You know he's got perfect control, and, yeah, some pitches are ridiculous, but he has to mix it up, speed wise. So it's a mind game thing going on out there. You try to figure out what he's thinking and look for something to work with."

"Even if that *next* one is one oh eight or one oh nine? Or sizzles in at one ten?"

"I'm not saying it's easy," says Costa. "I'm saying you have to be ready. Every pitcher makes mistakes."

"And can you give fans an idea of what that's really like out there, when you're standing in the box facing Frank Ryder?" The reporter is a woman. She could be grilling a politician. "Hitting is the single hardest thing to do in all of sports; isn't that what Ted Williams said? So how does it feel, knowing it's exponentially harder, and some say impossible, facing him?"

Costa sighs. "I'd like to say it's about adjustments. Mechanical adjustments and mental ones too. And it's true."

Costa shrugs.

"You don't sound so sure," says the reporter.

"You can't be sure about much," says Costa. "It's baseball."

Chapter 58

October fog floats in from Lake Michigan. It pours in over the outfield wall like white surf. Ryder wants to reach up and grab a handful of the ghostlike stuff, feel it in his hand. The fans in the bleachers look like smudges in an impressionistic painting.

The ball is damp. *Moisturized.* Each toss is a battle. Wrigley Field's swampish air wants Ryder to pitch harder. There is no *effortlessness* tonight.

His velocity is down. By the second inning, he's reached 106 once. The night is weighing in. *See, this is what the game would look like if you put some brakes on this guy.* It's hard to stay in rhythm. Ryder wants to overthrow, to punch back hard, but the penalty will be wildness and walks and mayhem and losing.

Ryder takes what the night gives him. His curveball adores the wet air. The spin on his curve bites hard against the humidity. It comes to the batter looking like an ice cream sundae and vanishes like a mean mirage. Each pitch is work, each batter is work, each inning is work. Each batter is a mind game. A duel of expectations. On the mound, Ryder's trance is a box of nothing. The box of nothing allows only two thoughts.

Now is one. This moment. This mound. This batter. This game.

This batter is the other. With each batter, Ryder ejects one cartridge of data in his head, inserts a new one. Torres. Costa. Foley. Bachman.

Barrett. Weaknesses, tendencies, sweet spots. Hot-zone charts pop in and out of his head like a PowerPoint presentation. *How did I start him last time? How should I start him this time? What's he looking for? What's he* not *looking for?* The batters try messing with his timing. They call time-outs. They pretend to bunt. They stare at their bats, talk to them. They retighten their batting gloves as if the Velcro somehow got loose between pitches two and three. *Yeah, right.*

It's to no avail.

When they stand in the box, Ryder throws.

They strike out.

All other thoughts are banished.

But . . .

One thought doesn't want to go away.

The thought raps at the door. At first, it's a gentle knock.

The thought is *yesterday.*

You overdid it.

His arm is angry.

It starts in the bottom of the third. With two out, he gives up an excuse-me, check-swing hit that turns Cubs fans delirious.

You do feel that twinge, right?

Ryder takes an extra moment behind the mound to rub down the ball. *Was it a bad arm slot that caused the twinge? His footwork?* Ryder replays the last pitch in his head, can't find the fault. The next pitch is twinge-free.

You're fine.

Back to the trance.

In the fourth inning, his arm grows heavy. The *ball* is heavy, as if someone replaced the cork with lead. He gives up another single and a walk, but they are separated by a strikeout and an easy grounder to second base. With two men on base, however, the Cubs faithful are sure this is their moment, their time.

"You okay?" says Lackland after the fourth.

"Fine."

"Looks like you're laboring."

"No," says Ryder.

"If the tank is empty—"

"No."

The Oriole hitters aren't making much headway. Two soft hits so far, no blood.

—∿∿—

Ghost fog swirling and still a scoreless tie, Ryder strikes out the side in the bottom of the fifth. Except on the third batter, his curveball dives into the dirt. Bachman swings. It should be strike three, but the ball caroms off Wyatt's shin guard and squiggles away. Wyatt tracks the ball down near the on-deck circle and thinks about throwing. Bachman is too quick.

Man on first.

Ryder stiffens. An extra batter is not something he needs. Extra work is not something he needs. And, if he were hooked up to a lie detector, he would have to confess that on the last pitch to Bachman he felt the same twinge—again.

This time, more of a *pop*.

Ryder has read plenty of accounts of Achilles' heels snapping and athletes reporting that they heard a pop. ACL tears too. Same thing. A *pop*. It always seemed strange to Ryder that you could hear a pop through all the skin and tissue; how would the sound even travel? But there it is, a distinct *chunk*, a ligament's alarmed yelp or a tendon's plea for mercy. Something.

He hopes to hell his face is keeping the secret. He wants to probe his right shoulder with his left hand but refrains. He wants to roll his arm or shake it out but refrains. He sticks to his routine.

Fuck the twinge. Fastball on the inner half, 106. Cutter on the outer half, 105. Curveball low, 102. Costa can't resist—and whiffs.

Four strikeouts, three outs.

—〰—

Ryder wills an Oriole hit. He deems it so, dreams it so. He imagines Orioles on base—a walk, a hit, a harmless hit by pitch. Perhaps one curveball could strafe a batter's jersey—no damage done. Anything to get some traction. He pictures a homer. He imagines a blur of orange on the base paths. The mood in the dugout is tight. Ryder wants time. He wants a break. An extra few minutes would be gold. Scoring five runs, for the time it would take and the mental cushion it would provide, would feel like a week's worth of rubdowns.

Steve Penny channels Ryder's plea. He connects on the first pitch from wily Kyle Holmes. The ball muscles its way up into the fog. The sound says *homer.* The arc says *homer.* On most nights, the ball would bounce off Waveland Avenue. Battling the spongy air, the ball ekes its way out of the park and lands in the overhanging basket above the ivy. A fan reaches down, plucks it out, and hurls it back on the field in one swift throw—to raucous applause.

The Oriole dugout erupts. Penny returns from his routine jog around the bases to bear hugs and shouts. *Hell yeah! Fuck yeah!* Ryder joins in the fist-pumping fray, but he's worried. The first-pitch homer was too quick. The next three Oriole batters go down without a fight.

Ryder drags his arm back out to the mound, shaking it to chase the hot tingling twinges. Or rattle the pain loose.

He needs to break the trance. He can't do it alone. He can't fight through it. His arm is raw.

And mad.

At him.

Ryder circles the mound, plays with the rosin bag, inhales fog.

The arm barks with every pitch. Three up, three down. One strike-out, two dink grounders.

The arm whines and balks in the eighth. The first two batters get to three-ball counts. *Back to back.* Ryder converts both to K's, but the crowd smells blood. Wants blood.

Ryder prowls the mound, paces down off the back between batters, stares out and up at the white swirls of mist. Breath comes hard. His lungs won't fill. His arm cries for relief. Cory Bayless starts to head over to say something; Ryder waves him away. Words won't help.

Ryder doesn't quite *get it*. What do those years of practice mean? What do those years of work and focus mean? What was the point? What is this *game*? It's everything, of course, and pure nothingness too.

Ryder strikes out the third batter of the inning, Chris Bachman, on five pitches. Bachman unstraps his shin guard and drops his helmet on the plate.

The dugout between innings is as quiet as a crypt.

He'd take fifteen minutes by rain delay or fog delay or an extended Oriole rally to let his arm reboot, rebound.

It doesn't happen.

Ryder walks to the mound for the bottom of the ninth.

Next is so soon.

Next is right after three little outs.

Stan Foley manages a sad grounder to third base. Mateo Torres hacks hard at all three pitches over the plate, comes up empty.

The Wrigley crowd rises.

They are . . . *cheering*.

Ryder looks up. He listens for sarcasm in the mix, for the cheers to turn to jeers.

No.

They are cheering *for* him.

What?

They are cheering for *him*. The cheers are legit. Heartfelt.

Kurt Costa waits a moment to step into the box. Ryder's teammates line the top of the dugout. A few clap. Ryder finds the friends-and-family section above first base, spots Maggie in her Oriole cap. Josh stands on one side of her, and their parents are on the other. And Coach Rush. Standing. Clapping. Maggie, bouncing on her toes, raises her arm as he looks up.

Ryder walks off the mound, removes his cap, and uses the sleeves on both arms to mop his forehead.

And he wipes his eyes.

Discreetly.

The crowd settles.

Costa steps in.

Ryder toes the rubber, strokes the seams on the baseball.

Accidents are accidents . . .

He feels the necklace on his chest.

We didn't choose to be born into a world where you don't get to control your own fate . . .

We're just here . . .

Ryder blinks.

For a flash, he hears the warmth and certainty of Gail Johnson's voice.

For a flash, he sees Deon and his powder-blue helmet.

For a flash, he smells the sweat and heat of Webb Bridge Park.

Deon.

Deon.

This one's for you, Deon.

Kurt Costa doesn't know it yet, but he doesn't stand a chance.

NOVEMBER

People ask me what I do in winter when there's no baseball. I'll tell you what I do. I stare out the window and wait for spring.

—Hall of Fame hitter, infielder, manager, and coach Rogers Hornsby

Chapter 59

Frank Ryder stands behind a wood podium on the grass halfway between the mound and home plate at Camden Yards. It's a strange spot—smack in between. He's a nowhere man in no-man's-land.

Ray Gallo stands to his left. Art Stone stands to his right.

Reporters swarm home plate. Buster Olney. Rex Coburn. The *New York Times*. A phalanx of video cameras.

The day is cool and damp. The day yearns for football and hot chocolate. Ryder wears a gray sweater, dark slacks. His chest shudders. It could be the temperature. It could be his nerves.

He leans into the cluster of microphones. "When we brought the World Series trophy home to the great city of Baltimore," says Ryder, "I took two weeks to reflect."

Ryder reads. It's the fifth or sixth draft of the speech. Maggie weighed in on every word.

"It's been an honor to pitch for the Orioles. I cannot thank the team enough for this incredible season and to the coaches, my teammates, and to my manager as well for all the support. No player in the major leagues could ask for better teammates. Not one."

A breeze flutters the corners of Ryder's pages. A female reporter cinches up her coat.

"You might look at the year I've had and think, of course, that I would want another year just like it and maybe fifteen more years after that."

Ryder looks up, efforts a smile.

"For most ballplayers, that would make perfect sense.

"I have discovered that I am not most ballplayers.

"What happened to me as a Little League pitcher changed my life. It changed my life, forever. I could not have asked for better parents to get me through what happened. I couldn't have asked for a better brother, my catcher that day, to get me through it too. To get *us* through what happened.

"But . . ."

Admitting this part was the toughest to explain to Stone and Lackland, and to Gallo too.

"But I suffered."

Ryder swallows—*hard*. Waits. Looks around.

"Of course, Deon Johnson's parents and Deon's friends can tell you more about suffering than I will ever know." Ryder takes a moment. For Deon. For Gail. For Cedric. "But I suffered. In my own way."

Ryder has told Maggie about Deon's ghost—the vivid sightings and surreal conversations as vibrant as the purple frames of Rex Coburn's glasses—but nobody else. If he told them all now about Deon's ghost, would they let him off the hook?

"My teenage years were the opposite of carefree. The overwhelming guilt—"

The word alone sends a tremor through his chest. He tilts his head back, sparking a machine-gun flurry of shutters.

"—the guilt meant my teenage years were not years of freedom and joy. They were years of pervasive sadness that I hid from everyone."

Ryder clears a critical hump. There's a *click*. There was a moment during the big downtown parade when Ryder looked at the masses and felt like he didn't belong to himself anymore, that everyone else owned the story. Owned *him*. There's a release now, a lightness.

"I have empathy for youth. There are many kinds of personal suffering because there are so many kinds of aches and pains in our world today—and I'm not talking only about the inner cities. Far too many teenagers have had happiness stolen from them, like I did. Far too many. I want to do something for them, even if it is only a small group at a time. I have a little dream. And I have an idea for realizing it, too, so I'm going to get out there and see if I can make it work."

Ryder sneaks a look at the reporters, to see if he can read how it's going over. He can't tell.

"Of course I love the game of baseball. With a World Series trophy, I love it more than ever. But I'm on the verge of ruining it—some say I've already done just that.

"I'll leave that now for others. The pitch-speed issue can wait for another day.

"What can't wait is pitchers hitting batters on purpose. *On purpose.* Since I have your attention, I'll take advantage of this moment and caution baseball—capital-*B Baseball*—to fix the problem now, before another player gets hurt. Or worse. This unwritten rule encourages assault, promotes assault, enables assault. It's designed to maim and injure. It's putting good players in the hospital and extended stays on the injury list."

Ryder looks up from his pages—and around.

"And it could get worse. It *will* get worse. There will be an accident that will be far, far worse."

Ryder shakes his head at the thought.

"How do I know? Because the ball that slipped out of my hands last June and hurt Billy Jaworski was an accident. The ball slipped. I had no intention of hurting him. And yet . . ."

Ryder shakes his head. He can still see Jaworski's lifeless feet. The key is to keep reading the words, one after the next.

No improv.

Don't look up.

"And yet it happened.

"The unwritten rules need to go. In this case, baseball will not take care of itself. Adults—and I think that's all of us—can do what's right and put a stop to this adolescent BS. When suspensions and fines are large enough to hurt the team as a whole and the individual player, too, the stupid stuff will stop.

"As for me, I know now what's going to make me feel good about how I spend my time. I know now that I want to help kids who need more opportunities. And I know that if I walk away, which I am doing—"

A collective gasp washes over the reporters like a hard wave crashing on a beach.

"—that I'll feel better about what I'm doing with my time.

"Does this make me some sort of hero? *Please.* No. In no way, shape, or form. I'm just being honest with myself.

"And of course I'd be glad to answer a few questions . . ."

NOVEMBER

EPILOGUE

Frank Ryder sketches on the tablet of lined yellow paper. He draws a rectangle for the white, six-bedroom farmhouse looming in front of them. He draws eight more squares for the cabins, four on each side, to be built in an arc.

"Thirty yards between the cabins—or maybe something more random, less of a barracks feel," says Ryder. "More scattered around down in the woods by the river. And the house will be for staff. And we'll build a new house in back, in the same style as the main house, for more staff."

"Completed by when?"

Marty Ash carries an old-school reporter's notebook, but he doesn't take notes. Ryder had debated with Maggie whether they wanted to invite the *New York Times* or ESPN. All Ryder knew was he wanted one reporter, not a throng. And he felt like he owed Marty Ash a favor. And an apology.

"Next summer," says Ryder. He is sitting in the driver's seat of a 1993 F-250, the door open. Ash is in the passenger's seat. It's a cool day in late November. The property, twenty-five hundred acres along the South Platte River, looks like it's hunkering down for the winter. "That is, if all goes well. Should be doable, I'm told."

"And the kids?"

"What about them?"

"Where do they come from?"

"From all over," says Ryder. "From all thirty major-league cities, for starters. Four kids per city—a hundred twenty in the first go-round."

"Age?"

"High school," says Ryder.

"Picked how?"

"We'll come up with a process," says Ryder. "We'll have staff here all winter—planning the sessions, figuring out logistics. Transportation. Programs."

"Like what?"

"Sky's the limit," says Ryder. "I can tell you that out here, the astronomy sessions at night will be intense. It gets very dark out here. And some of these kids have never seen stars—other than the movies."

"So, astronomy and what else?"

Marty Ash was always matter of fact.

"They are going to tell us," says Ryder. "We'll build it around their interests, their preferences. But we've talked about lots of things. Music—maybe have a few bands, a recording studio. Art. Lots of art. Wilderness treks. Camping. Environmental studies, especially with the river right here. Yoga. We might put in a field for soccer. Writing. Cooking. About two miles away is a working cattle ranch, and two miles the other way is a horse farm, and we're talking to both about some real-life opportunities. There's history to study all over the place."

"And the kids stay for how long?"

"To be determined," says Ryder. He doesn't want to sound certain about anything. "I'm no expert. It could be a full eight weeks—all summer. Or two four-week deals. And if there's a way to figure this out, we'll go year round, working with the school districts in those cities."

"Free," says Ash.

"Free to the kids," says Ryder. "Paid for by the league—and various donors."

"And you convinced the league of this?"

"We had a conversation," says Ryder. "Ray Gallo and I. Both of us."

"They didn't know then—that you were ending your career?"

"Correct," says Ryder.

"And you have no regrets, second thoughts?"

Ryder knew this question was coming. Ever since the news conference in Baltimore, it's been one of the central themes. The implied question: *How can you walk away from all that money?*

"No."

"So you must have been planning this before the season ended."

Ryder smiles. "A while. Yes."

"You were going to do this one way or the other?"

"The league buying in puts it on a bigger scale. Leave it at that."

"Why not pitch for a decade and then do this?" says Ash. "Add a ticket to the Hall of Fame as a cherry on top."

"The owners have plenty of money to make this happen. And think of all the kids who would end up in dead ends over the same ten years."

"You can't reach them all."

"I can reach ten more years' worth."

Ryder leads a tour of the main house, guarded by four massive cottonwoods. A recent renovation added giant windows for light. The kitchen is expansive, with a butcher-block island and long granite counters, double sinks, picture windows, two refrigerators, a walk-in pantry, and a wall full of pots and pans hanging on hooks. Ryder knew with that many teenage mouths to feed that a sizable kitchen would be the heartbeat of the entire operation.

"And I want you to meet the woman who will likely head up food services," says Ryder.

Gail Johnson is sitting on a high-top chair, a clipboard in front of her on the island. Marty Ash shakes her hand. Ryder explains she is visiting for now, but might move out later this summer.

"From where?" says Ash.

"Atlanta," she says.

Marty Ash isn't putting two and two together. That's fine with Ryder. Maybe he was the right choice.

"Bit of a different climate out here—you know that?"

"So I'm told," says Gail.

Marty's photographer, a tall woman draped in cameras over a sleeveless fleece parka, starts to take a photo. Gail Johnson holds up a hand. "Not until I sign a contract," she says. "If that's okay with you, Frank."

"Your call all the way," says Ryder. "Gail might teach some culinary arts—isn't that right?"

"Teach might be a stretch," says Gail. "More like show."

Ash turns back to Ryder. "And I understand you've got some talent helping you with other programs too."

"You mean my dad."

"Yes."

"Mom too," says Ryder.

"A family affair?"

"I didn't exactly see that coming," says Ryder. "But, yes."

"You all are going to move out here?"

"Wait and see," says Ryder. "Real staff first. I know Maggie will finish up her degree first, and then we'll see."

"And you're not going to miss all the limelight, all the attention?"

"Might seem hard to believe," says Ryder.

"Because you think they would have put in an artificial speed limit?"

"I have no idea what they would've done, what they're going to do," says Ryder. "The rule they need to fix is around the beanballs."

"*Hmmm, mmmmm,*" says Gail Johnson. She doesn't look up.

"You're worried."

"Goes without saying," says Ryder.

"And this is going to be enough for you?"

"Enough what?"

Ash searches for a word. Shrugs. "Satisfaction, I suppose. Fulfillment."

"Sure," says Ryder. "Plenty. The deep-down stuff."

"Hmmm, mmmmm," says Gail Johnson. Still, she doesn't look up.

—⁓—

"It'll come to him," says Maggie. She's back from a late-afternoon run. She's wearing a tight-fitting T-shirt the color of apple cider, tiny gray shorts, and her purple sneakers. Her dark hair is pulled back in a short ponytail. She's carrying a glass of ice water and a big smile. She kisses Ryder on the cheek. "Gail played it cool?"

"Cooler than cool," says Ryder.

Maggie takes a stool at the butcher-block island, the same spot where Gail made notes. Maggie sweats. Beams. "He'll wake up in the middle of the night and think *Johnson* and then *Atlanta* and he'll go, *Holy hell.*"

"He'll wake up in the middle of the night, and it will all connect when he realizes I'm no longer the story."

"He'll think you should have said something," says Maggie, "but of course you wouldn't have done that."

"No."

"That raises a question." She's been doing lots of anticipating and thinking about the activities they might end up running, the kinds of spaces and places they need to build. And prepare. "Something I've been wondering."

"Ask away." Ryder, too, has found his mind happily lost in planning. It's a near-giddy feeling of excitement mixed with occasional flashes of uncertainty. How is he so sure the kids will connect? That the plan will make a difference? "Just know that if I don't have the answer, I might concoct some pure fantasy BS on the spot."

"So nothing has changed in that regard—got it," says Maggie. "Are you going to invite reporters out to see the camp? Write about it? Do you want that?"

"Seems like that's an issue for a long way down the road."

"But it's something you should decide from the get-go. I'm assuming the last thing these kids want is for their stories to be splashed all over a newspaper or feel like they are being, well, exploited."

"We don't want that," says Ryder. "Or need that. You're right."

"It would change the whole tone around here. With everything. I mean, it might look like we're asking for more, when we've got everything we—"

Ryder holds his hand up—*full stop.*

"I can't think about that," he says.

"What?"

Ryder paces a small circle. He sits down opposite Maggie. He lets the moment fill him up. He promises himself he won't try to speak until he knows the words will come out clear.

Maggie stands up, comes around the table. She parks her sweaty self on Ryder's lap. She smells of sweet onions and cool spring air. She wraps an arm around Ryder's neck.

"I can't think about it." The words are raspy, but he forges on. "About how I got here, to a place where, yeah, we have—"

"Everything." Maggie whispers the word in his ear.

"And I get to meet these kids." Ryder pulls Maggie closer. "Find out what they're into."

"Yes."

"I can't wait."

"I know."

"I'm in the right place."

"Again," says Maggie.

"But I can't think about how I got here."

"No," says Maggie. "The 'What if?' game is an endless tunnel back in time. It's unforgiving. You're here, now. With me. With the kids. Well, the kids are coming soon."

"That reminds me."

"What?"

"There's something coming up on ESPN."

"I thought we were getting away from all that."

"We are," says Ryder. "We will be, I mean. Soon. But Josh texted me."

Ryder reads the text aloud:

ESPN has been teasing this interview all evening. Big tease. If it's for real, you don't want to miss it.

"Okay." Maggie is a hard sell. "How long we gotta wait?"

They have taken to staying out on the farm, alone with each other, on the weekends. They check on progress with the renovation, go for long dawn walks down country roads, and bask in the serenity of open space.

"You'll be pleased to know, Miss Impatience, that it's almost the top of the hour."

"Suspense," says Maggie. "How am I going to stand it?"

Ryder sits on the tattered old high-backed couch, now covered in a white sheet. The previous owners watched TV off a satellite service, and after some debate, Ryder and Maggie agreed to restart the service but only for limited use. The goal is to sink into farm living when they are out in the country. One big decision ahead is whether to have a TV room when the camps start—or maybe they'll build a movie library of DVDs and leave it at that.

Maggie sits next to Ryder with a plate of crackers topped with slices of cheddar. "I hope it's something cheesy," she says.

Ryder gives her a dead stare, clicks off the mute.

Nicole Briscoe starts off the show. On a giant screen behind her, a giant MLB logo morphs into a photo of a young pitcher in a Baltimore Orioles hat holding the World Series trophy.

"Yes," says Briscoe. "Remember him? The one and maybe only Frank Ryder? We all thought the Ryder conundrum was over when the star pitcher with four wins in this year's World Series and the owner of the most dazzling single-season pitching record of all time . . . walked away from the sport."

Briscoe pauses. Shakes her head like a disappointed mother.

"Not. So. Fast." Briscoe smiles. Raises one eyebrow. Slowly. "Two years ago, the Chicago White Sox signed a pitcher in the thirty-ninth round. From Tennessee. Let's just say that pitcher was a work in progress. Well, he's improved. He's still assigned to the Single-A Kannapolis—that's North Carolina—Cannon Ballers, but here in the hunch department? We don't think that's going to last."

The stage-wide MLB graphic dissolves to a round-faced kid with freckles under a baseball cap with the Cannon Ballers logo, a human cannon ball in flight. The cartoon figure's head is a giant baseball. He wears a helmet and goggles. He's got a Monopoly Man mustache. Minus the facial hair, Ryder can relate.

"Yes, the Cannon Ballers," says Briscoe. "Don't you love the names of baseball's minor-league teams? So playful, right? Well, take a long look at this face. That face belongs to Jack Jones. Jack's top pitching speeds were always impressive. One oh five. One oh six. But he was wild. Jones was sent to play winter ball in the Arizona League this fall, and something, well, clicked. We sent Buster Olney to Alamo, Tennessee, to catch up with Jack at his local town training facility, where Jack Jones is regularly lighting up the radar gun at one ten. And, wait for it, *above*. There is video evidence of Jack Jones throwing one fourteen. One. One. Four. You heard me right. And we've got the tape to show to you tonight."

Briscoe pauses.

Smiles again.

Waits.

Smiles.

"Buster?"

Once Maggie is deep asleep, her chest rising and falling in a restful rhythm, Ryder slips out of bed. In the upstairs bathroom at the end of the hall, he pulls on gray gym shorts and a ratty Metro State T-shirt. Downstairs, he digs out his cleats from the back of a closet and slips on a green flannel shirt. Ryder steps outside. He stands for a moment and takes in the chilly pungency of the night. The sky is clear. There might be more stars than the spaces in between.

The barn door groans at being opened and squeals on the close, behind him. Ryder flips a switch that fires up one naked overhead bulb. The light works as well as one match in a giant cavern, but it's enough.

Working with a hammer and saw, feeling his hands doing new things, Ryder has converted five horse stalls into one long chute. He built a mound with one-by-sixes, two-by-fours, and plywood—following plans he found online. He covered the mound with green outdoor carpet and ordered a genuine pitching rubber that's anchored at the top.

It's hard to round up catchers who will come work with you at odd wee hours of the night when you can't sleep, so Ryder has built a wood frame that approximates the size of Jose Altuve's strike zone. Behind the frame is a pile of loose hay that swallows each pitch with a soft gulp. All that's missing is the pleasing *thump* of a catcher's mitt.

Ryder sheds his flannel shirt, knowing that in a few minutes' time his body won't feel the chill of the drafty barn. He pulls his glove from where it's hanging from a nail and plucks one ball from dozens waiting in an old ten-gallon bucket.

Toes to fingertips, thighs to wrist, leg kick to release, Ryder's body knows the effort required for top speed. The timing. The torque. The reach.

It's music.

—⚉—

AUTHOR'S NOTE

I'm not a fan of baseball's use of designated hitters. I don't understand why major league pitchers can't hit. And hit well. (Exhibit A: Shohei Ohtani.) From a strategy perspective, sending pitchers to the plate as part of the lineup means managers have tougher decisions to make when it's time to boost the offense. I was raised in suburban Boston as a Red Sox and American League fan. However, I grew to appreciate the National League when the American League started with designated hitters in 1973. When I wrote *The Fireballer*, there were no designated hitters in the National League. When I sold *The Fireballer*, that was still the case. In March 2022, that all changed. The 2022 season started with designated hitters in both leagues, just as copyediting for this novel was wrapping up. This significant change in baseball's rules is further proof that baseball is always evolving. The same is true for beanballs. Major League Baseball could put a stop to pitchers hitting batters on purpose but, clearly, chooses not to. But I chose to keep this story set in a world where pitchers step to the plate for the sake of the story. I hope readers can suspend the reality of today's baseball rules and enjoy Frank Ryder's journey.

An additional note: the average pitch speed in all baseball has increased six miles per hour, from eighty-nine miles per hour to ninety-five miles per hour, over the last twenty years. That's the *average* speed for all pitchers. Today, one hundred miles per hour is not uncommon.

The fastest pitches recorded, by Aroldis Chapman, were two-tenths of a second under 106 miles per hour. During the 2022 season, Cincinnati Reds pitcher Hunter Greene, who is twenty-two years old, threw thirty-nine pitches at one hundred miles per hour or faster against the Los Angeles Dodgers. In 2021, Jacob deGrom threw thirty-three pitches at one-hundred-plus miles per hour in a single game. And the future for fireballers looks bright. University of Tennessee pitcher Ben Joyce, who was a junior during the 2022 college baseball season, routinely pitches baseballs at speeds that reach 103 miles per hour. Joyce has touched 105. If you haven't seen how quickly a baseball travels from mound to catcher's mitt at 105 miles per hour, a quick video search will give you the idea. Batters have very little time to decide whether to swing. And how to swing. Will a pitcher ever throw as fast as Frank Ryder? Who knows? The point is that pitch speeds are up. Like the vast majority of records in sports, Chapman's top speed is bound to be broken one day. Options exist to restore the balance in the favor of batters should Major League Baseball decide that today's pitch speeds yield a product that is not entertaining to fans. Combined with the failure to check beanballs, the baseballs thrown by these fireballers could prove dangerous. As mentioned, baseball evolves. Electronic umpires are likely on the way. Automatic runners are stationed at second base in extra-inning games (another abomination) in order to declare a winner more quickly and not face the prospect of fifteen-inning marathons. So something could be done about pitch speeds. But the top priority should be to banish the designated hitter. It's not going to happen, but one can dream.

ACKNOWLEDGMENTS

I consumed many books about baseball while researching and writing this story. Among the notable titles: *The Game from Where I Stand*, by Doug Glanville; *Buddha Takes the Mound: Enlightenment in 9 Innings*, by Donald Lopez Junior; *A Great and Glorious Game*, by A. Bartlett Giamatti; *Smart Baseball*, by Keith Law; *K: A History of Baseball in Ten Pitches*, by Tyler Kepner; *The Phenomenon*, by Rick Ankiel; *For the Love of the Game*, by Michael Shaara; *Sandy Koufax*, by Jane Leavy; *The Baseball Whisperer: A Small-Town Coach Who Shaped Big League Dreams*, by Michael Tackett; *Throwback: A Big-League Catcher Tells How the Game Is Really Played*, by Jason Kendall and Lee Judge; *Battle Creek*, by Scott Lasser; *Power Ball*, by Rob Neyer; *The Fat Lady's Low, Sad Song*, by Brian Kaufman; *Ninety Percent Mental*, by Bob Tewksbury; and *100 Things Orioles Fans Should Know & Do Before They Die*, by Dan Connolly.

I need to thank Irv Moskowitz, first and foremost. Irv planted the seed for this story, read every chapter in raw form, drafted key sections of dialogue, and steered me back on course whenever I got lost.

I also need to thank a large group of major-league friends who helped along the way:

Linda Hull, Keir Graff, Terri Bischoff, Stephen Singular, Christine Carbo, Wendy J. Fox, Danielle Burby, Brad Newsham (whose positive energy is apparently boundless), Barry Wightman (who helped with research and descriptions in two key scenes, particularly at Webb Bridge Park), Anita Mumm, Ben LeRoy, Mark Eddy, Alan Gottlieb, Mark Graham, Dominic DelPapa, Dick Cass, Steve Katich, Anita Miller, Greg Miller, Jason Shaffer, Shannon Baker, Janet Fogg, Sami Jo Lien, Gregory Hill, Chuck Greaves, Maddy Butcher, and my incredibly supportive and talented wife, Jody Chapel.

William Kent Krueger, Lou Berney, and Stewart O'Nan were all kind enough to read early versions and offer their endorsements. These were all generous and meaningful gifts from supremely talented writers.

Special thanks to agents Josh Getzler and Jon Cobb from HG Literary. Josh was an early champion of the idea, insisting that "it can't only be about baseball." Both Josh and Jon offered powerful insights throughout the writing process, and of course they found a home for Frank Ryder.

And, finally, heartfelt gratitude to editors Alison Dasho and David Downing for the significant improvements and keen analysis during the editing process. David's deep dive, in particular, was like a pitching coach demonstrating a whole new grip on the ball.

ABOUT THE AUTHOR

The son of two librarians, Mark Stevens was raised in Lincoln, Massachusetts, and has worked as a reporter, as a national television news producer, and in public relations. *Antler Dust* was a *Denver Post* bestseller in 2007 and 2009. *Buried by the Roan*, *Trapline*, and *Lake of Fire* were all finalists for the Colorado Book Award (2012, 2015, and 2016, respectively), and *Trapline* won. *Trapline* also won the Colorado Authors League award for best genre fiction. Stevens has had short stories published by *Ellery Queen Mystery Magazine*, by *Mystery Tribune*, and in *Denver Noir* (Akashic Books). In September 2016, Stevens was named Rocky Mountain Fiction Writers' Writer of the Year. Stevens hosts a regular podcast for Rocky Mountain Fiction Writers and has served as president of the Rocky Mountain chapter for Mystery Writers of America. Stevens also writes book reviews; follow them at https://markhstevens. wordpress.com. Today, Stevens lives in Mancos, Colorado.